A TAKER OF MORROWS

STEPHEN PAUL SAYERS

HYDRA PUBLICATIONS

ISBN: 978-1-940466-72-9

Hydra
Publications

Goshen, Kentucky 40026
www.hydrapublications.com

To my daughter Kaylee, who taught me anything is possible. This one's for you.

CHAPTER ONE

Saturday, December 2, 2017

The dank staleness of uncirculated air pressed against him, weighing him down. Robert Granville scanned the slick advertisements slapped starkly against Kenmore Station's greasy, stained tiled walls. A humid, musty wind blew in from the tunnel, scattering paper and debris. Swiping a hand across his stubbled chin, RG's gaze drifted to the man at the far end of the tracks.

8:25 p.m.

Five more minutes and it would be over. Everything. All he was or ever hoped to be. RG blotted his moist palms with clenching fingers, a cold sweat seeping from his pores. The underground station's buzz filtered to silence as he fought the images flickering in his mind, dark thoughts taking root.

How had it come to this?

Squeezing his eyes shut, he pictured Kacey on the front porch swing, their fingers intertwined and resting on her prominent baby bump. Twenty-four hours ago, RG had the promise of a fulfilling life, but now he paced the subway station's dusty concrete platform contemplating murder. The dream had spiraled into a nightmare—and he couldn't jolt himself awake.

8:26 p.m.

A faint metallic squeal crackled through the darkened subway tunnel.

The other man stood alone at the far end of the tracks. His long, dirty hair hanging below his shirt collar shielded an expressionless face, chiseled and stern from life on the street. He clung to several worn-out plastic bags overflowing with personal items. The man repeated his movements in a compulsive pattern, leaning over the tracks and gazing into the tunnel, then turning and walking in a circle, mumbling to himself.

RG studied the man, a plan formulating in his mind. He crept toward the far end of the tracks.

8:27 p.m.

His mind drifted, the stranger's words echoing in his head—a story about an exchange of souls. One for another. The stranger had told him to keep those thoughts far from his mind, but time had run out, and dying wasn't in RG's plans. If a train whizzed by at 8:30 p.m. and struck a man, death would be instantaneous; and if the timing aligned perfectly, it would deliver the required soul at the exact moment and satisfy the matrix.

Life could go on.

RG stared into the tunnel. His stomach seized imagining the train's fury as it exploded into the station, the man's wide eyes as he grasped the inevitable, a final scream interrupted, and a twisted, broken body strewn across the rails. He tried to exorcise these demonic thoughts from his mind, but continued to creep toward the far end of the tracks. His feet scattered shreds of trash littering the grimy concrete floor.

8:28 p.m.

Down the tunnel, the train's screech indicated it had made its way from street level to underground. Could it arrive at precisely 8:30? Doubtful, but he continued to slink toward the far end of the tracks. The homeless man repeated his ritual, his dirt-smudged boots licking the platform edge time and again, giving RG plenty of opportunities to act. It would just require a nudge.

8:29 p.m.

RG stepped closer. The sound of the train's churning wheels thrummed in his ears. The homeless man leaned over the tracks and peered into the tunnel. Moving within ten feet of him, RG withdrew trembling hands from his pockets. He could almost taste the city's stench wafting off the man.

What the hell am I doing?

The piercing scream ripped through the station, echoing off the walls and reverberating in RG's ears.

Twenty-four hours earlier, the car stereo had blasted Warren Zevon on WZLX as RG headed home from the university. Everything normal. Well, normal as in hands-clenching-the-steering-wheel-in-a-sea-of-angry-vehicles normal, his typical posture in a Friday afternoon Boston gridlock. He fought the overwhelming urge to veer into the open breakdown lane, jam the gas pedal to the floor, and relish that burst of acceleration, the tingling visceral rush. Instead, he inched along behind a three-lane wall of flashing red, his spiraling blood pressure thumping in his ears. Some people killed themselves with cigarettes, alcohol, or bad carbs, but RG accepted long ago driving in this city would usher in his demise, a slow death by daily commute.

Nosing the Subaru through a break in traffic, his iPhone lit up, Kacey's familiar ringtone inducing a non-traffic-related increase in heart rate.

RG snatched the cell from the passenger seat. "Can't live without me, eh?"

"Well, you're a close second to Dunkin' Donuts. Still on the road?"

He imagined her, reclined on the couch at her parents' oceanside home in Chatham, legs curled underneath her, hair tucked forgotten behind her ear. "You must be psychic. How can you tell?"

"Your voice has that I-90 whine to it."

RG shook his head. "So, just calling to taunt me?"

"I'm calling to see if you miss me."

"You mean since lunch?"

"Since dessert," she whispered.

RG's heart gave a quick flutter, thoughts drifting to their lunch date and brief detour back to the house. "You keep making me late for my 1:30 lecture and my students will start to suspect something."

"Just the co-eds, I imagine. Think you can survive the weekend without me?"

"It'll be close."

"See you Sunday, around dinner time."

"I'll have Chinese waiting."

"Perfect." She paused a beat. "I'll bring dessert."

A grin crept across RG's face as he disconnected. Coasting through his tidy Newton neighborhood, he maneuvered into the snow-crusted driveway and killed the engine. Parked behind the wheel, he stared through the windshield at his Tudor castle—well, not a castle in the conventional sense—but his home, his family's chosen kingdom. Most evenings, its silhouette looming in his headlights soothed him, but tonight, a sense of dread pressed against him, his feel-good moment with Kacey giving way to a familiar chomping at his gut.

Exiting the vehicle, RG skimmed the snow-scattered front lawn. He pictured a not so distant summer day, a tiny tyke holding a jumbo Glo-bat as he carefully lobbed the ball, leading to the inevitable home run, of course, the cheers his shrill voice would send vibrating through the neighborhood, announcing his pride. But, in that brief thrill, a cloud shadowed his imagined future and returned unsettling misgivings. He wondered if fatherhood had a twelve-step program to help him over-come his self-doubt. Kacey had reassured him, insisted he'd be a natural, that he had nothing to fear. But that's what all wives tell their husbands, as if they belonged to a secret society that teaches expectant mothers how to unknowingly guide their husbands through Fathering 101.

RG negotiated the slippery stone walkway, the brittle snow's crunch penetrating the quiet street's chilly calm. Grappling to corral his shoulder bag stuffed with exams and lab reports, a sheaf of papers clutched to his chest, he keyed the lock and entered under a shadowy cloud having taken away the moon's last sliver of evening brightness.

The house radiated a peculiar coldness, a strangeness he'd never encountered. He couldn't shake the fear gnawing at him, something more than his fatherhood jitters. Whatever lingered in the air encouraged him to hurry inside, to close the door before he succumbed to its aura.

The shifting papers tumbled from his grasp and scattered across the tiled floor. *Son of a bitch!* Tugging at his gloves with his teeth, he released his hands and unwound his wool scarf, draping it haphazardly on the hall tree. He reached to unbutton his coat, but a slight crackling halted him in his tracks. He recognized that sound. Graduating toward the living room, his breath caught in his throat as he glanced at the hearth, a flicker of orange and yellow gyrating across his features. Since when did fires ignite themselves?

His answer rose from the room's dark corner, a figure, a man whose face hid in the shadows but whose voice penetrated the whooshing fire's quiet comfort and broke RG's self-inflicted trance.

"Hello, Robert." The stranger advanced toward him. "You're late."

RG steadied himself against the entryway table as his heart lurched in his chest, the air thickening like a smothering rag over his face. With gradual boldness, he slid his arm against the wall and triggered the light switch. "What the hell—?"

"I feared we'd missed each other," the man interrupted. "That would have been a shame. You see, we have a problem to discuss." His face hardened as he stepped forward, shoes clicking on the hardwood floor.

RG's pulse quickened. "Who are you?"

"I wish I didn't have to be here, Robert." The stranger unfolded his hands from behind his back and stepped forward, "but I have a job to do."

As the man advanced, RG backpedaled, snatching the old-school, wooden baseball bat stashed behind the coat rack. He never imagined grabbing the lumber for anything other than Tuesday night softball, but now found himself flapping it back and forth in a hardwood batter's box.

The man took another step. "Death has come for you," he said, shaking his head, "and no Louisville Slugger will stop it."

~

July 1987

Sunday after church, Kacey rode in the back seat, her father driving, her mother beside him. With their weekly religious obligations fulfilled, the family headed to the Pancake Man in South Yarmouth. The little girl gazed through the side window at the world flying past, a rumble in her belly, wondering why pancakes always tasted so much better after church. Other restaurants in Chatham served a breakfast just as delicious as the Pancake Man's, but the family had created a Sunday tradition, and no one seemed to mind the extra miles together. One of Kacey's favorite games on their Sunday drives involved her mother or father pointing to a car and asking her to tell a story about it. Her imagination piqued, Kacey could weave a fantastic tale. Her parents added their own colorful details until the whole story collapsed into silliness.

The little girl loved Sundays and time spent with her parents. She also loved the restaurant, the air dripping with syrup and sizzling bacon aromas, the sound of plates and glasses clinking together as hurried waitstaff cleared them into plastic bins, the bell dinging when an order came up or the cash register opened, and the din of cheery conversations. Kacey's order never changed—the silver dollar pancakes—always just the right size. Plus, since they came in a stack of twelve, she could eat all day and never come close to finishing them. Her dad would get the apple and cinnamon pancakes with a side of potatoes—every time—with fresh squeezed orange juice. Her mother proved to be a mystery, though, always a surprise.

Today, Kacey and her mother played a different game once they arrived at the table. "Okay, honey," her mother said, "what am I getting for breakfast today?"

Having memorized the menu long ago, the little girl scrunched her face, trying to guess what her mother would order. "Hmm, you're getting the Belgian Waffles…with apple pie and a big glass of chocolate milk." She lifted her wide eyes to her mother.

"You're amazing, Kacey. That's exactly what I planned to order!" She gave a quick wink to her husband.

"I knew it," the little girl grinned.

"You know, Kacey, every day provides an opportunity for new adventures. Eating the same food all the time makes life too predictable and boring." She said this while peering at her husband. He glanced up from his newspaper with mock irritation, just a quick peek over his glasses, making her mother smile and Kacey giggle.

The little girl loved Sundays.

After breakfast, Kacey's parents sipped their coffee and talked about grownup things while she colored on a paper children's menu. An uncomfortable dizziness fell upon her, darkness sweeping across her vision like moving clouds drawing shadows across a patch of lawn. She dropped her crayon and stared straight ahead, unseeing—the pictures playing in her mind, like a movie. A movie about her family.

Only the movie wasn't a happy one at all.

Blood spattered their faces, and her mother lay sprawled in the road with her head dented in and her neck bent backward. Her father's crumpled body rested on the car's hood, halfway in and halfway out the windshield, his legs bent in places they didn't normally bend. A gurgling sound bled from his throat as he tried to breathe, like when he blew milk bubbles with her through a straw at the kitchen table. No sound came from her mother. A big white truck, decorated with a picture of cows and milk bottles, rested way too close to the car, steam billowing from its engine. People stood everywhere watching them, covering their mouths with their hands, gasping. No one moved. They just watched them. In an instant, the movie in her mind stopped.

Kacey lifted her head. The restaurant sounds once again swelled in her ears. Her father gave her a wink as he dropped a handful of bills on the table for the waitress.

"Okay, gang, let's hit the road." He slid from the booth.

Kacey crept under the table instead.

"Kacey, honey, get off the floor." Her mother reached for her under the table. "It's dirty under there."

"We can't leave yet." The little girl pulled away from her mother, grasping the table leg.

Her father's voice rose. "Come on. You're not a baby anymore."

"Honey, I told you last time, it's disrespectful to the people waiting to eat." Her mother shrugged at the hungry family waiting for their table.

"We have to wait."

Other patrons stared at them, shaking their heads. Her father folded his arms. "Kacey! Let's go!"

Kacey closed her eyes to see if she could replay the movie in her head, but she saw nothing. It usually didn't take long for the pictures to go away; she just needed to wait a while. If she waited and still saw the pictures, she needed to wait longer.

"Okay, I'm ready." She crept from under the table and reached for her parents' hands, walking them outside the restaurant and over to the car. Her mother and father exchanged a glance as they buckled their lap belts, whispering in hushed tones.

They eased into the heavy weekend traffic heading south on Route 28. They drove for a few minutes until they approached the intersection of 28 and Old Main. At a stoplight, her mother leaned over the backseat, smiling.

"Hey Kacey, do you see the milk truck up ahead with the cows and bottles painted on the side of it? Tell us a story about that one."

Friday, December 1, 2017

The man's cryptic announcement replayed in RG's head, leaving him unhinged, with a sense of foreboding he couldn't shake: "Death has come for you." *Death? What the fuck?* "Don't take another step you sonofabitch, or I'm swinging away!" He slapped the bat against his hand as he faced off against the stranger.

He sized up his unexpected visitor. The man wore the clothes of a different generation, crisp dark suit and hat, impeccably tailored, and thick horn-rimmed glasses. RG's gaze darted around the room, searching for Baron. He expected the growl rumbling in the back of its throat, the ears pinned against its coat, a guttural bark and the stranger pinned immobile against the wall. Finding the German Shepard asleep by the fireplace, all cozy and content, he blinked his eyes trying to hit reset.

He crept closer to the man. "I'm not gonna ask again. Who the hell—?"

"Please don't be alarmed, Robert," the man interrupted, taking a step closer. "You can call me Morrow."

"How do you know my name?"

"I know many things about you."

RG squinted at the man searching his memory, but he couldn't place him. He appeared harmless enough, and while RG possessed the advantage of youth, a college professor with a gym-bought physique didn't guarantee jack in a physical confrontation, even one gripping a Louisville Slugger. His heart continued to thump against his throat. "Listen, Mr.—"

"Morrow."

"Morrow, Mambo, Dumbo, doesn't fucking matter," RG asserted. "You're trespassing in my home and you need to get the hell out of here!" His hand shot forward, pointing to the door.

"Robert, you must listen to me. Death has come for you," he repeated, "and time is running short."

His hands tightened around the bat. "Are you here to kill me?" His eyes did a quick scan to see if the man brandished a gun, a knife, a rope, whatever the hell a person might use to kill someone.

"I'm not here to harm you. In fact, I've spent a good portion of my existence watching over you and protecting you."

RG grinned and lowered the bat. "I get it now. It's a fucking prank!" He pressed his hand on his chest and exhaled. "Who put you up to this? Johnny D? Matty? Well, tell them you had me going. You scared the shit out of me, old man."

"No one sent me. Now, please sit." Morrow directed him to the couch. "We need to talk."

RG hurried about the room, checking doors and windows, all locked, no sign of forced entry. A cold sweat erupted across his skin. "How'd you get in here, anyway? Someone give you a key?"

The older man chuckled. "I don't need a key, but if I did I would've grabbed it from the window ledge out back."

"How did you know...?" His voice trailed off.

Morrow shrugged. "I know many things about you."

This guy's good. Whoever hired him did his homework.

RG lowered himself into the chair opposite the intruder, throwing his feet up on the coffee table. "All right mister, show's over, but if you want to stay in character, be my guest." *Must be getting paid by the hour.* "You were saying?"

"This isn't a joke, Robert." Morrow snapped. "It's time to listen to me. As I said, I've spent—"

"Yeah, you've been protecting me, yada, yada," RG interrupted. "Protecting me from what?"

"From the whimsical nature of the life we're born into." Morrow cleared his throat. "Robert, you're scheduled to die tomorrow."

"Yeah, right." RG crossed his legs.

Morrow glanced at the floor. "Robert, in my capacity I have knowledge of those destined for certain fates. And it's your fate to die shortly after sunset tomorrow."

"Bullshit!"

"I can't tell you how sorry I am."

RG sprung to his feet. "There's no way you can know that! You're fucking wrong!"

"Let me show you something. Afterward, you'll understand I'm telling the truth." Morrow stood and crossed the hardwood floor to the fireplace. "Please come join me and watch the fire."

RG couldn't move, his shoes frozen to the floor. His eyes wandered to the spot he and Kacey huddled together by the fire on cold winter nights, the place they shared Chinese food in paper cartons, talked about their future. He hesitated, frightened of what he might see, but curiosity peered out from beneath the shadow of his fear. Leaning his bat against the couch, RG took tentative steps toward Morrow, needing to witness whatever secrets hid within the flames. He stared at the fire but observed nothing unusual. He turned to Morrow.

"Be patient."

As RG's gaze returned to the fireplace, a hazy three-dimensional shape formed inside the flames, an image of himself as a five-year-old playing at the beach. The moving picture grew before his eyes, reaching across the living room's hardwood floor, sand spreading underneath their shoes. The ocean extended far beyond the dwelling's confines, the house walls now just a vague outline against the crashing waves and cobalt sky. RG's mother beamed at her child from the living flashback, oblivious to her adult son standing mere feet from her. Helen Granville, gone ten years now, walked on the beach beside the boy he used to be, holding his tiny hand; beautiful, young, and full of life.

As a child, RG understood how losing his dad had changed Helen Granville. He'd watched her struggle to put on her best face for him, but he could hear her muffled cries at night through her bedroom door. In the morning, she never failed to pull out a smile for him, despite her pain—only it never lasted. In the resurrected memory dancing before his disbelieving eyes, the brilliant sunshine, soft sand, and healing ocean delivered a happiness to her he rarely witnessed. He blinked back the tears burning below his eyelids.

"Mom," he whispered.

"She can't hear you. She isn't here." Morrow lingered in the vision, waiting several moments before waving his hand in front of the hearth. Immediately, the ocean receded, the sand turned into hardwood flooring, and the blazing sun morphed into the compact fluorescent bulb in the overhead fixture.

Morrow placed his hand on RG's shoulder. "I accompanied you to the beach that day. For the past thirty-five years, I've served as your protector and guardian. We call ourselves caretakers. It's our job to protect you, and at your life's end, we help transition your soul to the next world."

RG continued to stare blankly into the fireplace.

Morrow sauntered to the living room window, staring out at the moon spattered front lawn. "I'm not of this world anymore, although I once lived here. I'm from the next phase in the ongoing soul journey, and I reside where most people on earth can't perceive. Few in your world can sense those who've crossed into my world, but in fact, we all exist on parallel planes and occupy the same space."

The reality of his situation hit RG like a hammer—as if fate had brought the Louisville Slugger crashing down on *his* head. His time had come, and tomorrow he'd die.

This can't be happening. This can't be real. He paced the floor, waiting for a hole to open and swallow him, to take him away from the insanity.

Morrow continued speaking, but his words filtered to silence, the sound muffled in his head. *I can't leave this world yet. I'm going to be a father, for Chrissake!* "Who the hell do you think you are coming here and telling me this?" RG rescued the bat and waved it in front of him. "You can't take me! I'm not going!"

Morrow swayed with his hands tucked behind his back, listening while RG continued his rant. Before long, he stopped shouting and lowered his head.

"Listen, Mr. Morrow, I need to get out of here. I need to see my wife, Kacey, before tomorrow. Before…"

Morrow stared over the rim of his glasses. "And you will, but there's more you need to know."

CHAPTER TWO

ay 1972

Victor Garrett stared at the IV hanging from his ten-year-old boy's arm and listened to his labored breathing. The doctors at St. Francis worked around the clock to keep Sam alive as Victor had begged them to. He lay beside his son and held him, as he'd done every day since entering the hospital.

Three weeks earlier, Victor Garrett had the life of a different man—a deacon at his local church, a devoted man of God with a career, and a loving wife and son. Today, he lived a broken man's life, a desperate creature without faith in God or humanity. Praying for miracles, Victor heard only silence. The doctors told him his son wouldn't survive.

So much for prayer.

When his son fell ill, Victor believed God would use Sam as a vehicle for His grace and healing, because a merciful and blessed God takes care of the righteous. Sam spent his days in bed, too fatigued to sit up. He stopped eating after solid food raged against his insides, dragging with it a trail of crimson blood. The bulbous lumps along his neck multiplied and spread as his cough brought more and more dark fluid from his lungs. When they'd rushed Sam to the hospital, the young doctor escorted Victor and his wife, Lucy, into a consultation room.

"Please, sit." The doctor lowered himself onto a stool, his elbows resting on his knees, his hands folded together. He stared at the floor.

The fluorescent lights whined like a buzz saw in Victor's ears as he waited for the doctor to break the excruciating silence, the wall clock's second hand ticking like a time bomb. Behind him, a photograph displayed a peaceful oak tree with the phrase 'prayers available upon request' below it.

"The situation's critical." The doctor lifted his gaze. "We need to perform aggressive treatments to help your son. We don't have much time."

Lucy's sobs and phrases like "stage five," "experimental treatments," and "pain management" rattled in Victor's head. He fell to his knees, envisioning the coming trauma Sam faced, the chemicals they'd pump through his system, the devices they'd use to cut out invasive growths and tumors, the cries his boy would make when pain would overtake him.

He wouldn't be able to do a damn thing to help.

Victor had spent time with the sick and dying as a deacon, a man of faith bearing comfort and peace, but the young cancer patients tested his faith. The jarring images of their emaciated bodies and sallow skin tortured him, haunting his dreams. Their hollow eyes beseeched him for a miracle, as if he could dial up God himself. The suffering he witnessed brought moments of doubt, the questioning of God's motives. Sometimes Victor could give children nothing but empty words from an ancient book, the false myth of everlasting life. Now he'd watch Sam die in the same horrible way, his God repaying him for his crisis of faith.

When the young doctor offered to pray with them, rage took root in his soul.

There'd be no more prayer.

Victor wailed into his pillow at night and silently cursed happy families with healthy children. Sam bore little resemblance to Victor and Lucy's beautiful only child—their golden one, as Lucy called him

—with freckles gathered across his nose, iridescent blue eyes, and beautiful blonde hair. Now a shell of the boy he used to be, Sam's once-sparkling eyes rested dull in their sockets; his hair fell out with each tousle; his ribs and sternum protruded visibly through pale ghostly skin. When he spoke to his father, he'd whisper a desperate plea to be at peace. Victor had lived by his son's side for the past three weeks, rarely eating or sleeping. He'd lost his job and bills were mounting, his entire world now a hospital room where a suffering child lay dying.

Victor touched his son's cheek as the boy's eyes struggled open.

"Dad," Sam wheezed. "I think…I'm ready now."

A shudder rumbled through Victor's body. For the past week, Sam had lost the will to stay alive. He no longer ate; a tube in his stomach provided nourishment to keep him alive. He slept more and more, barely speaking. "You can't go, Sam, you need to keep trying to beat this thing. You're getting stronger."

"It hurts now…all the time."

More morphine. Victor jammed the nurse's call button, unaware Sam already took the maximum tolerated dose. "We'll get you something to help the pain."

"No more!" Sam cried. He struggled to catch his breath. "Dad, it's time to let me go."

The words echoed in his ears. "Not yet," Victor pleaded. "Please stay with me. Don't go." Victor closed his eyes and mumbled, "I need you."

Tears formed in Sam's eyes. He lifted a frail hand to wipe them away. Victor reached over and held it, tenderly pressing a corner of the bedsheet against his son's cheeks.

Sam barked out a ragged, wet cough, his body shaking. "Go get Mom for me, okay?"

His son's command, although weak in its whisper against the room's orchestra of life-saving machines, resonated with a truth Victor suppressed with such resolve, it shook him to his core. The moment had arrived, all the time he'd been coveting, now over.

Victor's glance darted from Sam to the clunky bedside machine with plastic lines and wires snaking into his son's body. He scanned the front panel, hoping the nurses had forgotten to flick on a knob or switch, maybe a special button, that could save his son. Below the panel, a company name and location etched into the metal brought to mind a barren, snow-covered field on the edge of a dying city and a large, windowless factory billowing out plumes of smoke into the cold, gray sky. He wondered whether anyone in that city now sat beside their doomed child the way he did.

He leaned down, pressing his lips against his son's cheek. "You can let go now, Sam," he whispered. "I won't stop you anymore." He placed his hands on both sides of Sam's face and kissed his forehead one last time.

Victor found Lucy sitting in the hallway in her flowered dress, clutching a Styrofoam coffee cup, eyes fixated on the tiled flooring at her feet, head bowed in a prayerful pose, her hair forming a curtain to hide a mother's undefinable pain. Victor's chest heaved, his body numb, his legs unable to hold his weight. Lucy rushed to her son and spoke in soft, comforting tones, caressing his sweaty forehead. As Victor stood frozen in the doorway, her words turned to sobs, then agonized screams.

Sam was gone.

A deep burning filled Victor as if a flame had been lit inside his heart. His eyes rimmed with hot tears as he gasped to breathe, fire spreading through his veins, encircling his body. Victor succumbed to it, praying the heat would kill him.

But it didn't.

Instead, a vision flashed across his open eyes, rocking him backward. Victor steadied himself as the room pulled away and the moving images filled his head. Victor recognized the young doctor as he strolled through the parking lot to his car, but he'd aged, maybe a decade or more. His body sagged around the midsection, the skin around his face softer. The doctor buckled the Volvo's seat belt and checked his mirrors as he pulled out into traffic.

Then Victor became the man, viewing the scene from behind the doctor's eyes.

Victor winced as a violent jolt of surging energy threw the doctor across the car's front seat, a furious presence invading his physical space, pushing at his skin's surface, attempting to burst through it. A fire raged inside the man, the searing heat burning him from within. Sweat dripped into the doctor's eyes, or it may have been Victor's eyes, he couldn't tell anymore, blinding him as the car exploded down the road at breakneck speed, a speed far too dangerous for the narrow two-lane road. Flailing at the wheel, the doctor struggled to stay in his lane as it rocketed toward the double yellow line. He fought to slam the brake, but his foot remained glued to the gas pedal. Victor sensed his own hands wrench the steering wheel back to the left, sending the Volvo directly into the oncoming traffic.

The fire inside Victor weakened and burned out, his hallucination fizzling before him. The quiet hospital's buffed, sterile floors and neutral colored walls resumed in his vision, and Lucy's wails rattled in his ears. He held onto the wall to support his quivering legs, laboring to breathe. He caught a last glimpse of Sam as Lucy hoisted the dead child into her lap and rocked him, his empty body lurching in tempo with his mother's racking sobs.

Life had ended for Sam. He'd found his peace. There would be no peace for Victor.

A change had taken hold of him.

∼

Friday, December 1, 2017

RG's head swirled. His dead mother's youthful, living image still played in his mind. He'd been told of life after death—the answer to our ultimate question—and his own imminent death. His heartbeat roared in his ears against the logic. He dropped onto the couch and buried his face in his hands, not yet ready to die.

This is too unbelievable. My eyes must be deceiving me, or maybe this two-bit parlor magician has me hypnotized or something.

Morrow eased away from the window. "How about some fresh air?"

RG raised his head and glared at Morrow. He sure as hell didn't want to go walking with this man anywhere, let alone outside in the frosty night air, but did he have a choice? Maybe a walk around the neighborhood would give him an opportunity to lose the bastard. Without as much as a grunt, RG bolted from the couch and ripped his coat off the coatrack.

Once outside, they hiked along the winding, hilly street, RG oblivious to the finely manicured lawns powdered with fresh snow. His mind numb, he didn't notice the swirling brisk air or the full moon casting nighttime shadows before them.

Morrow glanced upward, scanning the trees and sky. "How I miss the snow. It's one of the beautiful things in your world…along with chocolate. Nothing in existence can compare to the wonder of chocolate."

"Chocolate? That's a kicker." RG groaned, picking up the pace. "My life's in question here, and you want to talk about chocolate? Wow. This keeps getting more absurd by the minute."

"Robert, I know it's hard to understand, but—"

"Quit calling me Robert," he interrupted. "It's RG. At least get that right." He slammed his hands into his coat pockets and tucked his neck down into his thick collar, as if he could slink between the coat fibers where Morrow couldn't reach him. The faster he walked, the faster he'd escape, but Morrow kept at his heels.

"So, you've come to be my caretaker." The guy had to have missed his bed check at the neighborhood psychiatric ward. "Tell me, what exactly is your job description?" *This should be good.*

Morrow stopped before the rusty gate leading into the neighborhood park, his calm demeanor making RG want to scream. "In my world, we're chosen for this calling. My mission has been to guard and protect you, and I've been beside you since your infancy, the day your father died. You can't see a caretaker, but you can sense our presence."

"You have an answer for everything, don't you?"

They entered the playground. Dropping onto a swing, RG grabbed the icy chain links suspended from the metal structure and stared at his caretaker standing before him. *If this guy's legit, he'll be a straight shooter, no room for inconsistencies or bullshit.* "Why did I need protection?"

"Well, accidents mainly. Caretakers manipulate your world's physical laws every day to prevent them, but for some unfortunate souls, we must also protect against darker forces. You see, an evil exists in my world. There are others," Morrow hesitated, "others who can pierce the thin veil between worlds. They travel back and forth and prey on the living. We call them jumpers."

"Jumpers?" *Really? How original?*

"They kill to avenge an unfulfilled human life. Many have unfinished business here or experienced an unspeakable tragedy." Morrow gazed out across the park. "The loss of a loved one, or a child. Many can't move on from the loss so they punish the innocent, take souls for their own pleasure."

"You know what this sounds like, right? Like you're off your meds?"

Morrow raised an eyebrow. "There are no meds where I come from."

No meds...no keys. "Hmmm. Truth, death, caretakers, jumpers...I'd say you need professional help." Silence pressed between them for a short time. "Then tell me...these spirits...how can I see you but not them?"

"Because caretakers have the capacity of embodiment in your world, jumpers do not. It's only allowed for us under dire circumstances, when death is moments away and we can ease suffering. Unfortunately, my visit tonight does not qualify as such."

"So, you've broken the rules."

"And I will pay a hefty price."

"Let me recap. They exist, but we can't see them. How convenient. So, how can we defend ourselves against something we can't see?"

"You can't." Morrow lowered his eyes. "Jumpers invade your physical space, taking complete control of the body. They initiate accidents. I know of no defense. But they're reckless, fixated on their mission with such intensity they're sometimes killed in the accidents they cause. You see, if a jumper doesn't escape their host before the host is killed, the jumper dies, too."

"It's good to know Darwin's theory applies across multiple planes of existence. Not that I'm buying any of this shit, just saying." *Does anything rattle this guy?*

"Only a caretaker can help you fend off a jumper. We can overpower them when we sense their presence."

RG stood, traversing the damp grass toward the park entrance, Morrow beside him. *Let's see how he handles this one.* "Does everyone have a caretaker?"

"Unfortunately, there aren't enough of us for everyone, but not everyone needs one." Opening the gate for RG, Morrow followed him out to the street. "Some people in your world possess a defensive power a jumper can't penetrate, but caretaker or no caretaker, no one lives forever. Sometimes accidents just happen, and sometimes it's your time to go, like it's your time now."

Continuing their walk, they fell into a wretched silence, the intensity as biting as the frozen air. After several minutes RG turned to Morrow. "Tell me, smart guy, since you seem to know everything, how's it supposed to go down tomorrow?"

"You know, I didn't have to come here and warn you."

"Then why did you? Why upset what little life I have left? Why make me suffer, think about my death and how it will disrupt everything...my life with Kacey, how it will crush the ones I leave behind? Thanks for that!"

"I'm sorry."

"Are you? Do you really expect me to buy your bullshit story?"

"It appears I've made a mistake—"

"That's the first thing you've said that makes any sense." RG stopped and pivoted to face Mr. Doomsday. "You think you can just pop into someone's living room and drop a bombshell like this and expect them to believe it? Well, I'm not falling for it."

RG stomped ahead, but stalled as his muscles numbed, his limbs faltering. Morrow placed his arm around his shoulder and steadied him. "Do you want to hear what I have to say about tomorrow or not?"

RG bit his tongue.

"Death can occur in an infinite number of ways, depending on the decisions and choices you make. A caretaker doesn't always know specifically where and how, but we know when. Still, if I told you where and how, you'd avoid the location, believing you could alter your destiny and cheat death." Morrow faced RG. "But make no mistake, death will occur—and yours will happen tomorrow night."

Fat snowflakes tumbled from the sky. RG ached as he witnessed the beauty of his little spot in the world, the uniqueness of this picturesque snowy night. Like everything else in his life, tomorrow it would be gone. For the first time, he could no longer think in years, months, or even days. He could no longer plan his life down to its final moments. He fought to grasp and tightly hold the world's beautiful things, searching for memories to comfort him, images he could steal from this life to take with him, but none surfaced, his mind empty, a void. It only let him concentrate on what he could control, the number of breaths in and out, placing one foot in front of the other to make sure he didn't stumble, fall to his knees.

But with each step, the veil slowly lifted. Soon, every captive moment and remembrance flooded back. The past rushed through his hair like the wind, conferring upon him an insufferable elation. He found himself in the eye of the hurricane, rendering a temporary peace.

The men circled the neighborhood and returned to the house. Stepping into the kitchen, RG grabbed a handful of Hershey's kisses from the drawer beside the stove. He placed them in the bowl on the living room coffee table, tossing one to Morrow and collapsing on the sofa, for the first time aware of his exhaustion.

"Why tell me about my death? Why come here at all? You're not doing me any favors."

"Nor am I doing myself any." Morrow seated himself opposite RG. "For my transgressions, I will likely have my caretaker status revoked, my powers stripped. I'd give anything not to be here and deliver the gut-wrenching truth." Morrow removed his glasses. "But I had to come back. You see, I didn't have anyone come forward to warn me of my fate. I never received the memo that evil had its sights set on me. I had no inkling I wouldn't make it home from work that awful day."

"What happened?"

Morrow waved his hand. "I've come back because I didn't get a chance to say goodbye to my loved ones, to hold my wife one more time and tell her I loved her, to kiss my…" Morrow's voice faltered. He stood and slogged to the bay windows, staring at the night pressing against the glass. "I came back to give you the chance I didn't have, to tie up loose ends, to have closure. Go to Kacey. Have one final moment together. But do not linger. You mustn't be with loved ones when your time comes, it could be dangerous for them."

"I won't. I'd never put her in danger," he assured him. But, deep down, he couldn't imagine leaving her, saying goodbye knowing he'd be walking away forever.

"And another thing. Your death won't be the end, you'll be moving on to another realm…where your father's waiting for you."

RG shifted, gave a few short chuckles as if trying to comprehend the insane, inconvenient invasion into his cozy life. He swallowed. "Do you know how I'll die?"

"I see many possible variations." Morrow unwrapped the candy and popped it in his mouth. "But they all take place tomorrow, Saturday, at 8:30 p.m. This I know for sure."

Chatham Police detective Mike Stahl rolled down the unmarked vehicle's window as he coasted along Main Street. Nothing screamed 'cop' more than a dark blue Crown Victoria four-door sedan, and Stahl didn't expect to fool anyone. After a taxing workday, he sped over to Carmine's for a deep-dish pizza, a not-so-nutritional staple in a single man's diet, but as he drove past the Village Market, Kacey Kearns— well, Kacey Granville now—stepped through the automatic doors, her distinct form forever ingrained in his memory.

Mike's breath caught in his throat and he let out a sigh. She looked beautiful as always, her wavy, shoulder length hair the color of late autumn's falling leaves. But something was different, the way she moved maybe? He pulled into the grocery store parking lot, dragging a paw across his perpetual five o'clock shadow, the first gray flecks reflecting in the rearview mirror matching their brethren tickling his temples.

Stahl eased the Crown Vic beside her as she loaded bags into her trunk. He stepped out into the snow. "Need a hand?"

Kacey glanced over her shoulder with a smile. "Michael Francis Stahl. I had a feeling I'd run into you."

His eyes widened as she turned to face him. "Oh my God!" His eyes drifted downward. "You have a…you're—"

"Pregnant?" She stepped forward and gave him a hug, her presence warming him despite the cold. "Seven months now."

"How are you feeling?"

"Well, I'm used to being fat and out of breath all the time." She laughed, snow accumulating in her hair. One sizable snowflake landed on her cheek, and he watched in wonder as the crystalline structure dissolved on her skin.

"I got this." Stahl hoisted the bottled water and remaining bags into her trunk. "Why isn't RG doing the heavy lifting?"

"He's back in Boston. I'm helping Mom and Dad."

"Well, aren't you the perfect daughter." He shook away the flakes accumulating in his hair. "How are Bruce and Sandie, by the way?"

"Oh, they're fine," she shrugged, "slowing down a bit."

"I always do a quick check on the property whenever my duties take me out that way. A lot of loaded memories…"

Her movement slowed at his mention of memories. Jamming his hands into his jacket, Stahl blew out a breath, uncertain if he'd upset her, blindsided her with the past. "Kacey, I'm sorry. I—"

"Don't be." Her gloved hand reached out and squeezed his arm, the awkwardness more biting than the chill air.

"I should be on my way." He turned toward the Crown Vic.

"That's right, you have a town to protect, don't you?"

He chuckled. "No doubt Chatham will erupt into chaos if I don't get back to work." Neither one spoke for a moment, but Mike broke the silence. "Great to see you, Kacey."

"You, too." Kacey took her mitten-clad hand and brushed the clinging snowflakes from his hair.

"And congratulations."

Kacey smirked and shuffled to the driver's side door, easing herself into the seat. She gave him a can-you-believe-how-pregnant-I-am eye roll, jammed the car into gear, and headed down Main Street. He stared as she drove away, her taillights fading into glowing specks on the asphalt roadway. Shaking the remaining snow from his hair, he returned to his car.

Stahl chewed his lip as he maneuvered the Crown Vic from the parking lot. His mind drifted back to the last time he'd seen her, dressed in black in a receiving line of mourners. His parents' deaths had shocked the community, to learn they'd met a drunk driver on the wrong side of the mid-Cape highway. But Kacey's presence provoked another kind of collision, his own run-in with rampant demons lurking behind *his* destructive addiction.

He could never erase the stain from his soul or forgive himself for what he'd done to her one night in a drunken rage, seizing her by the arm and sending her flying across their Boston apartment's kitchen floor. If he could just take it back, that one moment out of the millions they'd shared, maybe he'd never have witnessed the love drain from her eyes as she turned and slammed the door, bolting from his life. He couldn't help but wonder if Kacey would have walked down the aisle with him instead of Granville if not for the power his weakness had wielded over him.

He raked his fingernails through his hair, as if the past was a snarl he could comb away. Aiming the vehicle down Main Street toward Carmine's, he opted to take one more pass through downtown to check on the Friday night revelers. Kacey was right, the patrolman in him still very much alive when it came to his town.

Rumbling past the Chatham Squire, Mike recognized the Falmouth police chief's cruiser parked along Main—blocking a hydrant, of course—its rear end sticking out enough to gnarl traffic along the narrow street. *Chuck Brennan, the arrogant sonofabitch! Still thinks he owns this fucking town.* He debated digging out his old citation book and writing him a ticket, just to catch the look on his face. Instead, he urged the car forward and continued through town, a grin spreading across his lips at the thought. No need to stoke a dying fire.

As he wheeled into the parking lot behind Carmine's, Mike pulled the key, the dome light pitching shadows across the car's interior. He sat for a moment, reflecting on his run-in with Kacey, wishing happenstance could be more predictable, at least with her. Still, every encounter set him back further, breaching the wall he'd constructed around his heart, stone by stone, year after year. It would now crumble in the silence of his loneliness. He closed his eyes as the bulb dimmed, welcoming the dark and craving the numbing sedation of a Captain and Coke.

~

Chuck Brennan stumbled out of the Chatham Squire earlier than usual for a Friday night, but the number of drinks he'd put down during happy hour more than matched his typical night on the town. He'd made a habit of traveling from Falmouth to Chatham Fridays after work for the Squire's new lineup of bartenders: young, blonde, bouncy —just the way he liked them—and, rumor had it, in love with the badge. He'd heard a few war stories passed along from his fellow officers, and he'd been eager to get in on the action. As Falmouth's Chief of Police and a former Chatham cop, it wouldn't be long until *his* stories filtered through the grapevine.

Passing the Squire's stenciled plate-glass window, Brennan's reflection exposed a hard man with a generous midsection protruding over his belt, pushing a snug uniform to the edge of its seams. A big man at six-foot-four, and growing bigger, he had a reputation as a crude and intimidating police officer, and he made no apologies for it. He'd done his time as a Boston cop, come up through the ranks working the toughest Southie neighborhoods. At fifty-two, Brennan welcomed Cape Cod's slower pace for police work and its perks—

usually after hours—but he missed the city's action, the high-profile collars and headline cases. He feared he'd ride this slow-paced pony right to the glue factory.

As Brennan swayed along the Main Street sidewalk searching for his misplaced cruiser, a dark blue Crown Vic emerged from the opposite direction, rolling down the street with a purpose, clearly someone on the job. Focusing through the cloud of Johnny Walker Red, Brennan leaned forward, peering through the side window as the car rumbled passed.

Mike Stahl—the self-righteous prick.

Brennan had partnered with Stahl for a time, before he'd taken the Falmouth chief position. He'd taken him under his wing, showed him how things worked, how to take advantage of complimentary meals around town, enjoy free drinks after hours. But Stahl turned out to be a crusader, a company man who played by the rules, the poster boy for internal affairs.

Brennan spit on the sidewalk as he recalled Stahl's first year on the job, the night they'd responded to a late-night call to the Super 8 just off Route 28. They flew into the motel parking lot, tires squealing, aiming their patrol vehicle toward the crowd forming outside the room. Bright light spilled through the open door, shining through huddled gawkers trying to catch a peek, their bodies throwing oblong shadows into the inky black parking lot.

Brennan wiped his forehead with his shirtsleeve as he exited the air-conditioned car and stepped out into the humid July night. An ambulance idled in the parking lot, lights flashing. He nodded to Mike. "Follow me, rookie." Brennan sauntered through the throng of people crowding the motel room door, watching the EMTs inside.

"All right, get the fuck out of my way, you vultures. Back to your rooms!" Brennan growled at the onlookers, who immediately shuffled off, leaving Brennan and Stahl alone outside the motel room with the middle-aged hotel manager pacing back and forth, hand pressed against his forehead.

Brennan and Stahl entered the drab room, thrown together on the cheap, microwave and fridge, low-end flat screen TV resting on a wobbly chest of drawers. But this one featured an additional item not found in most standard rooms.

A dead body lying sideways across the bed.

The man couldn't have been more than twenty years old, wearing stained blue jeans and a Jimi Hendrix tee-shirt, his dirty brown hair matted and unkempt as if he'd been too preoccupied to shower, or care, in his final days. The scars in the crook of his elbow betrayed an unmistakable history, a habit ending the man's fateful journey. White powder packets lay next to a spoon and lighter on the nightstand, scorch marks infiltrating the wood.

"Sonofabitch picks the hottest night of the summer to OD. Jesus Christ," Brennan muttered, wiping his forehead again and leaning over the bed to better view the man's face. His lips had the same hue as his wide blue eyes, a vomit clot still coagulating in his open mouth, a thick, soupy trail winding down his cheeks, pooling behind his head like a lava flow from a volcano's crater. Half empty beer bottles and cigarettes still burning in ashtrays told the tale of people making a hurried exit.

Brennan dismissed the EMTs and requested the County Coroner. This body wouldn't be going to any hospital tonight. The way Stahl gazed at the stiff, eyes wide and searching, his feet fixed as if poured in cement, Brennan figured he hadn't run into many DOA's before. Brennan smirked, pointing to the dead man's shirt as he circled the room. "Poor bastard ended up like his hero."

The motel manager stepped into the room, speaking in a halting, melodic accent, the sweat noticeable on his brow. "Officers, this type of…activity doesn't happen in my motel."

Brennan wheeled, directing a pent-up venom at the man. "I don't give a fuck about your motel. You got a dead man in here with drugs all over the place. You're lucky I don't arrest you. Did you call for us?"

The man backed up. "For the ambulance, yes."

"You rent the room to this guy?"

"About an hour ago."

"All right, get the fuck out of here and wait for me in the office. You don't need to be here."

As the manager retreated to the parking lot, Brennan and Stahl secured the scene, checking every inch of the room. Mike pulled back a pillow to find a stuffed envelope full of cash under the rumpled bedding.

Brennan sauntered over to Stahl, holding out his hand. "Looks like we have more than just an overdose here."

"A 966, you think?"

Brennan rolled his eyes. *What? You memorize the codes, Ponch?* "Let me have a look at the envelope."

Stahl handed him the cash. "Would drug dealers just leave money?"

"Guy croaks with *their* drugs in his system, they're gonna bug out to avoid a murder charge. Amateurs, obviously. They panicked, forgot the cash." He fanned the bills in the envelope with his thumb. "Hmm. Enough to buy drinks for the next couple of years."

Mike gave a nervous chuckle.

Brennan shot him a condescending glance. "That's right, you don't drink anymore, do you? Well, it'll buy you a lot of milk, or whatever the fuck it is you do drink." Brennan glanced toward the open door and shoved the envelope in his pocket.

Stahl shifted his weight from his left foot to his right. "Um, what are you doing?"

"I'm relieving this man from the obligation to pay for a product clearly not performing to his satisfaction." Brennan winked.

"That's evidence of a crime."

"I don't see a crime. I see a kid wanting to be alone for a while to use, springs for a hotel room, winds up with bad junk. Another tragic Cape Cod heroin overdose, nothing new there."

Stahl rubbed the back of his neck. "Sir, I'm not comfortable with—"

"I don't think Jimi over there will be filing any complaints, do you?"

Mike swallowed. "Sir, we need to count it, put it in the report."

Brennan raised his hand and patted Stahl on the cheek. "Relax, son. I'll take care of it."

Hours later at the station, Brennan left a stuffed envelope in Stahl's locker, but found it back on his desk the following morning unopened. A message delivered.

Fuck him, more drinking money for me.

Stahl ended up making a minor stink, roiling the waters, talking to the chief, but it was his word against a veteran officer. The chief did honor Stahl's request for partner reassignment, and he ended up riding alone once gossip spread that he didn't play well with others, professional suicide for most rookies.

At least Brennan didn't have to put a bullet through Stahl's skull.

As Brennan stumbled along Main Street, Stahl's Crown Vic pulled into the lot behind Carmine's Pizza. Brennan reversed direction, hoofing it toward the pizza place. He squinted through the restaurant's smudged glass to focus on the lone figure seated in the booth. Stahl sipped his water and made small talk with the waitress.

Still riding alone, huh?

Brennan crept over to the car nestled in the lot's shadow, cloaked in darkness, and stood beside the driver's side door. He unzipped his pants and urinated on the Crown Vic's door and front panel, steam rising from the thermal puddle forming on the frigid ground.

"Just marking my territory, you sonofabitch!"

CHAPTER THREE

Saturday, December 2, 2017

RG woke with a start and dragged himself upright, feeling as if he'd been asleep for days. Shaking out the cobwebs, he swung his legs over the edge of the antique bed. The morning sun streaming through the window exposed a hidden dust particle blizzard floating midair. He rubbed his eyes, wiping away the remnants of a terrible dream, a nightmare of his own death foretold. *Caretakers, jumpers, where the hell did all that come from?* Breathing a deep sigh of relief, he stepped onto the plush bedroom carpet and shuffled out onto the landing.

Before heading downstairs, he took a brief detour into the baby room at the end of the hall. RG placed his hand over his stomach, getting acquainted with the uncomfortable knot living there. Father-hood can't be that hard, can it? The dog-eared pages of the parenting books Kacey left on his bedside table offered a smidgeon of reassurance. All those birthing classes he'd attended on diaper changing, feeding, swaddling—you name it, he could do it. But the paralyzing uncertainty about screwing up an innocent child's life the way his father's death had damaged his own weighed on his mind. With no role model and mentor, no make-the-hurt-go-away provider, RG would never be able to draw from, or echo, the unconditional and free-wheeling love he'd missed. What did he know about these things? Nothing.

He had to have faith.

He shuffled down the stairs but froze in his tracks at the sight of Morrow relaxing at the kitchen table, stirring a mug of hot chocolate, Baron dozing at his feet. RG's face crumpled.

"I'm sorry, Robert." Morrow blew steam from the mug. "I'm not a dream. It's time to accept the truth."

"Sonofabitch!" The reality of his impending death hit him like a blow to the gut. How could this all be for nothing, all his preparations, all his plans? He had news for Morrow: he wasn't going anywhere without helping his child take his or her first steps, hearing their chosen baby name tumble over their lips for the first time, or walking the kid into school on the first day of kindergarten. History wouldn't repeat itself this time. *Not gonna happen!*

"Look, Mr. Morrow," he swallowed. "I need more time."

"Sorry, it doesn't work that way."

RG collapsed into a chair at the kitchen table next to his so-called protector, his fingers tapping on his thigh. He reached out his hand for Baron to come to him, but the dog only raised an eyebrow, content to remain at Morrow's feet. *I'm going to have to demote the mutt from guard dog to lap dog. Traitor.*

If Morrow's caretaker claims were true, why couldn't he exercise his special talents to save him? "For Chrissake! You can travel across dimensions, create living images in a fireplace, but you don't know a way out? There must be exceptions. Think Mr. Morrow, please!" He closed his eyes and rubbed the back of his neck.

Time passed before Morrow leaned forward. "I heard a story once about a man destined for death receiving an unexpected reprieve." He reached for the bowl of Hershey's kisses.

What's the deal with Morrow and chocolate?

"At the moment of his scheduled death, he crossed paths with someone else meeting their demise at the exact same time, within mere feet of him. In the cosmic scheme, for every soul required, one must be delivered to satisfy the matrix. In this case, an exchange of souls occurred, one for another. The man went on with his life, shaken up naturally by what he'd seen, but unaware of his extraordinary good fortune."

A glimmer of hope radiated behind RG's eyes. He pushed the chocolates closer to Morrow. *Maybe they feed Morrow supernatural powers and solutions. Eat up, old man.* "But there's a chance?"

"I described an extraordinary case to show the situation's futility. No one could replicate such an event."

So much for the powers of chocolate. RG rose from the table and stepped to the window, staring out onto his backyard. "Don't people die in hospitals and nursing homes? I could go there at the right time and—"

"That's not how it works," Morrow cut him off. "In such places, simultaneous deaths occur frequently. You wouldn't be spared."

"I don't understand."

"Robert, the reprieve I described happened because a scheduled death and an unscheduled death happened together in immediate proximity to each other."

"Unscheduled death?"

"A random death. The result of human action, as opposed to determinations made, shall we say, at other levels."

RG paused, the gears turning in his mind. "If a person…engineered someone's death, would this be an unscheduled death?"

"It would be unscheduled, but we're discussing impossibilities here. No one could orchestrate an unscheduled death to coincide with a scheduled one. Keep those notions far from your mind. It would be murder."

The caretaker's final statement hung suspended over RG's slumped shoulders, the word 'murder' replaying in his ears.

"I know it's hard, but you must accept the inevitable." Morrow stood. "I must leave you now. Prepare as you must for this evening. I'll be with you when your time arrives."

RG nodded, staring at the floor. He had another news flash for Morrow: No way in hell—or the afterlife or wherever fate would supposedly send him—would he go quietly. Morrow could throw his bullshit rules to the wind. Right now he had to focus on the matter at hand, he had to find a solution, a way out.

As RG raised his head, Morrow fixed his gaze on him, reading the intent behind his vacant stare. "I'll say it again. You need to put those ideas aside. Understand? There's no way out of this. I've known you all your life. I've seen what's inside you. You're not capable of harming another person."

But despite Morrow's beliefs, RG wasn't sure who dwelled beneath the surface anymore or what such a person might be capable of. He'd do whatever was necessary to survive, to stay alive, no matter the cost. Morrow had shown him he still had a slim chance—and he had no plans to leave the world just yet.

After Morrow's departure, RG organized things as best he could, just in case. He left important paperwork on the desk for Kacey to find: insurance policies, property titles and deeds, tax documents. He contemplated penning a long letter explaining everything—Morrow, jumpers, and the next world—but this would raise far more questions than it would answer. Besides, how could he explain something he didn't entirely understand or believe himself?

He made the drive from Boston to Chatham in record time to watch Kacey take her afternoon walk along the beach with her mother. He settled in the dunes gazing at the ocean, hidden for the moment behind the willowy beach grass, marveling at the sea and sky's matching hues. As she approached the house, he hesitated, studying her face, her form, taking it all in. Images of her came at him like a shotgun blast, bits and pieces of a life assaulting his senses—the smell of her hands when she worked in the garden, the salty taste on her lips after a day at the beach, and the wet cotton candy they shared when Big Papi took Rivera deep through the raindrops. He relived the tremble of their first kiss and her warm breath against his skin. The memories picked up speed, flying past him now —shoes by the door, dishes on the counter, her body through the shower's frosted glass, sunglasses on the dashboard, her hair between his fingers, a shirt in the hamper with a single sleeve pulled inside-out, a million things about her simultaneously flooded him, defeated him.

Giving in to the overwhelming impulse to run to her, hold her, RG sprinted from the dunes, catching up with her as she and her mother reached the screen door.

Kacey jumped as his feet pounded on the wooden porch. "RG, what the—"

Before her words could escape, he hoisted her off the porch in an impassioned embrace and spun her in a half-circle. He kissed her and buried his face in her neck.

Sandie looked on in approval. "After all these years it's like you're still on your honeymoon. I'll just leave you two to yourselves then."

"I'm sorry to steal your time with your daughter, Sandie. I just couldn't be without her right now."

"Nothing to be sorry about, dear." She reached a hand to his cheek. "It's good to see you." Stepping into the house, she shouted, "Bruce! You could learn a thing or two from our romantic son-in-law." Her words muffled as the door closed behind her.

The couple stood on the weathered, wrap-around porch, the chilly wind rolling in from the sea, whipping their hair forward and back.

"What the hell are you doing here, RG?" Kacey wrapped both arms around him and kissed him with purpose. "I'm not complaining or anything." She kissed him again, giving his neck a familiar caress with her fingers. "Too bad Mom and Dad are in the next room."

"Never stopped us before," he whispered in her ear. He grabbed her hand and squeezed it twice, their secret language.

Kacey buried herself in the cocoon of her husband's embrace, their bodies in sync like voices in harmony, but he held her differently now, with a sudden urgency. Throughout their marriage, they had spent time apart because of his scientific conferences or her getaway weekends with old friends. He had a signature goodbye hug, passionate but with a childlike desperation.

"Are you going somewhere, RG?"

He continued the embrace until the dam broke inside, the sobs shaking his body.

"What's the matter?"

He quickly wiped his eyes and shuffled a few steps along the porch before collapsing onto the old wooden porch swing suspended from the ceiling joists. The metal chain links tightened and groaned as it took his weight. He looked out over the ocean, lost in a memory.

"Do you remember the first time we came here? New Year's Day, '08 or '09, maybe?"

Kacey joined him on the swing. "I don't remember the year, but I do recall a spirited New Year's Eve." She gave his ribs a playful poke.

"Do you remember what you said to me right here on this porch?"

"I remember the cold, shivering but not wanting to move from your side." She cocked her head to the side. "I said something about being in heaven."

RG shook his head, the professor in him taking over. "We sat right on this swing, you linked arms with me and said 'I can't imagine heaven being any better than this.'" He stood and leaned against the porch railing. "There's a heaven up there, or there's something—I don't know what." He turned away, staring off toward the sea.

Kacey crept up from behind, threw her arm around his shoulder, and leaned her head against him. "What are you talking about? What's going on?"

"You need to promise me something. If anything…" RG's voice trailed off.

"If anything…what?"

"If anything should…listen, Kacey." He forced a breath. "Promise me our child will always have a father."

She rubbed his shoulder. "Oh, I get it. Now that you're about to be a father, you're thinking about your own father. Listen, I'm sorry you lost him when you did, but nothing's gonna happen to us."

If only it could be so simple. "What do you love about me?"

"Everything. I've always—"

"Kacey, tell me what you love about me." She linked her hands behind his neck, resting her forearms on his shoulders, studying him. He'd lived with her long enough to recognize the attempt to read in his face the reason for his oddball behavior.

"What do I love about you? Okay. I love how my heart beats faster before you walk into the room, when I hear you in the kitchen first thing in the morning, or when you pull in to the driveway. The fireworks go off long before I see you. I love that after so many years, you still do things to me inside."

"A child needs a father, you know."

"Ours will have the best one ever. Why don't you stay here with me tonight?" She wrapped her arms around his waist.

"Your parents will be in the next room."

"Never stopped us before."

Her words roiled the hurt inside him, anticipating someday—long after she buried him and moved on with her life—she'd speak those words to someone else, allow another to love her.

"I gotta get back." His pulse raced and his mouth turned as dry as the surrounding sand. With nothing more to say, he gazed into her eyes, trying to capture everything inside her at once: her joy, her passion, her soul and spirit in one fell swoop, to take it all with him. He held her face in his hands, closing his eyes as he kissed her in the bristling wind." I love you, Kacey Granville."

"I'll miss you, 'til tomorrow." Her fingers wound around his, communicating a silent, final plea for him to stay.

He dropped her hand and walked over the dunes. With each step in the shifting sand, he fought the urge to turn around and take one more peek, but he didn't dare. If he caught a glimpse of so much as her shadow, he'd race back to her arms for good, putting her and her family in unacceptable danger.

Just keep walking, he told himself, keep walking.

≈

Driving back to Boston, RG cursed the stop-and-go traffic at the Braintree split for wasting his last day's precious minutes. At the I-93 tunnel, the traffic finally thinned out. He took the Storrow Drive exit to Kenmore Square, stopping at his office to send a few emails and organize his files. He considered the odd human need to tie up the most inconsequential loose ends in one's life.

The wall clock ticked behind him like a hammer, picking up speed. He tried Kacey's cell, but he couldn't get through. He checked his watch: 8:06 p.m.

Time had run out.

Butterflies fluttered inside his stomach. *This is it. Now I find out if Morrow fabricated all this shit…and if he didn't…*

"Mr. Morrow, are you there?" No response.

RG burst from his office and raced up Commonwealth Avenue toward Kenmore Square. The air smelled of city and winter, his heightened senses in tune with every sound, every car horn, and every passing conversation taking place under the artificial gray-black hue of the urban night. As he inhaled the cold air, every oxygen molecule energized him. His muscles fired up, alive and full of power.

RG hesitated as he reached the Kenmore T Station. He surveyed Commonwealth Avenue, considering following it into downtown Boston. On a whim, he descended the subway steps, nodding at the on-duty Metro police officer texting on his smartphone. *Might as well get on the T and ride for a while, see where it takes me.*

He passed through the turnstile heading inbound.

8:22 p.m.

His legs shook and his breath came in short bursts. He instinctively called Kacey for support, but he couldn't get a signal underground.

"Mr. Morrow," he called out, but received no response.

Alone.

RG bound down steps to the platform, nearly bumping into a family loitering near the platform's edge: a father, a mother, and a young boy. He excused himself as he moved past them, his feet scuffing along the dirty concrete. He caught a whiff of cigarette smoke as a heavyset, middle-aged man, breathing heavily, lumbered down the stairs to the platform. RG backed up to give him room, the man stubbing out his cigarette and nodding as he passed, taking out a handkerchief and dabbing at the beads of sweat on his brow. RG planted himself a comfortable distance away from the group.

His eyes wandered down the platform, fixing on the lone shape at the far end of the tracks. RG hadn't noticed the homeless man before, the station's gritty darkness camouflaging his drab, dirty contours. The man performed his repetitive ritual, leaning over the tracks and gazing into the tunnel, then turning in a circle, mumbling to himself. His boots danced along the platform's edge.

8:25 p.m.

RG checked his watch, dark thoughts filling his head, a plan formulating in his mind.

The man once known as Victor Garrett stood in shadow behind the riveted steel girder, unseen, burning with a vengeance out of control, fire rising from his simmering body's glowing skin. He gazed at the caretaker, leaning against the gritty wrought-iron railing along the stairs leading to the subway platform, watching his charge, Granville, standing with the others waiting for the train. Like the caretaker, Victor wasn't visible to the living souls congregating on the platform.

Might be fun to do some browsing while I wait for the action to start. Victor concentrated, penetrating the caretaker's mind, probing his thoughts and memories, careful not to alert him to his presence. He scanned the myriad living images pummeling him in an instantaneous visual barrage, combing for that special one. The one he'd seen before, up close.

The one he'd witnessed from behind the man's eyes.

The jumper cracked a rotting grin and closed his eyes as he fixed on the target mind-film, rubbing his pulsating skin as the images washed over him, bathing his senses.

Victor found himself back in the car with the doctor, reliving the man's final moments. The Volvo hurdled toward the double yellow line as the doctor struggled behind the wheel. He witnessed the soon-to-be-totaled Monte Carlo's grill approaching head-on at an incomprehensible rate of speed. The doctor's mind numbed, the outcome not survivable. Victor could taste the chemical fear flooding the doctor's bloodstream as the Volvo struck the Monte Carlo head on, driving the steering column into his sternum, shattering his ribs and ripping his lungs from the chest wall. Pieces of the man's life flew at him like the shattered glass now peppering him from all directions—a teenage girl's soft kiss in her father's Buick behind the Dairy Queen on Route 44; the whiz of a fastball he slammed into the trees above the left field fence during state finals; the swirling wind whispering through the wheat at his parent's farm.

Victor felt the bones in the doctor's arms snap as his body thrust forward into the instrument panel. The collision's rotational force spun him off the steering column and slammed him backward into the windshield. Above the shattering glass's explosion and the crumpling metal's screech, the doctor's wife whispered to him, her voice echoing softly in his head like a melody—the man's focus drawn not to the 'I love yous' and 'forevers' tumbling over her lips, but her voice's magical intonation, the secret gift she unknowingly gave him with her every spoken word. The driver's side seat ripped away from its mountings, launching toward the windshield and taking the doctor through it, his child's face crossing his vision, his joyous laugh filling his ears one last time. Spiraling through the air, Victor smelled freshly mowed grass along the road's shoulder before the body impacted the roadway.

The jumper released a pleasurable sigh, heat smoldering in his white-hot core. He disengaged from the caretaker's mind and stepped from the shadows.

"So, it's...Morrow now?" Flames licked the steel supports on either side of where Victor stood. Victor spoke to Morrow in an ancient language, deep inside his mind, a language not of this earth. Morrow responded in kind.

"There's nothing here for you, Victor. Robert's time has arrived, and I'm here to take him with me."

"How touching. You know, I've waited a long time for this, and *we're down to, what, the last five minutes now?"* Victor pulled his sleeve back to check a cracked and broken watch, a remnant of his former human costume. *"I wouldn't miss this for the world."*

"It's time to let it go, Victor. Your efforts to take him the past thirty-five years are over. You'll have to find other ways to spend your time now."

"You mean, find a hobby or something?"

"What the hell do you want?"

Victor's skin pulsated red, fire from deep within erupting on its surface. *"A front row seat, doctor. To see your charge die in front of you, without you being able to do anything about it. Like how you watched when my son died in front of me. You remember Sam, don't you?"*

"It's time you hear the truth, Victor. No doctor could've saved Sam. It's not anyone's fault your son's cancer was too advanced. If we'd found it sooner, maybe he'd have had a fighting chance, but we didn't have that luxury, did we? The only thing that could've saved the boy was a miracle."

"Miracles! A guilty, ignorant doctor's answer!" Victor's anger flared, raising the temperature further inside the humid station. *"And you don't get to say his name."*

Morrow remained silent.

"I've suffered for your mistakes. Now I'm here to watch you suffer."

Morrow's muscles tensed and his hands curled into fists. *"Suffered? You think you own suffering? Your anger and blame overshadow any real understanding of what it's like to suffer. You have no concept of pain. You don't suffer. You hate. If you want to talk about suffering, let's talk about everything you took from me out of some misguided vengeance you allowed to destroy everything you could have had. Suffering...please..."*

"Who's the misguided one here? How many other children did you kill, doctor? Or did you lose count? How many other mothers and fathers did you cripple inside?"

"I could ask you the same question. You've continued to take inno-cent children's lives in your twisted sense of justice."

The subway train screeched as it entered the tunnel, penetrating the station. *"And they're all because of you."* Victor scanned the subway platform, narrowing his eyes at the family with the young boy. His eyes fixed on Morrow. *"Let's carve another notch on your belt, shall we?"*

"Victor, no!"

The jumper disappeared inside the boy, taking over his body and hurling him high into the air as his scream echoed off the walls and ceiling. He plummeted with a sickening thud on the tracks below the platform.

~

8:30 p.m.

The high-pitched scream jolted RG from his intentions as the young boy flew onto the tracks. Dazed and still, he lay between the dirty rails five feet below the platform's edge, his body contorted in a most peculiar configuration.

The train's squeal rumbled louder as it made its way into Kenmore from Commonwealth Avenue. In moments, it would come barreling into the station, crushing the boy beneath its wheels. Without hesitation, RG leaped from the platform onto the tracks and charged over to the boy, careful to avoid the third rail. As he lifted him in his arms, the unconscious boy's head lolled backward, the shifting of dead weight surprising him, dancing an awkward jig to avoid stumbling. As he recovered and attempted to heave the boy upward, he lurched forward, pulled off balance a second time, a tug of resistance coming from the boy's leg. Glancing down, RG grimaced at the boy's foot wedged beneath the metal track and wooden tie.

Trapped.

The shrieking train reached a higher octave. RG's pulse quickened. He lay the boy back on the tracks and dropped beside him, working to free his wedged foot. The sweat on his hands and layers of subway grime coating the boy's high tops prevented him from getting a grip, his hands sliding off the sneaker like a bar of soap in a shower. His mind froze. *What do I do? I can't free him.* The parents' high-pitched wails rattled in RG's head.

The roar of the train now filled the station.

Untie his shoe, you fucking moron.

RG gave a frantic jerk to the laces, the loop catching on its counterpart, knotting the frayed strands together. *Fuck me!* He fell to both knees on the vibrating tracks, sweat dripping into his eyes, blurring his vision. He wiped it away with a grimy hand, making it worse. Working the knot with the thumbs on his shaking hands, he pulled and picked at the snag of entangled string until it reluctantly loosened and unwound. RG tore at the tongue of the boy's sneakers, releasing the tension, and pulled his foot from the shoe. Grabbing the boy in his arms, he hoisted him upwards.

"Help me!" RG shouted, as the shriek of the train filled the station. "Grab him. Hurry. Before we're both killed!"

The heavyset man rushed toward the platform's edge along with the boy's father. RG struggled to stay upright as a powerful whoosh of the rushing train shuddered the ground in an ever-increasing vibrato, their last seconds upon them.

"Hurry, man, we've got this." The heavyset man swayed at the platform brim, his boot tips protruding over the edge. Laboring to breathe, sweat dripped from his forehead. The boy's father crouched beside him, four arms stretching wildly to snatch the boy from the roaring, merciless wheels churning unknowingly to deliver a gruesome end. The heightened crescendo of their shouts and cries matched the escalating buzz echoing throughout the tunnel.

RG heaved the boy up from the tracks as the heavyset man latched onto the boy's jacket, dragging him to safety as the train hurtled with unbridled power into the station. He glanced up at the Government Center roll-sign above the front windshield, a station two stops ahead; the train would not slow down through Kenmore. He had one shot at leaping out of the coffin-shaped pit and onto the platform before being crushed under its sharp wheels.

The heavyset man reached for him, but RG's hand, slick with sweat and grime, slipped from his outstretched grasp, sending both men toppling backward. RG landed on his back in the pit across the track's wooden ties, his head pinging off the metallic rail, stars exploding before his eyes. The train approached at an unimaginable speed, the headlights blinding him.

He sprung to his feet, dizzy and wobbly. His muscles, alive and awake minutes earlier, now proved useless in his post adrenaline fatigue. The platform seemed much higher than it had been moments ago.

I'm not going to make it. This is how I die.

His muscles relaxed. As the halogen lights bore down on him, filling his senses with brilliant white, he found peace in the knowledge that if he had to go out this way, at least Kacey and the baby would learn he went down fighting to save a child's life, that maybe they could find meaning in his death. As he closed his eyes, two meaty hands grabbed him by the shoulders, plucking him off the tracks. The train thundered past in a deafening boom and swirling blur of green and white, missing him by inches. But the train door caught the open flap of his jacket, ripping it from his body, sending it flying under the train's slashing wheels and twirling RG and the heavyset man to the ground in a heap.

"I got you, buddy, I got you!" The heavyset man's arms remained locked around RG on the dirty platform.

"Holy shit!" RG shouted.

"I got you, buddy," the heavyset man cried, gasping for breath. His grip weakened, and he lay back on the platform, exhausted. The boy stirred as his mother dashed to his side.

Helping RG off the filthy subway platform, the boy's father gave him an awkward embrace and brushed the dirt from his clothes. RG craned his neck to peer into the pit, his tattered jacket lying in shreds across the tracks below, pieces still fluttering in the train's swirling wake. The woman shuffled over to him, holding her son's hand. She gazed up at RG with tears rimming her eyes and hugged him.

"Thank you," she whispered.

"Is everyone okay?" The Metro police officer jogged over to the group, his leather jacket creaking with each step. He knelt in front of the boy and gave his hair a tousle, turning him around to look for signs of injury. He inspected his misshapen forearm as the boy squeezed his eyes shut and let out a slight moan.

"You're one tough little kid." The officer gave the boy a pat on the back and turned to his father. "It looks like he has a broken forearm, but I can't find any other obvious injuries. He lost consciousness, so you're gonna want to have him checked out immediately."

A cry escaped the boy's mother. She stood over the heavyset man, lying still on the platform. She threw her hands over her mouth as the officer hurried to his motionless body, the man's eyes open and staring upward, unblinking. Static filled the air as the police officer keyed his shoulder mic and called the EMTs, dropping to his knees to perform CPR on the man.

RG checked his watch: 8:31 p.m.

"What the hell?" *Where are you, Morrow?* A few minutes later, the EMTs arrived and took over, but they could do nothing for the man.

RG stood in a daze, eerily detached from the scene before him. It happened. It must have happened—the reprieve Morrow called impossible.

He eyed the lifeless stranger, his savior, alone on the cold, dirty platform, his body now devoid of the mysterious intangible, the what-ever-it-is guiding the human suit. The strain must have been too much for him.

My so-called caretaker didn't save my life. The dead man lying on the cement did.

RG couldn't swallow, his mouth as dry as the dusty floor the man now shared with the subway roaches, but at the same time, life exploded within him. His muscles hummed with the energy of a caffeinated game show host, his senses heightened, brimming with kick. RG slammed a hand over his mouth to stifle a laugh escaping his lips, surprising him from somewhere deep inside. His eyes darted back and forth, but no one appeared to have heard.

Who was this man? He entered the subway as one of the faceless, nameless souls moving unnoticed through a crowded city, someone to navigate past, an impediment. Tonight, he'd saved a life, his recompense netting him a body bag—thanks for playing, we have some lovely parting gifts—while the man he died for turned out to be the showcase winner, allowed to live out his life with his beloved wife and child beside him. RG would witness those first steps now, hold his child in his arms and sing it to sleep in the still of an early morning. Every sparkling ray of sunshine tickling his skin from this day forward, a serving of gravy on a life that rightfully should have ended. At the same time, the sun had set on someone's father, son, brother, or uncle who missed the train home tonight.

The Metro officer approached RG, asking for a statement. The shocked and grateful family remained in the station as medics attended to the boy, securing his broken arm for the trip to the hospital and checking his eyes with a penlight for evidence of head trauma. With their boy beside them, the parents intercepted RG as he left the officer's station, the weight of the world lifted from their shoulders, but the trauma still evident in their eyes. They thanked him again as fresh tears created new tracks along their cheeks. They all avoided looking at the dead man on the platform.

RG waited as the couple gathered their son and left with the EMTs before trudging up the stairs and out of the T station, his feet plodding like cement blocks, his entire body weightless and heavy at the same time. The Boston University bookstore loomed in the distance but eluded him, appearing to stretch and lengthen, pull away from him with every step he took. He expected to hear the excited buzz of weekend night crawlers heading toward unknown adventures or the roar of buses and cars speeding through the swelling rain pools in the road's asphalt indentations, but the sounds of the city filling his head remained muffled, muted, as if strained through wet cloths. His head pounded and his insides ached, like a hand had reached into his midsection and roiled up his innards.

Something wasn't right.

He stopped on the sidewalk outside the bookstore to get his bearings as a light rain fell. He'd taken only a few steps when an unimaginable source of heat invaded his body, like electric prods, filling it with fire. He struggled to breathe and the rhythm section of his heart tapped out a strange, discordant backbeat, as if death itself had taken a turn behind the drum kit. Maybe Morrow had miscalculated his time of death and it had finally arrived. Maybe he hadn't traded souls with the man on the platform; the matrix had not received its spiritual deposit and had come to collect. As the simmering force spread through his insides, his body's boundaries pulled and stretched to their breaking point, the invading fury shifting to fit itself into his human dimensions. People passed on the street in slow-motion, the falling raindrops suspended in midair.

Inside him, a voice resonated. *"It's time we get to know each other."*

RG staggered, clinging to a trash receptacle, frantically peering one direction, then another, but he couldn't decipher the owner's voice, which appeared to emanate from his brain's center lobes. The voice dripped with contempt in a language RG had never heard, but somehow clearly understood. He pivoted, releasing his stronghold on the receptacle to flee whatever gripped his head, escape somewhere, anywhere, but the voice hounded him. *"It may not have ended tonight like I planned, but it will."*

Then he knew.

A swelling furnace bore through him with such intense heat, his entire body thirsted for relief, the cold night air offering no respite. He twirled about, stretched as if in a full-body cast, waving his arms and straddling the sidewalk with widening legs, fighting whatever possessed him. Another jolt rocked him as Morrow entered, wrestling for control of his body. Countering the hellish, burning heat, Morrow infused RG with a cool and soothing force. People passed him on the sidewalk in an infinitely slow cadence, wary of the odd gesticulations coming from the strange man, but oblivious to the internal struggle raging inside. Morrow displayed remarkable strength, yet a relentless force opposed him.

"Leave him, Victor," Morrow shouted in the same ancient tongue. *"He's under my protection."*

"Not for long," the voice said calmly.

In an instant, the infernal heat escaped RG's body with a violent shudder leaving him sprawled across the sidewalk. When he opened his eyes, Morrow stood over him.

"What happened?" RG asked.

"Come with me, we don't have much time."

CHAPTER FOUR

July 2007

Under a marble-blue sky, RG eased the beat-up Ford Bronco into Johnny D's beach house driveway in Falmouth, a stone's throw from the Atlantic Ocean across Surf Drive. Music wafted from two monstrous speakers perched on the raised weather-beaten deck, drowning out the comforting sounds of crunching shells and gravel beneath his wheels. He surveyed the growing crowd enjoying the abundant food and drink in the backyard. He couldn't recall when his gang of misfits last raised hell together, but they never missed the chance at Johnny D's annual Independence Day Shindig on Cape Cod.

This had been the first year of RG's adult life he hadn't spent the summer on the Cape. After earning his bachelor's degree, he'd perpetuated his carefree lifestyle with a slick move into graduate school. His carefully crafted scheme to put off the working world and salvage his summers looked good on paper, but backfired dramatically. Now as a research assistant and PhD candidate, he performed research, submitted abstracts and articles, and taught summer classes—a twelve-month-a-year commitment. With every lecture grudgingly delivered on a dazzling summer day, he fought his DNA, screaming at him to kick open the auditorium doors, throw off his higher education oppressors' shackles, and race across the Sagamore Bridge to freedom.

He'd grown up walking distance from Revere Beach, but even as a teenager, RG and his friends chose to pile in the back of Johnny D's beat-up Ford F-150 and endure the slow crawl south along a cramped Route 3 to the Cape. Johnny D's uncle owned a summer rental in Harwichport along Route 28 with no kitchen, no A/C, and a some-times-working outdoor shower. The gang spent their summers bussing tables, scraping million-dollar boat hulls, and perfecting at least five unhittable Wiffle ball pitches. At night, they snuck into the clubs in Hyannis and chased summer romances that blossomed and fizzled with alarming regularity.

Leaning forward against the steering wheel, RG peered at his friends gathered on the deck. Johnny D, his hair pulled back in his signature ponytail, balanced three Coors Lights and two mixed drinks while expertly navigating the screen door with his right elbow and knee. Two of the beers went to Matty Kelly and Donnie Goudreau, arguing like an old married couple while manning the grill at the deck's back corner. With a deep tan from years of surf competitions and a defining laugh—all snorts and pops—Donnie's nickname, Sun-Pig, couldn't have been more fitting. He could barely be seen through the thick, gray smoke billowing from the various meats he poked and prodded, but the tall and beefy Matty stood majestically above it all like a skyscraper in a fog.

"Well, look who finally made it," Johnny D shouted from the deck, waving a hand and tossing the third Coors Light in a tight spiral toward the car. Opening the Bronco's battered door, RG ducked as the bottle exploded against the roof, showering him with beer and glass and adding another scar to the aging vehicle.

"Are you out of your mind?" RG raced up the driveway with a grin and tackled a surprised Johnny D coming down to inspect the damage. Picking sides, Matty and the Sun-Pig jumped into the melee. Before long, RG emerged soaked with suds and bleeding from a scraped knee, his shirt torn at the collar, and his cargo shorts' back pocket hanging down his outer leg. Johnny D didn't look much better.

Johnny playfully pulled RG into a headlock as they walked up the deck steps. He'd grown up an only child, compelling him to claim RG as his unofficial adopted brother. This made him RG's best friend and vice versa, but among the Revere gang, the term could be used interchangeably. They'd all grown more respectable in the past few years compared to the unruly gang once unleashed on the unsuspecting Cape residents each summer, but somehow they already regressed in their few moments together.

"Hey, RG, get your ass over here!" Matty grabbed him by the scruff of the collar, nearly lifting him off the ground.

Attempting to free himself, RG reached back and locked onto Matty's muscled forearm. "Jesus, Matty. You grow out of another gym again?"

"Third one this year." He dropped RG in front of two girls at the deck's far end. "I've told you all about Livy." He threw a thick arm around her shoulder. "Say hi to her roommate, Kacey."

"Nice to meet you both." RG picked glass shards out of his tangled hair and attempted to stanch the blood dripping down his shin into his sock. With her near-auburn hair and a spate of freckles across her nose, Kacey immediately drew his attention. To keep from staring, he turned to her friend. "I've heard such nice things about you, Livy. It's like I already know you."

"I'm glad you could make it, RG." She winked an eye and tilted her head toward Kacey.

RG suspected Matty and Livy had conspired as matchmakers to set the two of them up. He sensed the weight of Kacey's stare and for the first time in a long time wondered how disheveled he appeared.

"You look like you've seen better days," she said, taking a sip from Johnny D's concoction.

"And I don't always look this good." He dabbed at his bloody limb.

"You can tell he tried today," Johnny D chimed in with a laugh. "I detect a hint of gel mixed in with the glass slivers and beer in his mop."

"I'm RG." Unsure what to do with his hands, he picked at the beer bottle's label, sending shredded shavings fluttering onto the deck.

"RG? Where'd that come from?"

"It's short for 'Royal Geek,'" Matty shouted.

"More like 'Real Gorgeous.'" Livy shot Matty a glance and raised her eyebrows.

RG turned a crimson hue as he faced Kacey. "It's Robert and Granville but no one calls me either. My mother told me I never looked like a Robert, so she always called me RG."

"Well, mother knows best. RG it is, then." Her grin sent a gentle dagger through his chest, her blue eyes twisting it for good measure.

With thumping speakers hampering their efforts at small talk, RG and Kacey moved to the other end of the deck, but not too far outside their friends' protective buffer. It wasn't long before the shared aspects of their New England upbringing—the Red Sox, fried clams with bellies, Dunkin' Donuts coffee—injected a comfortable familiarity to their conversation, as if they had a mutual friend. RG found himself paying far more attention to Kacey than the gang he'd come to visit, welcoming the cautious elation of learning another's secrets.

When she told him she taught third grade with Livy, RG chuckled.

"What's so funny?"

"I remember my third-grade teacher, Mrs. Susky, five-foot-four and wide as a doorway. If you misbehaved, she fired chalk at your head." RG flicked his beer bottle cap, skimming it off Johnny D's forehead.

"God, I haven't thought of her in fifteen years." The Sun-Pig took a sip from his beer and subconsciously sat up straighter in his deck chair.

"She hated us." Johnny D stared down at his shoes, rubbing the reddening welt on his forehead. "She was like Curt Schilling with that chalk."

Kacey smirked. "Hmm, I'm thinking you guys had it coming some-how." She draped her arm around Livy. "Today's third grade teachers are a lot different, though."

Johnny D threw an elbow into RG's ribs. "I'll say."

As the afternoon passed, RG caught up with friends and mingled with other guests, but he couldn't keep his eyes off Kacey as she glided through the crowd. She moved with the fluidity of the distant ocean framing her silhouette, unimpeded by the same internal scaffolding guiding his graceless, plodding man-gait. It was as though her body had received a software upgrade and been placed alongside the outdated prototypes glitching and crashing around her. Any hint of a glance from across the yard turned into an excuse to find their way back to each other and pick up where they left off. As dusk settled, the party drifted across Surf Drive to the beach. The bonfires burned in a controlled inferno and fireworks ignited the sky.

"Here's to Walt," Matty announced, raising his beer and clinking bottles with the boys. Whenever they came together, they acknowledged the Revere gang's absent member, now serving time in Plymouth County Correctional. With his imposing frame, it had always fallen on Matty to watch everyone's back, especially the bookish and bespectacled Walt Worthing, whose quick wit and sharp tongue often landed him in hot water. But now with iron bars and razor wire between them, he was powerless to protect the one friend who needed him most.

"To Walt," they replied in unison.

RG broke from the crowd and walked toward the water's edge, Kacey following. The pounding surf matched the firework explosions overhead, the salty breeze carrying burning wood and sulfur odors.

As darkness set in, the sky over the water drew RG's gaze, the spot where civilization's lights fail to reach, the place where the constellations and stars behind them are vivid and spectacular, like a million glowing grains of salt scattered across a black velvet cloth. Studying Kacey's eyes, he swore he saw a reflection of each one.

"I don't know if you know this, but Matty told me someone would be coming to the party tonight I should meet."

"Well, I bet she's given up looking for you by now. Livy told me about this guy too…an intellectual type, funny, good looking."

"Yeah?"

Kacey raised an eyebrow. "I don't think he showed."

A soft chuckle escaped RG's lips as he dropped his head. When he glanced up, Kacey stepped closer, their bodies brushing. She reached for his hand as he leaned in for a kiss, one she returned with fervor. As he held her close, the night opened with color, sparks shooting vertically from canisters embedded in the sand and spiraling across the blackened sky, the repetitive pops and bursts drowning out the sounds of the world around them. He couldn't have guessed their kiss would be the first of a million they'd share from Falmouth to Boston and everywhere they would ever be.

CHAPTER FIVE

Saturday, December 2, 2017

"What do you mean we don't have much time?" RG managed to mumble, his lungs burning like smoldering coal. He couldn't dispel the scalding assault he'd endured or the overwhelming loss of control. Morrow helped him to his feet, his legs holding him up like slices of Swiss cheese full of holes. He yanked on Morrow's arm until his sea legs reoriented to land.

"We're not safe here. Come on." Morrow secured his hand around RG's forearm and led him away.

They half-jogged, half-stumbled along the rain-spattered sidewalk toward RG's car. "What the hell just happened?" RG struggled to breathe between words.

"You've just met a jumper named Victor Garrett. He took over your body briefly before I expelled him." Morrow slowed his pace and stopped, using his hand to massage a stitch under his ribcage. "I need a minute, Robert."

"You and me both...maybe a few minutes." RG bent over and placed his hands on his knees. "Maybe a few days."

They took a moment to catch their breaths and walked the rest of the way to the car. With the engine running and heater on, they rested, the automatic wipers thwarting the accumulation of raindrops on the windshield.

"A jumper after me? What the hell did I do?"

Morrow stared out the rain-stippled glass, his eyes unblinking. "You've done nothing. He's come for you because of me. You see, Victor and I have a history." Morrow turned his head away, his eyes searching the night through the side window. "Years ago, in your world, I had to make a decision, and this decision may have contributed to his son's death."

RG remained silent, a thin fog forming on the glass inside the car.

"For decades Victor has stalked you, aware I'm your caretaker. He's spent his life trying to take you from me in retribution for my actions long ago." Morrow turned to face RG. "Tonight, he got to you. The evening's events distracted me, and I let me guard down. I shouldn't have. I should have been better prepared, but unfortunately, caretakers are not without fault."

RG stared straight ahead through the windshield. "You said I'd be dead at eight-thirty, but I'm still here. Why?"

"Because souls were traded tonight. When the man in the subway helped you and the boy off the tracks, exertion triggered a fatal cardiac event—a random death, the direct result of another person—and it occurred at the exact moment of your scheduled death."

"So you're saying I caused his death?"

Morrow nodded as RG lowered his head and rubbed his temples. "His body was far too damaged to sustain life much longer. His scheduled death was near. It may come as a surprise to you, but tonight's events gave him a great sense of purpose and fulfillment."

"How?"

"Sadly, the man accomplished little in his life, but tonight, as his soul slipped away, he found peace. He saved two lives, yours and the boy's. In fact, he saved your life twice, once by pulling you off the tracks and then through his own death."

RG pictured the man lying on the dirty subway platform. "I still don't understand why Victor showed up to watch me die under a train."

Morrow turned his gaze to the windshield. "He didn't come to watch you. He came to watch me, to taunt me with your death, knowing I couldn't protect you. When he saw the boy standing there, his arrogance pushed him to steal another innocent soul while he enjoyed the show. He didn't expect you to risk your life without hesitation." Morrow chuckled. "Such irony, by hurling the boy onto the tracks, he ended up saving your life."

RG lowered his head, his original intentions leaving a shameful sting.

"I know you had ideas, Robert, but your true nature won out. You laid down your life for another tonight, and no nobler act exists in your world than to sacrifice oneself."

The two men listened to the raindrops' staccato rhythm on the car's roof.

"And now Victor's after me?"

Morrow nodded.

RG rubbed the back of his neck. "What do we do?"

"Victor will return. His vengeance won't let him rest until he finishes the job." Morrow removed his hat and shook stubborn raindrops off it. "Unfortunately, I have only limited time to help you now."

"What?"

"A caretaker's responsibility ends at the time of a scheduled death. Through a miracle of fate, you still live. We'll have a brief transitional period before I'm called back to my world."

RG swallowed. "For good?"

Morrow nodded.

"How long are we talking?"

"A week, maybe two," Morrow offered. "I can protect you until then."

"So, I bought myself more time? That's it?"

"What? Did you think your death had been cancelled?"

"Well...hell, yeah. Souls traded, the matrix satisfied."

"True, but a jumper wants you dead."

"Well, after all I've been through tonight, I'm not in this to lose. I'm not giving up my life for any stupid revenge shit between you two. Not happening!"

"I don't think you have much say in the matter."

"You're wrong. I just demonstrated to the contrary. Look at me, I'm alive, no thanks to you! I'll defeat the jumper one way or another. You just watch."

"And how do you plan to do that?"

Morrow had a point, but RG never cowered from a challenge. He pondered his options, letting the rain take over the conversation for a moment. "Isn't that where you come in, Morrow? You impart a secret code or a whimsical weapon I can use against him?"

"I can teach you how to detect him and resist him, but I don't have any magical solution."

"If you don't know what will stop him, I guess I have no choice. I'll figure it out myself. Let's get the hell out of here."

Needing time to unwind, RG navigated side streets and back roads until he reached the house in Newton. Morrow fell asleep within minutes, barely stirring until RG turned into the driveway. He killed the ignition and relaxed a moment, the cooling engine's intermittent ticking soothing him.

The silence woke Morrow with a start. "My apologies, Robert." He straightened and readjusted his hat. "My struggle with Victor drained my strength."

RG helped him into the house and onto the living room couch, removing his shoes and retrieving bedding from the hall closet. He dropped into the chair beside him, eyes fixed on his caretaker.

Morrow raised his head off the pillow. "What's on your mind, Robert?"

"Just thinking, you know. The fate of a person's soul, its movement from one world to the next, how one ends up a jumper or caretaker."

Morrow propped himself up on his elbow. "I've only heard rumors really, theories. It's believed a jumper suffers a tragedy and can't let go or caused harm to someone and never dealt with it. Jumpers never quite ascend to the next world, ending up somewhere in an intermediate plane, unable to move on. Others say jumpers were born with wicked hearts and kill out of pure hatred and vengeance, or they rejected their faith and sold their souls. Truth is, we don't know."

"So, does that mean caretakers lived a good life?"

"Some propose there exists graduating levels to the final reward, and caretakers are closer to the last level before reaching the final good."

RG leaned forward. "You mean…heaven?"

"Heaven, hell, no one's sure." Morrow chuckled. "I'd be arrogant to believe I'm closer to one end of the spectrum than the other."

RG mulled over their conversation, wondering where his life fell along the continuum of good and evil. *I'm no fucking caretaker, that's for sure!* He'd had his share of bad moments, but could recall nothing he'd done to warrant banishment to the jumper soul heap. He breathed a sigh of relief and leaned closer. "What else can caretakers do?"

Morrow grinned. "We expel jumpers to their own realm when they invade a host body, and we track and recover hosts abducted from your world. Many of us have the power to probe the mind's history, construct portals to different dimensions or different times, even perceive the future."

"Pretty short résumé," RG smirked as he raised his eyebrow. "Were you with me tonight, on the tracks?"

"Of course, where else would I be?" Morrow reassured him. "It's a miracle you're still here, and I have a great story for my fellow caretakers. Now get some rest. Tomorrow we prepare for Victor's return."

RG killed the light and trudged upstairs, Baron following at his heels. When he reached the landing, he peeked between the iron balusters, Morrow's face assuming a more somber expression, as if he held back a key piece of information. RG pressed his lips together. *He hasn't told me everything.*

～

May 1972

Victor Garrett shoved his way through the St. Francis Hospital revolving door and out into a world no longer making sense to him. The sun shone brightly and springtime's burgeoning colors exploded all around him, but it brought him no pleasure. People passed, wearing the day's loud and colorful clothing, oblivious to the pain gnawing at the rumpled man's soul before them.

Victor saw no one.

He shuffled south toward Elizabeth Park. Following the winding walkway toward the pond, Victor collapsed on a wooden bench, a spot where he and Sam spent their Saturdays nursing melting ice cream cones and feeding stale bread to the ducks. He lingered all day and late into the evening. The dropping temperature and night's bristling chill brought Victor no discomfort, an internal heat swelling within him, a fire in his veins spreading warmth. His pain and fury instigated a guttural cry from a place so deep inside, it sounded as if it came from someone else—and it did.

A change had taken hold of Victor.

As Saturday night slipped into Sunday, Victor stared across the pond, chirping peepers at the water's edge interrupting the unholy stillness. A young boy, healthy and smiling, greeted Victor in a memory, the wind ruffling his blonde hair as he raced along the beach with his father, chasing seagulls they'd never catch, evading the waves racing them to the shore.

Then the boy stopped running and stared at Victor.

He appeared different now, thinner, with sunken eyes, his ribcage visible through his translucent skin. An IV bag attached to his skin dragged behind him, etching a trail in the sand as it pulled against a vein in his spindly, bruised arm, its contents leaking out into a small gritty puddle.

"I'm waiting for you, Dad."

Victor trembled. Tears stung his eyes. He clutched his stomach and lay on the bench as the sobs racked his body until his ribs ached.

At sunrise, Victor eased off the bench and lumbered out of the park toward his West Hartford home. As he stumbled up his driveway, Lucy rushed from the front door, her hands balled into fists. She met him in the driveway, pounding his chest and face, bloodying his nose. "You and your God!" Lucy spat, cheeks stained with tears.

Victor grabbed her wrists, preventing her from pummeling him further.

"You're both to blame." She glared at her husband with blatant malice, Victor returning an empty stare.

Her legs buckled and she collapsed onto the warm asphalt, moaning in agony for a son she'd never see again. Victor sensed the neighbor's faces pressed to their windows, silently watching the spectacle with the dawning knowledge the unimaginable had finally happened.

Ignoring his wife's writhing in the driveway, Victor entered the house and stepped into the kitchen, grabbing an unopened box of Quisp cereal, Sam's favorite. He stood at the sink and poured a hefty portion into a bowl. Finding no milk in the refrigerator, Victor added warm tap water and scooped the sugary nuggets into his mouth. Blood dripped from his nose and mixed with the water and cereal. Between bites he glanced above the stove at Jesus hanging from the cross with the quilted scripture quote from Ecclesiastics 21:5 below it—

'A prayer out of a poor man's mouth reacheth to the ears of God, and his judgment cometh speedily.'

Victor processed the words as he continued to eat, filling the bowl with cereal and water.

The vision came to him like a lightning flash. He stopped eating. His mouth hung open and globs of wet, half-chewed cereal dripped down his shirt and onto the floor. He instantly understood *the change*, what would happen to him and what it would create. He would shed his human form and allow the growing immortal force within to fulfill its role in the universe—a role equal to God Himself. Worlds would open to him as he completed his evolution from a simple man into a being beyond imagination—a *burning man*—glowing in the embers of a raging, eternal fire. He closed his eyes and glimpsed the path to his destiny.

Immersed in the vision, he didn't register his wife's cries as she dragged herself up the steps to the front door and into the kitchen.

"Why didn't you listen to me?" she sobbed. "Now our baby's gone!"

Victor replied to Lucy in a language he'd never spoken before, a dark and brooding tongue arising from the gut and resonating in the nasal cavity. Words from a language not tethered to place, time, or being sprung from Victor's mouth, a universal language every living creature everywhere understood, developed in a parallel plane many times removed from the realm it now appeared.

Lucy froze as Victor spoke the last words she'd ever hear. Her eyes widened and air vacated her lungs. "Victor, no! Please!"

Victor pushed her away with contempt, reaching up to her throat with both hands. His fingers pressed against her neck with blazing strength, heat rising and singeing flesh against flesh. Lucy lashed out against the beast attacking her, raking her nails across his face and carving jagged indentations into his smoldering features. The more she fought, the harder he cinched his hands around her throat, pressing until her eyes rolled in her head. She pounded him with her hands one last time, but asphyxiation weakened her. Her arms slipped to her sides, dangling from her shoulders like swinging pendulums.

The snap of her cervical vertebrae ripped the air as his powerful hands cracked her neck. He gradually released his fingers, noticing glowing pits of flesh where his fingertips had pressed her dainty neck. Gently, he pulled her against him, resting her head on his shoulder to steady her, but where he'd once embraced her with need and affection, loathing burbled from deep inside for the undeserved blame and coldness she'd showered upon him. He lowered her lifeless body onto the kitchen floor, staring into her open, hemorrhaged eyes.

When the vision ended, Victor poured more cereal and water into the bowl. He took two bites and regurgitated his stomach's contents onto the kitchen floor, splattering Lucy's clean, pressed shirt and recently washed hair.

Opening the basement door, he descended into the moldy darkness. Three steps from the basement floor, Victor pulled the chain on the light suspended above him. The sixty-watt bulb failed to illuminate the room, doing little more than cast dim shadows along the water-stained walls. Locating his hunting rifle, Victor loaded both barrels and shut off the light for the last time. He trudged back upstairs and seated himself on the floor beside his dead wife, careful to avoid the reeking pool of vomit.

Closing his eyes, Victor tried to imagine Sam running and laughing on the beach, but only a shrunken, sickly boy stumbling in the sand and gasping for breath, stared back at him. Jesus appeared before him, arms held out, gazing at Victor with a face filled with forgiveness and compassion. A moment later, His eyes filled with blood—his neck swollen, bruised and broken, bent crudely to the side. Victor positioned both shotgun barrels above the bridge of his nose and took a breath. The fire flared up again within him, comforting him. In the microsecond before both barrels exploded, Sam's voice filled his head one final time.

"I'm waiting for you, Dad."

~

Sunday, December 3, 2017

RG woke to the sound of an approaching car, headlights dancing across the darkened bedroom wall. "What the hell?" He checked the clock on the bedside table.

1:45 a.m.

He shuffled out onto the landing and glanced downstairs, surveying the living room. He spotted only a folded quilt placed neatly upon the couch cushions—no Morrow. The kitchen door leading to the garage slammed shut, and Kacey dashed up the stairs with Baron loping behind her. RG met her halfway and held her, kissing her for the first time in his new life, tasting on her lips the future he'd nearly lost.

"God, I'm glad to see you, Kacey," he mumbled between kisses.

She placed her hand on his cheek. "It's only been eight hours."

"Trust me, eight hours can seem like a lifetime." He kissed her again.

Kacey severed their embrace and grabbed his hand. She pulled him up the stairs and into their room, settling on the bed. Baron bounded up beside her, placing his paws across her legs and lowering his head onto them. Kacey rubbed the mutt's ears and kissed the top of his head.

"I had one of my dreams tonight." She paused, searching his eyes as if begging him to express his objection.

He should have expected this, but he'd been so preoccupied with saving himself, he'd forgotten it would be nearly impossible to hide the truth from her. She would know. She would see.

"A bad dream?" he said slyly.

"Why didn't you pick up your phone? I tried to call you a million times."

He rose and snatched his crumpled pants off the chair, digging his cell from the back pocket. "Sorry, I forgot to turn the ringer back on." He studied it again briefly. "But it doesn't say a million missed calls. Only twelve." He showed her the evidence, trying to lighten the situation. He didn't want to go where she wanted to take him right now.

"This isn't funny. You have to listen to me."

He lowered himself onto the bed next to her and draped his arm around her shoulders. Tremors flitted throughout her body. He didn't have to guess why.

"I am listening. It's just—"

"Aren't you concerned why I raced home?" she interrupted. "That I had a dream involving you? You can probably guess what happened to you in the dream, can't you?" She pressed a hand against her trembling lower lip.

RG had learned of Kacey's unique gift only a few months after they met. Walking along Newbury Street late one night after dinner, Kacey swooned, a vision stopping her dead in her tracks. When her eyes fluttered open, she pushed him back, warning him a car would jump the curb any second. He stood frozen as the exact vehicle she described veered off the road and onto the sidewalk, the precise spot he'd lingered just moments earlier.

Kacey confided in him about things she could see in her visions since childhood, tragedies she'd prevented. She told him darker powers called to her, powers existing deep inside, terrifying her. Her mind opened portals into unknown, frightening worlds beyond her comprehension. She refused to go there, to explore these overwhelming powers. And they'd agreed she'd banish them and lock them safely away. Better to let them remain dormant inside her than to rouse them from their sleep.

Kacey pulled away from him. "A voice inside kept whispering to me. 'He's gone. You lost him.'"

"You told me you weren't gonna go there anymore."

"It's not that easy. I can't always control these things. This dream was too vivid..." She closed her eyes.

RG sensed a painful image from her past had returned to haunt her. He couldn't imagine what it had been like to witness her college roommate's death in one of her foreboding dreams and being powerless to prevent it. He leaned his forehead against her and kissed her on the cheek as if he could make it all go away.

"Tell me what you saw."

Kacey took a deep breath. "You're not going to like this...but I saw you heading toward Kenmore Square in the rain. You stopped at the T station for a moment, then jogged down Commonwealth Avenue. When you reached the corner of Charlesgate, you rushed across the street...didn't even check for traffic...just kept running, and out of nowhere, this SUV barrels around the bend and hits you with such force, it knocked you out of your shoes."

Still immersed in her dream, Kacey's eyes launched a deserted stare.

"Why didn't you check the traffic?" She paused, as if expecting him to answer. "It was horrible...hearing your bones snap into pieces when you bounced off that car and landed on the road." She brushed the burning tears from her eyes and placed her hands on Baron's paws. "Then the strangest thing happened. Your body lay motionless on the pavement, but this well-dressed older man helped you up, and you simply walked away with him like nothing happened. I kept thinking I'd seen the man before. Your spirit looked back at me with this beautiful, happy glow on your face, all while the distraught driver trampled back and forth, muttering and crying. For some reason, I checked my watch. Half-past eight. Then I woke up."

Kacey gazed out the window. "I swear I saw you die tonight." He draped his arm around her and held her close as she rested her head on his shoulder.

"I'm not dead, Kacey. I'm right here, and I'm not going anywhere."

He reached down, enfolded her hand in his, squeezed twice, and promised something he couldn't guarantee.

Kacey leaned against him. "You know what this means. We can't go anywhere near Boston right now." She reached her arms around him and buried her head in his neck.

Brushing the hair from her eyes, RG replayed the dream in his mind. Kacey had seen him die in one of dozens of possible scenarios playing out tonight. She'd seen Morrow escorting him on to the next world. He'd made a split-second decision to descend the steps into Kenmore station instead of continuing up Commonwealth. If he hadn't, Kacey's dream would have happened in the exact manner she envisioned. He shooed Baron off the bed and out of the room, closing the door behind him, happy to finally have Kacey all to himself.

But the dream haunted him. Later, as RG drifted off beside his sleeping wife, he mumbled to himself, "So that's how I was supposed to die."

~

Victor slept on a dank, foul-smelling cave floor somewhere between the current world and the next. Blood and dirt caked the walls and ceiling, the trickle of water echoing through the cave as it dripped from the rocky outcroppings above and seeped down the walls. Scattered piles of excrement littered the floor. His nourishment consisted of rodents and small animals, their bones strewn about the cave, several half-eaten, others remaining alive in primitive traps. Nothing in this hovel represented a connection to civilization. Victor needed to rest and rekindle the simmering heat and energy fueling the burning man within. Adventures in Kenmore Square had left him drained and weak, the aftermath of sharing physical space with another requiring the unrelenting rage to subside.

In these moments, Victor enjoyed a peace and solace similar to what he'd experienced in the moments of sleepy comfort before waking in that other world, before the change, when he opened his eyes to a brilliant new day and surrounding family. He embraced these ephemeral, clear moments when he could reflect on things he'd done. Regret and remorse would temporarily arise, but they'd disappear when the rage returned. For Victor, the time of solace grew more fleeting with each jump. He welcomed the coming transformation, but also feared someday he'd exist solely as a force of blinding rage.

When Victor died and awoke to his newly found power, he navigated the astonishing variety of existential realms throughout the universe with one intent in mind: to explore opportunities to kill anyone fit for his fodder. Amazing prospects titillated his voracious appetite and intoxicated him with boundless choices, all for his taking. Too bad most jumpers had inconsequential exposure to such a smorgasbord. Wherever he traveled, he relished his purpose—to exterminate desperate souls clinging to life, to snatch them from a world where they no longer belonged. The place he once lived as a man had become his favorite hunting ground.

The fire ignited inside him, the solace coming to an end. His musings turned to Robert Granville, the man depriving him of his triumphant moment over Morrow. It wouldn't matter; Granville wouldn't be around much longer. As he reflected on this, a thought struck him like a hammer. He sat bolt upright on the cave floor.

Granville's death would make Morrow suffer, but his suffering would be too short. Granville would die, but he'd join Morrow in the next world. Where's the suffering?

Prolonged suffering for Morrow would be more sublime.

If he could make Granville suffer for a lifetime, then Morrow would, too. Victor's efficient but brutal cleansing might not be needed here, but instead, a subtler strategy. He'd visit Granville, not an invasion, but a light probe—a gentle exploration of Granville's mind to gain insight, devise a strategy.

Although still physically spent, a quick probing of Granville wouldn't require much effort, just a quick leap over to his side. Another replenishing and swelling heat rose within him as he shifted across planes. He couldn't alert Morrow to his presence in this realm. He had to get close, yet remain imperceptible. Victor found himself in

Granville's upstairs bedroom, the man asleep with his partner beside him.

He restrained the urges boiling inside him.

Examining his mind with a surgeon's precision, Victor sliced into Granville's thoughts, pried his way into his being. Doubling over with a visceral ache, his split-second scan brought immediate revulsion.

He squeezed his eyes shut as Granville's embedded reservoirs of joy, love, happiness, and gratitude flooded him—a teenager leaning against a car's rusty hood, music drifting from the radio; a boy's face pressed against a school bus window, his mother waving from the porch; a perfume aroma lingering on a worn T-shirt; a barefoot couple wading in the misty surf under a rainbow's double arc; a child on Christmas Eve and the weightlessness of anticipation.

As he surveyed the pleasant images, Victor unexpectedly vomited up a small spray of blood. He vowed to destroy Granville's joyous world. All of it. Yet somewhere within this nauseating contentment, the sweet fragrance of unimaginable pain and despair arose, not from Granville himself, but from someone close to him—a boyhood friend. Victor listened more intently, focusing his vision until the man appeared in his mind, a man living in fear, desperation, and agony; a breathtaking image of relentless misery.

The energizing glow of suffering invigorated him, and he wanted to know more.

CHAPTER SIX

October 2003

Kacey's scream jolted her from another nightmare, leaving her shaking and terrified. Scanning the dark room, she oriented herself to her surroundings. Her heart pounded and sweat dampened her skin, soaking the Patriots nightshirt. Familiar posters adorned the cramped dorm room's walls, *Third Eye Blind, American Hi-Fi*, and the Red Sox's Jason Varitek. Taking a deep breath, she willed her heart rate to settle back to normal.

"Oh my God." Kacey cupped her face in both hands. "What did I just see?"

She lay back on the pillow and closed her eyes, her body cooling as the sweat evaporated from her skin. For the next hour, she tried to shake the dream's unrelenting intensity. It may have been a dream, but it foreshadowed the undeniable, a vivid and tangible warning of impending death.

Her hand fumbled over objects on her bedside table until she found her cell phone. She prayed Marcy would still be awake. Knowing Marcy, she wouldn't be. Not wanting to risk her future by oversleeping and missing her early morning flight to Los Angeles, Marcy had sprung for a hotel room at Logan International Airport.

A Hollywood film director had noticed Marcy in her only TV commercial and requested she audition for a role in his film. Tired of constant disappointment from open casting calls, she couldn't turn down the chance of a lifetime, even if it meant falling behind in school.

Marcy mumbled into the phone. "Who's this?"

"Sorry, Marcy. It's me, Kacey—"

"Oh, thank God," Marcy interrupted, "I was afraid someone was calling to cancel my audition. What're you doing up so late, hon?"

Marcy's sweet tone always made Kacey's heart swell. She just had an unexplainable way about her. The boys fell all over themselves whenever she walked by and now a film director had fallen for her engaging smile. Who didn't love being around Marcy? She radiated a magic, leaving no one untouched.

Kacey closed her eyes, preparing for what she had to say. "Marcy, I had a dream about you and I just couldn't ignore it."

"It must have been a doozy for you to call this late."

Kacey pictured Marcy lying on her side with her phone wedged between the pillow and her ear. "It is, and you're gonna think I'm losing my mind."

"Probably, but tell me anyway. I'll be the judge. You know I'm always honest with you."

"You won't want to hear this, but you can't get on that plane tomorrow." Silence from the other end of the line. "You know I'm convinced you'll be the most famous actress in the world, but you have to change flights first."

"You're scaring me." A nervous flier to begin with, Marcy always performed a laundry list of superstitions before boarding a plane. Changing a flight would no doubt ratchet up her pre-flight anxieties. "Why should I change flights?"

Kacey took a deep breath. She would need to proceed with care. "Have you ever thought about fate and destiny?"

Marcy yawned. "I wouldn't be in an airport hotel right now if I didn't."

"That's not what I meant. If you had the power to alter your future, would you use it?"

"It depends. Does it involve tall, dark, and handsome?"

"Marcy, I'm serious. Haven't you ever regretted ignoring your sixth sense? Like when you know you should take a different route home but don't, then end up in a traffic jam?"

"I suppose, but what does that have to do with a silly dream and changing my flight?"

"It's time to listen to that sixth sense." Marcy might very well think differently of her if she continued, but she forged ahead regardless. "Marcy, what would you do if I told you I had the power to see the future…and change it?"

"Uh, I'd call one of those tabloid talk shows and have you booked on their 'crazy roommate' segment immediately."

"Marcy, be serious. Every now and then I have a dream or vision showing me things about to happen. I'm still alive because I've made decisions to alter my destiny."

Marcy's headboard creaked and pillows shuffled, followed by a deliberate sigh. "Hello, Mr. Povich. Yes, I have someone you just *have* to meet." She giggled.

"Will you please listen? I'm concerned about you."

"I heard you." Marcy hesitated. "So you can see the future? Then who's gonna win the World Series? What lottery numbers should I play?"

"My dreams don't tell me those things. They tell me who's going to die."

An exaggerated silence filled Kacey's ear, followed by soft sobbing. Panic crept into Marcy's voice, the sweetness gone. "What does this have to do with me?"

"By changing our behavior in the present, we can change our future."

"Bullshit!"

"Marcy, I need to tell you my dream and you decide for yourself. Okay?"

Sniffles replaced her sobs. "Fine, I'm listening."

In the dream, Kacey sat next to Marcy on her flight to Los Angeles. They'd been in the air for more than an hour.

The plane flew erratically, descending rapidly.

The captain informed the passengers they'd lost all hydraulics and backup systems, disabling the steering rudder and flaps in the horizontal stabilizer, requiring them to make a hard emergency landing. Marcy stiffened in her window seat with her phone wedged between her left ear and the headrest, sobbing and gasping for air, speaking to her mother as the earth moved closer and closer. Marcy whimpered, telling her mother she loved her.

Kacey moved through the aisles, scanning the frightened passengers' faces. Many huddled over their cell phones, desperate to reach loved ones, while others held strangers' hands, weeping. Snippets of conversation pelted her, "…tell the kids, I love them," or "…don't cry, it'll be okay," but mostly "…I love you," over and over again.

To Kacey's surprise, many passengers appeared calm, at peace. Next to each of these passengers, someone stood with their hand on their shoulder, soothing them. These standing figures appeared unreal, translucent.

As the plane lurched and dropped, passengers' cries filled the plane with the last sounds they'd ever make. Kacey turned to Marcy, sitting by the window, now off the phone and staring back at her. Their eyes met, and Marcy gave a tearful smile as the world exploded in a fireball of brilliant white light.

"Marcy?" Kacey whispered into the phone.

Silence.

"Marcy, listen to me. Something terrible happens to you tomorrow. I've seen it. Say something."

Marcy blew her nose. "The flight takes off in a couple hours. I doubt there's another one going out."

"There'll be tons of flights to LA. Let me call and find another—"

"For Chrissake, Kacey, I can do it!" Marcy interrupted.

"You'll do it?"

"I will if you hang up and let me!"

Marcy's exasperated sigh made Kacey grin. "Okay. Thanks for not thinking I'm crazy."

"Oh, I definitely think you're crazy."

"Call me back when—"

Marcy disconnected. Kacey lay wide awake as the minutes ticked by. She waited, wondering whether Marcy had chalked up the phone call to a lunatic roommate. Kacey grabbed her cell, holding it in front of her, unsure what to do. She placed it back on the night table. *I'm sure she made the reservation. She just forgot to call me back.*

~

Late in the morning, Kacey woke from a deep sleep. She dragged herself to the sitting position and grabbed the remote. She wiped her eyes as CNN's breaking news described the crash of an Airbus a319 from Boston to Los Angeles in Ohio farmland.

"Oh my God, it really happened!" Kacey held her palms against her face, numb, her breath coming in gasps. Could she have done something to prevent it? Who would have given her the time of day for a dream about a plane crash? *Yeah, and what size straightjacket do you wear?*

Kacey jumped from her bed and checked her watch. 11:30 a.m. Surely, Marcy's other flight had landed by now. She picked up her cell and dialed her number, waiting to hear Marcy's cheery voice tell her she'd listened, she'd arranged a different flight, and she was soaking up the sun in LA, but her call went straight to voicemail. So did the others she placed throughout the day. *She'll pick up, I just have to keep calling. She'll pick up...*

~

Sunday, December 3, 2017

Victor hovered over the man resting on the musty cot in the drafty six-by-eight cell. He'd learned much about Walt Worthing when he probed Granville's mind and introduced himself to his friends. The man's residual pain and humiliation had stained his senses, but he wanted to know more, relive the suffering through the victim's eyes.

Not to mention, this brand of entertainment thrilled him.

A quick probing would give Victor the required answers. He tapped into the man's thoughts and dreams, the reservoirs of joy, love, and gratitude encountered with Granville missing from Worthing's mind. Instead, he found a vast emotional desert; his sentiments, longings, and passions walled off from his current reality. Victor uncovered the sight, smell, and taste of desperation and agony.

Victor could tell Plymouth County Correctional wasn't a place for someone like Walt Worthing, a Boston College graduate from a good home in Revere. Victor caught a glimpse of the man's graduation day, his parents beaming with pride and envisioning a limitless future for their youngest son. Now he shared his home with the nation's most notorious criminals, Richard Reid, the shoe-bomber; New England crime boss, "Cadillac Frank" Salemme; and "Whitey" Bulger.

Worthing's fall from grace fascinated Victor, his slow descent into hell after knee surgery following a hard fall while skiing. A lineup of increasingly powerful opiates—Percocet, Oxycodone and Fentanyl—alleviated a persistent pain, but enabled an addiction.

He rode in the passenger seat of Worthing's car as he cruised the strip in Brockton after the prescriptions ran out and the cravings took hold. Victor welcomed the delirious numbing as he and Walt had their first chase of the dragon, the barb penetrating their veins and delivering a mind-bending rush through their bloodstreams. Afterward, they spent their endless days and nights searching for new friends at any, and all, Dunkin' Donuts parking lots dotting the South Shore, eventually disappearing into the world of nameless addicts surviving on the streets.

The film in Victor's head replayed the events solidifying Worthing's destiny. Sharing a ride with two other junkies he'd just met, Worthing pulled into a convenience store to grab a few snacks and top off the tank before finding a spot for a fix. Inside, he wandered the aisles of chocolate bars, cookies, and chips stacked on top of each other in colorful rows, while the other two men used the restroom. Worthing grabbed a Mountain Dew and Funyuns and brought them to the counter, his mouth watering spontaneously in a Pavlovian response to the satisfying cellophane snack bag's rustles.

"Anything else?" the young girl behind the counter asked.

"Put three dollars on pump two for me, will you, hon?"

"Sure thing...hon." The girl gave him a friendly wink and turned toward the register. She wore a funky jewelry assortment, a feather earing, two thumb rings, a nose stud, and several tattoos behind her neck and on her arms, including the name Brad between her thumb and index finger. An AP calculus book lay open on the other side of the register.

"Let me guess. Your boyfriend?" He pointed to her hand.

"Ex, fortunately." She wrinkled her nose at the tattoo. "You don't happen to have a machete I could use to cut this thing off, do you?" She made a chopping motion at her wrist.

Worthing smirked and reached for her hand. "There's an easier way." He turned it over and pointed to the name. "If you added a 'y' at the end here and a New England Patriots logo above, you'll be all set."

She leaned over the counter, her carefree laugh filling the store.

Before he could ask her name, the young girl's neck exploded, spattering his face with blood and leaving a metallic, copper taste on his tongue. She collapsed behind the counter like a marionette whose strings had been cut. His ears rang from the deafening blast. The two men he'd come with emerged from the back of the store, one with his extended arm holding what looked like a cannon in his hand. The second man raced behind the register and pounded on it until it opened, callously stepping over the dying girl.

Glancing over the counter, Worthing locked onto the girl's eyes, wide and staring, blood jetting from the gunshot wound to her neck. Her lips moved, trying to speak. She reached for him, the name Brad visible on her hand underneath a smattering of blood.

The gunman came up behind Worthing and tapped him on the back with his hand cannon. "Drive, asshole!"

For reasons he couldn't comprehend, Worthing grabbed the blood-spattered snacks and drinks off the counter as he turned and stumbled out to the car.

Victor fast-forwarded to the Suffolk County courthouse on an over-cast February morning. A trial judge, appalled at Worthing's cold-hearted actions—salvaging his food and ignoring a scared high-school girl slowly bleeding to death—handed down a thirty-year sentence for murder.

Worthing's prison life played out in Victor's head: the daily attacks behind the laundry, the beatings bruising his body and shattering his spirit. But then the images took a darker turn. Victor spun away in disgust as the assaults turned ugly—shocking images of unnatural things he'd never condone, horrific acts he couldn't bear to watch. Painful. Humiliating. Victor pulled himself from Worthing's mind, his probe over, a shudder flitting through his burning body. The undersized man would never survive another year or two, let alone thirty, with the atrocities he endured.

He entered Worthing with a skewering force, turning him inside out, straining his victim's skin and manipulating his bones to make room inside him. Angry at what he'd witnessed and with a sense of misguided retribution, he hurled Worthing across his cell, smashing him against the opposite wall with bone jarring force.

"Why didn't you fight back?" Victor spoke the words of another time and place, and although Worthing had never heard them before, he understood.

"Who are you?" Worthing replied inside Victor's mind.

"I'm a friend of a friend. I've witnessed your suffering."

"A friend of a friend, huh?" Worthing rubbed his neck. *"Hard to imagine you have many friends."*

Victor responded with a burst of flames through the man's battered body and hurled him across the room a second time, slamming him against the bars. Worthing offered no resistance to the force inside him, submitting to his fate.

He grinned, blood trickling from the corner of his mouth. *"Tell me who you are. At least humor me while you kill me."*

"Kill you? Your colleagues here will take care of that, you don't need help from me."

"Actually, I do. Please…"

Worthing's desperate plea triggered new ideas swirling through Victor's head. A grin crossed his burning face. *"You'd prefer death?"*

"To this living hell."

"You and your kind," Victor shook his head, *"so unfailingly naïve. Did you ever consider your hell may never end? This may be the best you get."*

"I'll take my chances."

"Get used to suffering," Victor whispered, wrenching Worthing's body with a painful twist. *"I leave you now to your living hell. Someday when you get out of here and get your life back,"* Victor said with a wink, *"I'll pick up where I left off. Then you'll know suffering."*

As Victor exited Worthing, he gave him one last push, throwing him against his sink and toilet. The violent impact left him unconscious with a concussion, broken wrist, dislocated elbow, and six broken ribs.

He'd also formulated a new plan for Robert Granville.

∾

Monday, December 4, 2017

RG awoke to a persistent tapping on his shoulder. He opened his eyes, Morrow held a raised finger in front of his lips.

"It's time," he whispered.

RG nodded, untangling himself from the bedcovers, trying not to disturb Kacey and Baron. He eased off the mattress, grabbed his clothes and sneakers, and followed Morrow, pausing outside the door to slip on his jeans and sweatshirt.

As they tiptoed downstairs, Morrow turned to RG. "Take us somewhere quiet where no one will interrupt us."

He led Morrow out the back door, their feet crunching a thin layer of crusted snow. In the property's back corner, they stepped into a tool-shed's cold, dawn-lit interior. RG caught a whiff of cedar and grass clippings. Above him layers of spider webs cascaded from the high, wooden joists and window frames. Pulling out two Adirondack chairs wedged behind an old garden hose and wheelbarrow, RG brushed them off and turned them facing each other.

Once seated, Morrow leaned in. "How would you like to start?"

"How the hell should I know? You're the sensei here. How about you teach me a Vulcan mind meld or something?" What did he know about forces outside his own world?

"I'm not sure I know that one."

"Maybe you can just spring for some body armor, anything keeping Victor from getting inside me."

Morrow chuckled. "It's not that simple. When a jumper comes for you, nothing can repel the initial invasion. It happens at the speed of light, and there's no defense."

"Then what the fuck are we doing?"

"Hear me out, okay? I can teach you how to perceive Victor's presence and how to prevent him from harming you once he enters your body."

"All right then, let's do this." What option did he have? He could either trust Morrow or he'd be screwed. A no-brainer.

Morrow adjusted himself in the chair. "Okay, let's begin by—"

"Wait a minute," RG interrupted. "What if he comes for Kacey?"

Morrow turned his eyes to the toolshed's weather-stained window. "Let's worry about you first. Protecting Kacey may be the least of your concerns."

"What do you mean?"

"She has powers Victor may not want to challenge, and they've grown stronger since her pregnancy. But she has deeper powers, potent ones she keeps locked away. She fears them, and she's never reached her full potential because of it."

"Her full potential?"

"Kacey has the soul and strength of a caretaker, although she doesn't know it yet."

"How could she? If you'd been terrorized in your dreams and visions as a child, you'd have done everything you could to stop it. What do you expect?"

"Well, that may be, but now she needs to harness her dormant powers. You're going to need all the help you can get. She'll be a formidable ally in fending off Victor."

RG hesitated. "I don't know. If anything happened to her—"

"I understand," Morrow interrupted, "but what if something

happens to you? Are you ready to leave Kacey alone, leave your child without a father?"

"You're pretty eager to put Kacey in harm's way!" he snapped.

"It's my job to protect you. I'm simply looking at all options."

"Well, don't be so generous with her life. If I have to sacrifice myself for them, I will."

"You need to talk to her and let her decide if she wants to help."

RG crossed his arms. "I'll think about it."

"This isn't going away any time soon. You can't keep her in the dark. When have you ever kept anything from her?"

"Never." RG lowered his head.

"Okay then, I've said enough." Morrow removed his glasses, breathed on them, and wiped them off. "This training today will teach you how to contact Victor mentally when he's close, draw him toward you and away from Kacey. When he's close, you'll experience dizziness, weakness, maybe nausea. It'll be sudden, like vertigo at the edge of a cliff. Victor has been close to you before, but my presence blocked these sensations. You'll experience his full power when I'm no longer there to intervene."

Morrow continued. "Okay, I'm going to shift across planes where you cannot sense me. Close your eyes and clear your mind of distraction. When you perceive my presence, reach out to me."

"Reach out to you, how?"

"With your mind."

"How?" He tilted his head.

"You must concentrate, and it will come to you."

RG leaned back in his chair and ran a hand through his hair. "All right, I'll try."

"Forget try…you must do."

"Who the fuck are you? Yoda?" RG mumbled.

"Who's Yoda?"

"Never mind." As he grappled with Morrow's vague direction, the caretaker disappeared, leaving the Adirondack chair empty beside him. "Great!" he muttered.

He closed his eyes and waited as the minutes ticked by, frustrated with Morrow and feeling nothing but the uncomfortable chair's hard wood seat and the dim shed's cold. Should he have sensed something by now? "Mr. Morrow." He gave an exasperated sigh. "Morrow!"

RG's eyes fluttered open. Back in his chair, Morrow shook his head. "You're not concentrating."

RG shrugged and held his hands palms up. "Well, I didn't know what to do, and I didn't know when you'd come back—"

"You aren't going to know when Victor comes back either," Morrow interrupted, "You need to focus to pick up subtle changes in energy." He rubbed his face with his hands. "Concentrate."

"Maybe you could throw me a bone here and teach me how to —" He turned his head toward Morrow, the chair vacant beside him. "Sonofabitch!"

RG grabbed a crumpled soda can off the floor and tossed it against the wall. "Dammit!" *The guy must be laughing his ass off right now.* Taking a deep breath, he attempted to empty his mind and concentrate.

He recalled the meditation classes he and Kacey took during her new age healing-veganism phase. Thankful it only lasted a few months, RG quickly reaching his limit of tolerance for kale and Enya. Still, he did learn to clear his mind and focus, a critical skill he'd needed now. With numerous swirling thoughts, including a few choice words for Morrow, he systematically banned infiltrating distractions one by one until he'd achieved a relaxed, uncluttered state.

RG experienced the fleeting overlap of wake and sleep, that moment when the mind falls into the night's first dream. Morrow's cool energy flew past him, engulfing him. *"Are you there?"* The energy source grew stronger. *"Answer me, Yoda."* RG smirked.

"Who's Yoda?"

He sensed Morrow's essence but couldn't see him. He remained keenly aware of his surroundings, everything from the morning's chill to the fragmented spider webs floating on the updraft. RG latched onto the caretaker's presence. *"I can sense you. It's like you're everywhere at the same time."*

"Good. See if you can keep me there," Morrow responded, testing him.

RG remained in the fleeting dream state for another minute, keeping contact with Morrow, but untethered distractions severed the connection. "I'm done Mr. Morrow. I lost you."

Morrow reappeared in the Adirondack chair. "You did wonderfully. You may not be such a lost cause after all."

RG glared at him. "Thanks for the vote of confidence." *You may be a powerful spirit, but you're a shitty teacher.*

RG stood from his chair and stretched.

"We're not finished yet. There's one more lesson for today, the most important one. When the jumper invades your space, you must learn to hold him. That way, he can't manipulate your muscles. Instead of controlling you, you'll control him."

"Will you show me how this time, or do I have to play twenty questions?"

Morrow raised an eyebrow, but held his tongue. "Your body contains millions of muscle fibers. Imagine contracting every single one, from the largest to the smallest. Imagine they're like tiny hooks. When a jumper invades, you must tense up and dig the hooks into him. This will hold Victor motionless." Morrow sat up straight. "Pretend I'm Victor."

Without warning, Morrow jumped inside him, channeling an internal heat and energy RG didn't expect, dredging up his earlier encounter with Victor. Withering under the heat and discomfort, he sought shelter within himself. Morrow exited and seated himself in his chair. Sweat leached from RG's face, arms, and back.

Morrow placed his hand on RG's shoulder. "Victor will bring the fires of hell with him, but you can't run or hide. He'll have you at his mercy."

Morrow re-entered him, once again with a heat and anger comparable to the jumper.

The violent invasion jolted him, and RG withered against the massive fury. He battled against it, recovered, and faced Morrow. He closed his eyes, imagining the muscles in his body tensing against the heat, the nerves activating individual muscle fibers and snaring Morrow, but he slipped away like a fish evading a baited hook.

"Shit!"

"Try again."

Straining harder, RG activated every muscle fiber he could to contain Morrow. The effect caught the caretaker off guard, paralyzing him momentarily, but he quickly regained control.

"Do it again." Tensing, RG held him for a few seconds longer before Morrow recovered. *"And again."* With each attempt, he prolonged his control against Morrow.

On his last try, as he held Morrow motionless, RG initiated a convulsive wave of pressure through his body, expelling Morrow into the Adirondack chair, knocking his glasses askew. Morrow shook his head, stunned.

"How did I do that?" RG lay back in the chair, drenched in sweat and grinning from ear to ear, satisfied he'd knocked Morrow on his ass.

"I planned to cover how to expel a jumper in a future lesson." Morrow rose from his chair and gave RG a clap on the back.

"Can I try again?"

For the next half hour, they practiced, RG holding Morrow and attempting to expel him. Morrow matched his efforts, but on the last try, he pushed with such gusto, Morrow flew across the top of the Adirondack chair and crashed against the toolshed wall.

"Ooof," Morrow grunted, his glasses and hat flying off his head and skittering across the wood floor.

"Holy shit! Are you okay?" RG rushed to help the crumpled caretaker back into his chair.

"I'm getting too old for this." Morrow positioned his glasses and hat back in place. "You did beautifully, but we must be careful, or we'll exhaust you. Let's pick it up again later." He massaged his neck. "Plus, I could use a breather."

Morrow reached into his coat pocket and unwrapped a Hershey's kiss he stole from the living room.

~

After work, RG came home bearing gifts from his and Kacey's favorite

Chinese restaurant—cartons of veggie lo mein, beef and broccoli, chicken wings, and plenty of white rice. Located at the end of a mostly abandoned strip mall in Watertown, China Palace rivaled the best Asian restaurants in Boston. Roughly the size of a Back Bay apartment hallway, the restaurant's peeling walls and brown-stained ceiling did little to deter eager patrons lining up all hours for a table. RG and Kacey visited with such regularity the owners sent them a Christmas card every year.

Kacey lined the various cartons across the living room carpet in front of the fireplace.

Ravenous, they traded boxes as the TV provided a forgotten backdrop of daily news. Laying by the fire, Baron rested his head on his paws, his eyes moving back and forth between the objects of his affection. Between mouthfuls, Kacey lolled on the couch's throw pillows while grading her class projects, her protrusion now a significant impediment to her leisure.

RG ate with one hand resting on Kacey's belly. With each kick his eyes widened, the incomprehensible wonder of his child resting inches from him, separated by a thin layer of skin, boosting his spirits.

The best of his world lay before him in his living room, but what RG had learned lately, including what the future held, tormented him.

A force of pure destruction, Victor waited, biding his time. RG faced a battle he couldn't afford to lose, but one whose outcome provided no opportunity to win. If he chose to shield Kacey from the impending attack, he would likely die. He had no illusions about his ability to vanquish this supernatural slayer, despite his success training with Morrow. If he died, his son or daughter would grow up without a father and a life plagued with a vague emptiness impossible to fill. RG had lived such a life and couldn't allow it to happen to his child.

If he fessed up and involved Kacey in the battle, as Morrow recommended, they might have a rare chance to conquer Victor, but the risk pounded him with guilt, the mission too dangerous for Kacey and the baby. Losing her would break him and darken his soul. Her loss would mean never meeting his son or daughter, never knowing his or her name, imaginative abilities, eye color or shape, dreams sprouting within his child's heart—and he'd be responsible. He could never live with himself.

If he and Kacey somehow successfully stymied Victor's attack, they'd constantly be wondering if and when Victor would come for them again. What kind of existence would that be? Surviving such a burden wasn't living. No matter what transpired, life would never be the same, and nothing he could do would offer relief.

RG surveyed his world—his beloved wife, his faithful dog, the fire casting warmth and light. The puzzle pieces didn't fit and the game couldn't be won.

Tonight, the calm before the storm.

CHAPTER SEVEN

Tuesday, December 5, 2017

Kacey opened her eyes and found RG lying next to her in a deep sleep. His face rested inches from her own, his cool breath against her cheek in an intermittent, predictable cadence.

On mornings like this, Kacey could curl up in the down comforter and stay in bed all day, reveling in the man beside her. Sometimes when she awakened before he did, she'd secretly watch him sleep, admiring familiar details about him, how his outer ear curved toward the lobe, his hair's soft strands flattened on his forehead, and his hands curled around the pillow. She could visualize in his face the boy he must have been, and she wondered whether his mother, Helen, ever sat where she did, doing the same.

She imagined places he explored in his slumber, the dreams he wouldn't remember upon waking, a secret life she'd never know. Today, she'd put her wonder and awe on hold, his odd behavior taking center stage—the mad dash to Chatham only to leave after ten minutes, and his conversation with himself on his way back from the toolshed yesterday she'd witnessed. For someone so damn rational, RG's recent behavior simply befuddled her, and she couldn't blame it on fatherhood jitters.

Sliding from under the covers, Kacey stood at the end of the bed, the morning sun tumbling in through the wide bedroom windows. She closed her eyes and warmed her feet on the sun-drenched carpet before padding downstairs to the kitchen, the floor's crisp, slate tile instantly cooling her temperate toes.

Kacey grabbed a mug and poured herself Dunkin Donuts decaf from her coffeemaker, strategically programmed to produce a ready-made placebo caffeine jolt at 7:05 a.m. each morning, a miracle of modern day living Kacey never took for granted.

Her heart fluttered as she ran her hands over the mug, a gift RG made for her at the Newtonville craft show last year. Instead of buying the mug she wanted, he'd manned the potter's wheel at the do-it-yourself craft tent, producing perhaps the ugliest clay formation human hands had ever shaped—smudged and misshapen, listing to the left, with an abrasive edge catching her lip with every sip. Kacey held the cup in her hand like a chalice, a reminder things you love don't always come in shiny packages. Sometimes the luster dulls over time, and rough edges can emerge, but no coffee ever tasted as good as when she sipped it from RG's lump of clay.

A shrill ring from the wall telephone interrupted her pleasant preoccupation.

"I'm sorry to call this early," a female voice on the line said, "but I'm trying to reach Robert Granville. Um, is he there?"

"Are you a student?" Kacey had broken the hearts of many infatuated college women calling to speak to RG for various trivial and contrived reasons. She could only pray this caller responded differently than the very persistent Brittany Thorne last semester.

"I'm Deb Skinner, the mother of the child he rescued from the tracks in Kenmore Square Saturday night. I was hoping to thank him."

She choked on her brew. "Who's this again?"

"We haven't met, but I'm calling about your husband's heroics the other night. My son wanted to see him again and thank him in person." She paused and added, "Truthfully? We all want to thank him again."

Kacey took another gulp of decaf, trying to make sense of this conversation. "Heroics? Wait a minute. What are we talking about here? Are you sure you have the right Robert Granville?"

"Well, I asked for Robert's name from the Metro Police officer in Kenmore Station."

Kacey teetered, but steadied herself before she lost her balance. She sat on the high stool abutting her kitchen's granite-topped island, moving her free hand over her stomach bump to calm her racing mind. "If I sound uninformed, believe me, I am. My husband's too humble for his own good."

"He didn't tell you? My son, Jack, fell off the platform just as a train came into the station. He says someone pushed him, but you know how kids' imaginations can take over after something like this." She gave a nervous laugh.

"Oh my goodness!" Kacey set her mug down before she dropped it. "That's horrifying."

"Tell me about it. Saying my husband and I were in a panic is an understatement."

"Your son's all right then?" She rubbed her belly again, sharing in a mother's fear.

"A broken arm, but the idea your child is lying on a subway track and about to be..." She drew a deep breath. "Before we could figure out what had happened, your husband jumped down onto the tracks and lifted him to safety right when the train came flying through the station. I've never seen anything that courageous my entire life."

Her heart swelled as she imagined RG jumping onto the tracks, risking his own life for someone he didn't know. That he selflessly saved a child's life stirred her emotions even more, and she blinked back the tears forming in her eyes. "How's your boy doing?"

"As good as can be expected. He's scared, says he doesn't feel safe."

"I can't believe what I'm hearing," Kacey mumbled.

"Mrs. Granville, is this the first time you've heard about this?"

Kacey searched for an answer. "He might have tried to tell me as I fell asleep."

"I completely understand, although none of us have slept the past few nights."

"Um, listen, I'll tell him you called to say thanks. I'm glad my husband was there to save your son." Kacey hung up the phone, sitting motionless at the kitchen counter.

Kacey's mind experienced the weightlessness of freefall just before gravity asserted itself. Despite adoration for RG's selfless act, she stared blankly ahead, her eyes transfixed to a spot on the opposite wall, deep fissures fanning out between her eyebrows. Taking a breath, she attempted to field the random thoughts and questions striking all at once. Why wouldn't he tell her he'd saved someone's life? It didn't make sense. One more piece of odd behavior she couldn't explain. *The sonofabitch!* She contemplated racing upstairs and dragging him out of a deep sleep, but instead shuffled into the living room and sat at the desk perched in front of the bay windows overlooking the front yard. Powering up the laptop, she clicked on the *Boston Herald* website and scrolled down through archived stories until she found the right one.

TRIUMPH AND TRAGEDY IN KENMORE STATION—Boston (AP) —Two men rescued a young boy from certain death in the Kenmore Square T station on Saturday night, pulling him from the tracks just moments before a speeding train pulled into the station. Jack Skinner, 12, stood along the platform's edge when he apparently lost his balance and fell onto the tracks. As his horrified parents, John and Deborah Skinner, looked on, an inbound train came barreling through the station heading for their son, dazed and lying motionless on the tracks below. Robert Granville, 35, a passenger in Kenmore Station, disregarded the imminent danger and risked his own life to dash onto the tracks, handing the boy to a second man, 46-year-old Ben Frasier. Frasier grabbed the boy, then pulled Mr. Granville to safety just seconds before the train's thunderous approach, but while this triumphant tale of bravery and teamwork should have been the year's feel-good story, tragically, Mr. Frasier suffered a heart attack and died at the scene.

Kacey lowered the laptop lid, closing off Kenmore Station's tale of horrors. The incident terrified her, not the uncertainty of RG's timely presence, but something unexplainable, something outside the danger he faced on the tracks.

Something had prowled Kenmore Station's darkened tunnels Saturday night.

Something dark. Relentless. Filled with hate.

As Kacey finished the *Herald* piece, a swirling dizziness descended upon her. Her vision faded as light drained from the room. She stared straight ahead, unseeing, as pictures played in her mind. Kacey found herself in a rainy and cold Kenmore Square with RG nowhere to be found. As she passed Kenmore Station, she squinted down Commonwealth Avenue to the spot where the SUV struck him in her previous dream. No RG. She backtracked and peered into the stairwell leading to the underground station. Her instincts told her that's where she'd find him.

She hesitated.

An urgency gripped her like a vise, but her pounding heart and shaking legs kept her frozen in place. She tried to invent a reason to avoid the descent into the inky blackness, but the vision pushed her forward. At the bottom of the steps, the dank, humid underground smell overpowered her.

This must be what hell smells like.

She swung through the turnstile, continuing her descent into the station. The walls flanking the stairs no longer displayed advertisements, train schedules, or route diagrams as on the level above. Craggy, rocky limestone outcroppings replaced the smooth concrete walls, and rivulets of water slalomed from ceiling to floor. Ancient dripping stalactites lined the stone ceiling above her, the dim bulbs illuminating the station now gone. The steps vanished in the darkness. Scattered at her feet, bloated, half-eaten rodent carcasses. After several minutes traversing the wet, slippery limestone, the ancient railway's tracks appeared before her, the scene jarringly out of sync with the subterranean cavern she'd entered. A few people milled about on the inbound platform, a young boy with his parents, a heavy-set man standing alone, a homeless man at the end of the tracks, and RG.

She called to him, her voice echoing off the cave walls, but her efforts proved futile.

The events Deb Skinner described on the phone played out before her eyes. When the boy flew onto the tracks, RG leaped into the pit to save him. Kacey's heart hammered in her chest as he struggled to free him, precious seconds ticking away as the train's screech grew louder and louder. *Hurry up! What the hell are you doing?* Tension crackled in the air, despite Kacey's knowledge of the outcome. But what if it ended differently in her dream? What if he didn't make it? She gasped in relief as he pulled the boy to safety, but threw her hands in front of her face as the train exploded into the station with RG still trapped in the pit. She wanted to run to him, but the heavyset man pulled him onto the platform with seconds to spare, the train spinning them both to the ground as it pounded through the tunnel. Immersed in RG's plight, Kacey hadn't noticed the two others perched on either side of the tracks viewing the scene, too.

She recognized the older man with the hat and glasses from her earlier dream, his presence comforting her. Kacey's intuition told her she'd be safe with him and he'd also protect RG. But the fiery-like man—the way her mind described the second man—he'd destroy him if he could.

He appeared more like an electrified monster than an actual man, a hellish ghoul, the spiritual embodiment of despair, pain, and anger. Her knees weakened and a cold sweat flashed across her skin—this creature the cause of her earlier trepidation. While the older man had a soothing presence, she couldn't be sure whether he possessed the same power as this raging demon.

Despite her proximity, the two remained unaware of Kacey's interloping presence. The burning man sneered at the older man, a taunting grimace, revealing cracked, quivering lips on his rotting face. Clearly, the old man and his flaming adversary found themselves engaged in an ongoing conflict, with RG serving as a pawn in their game.

As the two continued their posturing, Kacey drifted into a deeper consciousness. With her focus on the burning man, a thought stream leaked from his mind into her own.

A young blonde-haired boy with freckles dotting his nose dashed across her thoughts. He strolled with the burning man on a beach— long before his transition—when he lived in the world as a man, happy and smiling, filled with love for his boy. The name 'Victor' floated through her mind.

Flashes of the burning man and the older man together in an earlier time appeared before her. Victor listened in agony to the man seated on a stool, facing him in a white office, the fluorescent lights buzzing in a duel against a ticking clock. The vision shifted to Victor sitting beside the same young boy in a hospital bed—he called him Sam—nearly unrecognizable compared to the healthy, laughing child strolling on the sparkling beach with his father. Kacey wanted to penetrate the burning man's mind, but hit a barricaded, impenetrable door. She could see no more.

Victor's despair and the boy's illness saddened her, and she let out a sigh.

The burning man's gaze broke from the older man, alert to a foreign presence breaking through his fortified inner prison. He turned and glared at Kacey with molten eyes, her breath caught in her throat as a pressure pounded her chest like a rolling wave.

"He's beautiful, your son, Sam," she spoke into his mind.

The burning man smiled at her, momentarily disarmed, and the fire inside him diminished. Victor Garrett's human face flickered on and off beneath the rotting mask covering his burning self while he pictured a boy from another time and place.

But the moment flitted away, replaced by a spiraling anger at his carelessness protecting his thoughts. The flame inside his soul's furnace burned hotter, her fear mounting. Victor met her eyes, shifting his gaze to her belly. He spoke to her in a language she'd never heard before, but somehow understood. *"Congratulations,"* he sneered. *"It's a boy."*

Kissing her on the neck from behind, RG jolted Kacey from the vision, causing her to jump and send her full mug flying off the desk, shattering onto the hardwood floor. Kacey stared dumbly at the beautifully misshapen pieces strewn about, but she'd need to salvage something far more important than her broken chalice.

"Jeez, Kacey, you might consider switching to decaf." RG smirked, picking up the mug's clay chunks, heaping them into one hand, careful not to cut himself.

Walking into the kitchen, he stepped on the trash bin's floor pedal, the ceramic pieces resonating with an audible clink as he tossed them away. He returned to the living room with paper towels and knelt beside the chocolate colored puddle. "I'm heading in to teach my 9:30. My turn to grab us something for dinner tonight."

RG finished wiping up the mess and carried the dripping paper towels to the kitchen. He walked toward the door, but turned and jogged back to the living room. He kissed Kacey on the cheek and grabbed his professor bag, as she called it, the leather briefcase with the throw-over flap and buckles they picked out for him when he received tenure. Then he headed out the kitchen door to the garage, giving Baron a hurried moment of attention.

"Why didn't you tell me?" Kacey turned from the computer.

He stepped back into the house, peering over his shoulder. "Tell you what?"

"I saw what you did in Kenmore Station. I had another vision."

RG closed his eyes, unable to meet her gaze.

"We promised we'd never lie to each other, but you did." Her eyes bore through him. "You kept me in the dark. Why?"

He shuffled over to the couch and slumped onto the cushions, defeated. "I don't know, Kacey. I—"

"You nearly died, and it wasn't important enough to mention in passing? Did you have a nice day, RG? 'Fine, fine, and by the way, I just missed getting pulverized by a train. I saved a boy's life, though. How 'bout you?'"

RG stared at the floor.

Kacey persisted. "Who's the older man in the hat and glasses? I've seen him twice now." Kacey stood and moved to the window, peering out into the front yard.

"What older man?"

Kacey pivoted to face him. "No more lies!"

RG recoiled as if he'd been struck. "Okay, time to come clean, but this is gonna sound nuts. His name's Morrow. He's my, um caretaker."

She leaned toward him. "Your what?"

He rose from the couch and paced across the hardwood floor. "Sort of like a guardian angel. He told me he's from the next world."

"What? Heaven?"

"I'm not sure. At first, I didn't believe him, but he keeps making more and more sense to me. He says he's been protecting me since I lost my father."

"Is he real, or..." she hesitated, "from your imagination?"

"I don't know, but I think he's real. You've seen him twice, what do you think?"

"I'm not sure what's real anymore." She'd questioned her dreams and visions, whether actual or imagined, she didn't know, but for both to be imagining the same man seemed too coincidental. "In my vision, he watched over you in Kenmore Station. How long have you known about him?"

"Since last week." He described his meeting Morrow, seeing his mother on the beach with him as a child. He told her about jumpers from the next world and the caretaker's protective role.

"Why would he suddenly appear after thirty-five years?"

RG dropped back onto the couch. "He came to tell me my time had come; my scheduled death had arrived."

Kacey joined him on the couch. "Let me guess, the day you surprised me in Chatham?"

"Must seem obvious now, the way I behaved." He leaned his head on her shoulder.

"But you didn't die."

"At the precise moment of my death, I won a reprieve."

"I'm glad you came to see me, but why didn't you tell me? You didn't give me a chance to do something to stop it."

"Morrow said it was too dangerous, not to involve family or friends, that you and the baby could've died with me. I had to do it alone. Now with me alive, Morrow's caretaker responsibilities have ended. He can't protect me much longer."

"Protect you from what?"

"There's someone trying to kill me."

"The burning man?"

RG nodded his head. "His name's Victor. He once lived in this world. He blames Morrow for his son's death, and he wants Morrow to suffer like he has. So, now he's coming for me. I've been working with Morrow, learning to defend myself against him."

Kacey closed her eyes, recalling all she'd learned in the vision. "Morrow worked in a hospital as a doctor, and Victor took his dying son to him for treatment."

"Morrow didn't tell me that," RG said, rubbing his chin, "he only mentioned they had a history and Victor blamed him for his son's death."

"I just met Victor in my dream. I talked to him about his son."

RG's jaw dropped. "You talked to him?"

"He told me we're having a boy."

"A boy?" His eyes widened as the words rolled off his tongue. "He said this?"

"Well, in a threatening way. It's not like he planned to throw us a couple's baby shower or anything."

RG grinned, but only for a moment. He rested his head against her belly as Kacey reached her arms around him and held him. The breeze picked up outside, the soft tree branches scraping the siding punctuated the silence.

"I still don't understand why you didn't share all this," Kacey said. "Maybe this is what my power has been meant for all along."

He searched her eyes. "I needed time to formulate a plan. I thought if I fixed things you wouldn't need to know. But I fixed things all right. Now I have no idea when he's coming. Besides, I didn't think you'd believe me. Hell, I still have trouble believing it myself."

A small piece of her chalice still lay on the floor by the desk, overlooked during RG's cleanup. She went over, picked it up, and dropped it inside her pocket.

"It's gonna be all right." She returned to the couch and took his hand, squeezing it twice. "Anyway, I'm proud of what you did in Kenmore Station."

RG flashed a humble grin. "I guess I saved a life. Morrow said you've been saving people all your life, that you have the powers of a future caretaker. Morrow says not to fear your gift."

"Easy for him to say. Morrow doesn't appreciate how scary it's been to deal with all these years...or maybe he has. He could have a point. I admit I'm a little curious. Maybe it's time I learn more about these powers, you think?"

He didn't answer.

"Ever since my pregnancy I've felt the dream-thing getting harder to control. Maybe your friend Morrow is right. If he has answers or can help me fully understand what's happening, I need to meet him. I could learn what he's teaching you and tell him about an idea I have."

"What idea?" RG raised an eyebrow.

Kacey rose from the couch and paced the hardwood floor. "Well, in the vision, I had access to the burning man's mind and read his thoughts."

He swallowed. "Christ, Kacey, Morrow hasn't even been able to get a glimpse inside his head."

"I witnessed things he didn't want anyone to see. I gave myself away when I showed sadness for his loss."

"You took a pretty big risk with someone you describe as the burning man."

"Well, he responded to my kindness for a brief moment." Kacey shivered. "I couldn't see everything inside him, though. He had things hidden behind a door to his mind."

"You don't want to go in there."

The wheels turned inside her head, picking up speed. "We need an edge. If I can enter his mind and catch him off guard, I might find out what he's planning."

RG ran a hand through his hair. "I don't know, Kacey..."

Grabbing his face with both hands, Kacey spoke in a voice clear and strong, the fierce resolve and power inside her Morrow had described jetting to the surface. "Listen to me. We're in this together now and you need me, especially if Morrow can't protect you much longer. When he's gone, I'm all you've got. And after what I saw tonight, there's no way you can handle Victor by yourself."

RG stood and paced to the fireplace, leaning his head against the mantel. Kacey sensed his racing mind trying to come up with another option, a scenario he hadn't considered yet to protect them.

"Okay, you win." He turned to face her, exhaling sharply. "What's the point in arguing, you'd have gotten your way in the end."

"You're damn right!"

RG roused a defeated smile. "Let's talk to him."

Chuck Brennan strode down the hall and through the Falmouth Police Station's main floor, the familiar symphony of ringing telephones, pinging devices and computers, and the muffled cacophony of conversations greeting him like the comforts of home. He rubbed a calloused hand across his walrus mustache as he veered into the break room, dueling walls of vending machines bracketing a refrigerator, microwave, and coffee maker. He slammed a chair out of his way, the legs sticking on the bright vinyl flooring.

Brennan poured a cup of day-old Joe from the stained Mr. Coffee and dropped into a hard, plastic seat at a table with a group of his comrades; Fred Dodd, a veteran officer; and Sam Gibson and Wally Krug, two rookies joined at the hip straight from the academy. The three officers hunched over an article in the *Herald*, Krug standing and leaning over the others to get a better view.

"If you're all trying to convince me you know how to read, you're working too hard." Brennan chuckled, blowing steam from his Styrofoam cup.

Dodd gave him a smirk and slid the sugar dispenser toward of him. "You mean you don't just look at the pictures?"

"You gotta check this out, Chief." Krug slid the paper toward him. "Un-fucking-believable."

Brennan shook a flurry of granules into his coffee. "What is it? You guys got a picture of Michelle Pfeiffer or something?"

"Michelle…?" Gibson glanced at Krug, who shrugged.

Brennan patted his pocket for his readers and settled in over the paper. "Never mind."

Dodd took a sip from his coffee. "So, this kid falls onto the tracks in Kenmore and—"

"Trains coming right at him," Gibson interrupted. "Some guy jumps down and pulls him to safety. Almost gets crushed."

Krug shook his head. "Un-fucking-believable."

Brennan turned his attention to the paper. As he read, beads of sweat popped out on his brow, his elevated heart rate hammering in his throat. Squeezing his eyes shut, Brennan fought the traumatic images seeping from his unconscious, half buried in a never quite forgotten past. For a moment, he kept them at bay, struggling against their insidious ability to hijack his attention, like a hand reaching out and grabbing his chin, forcing him to look. *Please make it stop!* Brennan pictured the high-speed impact of two vehicles, the sound…

"You all right, Chief?" Dodd asked.

Brennan clasped his shaking hands together under the table as he labored to breathe. *Get out of my head!* The image of the crumpled Jeep Wrangler on its side, its back wheel spinning…

"Yeah, I'm fine."

Dodd stood and silenced his chirping phone. "You never know who's gonna end up being a hero."

"You guys mind I take this?" Brennan folded the paper under his armpit as he rose from his chair. He had difficulty swallowing and couldn't hide the flutter in his voice. *Relax, it'll go away.* The passengers clawing at the windows, the sound of their scraping nails…

"You owe me a buck-fifty," Dodd grinned, clapping Brennan on the back as he stepped into the hallway.

Brennan forced a grin as he swiped the back of a wobbly hand across his forehead. He trudged down the hall on unsteady legs, the station's floor swimming before his eyes. He concentrated on the task at hand, putting one foot in front of the other. *Just make it back to your desk, keep it together.*

Retreating to the safety of his office, Brennan pressed the lock on the doorknob and dropped into his chair, his shirt tacky, wallpapered to his chest and back. He laid the paper out on his desk and scanned the article again. Before he finished, his stomach seized, a surge of coffee-flavored bile erupted from his mouth.

Brennan lowered his head, clasping his hands over his ringing ears, trying to hold off the onslaught. He found himself thrown back into his rookie days with the Boston PD, inching along the Mass Pike with the other Monday morning commuters, his partner, Hal Witten behind the cruiser's wheel.

"You should've seen Tyler." Witten had said, waving his hands, quite the animated storyteller. "Kid's covered in white flour from hair to feet, his sister Maggie's trying to hose him off in the driveway." His booming laugh had filled the vehicle.

Brennan chuckled as Witten recounted his ever-mischievous kids' adventures. They sipped their Dunkin' Donuts coffee as they crawled toward the tollbooth, the sun burning through the morning's last wisps of fog. The white noise from revving engines pressed in on them through the open windows, drivers jockeying for position as they funneled through the highway turnstile.

A red Jeep Wrangler with three twenty-somethings inside idled in the lane next to him, heading into the city. As Brennan's eyes drifted toward the pretty young thing behind the wheel, an ascending roar filled his ears. A flash of silver flew past him on his right, a U-Haul traveling at breakneck speed heading directly toward the tollbooth, its driver in some sort of distress behind the wheel. Before Brennan's mind grasped the outcome's inevitability, his partner's voice escalated.

"Holy shit, Chuck!"

The U-Haul rammed the Jeep with a deafening impact, launching it forward, slamming it against the tollbooth's raised concrete edge and flipping it onto its driver's side door, flames belching from the ruptured fuel tank. The Jeep's pretty driver fumbled with the handle on the crushed passenger side door, the two others clawing at the roof and windows, desperate to escape the encroaching flames. The scratching sound…

"Let's go!" In an instant, Witten leaped from the cruiser and advanced on the overturned Jeep, flames licking its outer edges. The passenger's screams mounted until they dwarfed the traffic's steady din. Brennan sat frozen, staring through the windshield, his body tethered to his seat.

"Chuck, get your ass over here!" Witten shouted over his shoulder, tearing off his jacket, beating the growing flames racing up the Jeep's exterior. Struggling to open the suddenly weighty door, Brennan's weakened body trembled. In slow motion, he managed to place his feet solidly on the pavement, his brain sending bursts of signals to his waiting muscles, but his feet remained encased in cement.

Witten sprinted to the cruiser, grabbing the shotgun affixed to the driver side door. "What the fuck's the matter with you? People are burning!" He paused for a moment, meeting Brennan's eyes, a bewildering look wreathing his features.

There's nothing you can do, they're all gonna die. In the time it took for his eyes to break contact, Witten's face had gone from concern to disdain.

Witten raced back to the Jeep and wedged the rifle butt against the crack in the door, attempting to pop it open. The victims' screams intensified as flames snaked into the Jeep's cabin. Brennan eased himself back inside the cruiser, lowering himself into the passenger seat. He closed the door, and rolled up his window. His eyes and heart hardened in ice, a familiar defense he'd adopted when scolded as a child.

Witten managed to pry the Jeep's door open as the rifle butt snapped in two. Diving into the fiery interior, he pulled the passengers to safety, suffering second- and third-degree burns to his arms, hands, and face.

Rushing back to the cruiser, Witten shot the catatonic Brennan a nasty glare. "What the fuck's wrong with you?" He reached in and popped the trunk to grab the first aid kit and went about tending to the victims' injuries, relinquishing his medic duty after the EMTs arrived. Only after each victim was safely loaded into the ambulance and on their way to the hospital did Witten allow the first responders to treat him.

The stories in the following days' *Globe* and *Herald* only mentioned one police hero, lauding the bravery and sacrifice of Officer Hal Witten, humbly accepting a commendation standing on city hall's steps with the governor.

Witten didn't bother asking Brennan what happened to him that day. He never asked him anything again. The following two weeks, they drove in wretched silence while the department processed Witten's request for reassignment. His former loyal partner didn't mention the incident to anyone as far as Brennan could tell, but he suspected it wouldn't be long before Witten blabbed. These things get around. Unfortunately for Witten, he took their dark secret to the grave in a hail of bullets a month later, a senseless shooting outside his home as he returned home from work. No suspects. No witnesses.

No one ever found out where the bullets came from, but one cop didn't want his secret shared with the world.

Fuckin' heroes, who needs 'em anyway!

CHAPTER EIGHT

Tuesday, December 5, 2017

From RG's fourth-floor office window, Boston dazzled like a touched-up image on a travel brochure. The Harvard cupola hovered in the distance to his left, pasted against the cloudless sky on the Charles River's Cambridge side, MIT's Great Dome to his right. Between them, cars, buses, and bicycles dotted the roadways along the river, delivering people to their destinations in a chaotic yet coordinated migration. He never grew tired of watching his city wake to a new day from his elevated private viewing room.

RG powered up his computer and opened his class notes, hopelessly unprepared for his morning lecture. His topic on the stages of cellular respiration—glycolysis, the Krebs Cycle, oxidative phosphorylation—didn't lend itself to a lack of preparation. He pulled the textbook from his professor bag and crammed, refreshing his memory on the cycles and sequences of substrates, enzymes, and coenzymes; and the change in free energy in each step. By the time he strolled into class, he had confidence he could teach his students something.

Of course, if all went south, he could rely on the fact most undergraduates weren't listening anyway.

After class, RG returned to his office and reclined awkwardly in the chair of his ergonomically correct work station. He cracked his neck to both sides and closed his eyes, calculating the number of classes left to teach before finals the following week. Disappointed with the result, he checked his email. A dozen open access journals trolled for contributions, but he deleted these solicitations along with several others bypassing his spam filter.

He frowned when the last email popped up, a message from Wendell Abernathy, the Associate Dean of Research. "God, this can't be good."

Wendell Abernathy resembled a million dollar Lamborghini with a four-cylinder engine—physically striking, but without much under the hood. The son of legendary Harvard physicist Alistair Abernathy, Wendell disgraced the family name when Harvard fired him for research misconduct. He'd landed at BU as RG's immediate superior after Alistair called in a favor from a close friend on the Board of Trustees. RG had been a vocal critic of the Abernathy hire, and now Wendell never missed an opportunity to make his life difficult.

They'd first met in the rec center soon after Abernathy took the position. A basketball had rested under the man's arm, but he wasn't there to shoot hoops. He'd cornered a young female student beside the water fountain, running his own full court press.

Spotting RG, Abernathy strode with purpose across the gym. "Granville, I'd like a word." The clunk of weights and the whirring motorized cardio machines barely interrupted the sound system's thumping backbeat. He placed a hand on RG's shoulder and gave him a crooked grin, eyes darting back and forth at the youthful female forms working out around him. "God, they're like little pieces of candy, aren't they?"

RG recoiled at the puff of stale breath wafting toward him, ineffectively masked with a handful of mints. Stepping backward, he freed himself from Abernathy's grip. "That's the difference between you and me, Wendell. I see future professionals, not something to snack on. What do you want?"

Abernathy's eye twitched as he sized up his adversary. "I figured we got off on the wrong foot. I can't imagine how it must feel to find me in a position and a pay grade above you after trying to block my appointment here." Wendell smirked. "Things can be awkward sometimes."

"I hadn't given it much thought, to be honest."

Abernathy snaked his arm around his shoulder and leaned close. "Well, maybe you should. It's important you understand our college's hierarchy. The gleaming new laboratory space you have, it could very well be moved across town to one of our older buildings. Anytime, for any reason."

Gripping his towel tightly, RG's blood pressure ratcheted upward. "I've obtained more than enough grants to justify—"

"Oh, don't misunderstand me," Abernathy interrupted, "it's your laboratory for now, but even the best researchers find themselves without funding at times. Hopefully, you'll keep it up. If not, I'll gladly add a few more classes to your schedule."

RG glared at him, turning to leave before he lost his cool.

Abernathy followed him down the hall. "Nothing to say, Granville? I'm surprised. You certainly had a lot to say before my hiring."

RG spun and approached Abernathy, blood jetting through his veins.

"Oh, thanks for reminding me. I do have something to say, Wendell." He stepped up close and positioned his face inches from Abernathy's, wrinkling his nose as he inhaled. "Don't skimp on the breath mints."

Abernathy had laughed and threw an Altoid into his mouth, flashing RG his perfect teeth as he'd gazed around the gym. "Trust me, this won't be the only candy I have today."

RG leaned back in his office chair and rubbed his eyes, forcing his readers up onto his forehead. He accepted the electronic request for a meeting, already dreading the dance he'd have to do with Abernathy in the morning. He closed his email and punched at his office phone's flashing message light.

"Sorry to bother you at work, RG, but it's Mike Stahl. Give me a call at the Chatham Police Department when you get a minute or you can reach me on my cell anytime." He provided both numbers and thanked him before hanging up.

RG threw the receiver back on the headset with a thunk. *Christ, another one of my favorite people.* His blood boiled when he thought of him. Mike Stahl, Kacey's first love and the drunk who once tossed her across a room. The guy always found excuses to run into Kacey accidentally on purpose, edging his way into her life. Every time RG visited Chatham, Sandie would mention to Kacey how Mike had taken care of her parking ticket or how he'd helped Bruce with a zoning issue on one of his properties. No one could be that nice without a motive. RG viewed it as an intentional plan to stay in her life.

He grabbed the phone, stabbing at the keys. "It's RG returning your call," he snapped, skipping pleasantries.

"Hey, RG, thanks for calling back. Might as well cut to the chase here. I have information about a friend of yours, Walt Worthing. He suffered serious injuries during an incident in his cell, including a cranial fracture."

A shudder spiraled into his core. "What happened?"

"Too early to know. He's still unconscious."

"How did you know to call me?"

"Well, when I met you guys down in Falmouth a few years back, you all talked about your friend in Plymouth County. Didn't sound like a guy taking too well to prison. I caught the name and kept an eye on him, that's all. I talked to the warden, Tom Gooden, about getting him his own cell after the, um, trouble he's had."

RG lowered his head at Stahl's reference. "You helped him?"

"Well, Tom makes all the decisions there, he's the one who made the accommodations." Stahl hesitated. "That's what makes this strange, RG. All this happened late at night when he was alone in his cell. No one could've gotten in after lights out."

RG pressed Detective Stahl about the facts, access to Walt during the time of the incident, whether video surveillance existed, or whether injuries could've been self-inflicted. His responses left RG with more questions than answers, and the answers he could provide brought no comfort. "Thanks Mike, I appreciate your letting me know."

RG leaned forward in his chair, his hands shaking as he dropped the phone into its cradle.

∾

The drive down Route 3 to Plymouth took less than forty-five minutes; RG drove with a vengeance through heavy traffic, pulling into the penitentiary located uncomfortably close to a Subway, Home Depot, and Panera across the street. He sat for a moment contemplating the bizarre collision of worlds. His stomach sank as he surveyed the walled compound and its multiple gates topped with the razor wire, a building designed to house the worst of humanity—and one of his best friends lived here.

This would be difficult. The prison stood as a stark reminder of how close one can be to the unimaginable. He grew up with Walt; his family lived a few streets over. They went to the same church and schools. *How the fuck did Walt end up here?* RG still couldn't comprehend it. If it happened to Walt, it could happen to anyone. He climbed the steps to the front door of the lockup, bracing himself against the bitter wind, wondering how he'd survive in a place like this.

The simple answer: he wouldn't, and he knew it.

Entering the prison, he received his visitor's pass and waited for a corrections officer to escort him to the infirmary. Mike Stahl had called in a favor, arranging special visits for Worthing's close friends and family. After a lengthy wait, RG finally made his way through metal detectors and into the heart of the prison. The deafening noise reverberated in his ears, the buffed cement floors and concrete walls amplifying the slightest sound. A smell permeated the air and mobbed his senses, the odor of desperate men living in a savage environment. Prison staff patted him down or waved him with a wand before entering each part of the facility. RG tried not to stare at the inmates as he passed through each holding area, but he couldn't help himself. His calm demeanor belied a powerful visceral reaction to the place.

A danger existed for any civilian entering a prison, but RG had no fear. His escort bore a striking resemblance to the old WWF wrestler

Stone Cold Steve Austin, large and imposing with a shaved head and goatee, eyes dark as onyx, silent the entire journey through the penitentiary's intricate labyrinth. RG smirked. *Talk about caretakers. This guy might give Morrow a run for his money.*

After traversing an array of winding corridors and stairwells into the slammer's bowels, RG and Stone Cold arrived at the Infirmary. He awaited completion of visitor protocols before the nurse directed him into the room. Worthing rested on an adjustable hospital bed, covered in bandages and casts, IV fluids dripping into his rope-like veins.

"You need to keep your conversation short," the nurse reminded him, "he's heavily sedated right now."

Walt had stayed sober during his incarceration, despite available drugs circulating on the inside. RG hoped the opioids didn't reignite the addiction Walt had fought hard to overcome.

"Is he awake?"

"He's been in and out, mostly out." The nurse checked his IV lines, blood pressure cuff, and pulse oximeter. "If he does wake up, he may not be up to talking."

Stone Cold pointed at a metal prison chair next to Worthing's bed. RG took a seat while the guard posed beside the cramped room's doorway as if Walt would hop out of bed and make a run for it. He studied his friend's face, merging the boy and teenager with the man beneath the cuts and bruises.

Before long, Worthing's eyes fluttered open, glassy and disoriented. "RG, man…that you?" He winced.

"Yeah, Bud, it's me."

Worthing rolled his head deep into the pillow. "How'd you get in here?" he slurred. "You try to rob a gas station?"

"Not without getting your advice first."

Walt grinned and closed his eyes. RG rested his hand on a bandage-free part of his arm.

"I'm glad you came, RG." Walt tried to sit up, flinched, and lay back down.

"Easy, man. Just relax."

"I can't."

"Can you tell me what happened?"

A single tear escaped Worthing's eye and stretched down onto the pillow. "You wouldn't believe me if I told you."

"Try me. No sense in protecting the bastard who did this."

"It wasn't like that." Walt gasped for breath, his broken ribs sabotaging his efforts. "I know how this must sound, but some kind of force got inside of me Sunday night."

"Inside you?"

"A burning force took over my body." Recounting the events occurring in his cell, Walt paused at times, his injuries and medication levels skewing his recollection.

RG's heart tap danced in his chest as he nodded his understanding.

Worthing closed his eyes, searching his memory. "He spoke inside my head and said, 'I'm a friend of a friend,' but he was talking about you. No doubt in my mind." His hand shot forward and grabbed RG's shirt, yanking him closer to his beat-up face. "Listen to me! He's coming for you next. You gotta run! Just take Kacey and—"

"Calm down, man," RG interrupted, waving off the nurse hurrying into the room.

Beads of sweat shimmered on Worthing's brow. "You gotta believe me, man!"

"I do, Walt." RG leaned over and whispered. "I know who it is."

Worthing released him, dropping back onto the pillow exhausted. "You gotta get away, far away..." Walt's eyes flickered and he drifted off to sleep, the nurse glaring at RG as she fussed with his IV.

He placed his hand against Walt's forehead and stood up, signaling the guard. He gazed down at his battered friend.

Where do you go when far away isn't far enough?

RG arrived home at 4:15 p.m. and made a pot of fresh decaf. Whatever he'd done to wrong Kacey, real or imagined, she'd forgive if she came home to fresh, steaming hot coffee. He moved to the fridge, deliberating whether to pull something together for dinner and earn an extended absolution. He opened the door and stared, amazed at how much food they had and how little they had to eat. As he punched in the number for China Palace, Morrow emerged from the walk-in pantry next to the fridge.

"Jesus…!" RG dropped his cell and clutched his chest, letting out an exhale.

"I'm sorry Robert, didn't mean to startle you. I wanted to fill the living room candy dish. It appears I've eaten a few more than I—"

"How can it be no one has invented chocolate in the next world?" RG gathered his cell from the floor and turned it over in his hands, inspecting it for damage. He glanced at the silver wrappers littering the living room coffee table. *I'm losing weight from all the stress, but this sonofabitch is happily packing on the pounds. His friends back home won't recognize him.* "You could make a fortune over there, you know." He opened a drawer next to the stove and produced a bag of Kit Kats. He tossed them to Morrow. "It's an upgrade over what you've been eating."

Morrow unwrapped one, breaking off a piece and throwing it in his mouth. He closed his eyes. "This will definitely do." Moving into the living room, he poured the bag into the coffee table candy bowl. "Kacey won't mind if I place a few of these out, will she?"

RG seated himself at the kitchen table. "Listen, Mr. Morrow, someone nearly killed my friend in his prison cell Sunday night."

"I'm sorry to hear it. Your prisons are such violent places."

"I went to see him today, and after what he described, I'm sure it was Victor. My friend said a force attacked him from inside his body and a voice told him, 'I'm a friend of a friend.' It sounds like a taunt from Victor."

Morrow rejoined RG in the kitchen. "I wouldn't put it past Victor to get to you through your friends."

"Who else could it be? They said he was alone in his cell when it happened."

"But he didn't kill him." Morrow peered out the kitchen window, his hand on his chin. "Why not?"

"Does your caretaker magic let you protect others?"

Morrow shook his head. "We only get one assignment."

"But what do I do about my friends? They could be in danger."

"You can't tell your friends a supernatural serial killer's after them. They'll think you're crazy."

"But I've known them all my life. They'll believe me."

"Wait until your friend gets better. Maybe you can all meet and your friend's corroboration will convince them. That's my best advice. Time's running out and it's my mission to get you prepared. We better continue our training"

"And what'll this training do? If the burning man comes for us, we have no way to stop him. We can only hold him and expel him. He'll come back. What kind of life will it be, constantly looking over our shoulders, waiting for the next assault?"

Morrow folded his arms. "Listen carefully and understand the gravity of your situation. First, you must survive this assault, and there's no guarantee you will. You won't get a second chance if you're not ready before I leave. You'll die, and Kacey will, too. What kind of life would that be?"

RG shifted his weight from one foot to another.

"Second, you're looking for a permanent solution when there isn't one. If you can hold him, if you can expel him, you stop him. For now. He may go away, he may not. He may learn he can do nothing more to you and move on. I cannot tell you the future, but this is your life from now on."

"Well, that's just fucking great!" RG lashed out, swiping at a pile of mail on the kitchen counter, sending envelopes across the living room floor.

Morrow folded his hands behind his back. "Are you done?"

"I haven't even started! You say you're a caretaker, but I'm not seeing much caretaking. First, I survived in the train station by a pure miracle, dumb luck, with no help from you, thank you very much! Next, you're trying to recruit help from a woman seven months pregnant, and now, the training sessions we *are* doing won't do a goddamn thing against Victor. I'm going to die anyway. Caretaker my ass!"

Morrow dropped into a kitchen chair, removed his hat, and placed it on his knee. "Just because I come from the next world, doesn't mean I can perform miracles. Doesn't mean I don't wish I could." He ran a hand through his hair. "Maybe I should never have come back."

"What do you mean *maybe*?" RG plopped down beside Morrow, both men staring off in different directions. He wanted his words to sting, but Morrow's pained expression left him regretting what he'd said. Leaning forward in his chair, he rested his elbows on his knees and blew a loud exhale. He turned toward Morrow.

"Are you still willing to teach me what you know?"

"Of course, Robert."

RG stood and gazed out the window toward the toolshed. "All right. Let's go."

Late Tuesday evening, RG sat in his dark office, the only light filtering his world coming from his Dell monitor's soft glow. He'd worked straight through dinner and hadn't eaten since grabbing a soft taco at the food truck late morning, but he didn't care about his rumbling belly. What he did care about was his training session with Morrow and whether he could depend solely on iffy exercises to defeat the burning man. Victor had to have a weakness, something even Kacey couldn't access. RG had to find it.

He Googled the name Victor Garrett and waited. Page one of 9,540,000 results: Victor Garrett Facebook; Victor Garrett, Texas Real Estate Broker; Victor Garrett, Chiropractor; Images for Victor Garrett; Victor Garrett Discography, complete your Victor Garrett record collection. *That's just what I need, the burning man sings his greatest hits.*

"Who were you, you sonofabitch?" His hands flew across the keyboard adding an additional word to the search engine, D-E-A-T-H, bringing it down to 485,000 results. RG shook his head. "Well, now we're getting somewhere."

Leaning back in his chair, he rubbed his eyes, searching his memory for the name of the boy. He leaned forward and typed S-A-M.

He hit enter and waited, search results jumping down to a manageable one hundred. He spent the next hour scrolling through the Google entries, stories depicting house fires, boating accidents, and electrocutions splayed out on the web for public consumption, but nothing about his Victor Garrett.

RG continued to scroll down the list until he came across a brief story out of West Hartford, Connecticut, in May of 1972, the murder-suicide of Victor and Lucy Garrett following the loss of their son, Sam. This possibility boosted him forward in his chair, but he'd need to find the entire news item. He checked his watch and logged onto the Boston Public Library's website for their operating hours. He could get there with an hour to spare if he hurried. A 9:00 p.m. closing wouldn't leave much time, but he could get started.

Grabbing his coat, RG dashed out of the office, determined to score some answers.

After braving a crowded T and playing Frogger with the Boylston Street traffic, RG reached the massive library on the corner of Dartmouth in record time. The building took up a full city block, with Renaissance-style architecture, arched entryways and windows, appearing more magnificent under city lights and a glowing full moon. Behind its fortress-like walls, it featured a landscaped courtyard and fountain accessible only from the inside, a peaceful oasis—with Wi-Fi, of course—all hidden from a chaotic city.

Throwing open the main door, RG scanned the cavernous space, immediately overwhelmed. A former expert at navigating library services during his graduate work, he hadn't set foot inside one in years, online research journals now available and downloaded with the click of a mouse. He stood frozen at the front door, unsure which direction to go. With work stations and desks scattered throughout the floor, RG couldn't differentiate librarians from patrons. After scouring the room, he located the help desk from across the broad expanse of industrial grade red carpet. He hurried across the room, only to have a nimble, matronly woman cut in line as he arrived.

Her eyes bore down at the college-age girl behind the desk, the name Mariel pinned to her Buckle fringe cardigan sweater.

The woman's voice rose to a level designed to draw attention. "There's been a scheduling conflict this evening, young lady. According to this program, you scheduled my favorite author to speak here tonight." She waved a sheet of paper at Mariel, now in partial cowering mode. "But it appears he won't be speaking until next week. I've spent money on parking, gas, and tolls, and I want satisfaction!"

Mariel searched through her desk drawers. "I think there's a form somewhere…"

RG checked his watch. *I don't have time for this shit.* He pulled out a twenty and dangled it in front of the woman. "Will this help you out?" *Help you get the hell out of my way.*

The woman pivoted with a stern look. "Well, aren't you a disrespectful young man? I have other issues to discuss with the library, and I will not be—"

"Twenty bucks to beat it," RG interrupted, suspending the green bill midair. She faced off against him like a gunfighter in a spaghetti western.

He flinched as she plucked the twenty like Grasshopper snatching the pebble in Kung Fu. She narrowed her eyes at him, slowly stepping out of line to move behind him.

Lady could've slapped me in the face and still taken the twenty before I reacted! Slowing down, old man.

RG grinned at a surprised Mariel behind the help desk. "Hi, I need to find a newspaper article from May 1972."

"What paper?" She positioned her glasses and squinted at her computer.

"The *Hartford Courant*."

She tapped on the keyboard, her tongue dancing along the corner of her lower lip. "Okay, here we are. *Hartford Courant*, 1837 to 2004. You're in luck. We have it on microfilm. Are you familiar with the microfilm room?"

He shook his head.

She rummaged through desk items and produced a laminated card mapping out the library's layout. As she pointed to the top half of the card and opened her mouth to speak, a brief spark glowed in her eyes.

"Hey Fran." She turned, calling to a mousy colleague pecking away at a computer screen across the room. "I need to show this man how to use the microfilm. Can you take care of this woman in line behind him?"

Before receiving a response, Mariel hurried away from the desk, motioning him to follow.

"You must not like Fran very much."

"I owe you twenty dollars."

Mariel led RG along the carpeted main floor area to the elevator. They descended two floors to the basement. Here, remnants of an earlier remodel adorned the ancient space—1980's style metal desks and tables, colorful desk lamps, cement floors and buzzing overhead lights. Mariel seated him behind a microfilm reader in the first room of the warehouse-size basement while she left to retrieve the appropriate silver halide spool for the year he'd requested.

"The machine scans and prints. Just click the icon right there." She pointed to the screen. "We close in forty-five minutes."

"Thanks for your help, and good luck with Fran."

Mariel rolled her eyes as she left, leaving him sitting alone in the dimly lit room.

He had no idea where to start his search. He had forty-five minutes to scroll through thirty days of Hartford news hoping to stumble across Victor Garrett's name somewhere.

Scrolling through archived newspapers, RG found himself transported to another era. The black and white pages flashing across the screen depicted a world long extinct, a time capsule buried just for him —school board elections, fundraising efforts to renovate the Mark Twain house, revitalization of the crime-ridden North End—drawing him into a small city's big dreams, fulfilled or forgotten over forty years. RG lived for a moment through its history, as if it were happening, as if any of it still mattered. He experienced the odd sensation of dissociation, glancing up and briefly wondering where he was, not quite sure why he sat alone in the Boston Public Library on a Tuesday night.

Checking his watch, RG found he only had fifteen minutes until closing. He buckled down and scrolled furiously through the May headlines. Finally, on May 26, he found what he came for. The head-line splashed across the front page of the *Courant*.

'MURDER-SUICIDE' TRAGIC END TO FAMILY SUFFERING— Hartford (AP)—A husband and wife, found dead in their home on Trout Brook Drive in West Hartford Tuesday, appear to be the victims of a murder-suicide. West Hartford police responded to a call at the home of Victor and Lucy Garrett after neighbors reported what appeared to be a domestic dispute between the couple. When police arrived, they found Lucy Garrett, 39, strangled to death and her husband Victor, 42, with a gunshot wound to the head. Neighbors gath-ered on the street, shocked to learn of the tragedy. Next door neighbor, Marjorie Swain, spoke to the *Courant*. "The Garretts were such good people, churchgoing folks. But they lost their son, Sam, and I guess they just couldn't go on without him." Sam Garrett, 10, died the previous day from advanced cancer complications. Lead detective from the West Hartford Police Department, Manny Markham, commented on the investigation. "We're following all leads at this point. We're not sure of the motive, but we're gathering evidence from friends and co-workers and should be able to clear the case shortly." Garrett had been employed at Connecticut General Insurance Group in Bloomfield, but had recently been let go. CG would not comment on the firing, but a source told the *Courant* Garrett had not been to work in several weeks due to his son's illness. Garrett served as a deacon at St. Timothy's Church in West Hartford for fifteen years before his death.

The lights flickered above RG's head, sending a shockwave through his body. He half expected Victor Garrett to burst into the room, but a voice over the intercom calmed him, merely a reminder the library closed in five minutes. He exhaled, grabbed his jump drive, and inserted it into the USB port, scanning a copy of the article.

RG leaned back in his chair, "I found you, you sonofabitch!"

CHAPTER NINE

Wednesday, December 6, 2017

RG exited the elevator, his shoes clicking on the buffed, hardwood floors of the hallway housing the college's administrative offices. *We get cheap tile and the suits get Hand Scraped Birch. Why am I not surprised?* His feet tapped their way to the far end of the corridor, announcing his presence to every head in every open office. He nodded at each pair of upturned eyes as he scooted down the hall. Approaching Wendell Abernathy's open office door, he poked his head inside.

The man reclined in his custom leather chair, bedecked in an ice-blue button down shirt to highlight his dazzling and expensive smile, and sporting a thick mane of carefully coiffed hair. Abernathy's eyes stared out the window, facing down, not out at the scenic white gothic structures framing the quadrangle or on the Charles River's deep blue ripple as one would expect, but more than likely at a group of girls congregated on the yard, by the looks of his predatory grin.

RG knocked on the half-opened door to break the lecher's trance. "Not disturbing anything, am I?"

"Come in," Wendell pulled his gaze from the window as he feigned leafing through a stack of papers, not bothering to look up.

"Good morning, Wendell." RG used his well-rehearsed non-confrontational tone.

Abernathy's feet rested on the ornate oak desk that, rumor had it, once belonged to his father, delivered from Alistair's office at Harvard the day after a janitor found him slumped over it, dead. RG noted the massive oak desk's blemishes and deep gashes. The stories surrounding Abernathy's desk had made their way through the college, told and retold at faculty gatherings and happy hours from Cambridge to Brighton. They say he used it for power, as his father had before him, the unsightly scars across its surface intimidating junior faculty and staff. The chairs facing the desk, noticeably smaller than his own, forced visitors to gaze up at Wendell during conversation.

"Please sit." Abernathy pointed at the chair in front of the desk, already preparing his advantage.

"I think I'll stand."

RG loomed over Abernathy, irritation blooming across the man's features. Wendell stood, the two men facing each other awkwardly.

"Makes you wonder whether you need such a big chair if you're going to stand in front of it." RG flashed a wide smile.

Abernathy's face flushed crimson as he lowered himself into the chair. "Suit yourself." He shuffled his papers trying to regain the upper hand. "I'll get right to the point. We have a problem."

RG frowned. "What about?"

Abernathy let out a breath. "We have a female student alleging you made sexual advances toward her during the spring semester."

"What?"

Abernathy fished a pair of glasses from his jacket pocket and glanced at the folder in front of him. "The student claims she visited you during office hours, you closed the door and promised to improve her grade in exchange for sexual favors."

RG stood slack-jawed at the allegations, struggling to catch his breath. "Who said this?"

Smugness crossed Abernathy's features. "I'm not at liberty to reveal any information at this moment. I'm bringing this charge to the Title IX office and upper administration of the college. Once they ascertain the claim's validity, we will be in contact with you about your options."

"My options? What the hell are you talking about? When's this meeting? I have a right to be there." RG spoke in a clipped tone, his decibel level rising.

"Not according to the rules of shared governance at Boston University. The committee will notify you of their decision. You have the right to appeal the decision, the process clearly outlined in the faculty handbook." Abernathy shook his head. "We have a serious situation here, Dr. Granville. I understand you're going up for full professor this year, correct?"

"You know I am." He crossed his arms, the vein in his temple throbbing with each heartbeat.

"The process will take several months, whatever the outcome. I have no say on your promotion, but an addendum will be added to your dossier regarding the pending nature of the charges. Each committee and office voting for or against your promotion will have access to this new information. If there's a finding against you, it will fall to my office to initiate the process of removing you from the university in accordance with the moral turpitude clause in your tenure agreement."

A burning spread through RG's face, the blood rushing to his head.

Abernathy leaned back and parked his feet on the desk, shaking his head. "I feel for you, Dr. Granville. In today's climate, sexual assaults and harassment on college campuses are difficult to overcome."

"Who is she?" RG narrowed his eyes at the man, his jaw clenching.

Abernathy ignored him. "In addition to her testimony, we have phone records of numerous calls to your house at rather unusual hours." He smirked.

His head spinning, RG gazed out the window, struggling to recall anyone with a motive to invent such an accusation. "The only student who kept calling me last spring was Brittany Thorne…all intercepted by my wife." RG nodded, turning from the window. "It has to be her. And the only conversations I had with her were in class when I encouraged her to seek extra help or tutoring. It's not my fault she didn't heed my advice and withdrew from the program."

"Maybe the psychological trauma she received from you led to her withdrawal." Abernathy leafed through more papers on his desk, dismissing RG.

"Hold on a minute," RG muttered, "now the dots are connecting." He paced in front of Abernathy's desk like a caged animal. "Wasn't that Brittany Thorne I saw getting into your car last week?" He stopped. "Young girl, dark hair? Sure fits."

RG placed his fists on the desk and leaned toward Abernathy, heat traveling through his neck and into his jowls. "You sonofabitch! What did you do? Threaten her?" he shouted, jabbing his finger across the desk. "Or did you promise her she wouldn't flunk out? Or maybe there's more to it than that. What was she doing in your car, Wendell?"

"I don't know what you're talking about." Abernathy's voice wavered, a subtle tell. He struggled to swallow.

"You've been out to get me since day one." RG's fingers coiled into tighter fists. "You better be prepared for a fight on this, and you better hope my lawyer can't obtain any phone records or garage camera recordings, showing you with Brittany and your hand in the cookie jar." He burst out of Abernathy's office, slamming the door behind him.

As RG stormed down the hall, his shoes' reverberation against the Hand Scraped Birch brought curious heads peering out from behind office doors.

Returning to his office, RG dropped into the chair behind his desk, but couldn't stay seated. His rage had him dancing around like a live wire, signals from his nerves zapping every muscle in his body. He paced back and forth in his office until the heat seeped from his core and his breathing returned to normal. As his heart rate stabilized, the phone rang. He snatched it from the cradle, ready to bite the head off the unsuspecting caller.

"Yeah, what?" he snapped.

"Jeez, dude. Tough day?"

RG collapsed into his chair. "Johnny D, sorry man, I thought you were someone else. Shit's hitting the fan and I'm just on edge, that's all."

"Then I guess my timing's perfect to rescue your ass. I've got a cold six-pack and Indian stir-fry. Come down, you can vent while we review your investment portfolio. Bring Kacey, get her away from Chinese food for a while. What do you say?"

"I don't know, man. Things are so screwed up right now."

"I know you, RG. You can't resist my cooking…or my sage financial advice."

Johnny D owned his own construction business, but had managed RG's investments for years. Any other time, he'd be all over it, but not when preoccupation with life and death consumed him. Maybe that was the point. Kacey would need more than a life insurance policy to live her life without him. Maybe he should rely on Johnny D to handle Kacey's financial survival.

"She's busy wrapping up school. I guess she won't mind if I'm MIA for a bit. Sure, I'll swing by. Counting on you to make me rich."

Three hours later, Johnny D met RG in the driveway below the deck, tossed him a Coors Light, and gave him his patented man-hug. "Glad you made it, brother. You look like someone just handed you a death sentence."

"Asshole at work is making it his mission to royally screw me over." He kicked the car door shut.

"Join the real world, man, you've been living in the ivory tower too long." Johnny D took a long pull from his beer as they climbed the stairs and stepped into the house. "I've built entire additions for people who still haven't paid me yet."

"Well, this may cost me my career." RG recounted his earlier meeting with Wendell Abernathy.

"Don't worry about that prick. People recognize bullshit when they hear it. The great Bard nailed it when he said 'the truth will out.' It always does."

"*Hamlet?*"

Johnny D frowned. "*Merchant of Venice*. Some college professor you are." As they made their way through the sun room and into the kitchen, Johnny D handed RG a large serrated cutting knife. "Now give me a hand cutting up vegetables. I'm making Aloo Matar with onion culcha and I need a sous chef."

During the next half hour, aromatic spices filled the kitchen as the two friends drank beer and listened to Tom Waits' gravelly vocals from another thoughtfully arranged Johnny D music mix.

"Gotta tell ya, brother, we didn't do too well last month." Johnny wiped his hands on a towel and pulled a file from his desk in the sunroom, handing it across the counter to RG.

His eyes widened. "Whoa! That's everything I invested!"

"I know. Your buddy's start-up went belly up."

Against Johnny D's advice, RG had directed him to invest ten thousand dollars in a biotech firm in Cambridge, hoping to catch lightning in a bottle. *Sonofabitch!* "And I talked Kacey out of a Bahamas vacation." He chugged on his beer, the smell of food stirring a sickness in his gut.

Johnny D loaded up two plates with Indian food and grabbed two more Coors Lights from the fridge. "Well, I got some thoughts about how to recover a little bit every month, it'll require a little more aggressive strategy, but we'll have you on that tropical sand before you know it."

"God, I'm a bonehead! Whatever you think will work." RG clinked Johnny D's bottle with little enthusiasm, his loss of both appetite and revenue going hand in hand.

As Johnny D explained his plan in more detail, the different asset allocation he'd require, and the blue-chips stocks poised to perform well in the coming year, RG perked up. *Maybe there's a light at the end of the tunnel after all.* He dug a fork into the steaming mound of rice and potatoes. "By the way, I went to see Walt yesterday."

"Yeah, I did, too." Johnny D broke off a piece of onion culcha. "Mike got us in to see him pretty quick."

"God, I want to hate the fucking guy." RG took a long chug from his beer. "Turns out he convinced the warden to give Walt his own cell after…the trouble."

"That's solid." Johnny D nodded his head. "Listen, I understand you can't forgive him, I don't blame you. But people change. In my line of work, I run into more recovered alcoholics than you'd care to imagine. They all live with demons."

RG stopped eating and dropped his fork. "Listen, there's something strange about what happened to Walt." He cleared his throat. "When all this went down, every cell door had been locked. Walt's, too. No one could've been in there with him. After the incident, the guards accounted for every prisoner on his block, each one locked in, secured." RG leaned back in his chair and ran his hands through his hair. "Mike told me the guards arrived at Walt's cell immediately after they heard the commotion and found him alone."

"Alone?" Johnny D stared at him. "Could the guards have done it?"

"I asked Mike about that, but he told me they have time-stamped surveillance putting them in the guard station during the incident. They can't make a move without being recorded."

"It doesn't make sense." Johnny D stared into his beer bottle. "Unless he did it to himself. He's wanted out for a long time."

RG contemplated telling him the truth, that the burning man had started with Walt and would make his way through his friends. He considered telling Johnny D about Morrow, caretakers and jumpers, and life after death, what happened in Kenmore Station, how he cheated death through the unscheduled death of another, and his encounter with Victor. But how would it help? Johnny D couldn't do anything to protect himself even if he did know. Besides, Johnny D would never be able to handle anything so cataclysmic or accept evidence a supernatural world existed. He'd pick up his cell and dial 9-1-1 for the men in white coats to take him far away. *Now isn't the time.*

RG pushed himself away from the table, grabbed his beer, and walked over to the kitchen window, staring out at the beach across the street, stars hovering above the ocean. He gave a quick glance back at Johnny D. "Yeah. Maybe Walt did it to himself."

He joined Johnny D at the sink, scrubbing plates as Johnny loaded the pots and pans into the sink. "Thanks, man. I needed this."

"What, you needed someone to lose ten grand for you?"

RG grinned, grabbing his keys and placing his beer on the counter by the sink. "Actually, I didn't need that." He clapped Johnny on the back and stepped toward the door, lingering a moment as a wave of nausea rose in his throat. *Must have eaten too fast. Hard not to when Johnny D does the cooking.*

"Give Kacey a hug for me." Johnny handed RG a container of leftovers. "And make sure she gets some of this."

"I will." He paused for a moment at the open the screen door, watching Johnny wipe the countertops and place the rest of the dishes into the sink. *Now isn't the time, RG.* He marched down the porch steps in the cold darkness.

CHAPTER TEN

Thursday, December 7, 2017

Early the next morning, RG hopped in the car, set his GPS, and hit the highway west toward Connecticut, taking I-90 to the Sturbridge exit and following I-84 into West Hartford. The police had been reluctant to discuss anything about the Garrett case over the phone, but RG had confidence a face-to-face meeting would help his cause.

He needed answers, and he couldn't get them in Boston.

After an hour and a half in the car, he took Farmington Avenue to Raymond Road, arriving a few minutes after 10:00 a.m. at the West Hartford Police Department, its sparkling glass façade looming over a red brick foundation. RG mounted the steps and entered the palatial structure through a gleaming set of double doors.

At the main desk, he struggled to view the desk sergeant's name tag hidden behind a massive Starbuck's coffee. Sergeant Delmar James had a telephone propped under his chin, his fingers flying across the keyboard of a state-of-the-art computer with dual screens, taking up far too much of his work station. He raised his eyes from the screen as his fingers eased their assault on the keyboard.

Taking his cue, RG cleared his throat. "Sergeant James, my name's

Robert Granville, and I'm trying to track down information about a murder-suicide case from the seventies."

Holding up a finger, James spoke into the receiver. "Let me call you right back." He hung up the phone, sizing up the man on the opposite side of the desk. "Sir, police reports aren't typically public record, but you can get them." The sergeant reached into a drawer and came out with a handful of forms. "You need to fill out—"

"Excuse me," RG interrupted, "I guess I wanted to talk to someone who might have worked on the case."

"You call the other day?"

RG nodded. "The Garrett case."

"Like I told you over the phone, that's a forty-five-year-old case, whole new generation of officers here now. If you don't want the police report, there's a library around the corner. You'd probably get more information from old *Hartford Courant* articles than you would here." He picked up the phone and turned back to his computer screen.

"I've already exhausted that approach. Have you heard of a detective Markham?"

Sergeant James exhaled and eased the receiver back into the cradle. "Long gone, injured in the line of duty oh, thirty years ago."

"You have any idea where he ended up?"

"Where no cop wants to end up, in a wheelchair…and on the wall." He pointed to plaques and framed photographs hanging by the station's entrance—Connecticut's 'Wall of Heroes.' "Didn't know the man personally, but I see him every morning."

"Where do I find him?"

"Like I said, I didn't know the man." Sergeant James continued working the keyboard.

RG's stomach sank, his fact gathering mission going nowhere fast. "Listen, I just drove down from Boston. Maybe not the smartest thing, but if you could think of anyone with information to help me… anything, I'd appreciate it."

Sergeant James' eyes softened, a flash of sympathy crossing his face. "Have a seat and let me check on something." He stood, directing RG to a waiting area with a leather chair and small couch, a countertop with a Keurig single-cup coffee maker, and a fridge with bottled water. RG marveled at the level of customer service. *I might as well be waiting for an oil change.* The police stations he'd grown familiar with on Cape Cod and Revere during his youth certainly didn't have such welcoming accommodations. At least today's parents could be relatively comfortable waiting to bail out their wayward teens.

After Sergeant James left, RG approached Detective Markham's photograph on the wall, his fresh face and gleaming smile frozen in an eternal pose, oblivious to the life-altering event stalking him from the not-so-distant future. His smile would soon change, as would his world, and everyone else's on each plaque in front of him.

He moved closer, reading the text under Markham's name, recounting his service to the community. The text on each plaque closed with a quote, something meaningful to each officer or the surviving family members. At the bottom of Markham's plaque: 'A lake carries you into recesses of feeling otherwise impenetrable'—Wordsworth.

What the hell had happened to him?

As RG stood lost in thought, Sergeant James returned with a silver-haired man in a crisp uniform standing at attention. He appeared much older than the other officers manning their desks, a glistening badge clearly earmarking him as the headmaster of this tight fraternity.

The man extended his hand. "I'm Lieutenant Gordon Walsh, Chief of Police. Would you follow me please?"

Before he could introduce himself, RG found himself hoofing it down the hall at full tilt, struggling to keep up with the man's purposeful gait, like a puppy trying to keep up with its master. Walsh directed him into a glassed-in office and seated himself behind a massive desk in front of an expansive window, the abundant morning sunlight flooding his spotless work station. With the roll of his wrist, he directed RG to take a seat.

"To whom am I speaking?"

The man's strict tone forced him to sit erect in his chair. "I'm Robert Granville, I came down from—"

"You a reporter?" Walsh interrupted.

"College professor."

"What's your interest in the Garrett case?" Walsh divided his attention between RG and his computer, typing a flurry of words before hitting enter and leaning back in his chair.

RG stumbled, not having planned in advance what he'd say. He couldn't come out and tell a stranger all that had happened. "Well, my criminal law class researches various high-profile murders in small towns. I wanted more insight into the case than I've been able to find through traditional searches."

Walsh raised an eyebrow as he tapped away at the keyboard.

RG shifted in his chair. *He knows I'm lying.*

Walsh raised a hand to point at his computer screen. "Says here you're a professor of health sciences at BU. I can't imagine criminal law fits into the curriculum anywhere."

RG's face flushed with heat.

Walsh leaned back from his desk. "Why don't you tell me why you're really here?"

He hung his head. "I apologize, Lieutenant, but sometimes the truth can be harder to swallow than a lie. Truth is, I have a personal connection to the case."

Walsh narrowed his eyes. "You're a young man. This case happened way before your time."

"It did."

"Family connection or—"

"I wish I could tell you more, but I can't. I'm not lying to you, promise."

"Well, you're not telling the truth, either." The lieutenant rested his elbows on the desk. "Listen. Detective Markham took me on as a rookie and showed me the ropes. I owe him a lot, including his privacy."

"What happened to him?"

Walsh rose slowly from his chair and turned toward the window, his gaze failing to reach beyond the glass. "The Garrett case happened to him. He didn't talk much about it, but he did tell me Victor Garrett played a role in his accident. As crazy as it sounds, I believe him. The man's had a rough go of it, and I won't be the one to open up those wounds again. I'm sorry."

"Do you think he'd at least take a call from me?"

"Even if he did have a phone, it would be a longshot. And you won't find him in any directory."

"Please, help me. I just need to talk—"

"Let him be," Walsh interrupted, fixing him with a stare. "And you need to let this go, whatever it is. It may sound cliché, but cops get hunches, and it helps us solve cases. My hunch is this case had a dark side. You can go ahead and dig, but some things should stay buried."

Walsh stood, signaling the meeting had ended. He escorted him from his office and back down the hall. At the front door, Walsh rested a hand on RG's shoulder. "I'd wish you luck finding Markham, but I'd be lying to you. My advice, go back to Boston, let this thing go."

RG thanked him and headed toward the door.

"Why do I get the feeling you haven't heard a word I've said?"

"I've heard every word, and you're right about your hunch. But I can't stop until I find answers." RG burst through the double doors.

Walsh called to him as he bounded down the steps. "If you track down Manny, he's more likely to talk if you bring him Miller High Life, cans not bottles, and a carton of Marlboro Lights."

RG stopped and acknowledged Walsh with a grin.

"And make a lot of noise when you come up the driveway. If he thinks you're sneaking up on him, he's likely to shoot you."

RG collapsed in the Subaru's front seat and leaned his head against the headrest. He checked his watch. 10:45 a.m. He had the rest of the morning and afternoon to find a man in a wheelchair without a phone who could be living anywhere. Once found, he'd have to convince him to spill his guts to a complete stranger about a forty-five-year-old case he'd barely spoken about to his own partner. *Yeah, good luck with that!*

He had little to go on besides the man's name, other than he'd been injured on the job and ended up in a wheelchair. If he lived anywhere

near West Hartford at the time of the accident, he'd likely have spent
time in a rehabilitation hospital. RG would have to find the facility
treating Markham thirty years ago, and if, through divine intervention,
someone remembered him and had his records, he'd have to convince
them to volunteer personal health information and break a few federal
laws. *Everything shaping up for a major success today. Fuck me.*

RG drove the hundred yards to the Noah Webster Public Library on
Main Street, around the corner from the police station. He slipped into
the quiet building and settled behind one of the new computers lining
the middle section of the first floor. He accessed the internet and stared
at the screen. Starting with the obvious, he googled 'Manny Markham,
West Hartford Police Department,' getting a number of irrelevant hits,
but nothing about the injury.

Modifying the search to include 'accident,' RG hit on a handful of
stories referencing a July, 1984, accident leaving a police detective
paralyzed. A microfilm expert now with his second library visit of the
week, he grabbed an armful of spools from three different Connecticut
newspapers, the *Courant, New Haven Register,* and the *Record-Journal,* and settled himself behind the microfilm reader.

For the next two hours, RG scrolled through each paper
searching for anything on Manny Markham, his injury or rehab facility, but had no luck. His eyes burning and on the verge of throwing
in the towel, RG inserted the final spool of microfilm from the
Record-Journal. In the society section, he located a full-column
photo and story describing a fundraiser for Markham's medical
expenses. Peering at the photograph, RG recognized the man on the
'Wall of Heroes,' imprisoned in a wheelchair, surrounded by Hartford Hospital staff. RG leaned forward to decipher the writing across
the front of his tee-shirt, 'Bluegill Roundup-1982, Candlewood
Lake.'

First, the Wordsworth quote, now the tee-shirt. He had a feeling
he'd find Manny Markham within a stone's throw of water.

Working against time, RG hurriedly printed the picture and googled
Candlewood Lake. *Damn! Does it have to be the largest lake in
Connecticut?* First stop, Hartford Hospital. He rubbed his computer-

strained eyes, unfolded himself from the chair, and stretched his limbs before exiting the library and climbing into his car.

Typing the hospital address into his GPS, RG followed the light I-84 traffic into Hartford, taking the Capitol Avenue exit and sprinting down Main until he spotted the building to his right. He arrived in just under fifteen minutes, pulling onto the grounds of the 150-year-old facility and into a parking spot not designated for physicians or administrators. He never understood why the sick were banished to the distant parking spaces while the healthy staff scored the good ones.

Checking the directory on the gleaming first floor, with its stainless-steel check-in desks, high glass windows, and modern sculptures, RG followed the arrows to the rehabilitation clinic, housed in the basement. He exited the elevator, the clinic sprawled out before him, numerous blue-padded tables and plinths, exercise equipment, multiple harnesses suspended over treadmills, and a team of physical therapists and doctors working the floor. The room buzzed with activity, therapists moving from patient to patient, praising their efforts and shouting out encouragement.

As he stepped through the clinic to find the registration desk, a hand reached inside his heart and gave a slight squeeze, sapping the spring in his step. He tried not to stare at the damaged men and women, teenagers and children, scattered about the room. Unknown acts of God or split-second moments of foolishness or distraction had changed their lives in an instant, provoking a vague guilt for his unfettered ability to place one foot in front of the other and stride past the broken bodies before him. He subconsciously slowed down in an effort not to flaunt the normalcy he took for granted.

At the desk, a handsome woman in her mid-fifties greeted RG with an open smile. "What can I do for you, sir?"

"Hi, um, I wondered if you can help me with something." RG fumbled in his jacket pocket for his print library photo. "I'm looking for information on a patient from about thirty years ago, a police officer with a spinal cord injury. I have a picture of him right here. Anyone here might have known him?" He spread the folded paper out on the desk in front of the woman.

The woman leaned forward, squinting at the picture. "What's his name?"

"Manny Markham. Came here in July 1984. Looks like he stayed here a month or so."

"Are you family?"

"Not immediate family." *Here come the lies again. What the fuck, RG?*

"Sir, HIPAA laws do not allow any medical facility to release information to anyone not on the patient's designated list, and we purge all medical records ten years after the final visit. I'm sorry, but even if we could, this man's records are long gone."

"I figured they might be. Anyone still working here who might have any information about him?"

"Long time ago," she said, shaking her head. "Most of our staff weren't even born yet. I'm sorry."

"Thanks anyway." RG's heart sank as he turned and shuffled across the clinic, back to square one. He could take a drive to Candlewood Lake and hazard a guess at which of the five towns surrounding it Manny Markham lived in, if he lived in one of them at all. Maybe he could walk around each one, stop into the local businesses and see if anyone had heard of him. Impossible. His plan would take days, and he had classes to teach tomorrow. Time to call it a day, head back to Boston.

"Sir!" The woman behind the desk hurried to catch up with him, eyes still glued to the photo in front of her. "You know, I recognize one of the therapists from this picture. She's long retired, but still lives over in Bloomfield." She pointed to a fresh-faced girl smiling beside Markham. "Name's Donna McCaffery. She might be able to help you."

"Donna...?"

"McCaffery. I hope that helps."

RG thanked her, grabbed the photo, and climbed the stairs to the hospital's first floor. On the long walk to the car, he located Donna McCaffery's Bloomfield address on his device.

In thirty minutes, he sat in in front of Donna's farm house on Mountain Road, staring at a young girl in a photo. *God, let her be home!* He exited the car, approached the well-maintained ranch property, and knocked on the screen door.

A woman wearing a friendly smile answered. "Hi there. What can I do for you?" She had to have been in her fifties, but she could've been a decade younger the way genes and good habits contributed to youthfulness. She'd let her hair go gray, but it took nothing away from her youthful spirit, reflecting the confidence of a woman content with the journey, comfortable in her skin.

RG glanced at the photo, marveling at the mystery of time. A beautiful young woman hid inside the older one standing before him, but he couldn't say exactly what differed between them. "Are you Donna?" he asked, handing her the photo.

"Who else would I be?" She laughed, glancing down at the picture.

"Do you know this man? I'm trying to track him down."

As she gazed at the photo, her hand reached up to fix her hair. RG couldn't tell if her momentary sigh lamented the passage of time for the younger version of herself in the photo or grieved for the man staring back from thirty years ago.

"Oh, my God. It's Manny." She looked up at RG. "I'm sorry. I just saw my past staring me in the face. I used to be Manny's physical therapist."

"Manny's my uncle. I've lost touch and I'm trying to locate him." RG surprised himself at how easily the lies tumbled off his tongue.

Donna's eyes lit up. "Don't tell me, you must be Janey's son. Oh, I can't recall your name, but I do remember you running around the clinic when she visited Manny."

"It's Robert. Nice to see you again, Donna. Can't say I remember you, though, long time ago." *Fuck.*

"This is so amazing, don't you think?" She pressed her hand to her chest, still eyeing the photo. "Do you want to come in? Do you have a few minutes to catch up?"

"Of course." He hated what he'd have to do, playing with someone's emotions, but he needed answers. And he'd get them by whatever means necessary.

Donna welcomed him into her tidy home, seating him on the living room chair beside the fireplace. The room had a lived-in air, bright and open, hardwood floors throughout, separated from the spotless kitchen by a half-wall. The furniture appeared worn, but comfortable, a house used and enjoyed for many years. "Coffee?"

"If you're having one." As she fumbled with the filters and added water to the old-fashioned coffee maker, they made small talk. He contrived a family history, answering questions about a mother he didn't know, places he'd never lived, trying to insert a thread of truth he could recall if he had to backtrack. He prayed Donna didn't know things he himself didn't.

She returned from the kitchen with two mugs and warm croissants. She took a seat on the couch opposite RG. He took a sip from his coffee, but when he raised his head, a tear had tumbled over her cheek. She used a napkin to wipe her eyes. "I'm sorry."

"Don't be. I'm guessing you were more than my uncle's therapist."

"I'd just turned twenty-four when he came to us. I worked with him every day for six weeks. We'd work for an hour, but talk for two or three. I guess they call it the Florence Nightingale effect, but I fell in love with him."

Another tear jumped from her eye. RG moved to the couch, reaching over with his napkin to blot her cheek.

"Thanks. Just sitting with you brings him closer to me."

He reached over and squeezed her hand. *You're a class-A shit, RG.*

"He had such a great heart. He'd tell me about taking his boat out and fishing at the lake house." Donna dabbed at her eyes with her napkin. "Manny would stare at his legs and say how the thing he'd miss most would be the walks around the lake at night. He once told me the water would get so still you could see the stars reflected on it. I had this dream I'd see it with him someday."

"What happened?" He found himself drawn into her story, forgetting why he'd come.

"Manny could sense my feelings for him, and he told me he couldn't condemn me to a life with...half a man. He left the facility soon after. I often dreamed of going up and trying to find him, but it wasn't to be."

"I remember going up to the lake with him, but I can't remember where. Wasn't it Candlewood Lake?"

"Manny used to do fishing tournaments up there, but he lived on a lake in New Hartford."

"They have lakes in Hartford?"

"Not Hartford, New Hartford. Lake McDonough, about forty minutes northwest, straight shot up Route 44."

"That's right." He stared into his coffee, a tingle growing in his stomach.

"It sounded like paradise. Manny would describe sitting out on the deck in the evenings, the water absolutely still, and the night so quiet it seemed unearthly. Have you ever heard quiet like that?"

"Not living in the city."

"I've often wondered what absolute silence must sound like."

"So where on the lake did he live?"

"He never told me where. I guess he figured I'd come find him." She laughed and gazed at her croissant, still untouched. "He did say his house sat right below a place the kids called 'Chicken Ledge,' a short cliff wall, leaning out over the water. They'd stand on top daring each other to jump. Manny said the drop may have been only twenty-five feet or so, but seemed like fifty when you leaned over the top." Donna gave a short laugh, curling her hair around her ear with her hand. "Kind of a rite of passage for generations of kids. You find Chicken Ledge, you'll find Manny."

RG placed his coffee cup on the table in front of the sofa. "Donna, I need to get going. If I find him, should I tell him…?"

She shook her head, wiping one more tear from her eye.

"Can I help you with the plates?"

"Just leave them. Good luck, Robert. I'd walk you out, but I think I'll just sit here a while."

RG leaned over and kissed the top of her head. "Thank you."

As he walked toward the door, Donna stood. "Who are you, really?"

"I'm Manny's nephew." He turned the handle and stepped from the house.

~

After getting off Route 44, RG weaved the Subaru through the tall and sturdy trees lining the winding dirt roads, bouncing through deep potholes filled with rain from a previous evening shower, their contents painting the car's bumpers a muddy brown. The afternoon sunlight shimmering above the majestic trees had surrendered its attempt to penetrate the thick pine needle canopy, leaving the dense woods in perpetual shadow. Peering through the windshield, RG passed house after house, searching for the cliff wall Donna McCaffery described. After a painstaking search down every branching road surrounding Lake McDonough, a rocky plateau appeared through a break in the trees, looming over the water, adjacent to a house perched at the edge of the lake. He stopped in front of a dented mailbox secured to an old piece of timber, a faded number stenciled along its side.

This had to be it.

Pulling into the gravel driveway, RG approached a diminutive lake house in a terrible state of disrepair, with bowed roof, cracked windows, and crumbling brickwork on the chimney and walkway. The dwelling's rotting wood siding made it difficult to discern its actual color. The house's position beneath the thick pines left it in nearly constant shade, the roof shingles covered with a damp moss and ivy layer.

Heeding Chief Walsh's advice, RG revved the engine, leaned on the horn, and slammed the door twice before approaching the house. He stepped tentatively toward the screened-in porch, the walkway littered with spent oxygen tanks and garbage resting mere feet from the worn plastic barrels secured beside the garage.

He knocked on the screen door, rattling it against the metal doorframe.

"Who's there?" A raspy voice barked from behind the porch's window curtain.

RG lifted the carton of Marlboro Lights as the curtain fanned back, revealing the ravaged face of what may once have been a handsome man. He spoke through the glass. "My name's Robert—"

"Yeah, yeah, Grandview, Grayson, whatever?"

Manny Markham maneuvered the wheelchair backward and cracked the door, allowing RG to get a better look at him. His white hair, matted and unkempt, tumbled over his forehead, his yellowing eyes betraying the evolution of an alcohol-poisoned liver. Ropy arm muscles pushed against his tattered flannel shirt belying the build of a man in a wheelchair, but his considerable paunch more than made up for it. After thirty years of immobility, his spindly legs looked almost unnecessary. He bore little resemblance to the man with the gleaming smile on the 'Wall of Heroes' back in West Hartford.

"It's Granville, sir, Robert. I wondered if...hey, how did you know—?"

"Walsh informed me you might be coming," he interrupted, grabbing the carton of smokes and resting them on his lap. "Got anything else for me?"

RG handed him the beer. "He said you didn't have a phone."

Markham showed him his iPhone X. "I just don't answer it."

RG shook his head. "I don't want to trouble you, but I wondered if you had a moment to talk with me about an old case you worked on, the Garrett murder-suicide."

"I don't think you understand what you're asking, what you might be opening up."

"I think I do."

Markham cracked open a beer. "The less you know about him the better."

"Listen, I have a family connection to—"

"You're lying." Markham moved to close the door.

"Wait!"

"I learned everything about the Garretts' life, and I guaran-fuckin-tee no Boston University professor had any family connection to them."

"How did you know I'm—?"

"I'm a detective." Markham waved his iPhone and pushed the door closed, but RG stuck his foot in the jamb. Markham's eyes growled at him.

"Please!" RG lowered his head, eyes fixed on the floor. Having nothing to lose at this point, he came clean. "Look, this will sound nuts, but my wife has seen Victor Garrett in her dreams, and I've had him in my head. We need to learn everything we can about him."

Markham sunk in his chair, his face assuming a somber expression. "You'd better come in, then."

RG followed Markham's wheelchair through the dank, cramped house, years of refuse—newspapers, pizza boxes, brown grocery bags —stacked precariously on either side of the pathway the chair had forged through the wood-paneled rooms. Rancid cigarette and spilled beer odors permeated the furniture and carpeting, like a college bar at daybreak. Despite the squalor, Markham's back window framed a spectacular lake view, sunlight sparkling off the crisp, clear water. A recently build wooden ramp wound through a scattering of pine trees from the dock to the back door.

Markham sidled his chair beside a large oxygen canister. Positioning the nasal cannula prongs into his nose and adjusting the tubing, he gave the valve a quarter turn, an oxygen hiss filling the silence. RG tried his best to hide his terror as Markham proceeded to light a Marlboro and inhale deeply.

Not hard to figure out how it would end for this bastard.

"How'd you find me?"

RG seated himself on the edge of a worn sofa, its spotted brown cushions stained with God knows what. "I ran into Donna McCaffery."

Markham lowered his gaze, turning away. "How is she?"

"Still misses you."

Markham took a gulp from his can of beer as his face hardened, his moment of melancholy dismissed. "You've come a long way for answers. You may not like the ones I have."

RG leaned forward. "What happened that day in the Garrett house?"

Markham took a deep drag on his smoke and cracked open another High Life. "You aren't just gonna go away, are you?"

"Nope."

He popped the tab on a second can and handed it to RG. "Then you might as well join me."

He nodded and took a sip.

Markham closed his eyes, maybe to block the memory or maybe because he couldn't forget. "One of those crime scenes you never want to see again. But, unfortunately, you do. The man worked at an insurance company, but just to pay the bills. He'd been a preacher at heart, deeply religious man, a deacon at a local church. His wife, Lucy, also pretty devout. She played organ at the weekend services."

"And their son?"

"Sam, ten years old. Died a day before the killing, his body ravaged by cancer. They'd rushed him to the hospital three weeks earlier. Doctors told me Victor Garrett stayed in the hospital with the boy until he died, never left his side."

"Must have been a pretty aggressive cancer?"

"Actually, the docs told me it likely took a while to develop, but the Garrett's brought him to the hospital late, and he didn't have much of a chance. You'd think they'd have noticed the symptoms, though. It would've been pretty bad."

"Did you ever talk to a Dr. Morrow? I think he might have been one of his doctors."

"I don't remember a Morrow, but a bunch of 'em worked on the kid."

"The *Courant* article suggested he couldn't face life without his son, so he decided to call it a day, take his wife with him. What do you think?"

Markham took a gulp from his High Life and dragged a sleeve across his mouth. "Well, it's more complicated than that. Something else happened in that house." A fast-moving cloud crept over the lake, blocking the sun, a rolling shadow skating across still water.

"You see, murder-suicides usually involve a gun. Quick and painless, no prolonged suffering. But Garrett used his hands to break her neck. They also found unexplainable scorch marks along the skin. It's like his hands were on fire or something."

RG swallowed, his heart beating in his temples. The burning man's first kill.

"We also found Victor Garrett's blood in the basement, before he shot himself. He'd been bleeding when he went to retrieve the shotgun he used on himself."

"Maybe an altercation?"

"Could be. We have conflicting eye witness accounts of Victor and Lucy in the driveway, minutes before the gunshot. One neighbor says she collapsed in the driveway as Victor held her. Another says she may have hit him."

"I searched through Connecticut court records online from May of '72. Couldn't get much detail because they only archived the files back to '09, but I did find a protective order with the name Victor Garrett on it. Did you find a history of domestic abuse?"

Markham gazed upward in thought. "If I recall, the order hadn't been taken out to protect Lucy, but the boy. Right before they rushed Sam to the hospital, she'd filed an order of protection stipulating no contact between Victor and his son. They must have come to an agreement because Victor never left the boy's side afterward. Maybe the altercation stemmed from the protective order, some bad blood remaining. We'll never know. Confusing, because all evidence suggests he'd been a devoted father."

"Did you talk to any of his friends at work?"

"Didn't have any. He scared 'em off with all his religious talk. He had old school *Bible* training, strict interpretations, fire and brimstone, all that stuff. When he stopped showing up at the office, they fired him, pretty relieved to have an excuse to do it, too."

"Any evidence of mental health issues before Sam got sick, before he killed Lucy?"

"Tried to locate medical records, find out if he'd been seeing a shrink or something, maybe get a hint at what set him off, but we couldn't find anything on the guy. And when I say anything, I mean we couldn't find *any* medical records, nothing within a fifty-mile radius. No hospital visits, no regular checkups, nothing. He lived in West Hartford for over fifteen years and as far as we could tell, he'd never been to *any* doctor. Strangest fucking thing."

"So, he just snapped?"

Markham drained the rest of his High Life and turned to RG. "I don't think so. Something had been eating at him in the weeks and months before his death."

"How do you mean?"

Markham wheeled the chair closer to the window overlooking the lake, Chicken Ledge reflecting a spotlight of sunshine onto the water. "During my investigation, I stumbled across something in Victor's personal effects from the hospital room. He had this book, well, more of a crude journal. In the months before Sam died, the dated entries showed the rantings of a religious fanatic, disgust at the secular world, people and their sinful ways, most entries incoherent and close to illegible. Nothing dangerous, but maybe a bit disturbed." Markham threw another can of beer to RG, only three sips into his first one. "But in the final weeks of his life, sitting beside his dying son, the entries grew darker.

"Pictures appeared, sketches really, drawn in pencil or sometimes crayon, as if he grabbed the first thing he could write with to purge the images in his head. Beside them, he provided a few words, descriptions of places, names of roads, other vague details."

"What did he draw?"

"Brutal images of death, murder. Didn't give it much attention at the time. Chalked it up to the rantings of a man losing touch with himself...the world." Markham turned his chair to face RG. "But a few years after the Garrett case, I'm at the station and a story comes across the wire about a ten-year-old boy snatched off his bicycle in Wallingford. Tragic case, happened on an old dirt road, beside an embankment leading down to a shallow stream called Grover's Creek. Kid was last seen wearing a striped shirt and jeans." Markham grabbed another High Life and popped open the top, taking a long gulp. "I get this burning in my ears...Grover's Creek. It rings a bell. I've heard of it somewhere. The name's haunting me all day, making those little hairs on my forearm stand on end. You know the feeling? Something tells me to go through the Garrett case file, so I start flipping through the book's pages."

"And?"

"About halfway through, I see it. Pencil drawing, pretty faint. He's drawn a boy lying in a creek at the bottom of an embankment, striped shirt, overturned bicycle. There's an arrow pointing toward the water with the words Grover's Creek next to it. He's also written 'June morning.' Happened in June of '75, Victor's been dead for three years at this point."

RG froze. "Visions of death and murder, detailed in a book."

"Page after page."

"What did you do?"

"I studied the fucking thing, trying to piece together images with places I might recognize, anything to head off a tragedy. But his sketches didn't offer much, and I had no way of knowing when any of these things would happen. Later, I discovered most of the images had already occurred in the preceding three years. I matched his pictures to fifteen murders, but the book had many more drawings and sketches."

"Oh my God." RG contemplated the eerie connection between Victor Garrett and Kacey, both haunted with visions of death. Only, Kacey worked to change the outcomes; Victor went another direction.

"So, one night I'm sleeping, and I fall into this dream." Markham's eyes clouded over, lost in his recollection. "But it's like no dream I've ever had. This one's as real as you and I sitting together. I'm in the Garretts' kitchen, in the exact spot where he pulled the trigger. I'm convinced Victor took me back there somehow. I get this feeling like someone's sneaking up on me. You know how when someone's behind you, you don't notice anything for a while, but then you do, something don't feel right? I could sense the air move in the space surrounding me, like a hot wind. Victor's standing right behind me, I'm sure of it. My heart jumped into my throat, and I spun around expecting to see a dead man with his head blown off, but wasn't nobody there. As I relaxed, he whispered in my ear, way up close, right in the middle of my head."

Tears brimmed at the corners of Markham's eyes.

"What did he say?"

Markham wiped his eyes with his sleeve and took a deep puff from his cigarette. "I know how this will sound, but I'm just going to say it. The voice spoke in a language I'd never heard before—"

"But you understood every word," RG interjected, finishing Markham's sentence.

The two men's eyes met as a flock of birds skimmed across the glass surface of the lake.

"Victor told me, 'You're in the book,' and then I woke up, shaking, drenched in sweat. I tried to put it out of my mind. But Victor had sealed my fate, and it would only be a matter of time before my number came up. I practically had his journal memorized, and not a single picture had a happy ending."

"But you're alive. You outsmarted him and cheated death."

"I may have cheated death, but this isn't what I call a happy ending." Markham stared down at his legs. "He must have figured with me in this chair, I'm not worth finishing off."

Markham pulled out another Marlboro Light and struck a match, but his shaking hands couldn't get the tobacco to catch. RG stood and reached for his hand, steadying the flame. The setting sun had changed the angle of sunlight coloring the room, illuminating Markham's face as he stared out the window.

"July, 1984. I'm breaking in a new partner. You met him, Gord Walsh, now the chief but at the time a detective, third grade. We're working a kidnapping, and I head out to question a suspect, real long-shot in my opinion, just trying to knock people off my list, you know. I tell Walsh to stay at his desk, keep digging on other leads. This guy I'm going to question lives out near Granby. Back in the '80s, it's nothing but tobacco fields out there. I'm rolling down this dirt road when I see one of those tobacco barns up ahead, about a hundred yards from the suspect's house. The sun's nestled just above the roof, tobacco netting covers all the fields for miles, and my car's kicking up a shit-load of dust, nearly blocking out the late-day sun."

Markham took a deep drag from his cigarette. "I'm driving along and I slam on the brakes. I must have skidded twenty feet. I've seen this picture before, from the exact same angle—tobacco barn, netted fields, dusty haze above the barn roof, house in the distance. It's from Victor's book. In his drawing, though, there are two bodies in front of the barn, a man and a child.

"I'm the man in the picture, a fate Victor foretold when he whispered in my ear." Markham opened the last of the High Life cans, disappointment etched across his features.

"I understood right then and there the guy's holding the boy captive in the barn and he's about to die. I've never known anything with greater conviction. But Victor's drawing tipped me off. I already know how it's gonna end. If I follow police procedure—the way I should have—Victor's premonition comes true. I die and so does the boy. So, instead of heading to the house, knocking on the door, walking up to the barn, announcing myself, and getting killed, I'm gonna make changes to the script. Fuck procedure, fuck the badge, and fuck Victor.

"I get out the car and race the hundred yards through the tobacco fields to the barn. When I get to the door, I can hear the boy's cries from inside. I threw open the door with my gun drawn ready to shoot the bastard, but once I see the boy and his condition, I get distracted. He's chained against the far wall..." Markham's voice catches in his throat. "He's...he's...in bad shape. I'm just staring at him, when I catch the bullet, severs the spinal cord and my legs dropped from under me. Didn't even hear the shot. They say you never hear a bullet with your name on it." Markham faced RG. "I understood right away I'd never walk again. I had no idea I'd gotten off a shot, but it caught the guy in the throat. Lucky, that was. He bled out right in front of me. I watched him die from close up. Didn't mind, either."

"What happened to the boy?"

"Well, everyone said I saved his life. I guess I saved my own life, too, but neither one of us would ever be whole again. I gave him a chance to live out whatever semblance of a life he'd have after his nightmare, I guess. Doesn't make me a hero."

"Actually, it does."

Markham crushed the empty High Life can in his hand and tossed it onto the mound of refuse beside him. "Walsh and I ended up burning the damn book. Maybe if I'd done it earlier, none of those images would have—"

"Don't put that on yourself," RG interrupted. "How could you have known?"

"I don't know. I guess someone has to take the blame. Makes all this," Markham gestured around the room, "palatable, knowing I deserve it. Penance maybe."

RG stood and rested his hand on Markham's shoulder. "Doesn't have to be this way." He took the folded picture from his jacket pocket and placed it in Markham's lap.

Markham held the picture close to his face, tracing his finger across a face staring back at him. "What are you going to do about your wife's dreams, the voice in your head?"

"I guess I'm gonna throw open the barn door on Victor, catch him by surprise."

CHAPTER ELEVEN

Thursday, December 7, 2017

Mike Stahl sat behind his desk in the Chatham Police Department staring at the second of two egg sandwiches in front of him, an oily brown stain pooling across the parchment paper. He frowned, wiped his hands with a napkin, and washed down the remnants of the first sandwich with a large gulp of lukewarm coffee when the phone rang.

"Mike, Chuck Brennan."

Stahl exhaled, leaned his head back, and squeezed his eyes shut.

"Not my idea to call you, but the BCI guys told me you're the only one available right now, and we got a mess over here in Falmouth."

Police departments across the Cape regularly called on Mike Stahl due to his training in forensics and crime scene investigation with the Bureau of Criminal Investigations. In a region where police officers babysat million-dollar summer homes and wrote tickets to out-of-state tourists, Stahl's experience as a Criminal Investigations Officer was invaluable, especially when a mutilated body surfaced.

"Thirty-five to forty-year-old male pretty much beheaded. Wonder whether you could get out here and give us a hand."

Stahl pushed the sandwich aside as he imagined the crime scene.

He could tell it pained Brennan to have to ask him, and he made sure to prolong the agony a bit longer. "Crime scene secured?"

"You questioning our capabilities?"

"Easy there, Chuck, just need to know what I'd be walking into."

"Our boys are at the house now. It's all taped off, waiting for you. What's it gonna be, Stahl, you gonna get off your high horse and help us out or not?"

He propped the phone underneath his chin and shoulder as he checked his watch. "Your crime scene isn't the only thing I have on my calendar today, Chuck. You might be a little more pleasant, maybe say 'please.'" A long silence followed. Stahl could almost hear the steam coming out of Brennan's ears. "Who discovered the body?"

"Co-worker went to pick him up for work and found him."

Stahl looked down, contemplating why he'd ordered the second egg sandwich. "You holding him there?"

"Um, well, Mike, he seemed pretty shook up, so we let him go home. We have his name. We can get him if we need to."

"Jeez. You let your only suspect go?" Stahl shook his head. Personal history aside, he bristled at Brennan's sloppy police work.

"Well, he called us about the murder, so we figured…" Chuck's voice trailed off.

Stahl finished the last of his coffee. "Okay, keep everybody out of the house until I get there. Where am I going?"

Brennan gave him the address.

He stood and swept the uneaten egg sandwich from his desk into the trash bin. "I'm heading out now."

"I'll let BCI know superman's on his way."

"Kiss my ass, Chuck." Throwing an arm through his coat sleeve, Stahl hustled down the hall. He directed his conversation to the desk sergeant. "Hal, I'll be out for the morning, heading to Falmouth. Hold down the fort for me, okay?"

Hal raised an eyebrow, but didn't look up from his crossword puzzle. "Don't I always?"

Stahl grabbed what he'd need for his forensic examination and descended the granite steps to the parking lot, bracing himself against the brisk, swirling December air. He considered taking Route 28 into Falmouth but opted to navigate the backroads and connectors to the mid-Cape highway. He turned up the heat and cracked the windows, shaking his head as he anticipated the state of the Falmouth crime scene. He called Russ Randle, chief medical examiner at the County Coroner's office, to see if Brennan remembered to contact them.

"Haven't heard from them yet," Randle told him. "But we'll meet you there inside of an hour."

Stahl disconnected, a shadow of irritation crossing his features. As he exited Route 6 and approached Falmouth, he snapped off the police radio, letting the car go quiet, mentally preparing himself for the job ahead.

Stahl directed the Crown Vic along Scranton Avenue past the harbor. He hung a left onto Shore Street heading toward Surf Drive, with Martha's Vineyard straight ahead over a short expanse of ocean, close enough you could almost reach out and touch it.

As he searched the house numbers for the address Brennan provided, it dawned on him he'd been in this neighborhood before. He recognized the house, the presence of police cars and crime scene tape now unmistakable indicators of violence and death. After all his years on the job, Stahl had never hardened himself to the sight of death. A body, once filled with the intangible qualities of life, reduced to mere matter, still had the power to shock him. But today would be different. Today, the body belonged to a man he'd spent time with, who'd opened his home to him. He fought the urge to turn the car around, floor it to Chatham, and settle back behind the comfort of his desk.

Chief Brennan laughed with his patrolmen on the house's raised weather-beaten deck, a glazed cruller in one hand and coffee in the other. Screw Brennan. Let him and his crew fumble through the case. He eased the Crown Vic over the driveway's gravel and shells, rolled up the windows, and turned off the engine. He'd do his job, he owed it to the man inside the house.

He sat for a moment, a memory transplanting him into the past.

Five years earlier, Stahl's then-girlfriend had roped him into attending an engagement celebration for her old friend, Kacey Kearns, and her fiancée. He hated these types of events, but of all the engagement parties he didn't want to attend, this topped his list. He'd had no desire to meet the man about to steal the woman of his dreams. The emptiness in watching the love of his life say 'yes' to another man struck him as deeply as it had then.

Stahl leaned over the steering wheel and gazed upward through the smeared windshield, picturing Kacey on the raised deck, RG and his close friends surrounding them. The two had shared a secret language communicated through subtle gestures, laughs, and touches; a language Stahl had been fluent in years before. Before he'd stepped from his car, he'd had the wind knocked out of him.

She'd come right up to him, took hold of his hands, and let out a sigh. "Michael Francis Stahl. I'm glad you changed your mind." Before he could think of anything to say, she led him by the elbow into the house. "I want you to meet someone."

Stahl's heart sank, but he'd prepared himself for the moment, practicing what he'd say and how he'd say it. He'd smile, make eye contact, extend his hand, and give RG a strong handshake. He'd hold it together.

Kacey led him through the screen door into Johnny D's house, through the sunroom and into the kitchen. Across the Linoleum floor, Mike spotted him. He sensed in RG's eyes both surprise and contempt for the man at the other end of the room.

"Wasn't expecting you." RG blew past Mike's outstretched hand, the muscles in his jaw clenching. He placed a hand on Kacey's elbow and marched her onto the deck, the room temperature plummeting after the frosty encounter.

"Congratulations to both of you. I wish you the best." Stahl muttered his memorized greeting under his breath as he stood alone in Johnny D's kitchen.

He stared at the floor. He couldn't blame RG for his behavior, the man had reasons to hate him, Kacey no doubt confiding in him about what he'd done to her when he'd been drowning in the bottle. For some sins, redemption couldn't be earned, and maybe wasn't deserved. He'd secretly longed for absolution from RG, the chance to release the heaviness from his heart, to unburden himself of the one drunken act forever defining him.

It didn't happen.

As Stahl had stood in the kitchen, a man emerged from the bathroom down the hall, hair pulled back in a ponytail. "You must be Mike. Glad you could make it. I'm Johnny D."

Stahl flinched as a pair of knuckles rapped his car window, snapping him out of his reverie. He climbed out and greeted Russ Randle. As a CIO, Mike often worked with Randle, processing crime scenes, and had developed a friendship over the years.

"Hey, Russ, how's the family?" Mike clapped him on the back.

"Just keeps growing somehow." Russ and his wife had recently welcomed their fourth daughter to the brood, but he'd confided to Mike he wouldn't quit until he had a boy.

"Thanks for the gift, by the way. Sherry thought you might have been making a statement with a mustache pacifier, though." He gave Stahl a playful punch.

"She knows that's as close to a son as you'll ever get."

Chuck Brennan lumbered down the steps from the deck to the driveway, interrupting the moment. He wiped his hands on a napkin, tossed it on the lawn, and hitched up his sagging pants over a generous midsection. Brennan approached Stahl like an old friend, his arm extended from his body, giving him an exaggerated, welcoming handshake. "Hey, Mike, great to see you."

"Chief." Stahl shook his hand, confused by the hearty welcome after their earlier phone call.

Brennan escorted Stahl and Randle up the steps and introduced him to two bright-eyed officers. "I have a couple of rookies with me today, and I figured it would be as good a time as any to show 'em how we handle a crime scene." He threw a meaty paw on Mike's shoulder.

Stahl established the pecking order immediately, scuttling Brennan's attempt to align with him and elevate his status at the crime scene. "Okay, I'm the CIO and Russ is medical examiner. You three will answer directly to us. Make sure you don't do anything to compromise the scene's integrity. Don't touch anything or step anywhere

without instruction from Russ or myself. And remember, it's manda-
tory to call the coroner any time a body's discovered. Immediately." He
fixed his gaze on Brennan.

His face flushed a light shade of red. "You listening, boys?"
Brennan glared at his two rookies sternly. The officers glanced downward, shifting their weight back and forth.

As Stahl led the group into Johnny D's house, the copper-iron
smell of blood hit them as if they'd walked into a wall. After taking a
tentative step through the doorway, one of the rookie officers
backpedaled from the house. He leaned over at the waist, gasping for
fresh air, his hands on his knees.

The body of Johnny Delvecchio lay beside the kitchen table in a
thick crimson liquid pool covering half the floor. Stahl stepped carefully into the kitchen and found himself in the exact spot he'd met
Johnny D five years earlier. He surveyed the grisly scene, noting the
deep lacerations to the victim's neck and the serrated knife beside the
body. The spine had been partially severed at the level of the fourth
and fifth cervical vertebrae, nearly separating the head from the body.

Clearly a savage act of extreme prejudice, the type of excessive
violence occurring most often when love and hate became blurred.
Stahl's experience convinced him love and hate don't simply reside at
two different ends of an emotional spectrum. The line doubles back on
itself with the two emotions sitting side by side, often switching places
in an instant.

"What do we know about Mr. Delvecchio and his personal life?"

Brennan stepped forward, a handkerchief held over his nose and
mouth. "Well, Delvecchio had a pretty loyal following in this town,
especially from the ladies. I'm not aware of anyone having a beef with
him. How about you guys?" Brennan turned to his rookie officers only
to find both on the porch, bent over at the waist, hands on their knees.

"Explore that angle, Chuck. And let's have a talk with the guy who
found him. He might have insight into his personal or business interactions. Maybe he had enemies." Stahl looked at the lifeless body swimming in its own fluids. "Russ, you want to call it?"

Mike stepped back while Randle made the determination of homicide as cause of death. Stahl and Randle then invited the rookie officers back in to help process the scene. Brennan moved through the house, taking up space. While reading through Johnny D's mail, seemingly for his own entertainment, he stumbled across a stack of financial statements. One in particular documented significant losses for one of Johnny's clients. "You recognize any of these people?" Brennan addressed his officers as he began reading off names.

Stahl's ear pricked up. *I'll be damned!* "Chuck, I'm familiar with Robert Granville. He's a close friend of the victim."

"How do you know this Granville?"

Stahl walked over beside Brennan. "I met him at this house with Mr. Delvecchio about five years ago."

"You knew the victim? I'm sorry, Mike." Russ frowned.

"I only met him the one time. Still, it's a shame."

Brennan read the financial statement with greater interest. "It looks like Granville lost money last month, a lot of money." Brennan tilted his head and frowned. "Could be a motive. We'll definitely run prints on the knife." Brennan had moved on from searching for any evidence and now browsed through Johnny's music collection.

Stahl paused, reflecting on Robert Granville and his close-knit group of friends. The guy had been an asshole to him, sure, but he'd observed them up close. He'd watched them together. Maybe he silently wished he'd had something to do with the murder—for his own selfish reasons—but no way on earth it could be true.

Over the next several hours, they collected physical evidence, performing blood spatter analysis, recording and measuring finger- and footprints, the positions of all evidence diagrammed, photographed, and video recorded. They recovered and catalogued biological samples for lab work and interviewed neighbors. Eager to wrap things up, Stahl addressed the officers. "Next step guys, with evidence collected and documented, everything needs to get to BCI in Barnstable for forensic analyses. Chuck, follow up with the co-worker and see if he has an alibi for last night. I'll give Granville a call and break the news about his friend and verify his alibi. He's gonna be pretty broken up about this. They were close."

"Hmmm, a crime of passion?" Brennan raised an eyebrow.

Stahl considered the thin line between love and hate.

～

Victor dozed, exhausted from the violent encounter with Johnny D. He'd been there with Johnny D and Granville as they'd cooked and ate, shared drinks together. Victor had learned everything about Johnny D the instant he'd tapped Granville's mind days earlier. During his probe, the burning man had learned of Johnny D's dreams, his failures, and his darkest fears. When he'd visited him last night, he'd considered him an old friend, and he'd been remiss for not stopping by to say hello earlier.

For now, his rage abated. Peace settled in when he thought of Sam. How he'd cherished those mornings when Sam had shuffled into the bedroom at the crack of dawn, his hair in tangles. He'd loved it when Sam would crawl under the covers between Lucy and him and fall asleep. Victor would stare in awe at his son, realizing that one day, he'd grow up, and these fleeting moments would be gone forever.

He'd become a teenager, face the excitement and angst of girl-friends and breakups, schoolwork and sports teams. He'd learn to drive, take the SATs, graduate high school, and head off to college where he'd grow into a man, find the girl of his dreams, and bring her back to meet his parents. A beautiful wedding would follow, with a special toast from a proud father. Victor had imagined his son pursuing his own path, settling into a career, starting traditions with his own family.

But that future never came.

When Victor found himself at peace, during the solace, the enduring pain of his son's loss reappeared—the Yin and Yang of solace, peace but suffering, joy and pain. Soon the rage would return and all emotion would be gone.

Maybe that was best.

Victor reviewed the previous evening's events. He'd dispatched his old friend Johnny D humanely, no need to torment or prolong his suffering, a mere pawn in a new game. He'd faced Victor with courage and put up a valiant fight, earning Victor's respect. He cared deeply about life and had much to lose, unlike his friend Worthing who'd given up, begged to die. Victor almost regretted making him pick up the serrated knife, place it to his neck, and cut until he'd severed his spinal cord, inducing his own paralysis.

Victor had gazed deep into Johnny D's mind as he passed from his world. The things he'd miss most, the simple pleasures—the weight of ocean air, the smell of freshly sawed wood, the heartache of a minor chord, a woman's intimate smile. He only asked 'why?' but didn't beg or plead as many do. Anticipating the encounter's inevitability, Johnny D spoke to Victor as a man understanding the nature of life and death. He'd remained inside Johnny D as long as he safely could—a show of respect as the life drained from his body.

Johnny bled out before Victor could explain his death represented the first step in his plan for Granville. A grin crossed his lips, but he had more work to do to make it happen, and he'd have to be more careful.

The minutes passed, solace slipping away. Fire and rage inside him returned. Victor's musings turned to the woman who'd appeared in the dream, the pregnant woman watching him at the railway station—the beautiful one, he thought—Granville's wife. Somehow, she'd entered his mind and stolen his thoughts, something a caretaker as powerful as Morrow himself couldn't do. When she'd said Sam's name, he'd wanted to reach out, talk to her about his boy, but the rage flared up again.

He'd have to guard against her abilities, her power to see inside him. She could prove to be detrimental to his mission. Victor had no worries about Granville: weak, soft, and nurtured in his caretaker's shadow. Victor would crush him with Morrow out of the picture. The woman, though, would be a formidable opponent. Victor imagined squeezing the life out of her and her baby boy right in front of Granville. He might even force the professor to kill his own wife and child, something worth watching.

He sat up, wide awake, the burning man itching to get to work.

~

August 1988

The little girl went off to bed. She'd brushed her teeth, combed her hair, and received kisses from her mom and dad, making her feel safe and warm. After they left her room, Kacey looked forward to her time alone, to dream about the Pancake Man, her favorite place in the world. Sometimes she'd dreamed about it the same day she'd eaten there, and she still woke up looking forward to the next visit.

Kacey's dreams differed from those of her friends. They didn't have dreams during the day when everyone else was awake like she did, and their dreams didn't divulge all the gruesome things that would happen. Sometimes, Kacey's dreams came at night after she'd fallen fast asleep, waking her with screams. But not anymore. She'd learned to cope with the burden and protect her loved ones from the horror she witnessed in her head.

Most days, she looked forward to her dreams, especially the ones in the restaurant. She would observe her family at a distance, like watching a family video; they'd smile at each other and eat apple and cinnamon pancakes, mountains of fried potatoes, French toast, and of course, Kacey's favorite, silver dollar pancakes. The dream would end when her mom, dad, and the dream version of herself exited the restaurant. She ached to go with them because they appeared so happy, but something in her head told her not to. She wasn't supposed to leave the restaurant.

Tonight, Kacey decided to try.

As she fell asleep, Kacey had a feeling she'd visit her family again. Before long she found herself in the bustling restaurant, voices echoing from the kitchen, workers running back and forth setting tables, dirty plates and glasses clattering as wait staff tossed them into plastic bins. She stood beside a booth, watching her family order breakfast. Like her other dreams, she enjoyed the familiar conversations, anticipating who would laugh first at her dad's silly jokes. When her family finished breakfast and slid from the booth to leave, Kacey followed them toward the door.

They twisted through the crowded aisle, jostling their way through waitstaff and families waiting for a table. Kacey strolled beside her dream-self, imagining what it must be like to have a sister. Her twin glanced over and flashed a wide smile, but as they reached the door, fear descended upon her like a shroud. She shook her head. Kacey froze, unsure what to do, only inches from the door and desperate to leave with them. As the door opened and her family stepped from the restaurant, Kacey craned her neck, peering into a brilliant whiteness so vast and empty it frightened her.

Standing at the door, a gentle force drew her from the restaurant, as if someone had snaked their arms around her midsection and tugged at her to come outside to play. If she took her hand off the door she'd be swept away, forever lost in the dazzling brightness. Struggling against the determined force pulling against her, a voice whispered inside her head: *Everything will be fine. Come play with us. Let go of the handle.* Laughter rang in her head, but soon the sound shifted into a low growl, her fear returning. With all her might, she pulled the door closed and stumbled backward to the restaurant's safety, melting into the crowd of patrons. Her family sat in a booth, ready to order breakfast again.

She wandered over to them as they ate a second time, vowing never to try and leave the restaurant again.

~

Friday, December 8, 2017

RG yawned, his feet perched on his desk as he reclined in his chair. Once again, he'd not fully prepared his lecture for his sleepy students enrolled in his 8:30 a.m. Exercise Physiology class. Defending himself against a vengeful serial killer from the afterlife had taken precedence lately. No last-minute cramming today; he'd wing it with his Power-Point slides, certain to ease his students back to sleep. Only a few more classes before finals, he told himself. Exhausted from his travels to Connecticut and a serious lack of sleep, RG leaned his head back against the plush leather desk chair and nodded off in an instant.

Minutes later, the ringing desk phone jerked him awake. He grabbed it and checked the time: five minutes before class.

"Hey, RG, Mike Stahl again."

He readied himself for anger and resentment at the sound of Stahl's voice, but envisioned Walt in his private cell and recalled Johnny D's words about people living with their demons. RG allowed himself a peek over the wall of his ancient rage.

"Hey, Mike, I wanted to thank you again for getting us in to see Walt and for keeping an eye on him over the years. You didn't have to do that."

"Maybe not, but…" Stahl took a deep breath. "Listen, I'd give anything to be calling under different circumstances. I'm not sure how to say this, but your friend Johnny Delvecchio is dead. I didn't want you to find out about it on the news."

Johnny? Johnny D? Not possible! He pounded his fist on the desk to wake himself up, but the room pulled away from him, the light fading in his vision; and for the first time in his life, he couldn't remember how to breathe.

"Are you still there?"

Tremors spread from RG's hands to his arms and finally to his legs until his body shook out of control.

"RG, come on, man."

He held himself to keep from shaking. "What happened?"

"Someone murdered him in his home Wednesday night."

RG could hear Stahl's words, but he couldn't process them. Victor's evil rampage overwrote any reaction, forcing him to admit that the jumper had killed Johnny to inflict emotional turmoil on him one death at a time. The thought almost made him laugh hysterically before a primal scream threatened to shatter the silence, but he held it together long enough to ask, "How did it happen?"

"Are you sure you want to hear this?"

"No, but you're going to tell me anyway." *I didn't even warn Johnny. I said nothing.*

"The cleanest way I can describe it…" A rumbling noise, Stahl's obvious attempt to clear his throat wouldn't lessen the traumatic detail. "Uh, well, someone cut his throat."

"Shit." RG squeezed his eyes shut, warding off any picture he might conjure to visualize Johnny's gruesome mutilation, the horror sending a sharp sting across his own neck. Did Victor exact his punishment with a painful, slow, cutting force? *Oh, God.* About to crumble, he dropped the phone, Stahl's voice still droning. Somehow, he grappled to retrieve the device as anger spread through him. It was his fault, all of it.

I knew it would happen and I didn't do a goddamn thing!

He listened midstream. "…kitchen knife…" One he and Johnny had cooked with? He didn't say it, just kept listening. "…you're better off remembering him the way he was."

"It's not real. It's just not real."

"And it's about to get worse, trust me. Can you help us with locating his next of kin? Any brothers or sisters?"

"Just me," RG whispered.

"Unfortunately, I'm involved in the investigation. The Falmouth Police are running down potential persons of interest. They found a list of Johnny's investment clients and saw you lost a bunch of money last month."

"So, what's that got to do with anything? Is there a law against losing money?"

"Well, I know you couldn't have done it, but I still have to follow protocols. The money thing's a red flag, I just need your alibi so I can get them off your radar."

RG slumped in his chair, official business taking him down another depressing road. Couldn't a guy just grieve a minute first? "What do you want to know?"

"When did you see him last?"

"Well, Wednesday night. Johnny and I whipped up a gourmet meal and hung out a while."

Stahl paused before he replied. "At the house?"

"Yeah, headed home about nine or so."

"Just a guy's night? Any particular business you discussed?"

A subtle hint of interrogation entered Stahl's voice. RG chose his words with care. "Well, I wanted to talk with him about a few things—work, our visits with Walt, typical stuff."

"Hey, I know this is upsetting enough, but the sooner we get business taken care of, the sooner we can find Johnny's killer. Do you mind providing fingerprints and DNA to eliminate you as a suspect?"

Thoughts peppered RG's mind as he tried to process what he heard. They would find fingerprints along with a financial motive for murder. He'd watched too many late-night episodes of *Forensic Files* with Kacey, well aware how law enforcement operated. Once that happened, they'd zero in on him. "You know my prints are going to be all over the place, Mike."

"No need to be nervous. Once they see the knife's clean—"

RG interrupted. "Mike, my hands touched everything, knives, plates, countertops. We cut vegetables for God's sake." RG's decibel level rose, surprising himself with how guilty he sounded. "Do you think I could ever kill my best friend? That I could do something so awful?" Now he sounded desperate.

"It's not what I think. It's what the evidence says. You said your hands could've been on the knife?"

His voice betrayed a subtle change, sounding more and more like a cop. Stahl had called as a courtesy to tell him about Johnny, but it might not take much to shift his impression of him from grieving friend to murderer. Once he'd made that jump, Stahl would have a deep-seated motivation to see him put away. Forever.

"What do I do?" RG rose from his chair, but he struggled to hold himself upright.

"Given the circumstances, it's best if you talked to the detectives in Falmouth on your own."

"On my own?" RG couldn't believe his ears. "You mean, instead of them arresting me?"

"There isn't enough for a warrant right now, but you don't want to get them thinking you're being evasive."

"Should I get a lawyer? Does it make me look guilty?"

"A lawyer's never a bad idea." Stahl cleared his throat. "Listen, it's not often a beach town like Falmouth has such a savage murder occur. They're gonna want to clear this. The chief used to be a pretty tough interrogator back in the day. I'm sure the detectives taking your statement are going to be well trained, maybe try to trip you up in there. I'd bring a lawyer if you have one. One way or another, you need to get out ahead of this thing."

"Fine. I have nothing to hide. I'll head down there and give them whatever they want."

"I'll call Chuck Brennan, Falmouth's police chief. I'll tell him to expect you. I'm sorry about Johnny. I really am. He seemed like one of the good guys."

"I appreciate your telling me this personally." RG hung up as a second wave of nausea rose from nowhere. His stomach seized. He grabbed his garbage can and heaved up his breakfast. After several minutes, he stumbled from the office.

There would be no class today.

RG jumped in his car and hightailed it out of Boston, uncertain how he felt, what to do, or whether he was stuck in a hopeless situation and had lost the battle before it had even begun. He drove randomly, searching his soul for answers, trying to get a grip on a reality he'd never fully accept. He didn't want to be around anyone right now. He didn't trust himself not to fall apart in front of those who expected him to be strong…because he wasn't. He operated out of fear and pain, lost in an unfamiliar landscape, his compass no longer pointing north, nothing to guide him back to normal. Normal had just left the planet and wouldn't be coming back.

He closed his eyes. Johnny D gone. Not possible. He was just here.

Please, when I open my eyes let it be a broken compass. Let Johnny D still be alive. Please.

He did open them. But Johnny was still dead.

In his misery and numbness, he pulled up to the battered, two-family clapboard house on Beach Street in Revere where Johnny D once lived, the rusty metal basketball hoop still hanging at an angle from the aged wooden pole at the back of the driveway. Maybe if he sat here long enough and called for Johnny to get his sorry ass out here and play, the compass would realign. But sitting behind the steering wheel, eyes closed, memories tainted with the humid, insect-filled buzz of distant summers' choking heat, couldn't change the truth. He'd never hear Johnny D's voice again, watch him pull back his god-awful, out-of-style ponytail, or share his soul's secrets. Johnny D was gone, and it was his fault.

He took one last look at the decayed property and tried to find some ounce of comfort in knowing Johnny D's life happened here, and *he* had been a part of it, that he'd been a better person because of it. He studied the sagging front porch, wondering if Johnny's shadow still lingered behind the front door. Had Johnny's spirit misted through those walls and rooms, taking one last look around, making one final bow to the tangible side of a physical life before passing on?

In a brief, fleeting instant, RG whispered, "Johnny D? Are you there, brother? Please. You can't bail on me now. We were supposed to grow old together."

A guttural rumble escaped his throat, and he fell over his steering wheel with a grief he'd never wanted to meet or know, realizing if he didn't rid the world of Victor, this would be the torment awaiting Kacey. He wiped his eyes with his shirtsleeve, a raw determination taking hold, reigniting enough anger to stop the burning man once and for all. Victor would not win. He would not kill one more person on this earth—not his friends, not his wife, and damn sure not his child—if he had anything to say about it, no matter if it cost him his life. RG vowed to take him down.

I'll bury you, motherfucker!

He would need to grieve, but now wasn't the time. He pulled out his cell phone and found the number for the Falmouth Police Department, telling them he would be coming down to make a statement. RG shot back onto the highway and headed south.

"To hell with lawyers," he said. "I've got nothing to hide."

CHAPTER TWELVE

Friday, December 8, 2017

From more than just the overcast sky's gloomy umbrage, RG drove under the weight of his own cloud. He pulled into the Falmouth Marina and parked at the Flying Bridge restaurant, then hiked across the green to the Harbor Master's office nestled beside the dock.

The cramped office may have been as old as the harbor itself, with weathered shingles and a window doing little to brighten the room. A single bulb dangling from the ceiling struggled to illuminate the shadows lurking in each corner. Seated behind his desk, Matty Kelly's huge hands hid his face. Work towered in piles in front of him. He raised his head when RG walked in, the creaky wooden floor betraying his arrival. Without saying a word, Matty stood and gave him a bear hug, nearly knocking the wind out of him.

"It's good to see you, brother." RG clapped him on the back.

Matty broke away, grabbing tissues from the box on his desk, his eyes red with grief. "What the hell you doing here?" Matty wiped his face.

RG glanced around at the nautical décor and hundred-year-old photographs of the harbor and fishermen who worked these waters.

"The police want to ask me a few questions. I didn't tell you, but I had dinner at Johnny's on Wednesday night, right before it happened. I'm heading to the station at noon."

"Shit, man. Who'd you talk to there?"

"Some guy named Daniels. He's going to take my statement."

Matty reached out and snaked his huge paw behind RG's neck, leaning in close. "Listen man, the police chief, guy named Brennan, he can be a first-class prick. Likes to flaunt the badge, if you know what I mean. Expects a free drink everywhere in town."

"I'm here to answer questions, not buy him a drink."

"I'm telling you to be careful. He won't be too fond of a professor coming down from the city to mingle with the unwashed masses, I imagine."

"Jeez, Matty, I'm from Revere for Chrissake."

"I'm just saying, dumb down those big words you use." Matty raised his eyebrows. "Understand?"

"Listen, I'm meeting with Daniels, not Brennan, and I already spoke to him on the phone. Look, I'll be in and out in twenty minutes. That's all it'll take to eliminate me as a suspect. Just protocol." He offered Matty a smirk. "What do you say we head over to the Boat House? Hungry?"

"You have to ask? I'm always hungry." Matty wiped his eyes with his sleeve.

They strolled up Scranton Avenue to the restaurant shadowing the end of the pier. They both ordered fried clam strips and french fries. Despite the biting cold, they sat outside at a table overlooking the harbor. The golden sun had finally shoved through the cloud cover and warmed their faces. For the moment, the tasty food distracted them from the weight of Johnny D's death.

"Why didn't you call me when you heard?" RG picked at his plate.

"I'm sorry, man. I don't think I really believed it until I saw you today." He reached across the picnic table, stole a couple napkins from RG's tray, and wiped his eyes. "I'm not sure I'm ready for this."

"How's the Sun-Pig?"

"Inconsolable. We figured the gang would always be there, you know. Get our families together on holidays and our kids would grow up together, that kinda shit. But now…"

RG gazed from the pier across the unending ocean, at the commercial fishing boats heading out to earn a day's wages on the choppy water. The low tide exposed a dead fish, seaweed smell wafting from beneath the dock. RG turned to his friend, the one in the gang with the biggest heart to go along with his comparable frame—the guy with dreams of settling down and being a father when the rest of the gang traded in girlfriends every week or two. "I promise you, Matty, our kids will grow up together."

He stared out across the water, unsure whether he'd be around to see it.

RG pulled into the Falmouth Police Station a few minutes before noon, ready to end the fucking nightmare and concentrate on saving his own life. He climbed out of the car, forced the air from his lungs, and hiked across the parking lot to the building's front door. With its ocean-blue shutters, the structure appeared more like a New England vacation home than a police station. *Place could probably generate revenue as a summer rental, ease up on all those traffic tickets.*

He opened the door and approached the front desk. Pinging emails and ringing telephones created a comforting white noise to the bustling station. The desk sergeant pointed to the chairs lined against the wall. RG glanced around for a coffee pot and bottled water but didn't find either. *I might have to move to Connecticut if I'm gonna spend any more time in police stations.*

After a lengthy wait—not the twenty-minute in-and-out RG had guesstimated—a man exited an office from the far end of the hall and stopped at the front desk. He conferred with the desk sergeant, speaking in hushed tones as they eyed him. When they finished their conversation, the man approached with a manufactured smile. He had a youthful appearance and welcoming face, blonde hair styled in a brush cut. He wore a brown suit he could've found on a sales rack and shoes showing their age.

"Mr. Granville, I'm Detective Chris Daniels. I talked to you on the phone earlier. I'll be taking your statement today."

RG shook his hand. "Nice to meet you, Detective Daniels." *Maybe.*

"There are a few preliminary steps before we begin." Daniels extended his arm, directing RG down the hall to a cramped room where the detective offered him a chair. "Are you willing to provide fingerprints and a blood and saliva sample for DNA analysis?"

"That's why I'm here."

RG spent the next twenty-five minutes being inked, swabbed, and prodded with needles. Daniels escorted him into a dingy white room with a single door, a table with three chairs, and a one-way mirror. Offering him a seat, Daniels took the opposite one and glanced at his clipboard. RG gazed around the room with its stained ceiling tiles and scuffed floor, a hint of old sweat and cigarettes adding to the room's stagnant aroma.

"Mr. Granville, I'm aware you've lost a friend, and this is the last place you want to be, but your help today will bring us closer to finding whoever did this." Daniels consulted his papers. "We need to wait until Chief Brennan arrives to conduct the interview. Anything I can get you? A soda, cup of coffee?"

RG swallowed. "Chief Brennan? I thought you'd be taking my statement." *Fuck me.*

"Well, turns out the Chief wanted to work with me on this case, make sure we get this right."

The first drops of sweat formed on his brow, the decision to do this alone now weighing heavily on his mind. How bad could it be? *Relax, I've got nothing to hide, and it's time to put this behind me.*

After prolonged, uncomfortable silence and small talk with the detective, Chuck Brennan strode into the room, a thick, red licorice strand dangling from his mouth. He cradled a large Dunkin' Donuts coffee, a napkin wedged between his index and ring fingers. "Good afternoon, Detective." He hitched up his pants and took a seat beside Daniels, plunking his coffee down as if he were matching it up to an imaginary hole, then silenced his smartphone. Once situated, he directed his gaze to RG. "You must be Robert Granville, the hero."

"Pardon?"

"Read about your heroics in the subway. I'll bet you're just the talk of the town."

"Well, I don't know about that."

"Anything we can get you before we begin?" Brennan asked.

"Detective Daniels already offered, but thank you."

Brennan studied him for a moment. "So, what do you do, Mr. Granville?"

"I work at Boston University."

"So, it's Dr. Granville?"

"Only to my students, sir."

Brennan plastered on a smile. "All right then, Mr. Granville, let's get started here. The Falmouth Police Department thanks you for coming in today. We're here to talk about the events of Wednesday, December sixth, the night of John Salvatore Delvecchio's homicide. We understand you visited Delvecchio's home on Walker Street the night in question, correct?"

"Until about 9:00."

"Tell us about your interactions with Mr. Delvecchio."

"Johnny D and I go way back, closer than brothers. We talked about an issue at work. He's a good listener…or was a good listener."

"How come you didn't just call him?" Daniels stared at him.

RG hesitated, drawing a blank on the simple question. "Well," he stammered, "if you'd eaten his food, you would've found excuses to visit him, too. Ask anyone. He could whip up a gourmet meal worth dying for…" *Shit.* He wanted to zip his mouth shut before he prattled his way into handcuffs.

Brennan and Daniels met his response with stony silence.

RG filled the temporary lull. "Look, tell me you don't ever vent with your buddies or share a meal and a couple of beers. It's normal. When I left and headed back to Boston, he was loading his dishwasher."

"Venting? What about?" Brennan pulled out another licorice from his pocket, pulling on the strand until it snapped into his mouth.

"I don't see what that has to do with anything."

"We cover every base. What was so important you couldn't discuss over the phone?"

"A situation at work, nothing involving Johnny."

"Have you ever been angry at Mr. Delvecchio?" Daniels asked.

"Of course. I've known the guy since kindergarten. Hell, we go at it just like anyone, but he's always been my closest friend." *My brother.*

"Could Delvecchio have done something to upset you?" Brennan leaned forward.

RG shook his head. "Not a thing. In fact, once we started cooking and talking, I'd forgotten about my work troubles."

For the next thirty minutes, RG fielded their open-ended questions, trying not to reveal too much. Brennan and Daniels sometimes asked the same question in different ways, trying to trip him up, but he had consistent responses to each query.

Brennan and Daniels sat for a moment and consulted their notes. Every question they asked, he'd answered. RG leaned back and relaxed.

A knock at the door interrupted the silence. The desk sergeant came in and whispered into Brennan's ear.

"Please excuse me, Mr. Granville." Brennan nodded to Daniels and the two of them exited the room, leaving him alone. The minutes ticked by, but no one returned. Aware they were watching him, RG fought the urge to get up, cup his hands, and peer through the one-way glass. Having multiple eyes crawl over him made his skin itch. If their strategy included ways to ratchet up his anxiety, it worked. The room temperature spiked, parching his throat more and more with each passing minute.

After another twenty minutes, rounding his so-called short stint up to two hours, Brennan and Daniels sauntered back into the room. Brennan carried a manila folder in one hand and a coffee refill in the other. Daniels also had a cup of Joe, both settling in for another round of questioning. Brennan dropped into his chair and cracked the folder, reading silently.

RG broke the interminable silence. "Can I get something to drink, an ice water or cold soda?"

Brennan continued to read, sipping his coffee. "You can wait," he snapped, not bothering to look up from his papers. Brennan stood and positioned himself behind RG, placing the folder on the desk in front of him.

As Brennan leaned over his shoulder, RG smelled the coffee on his breath mingling with cheap aftershave.

"We have a preliminary comparison of your fingerprints with those on the murder weapon." Brennan's voice no more than a whisper. "Now the official results won't be available until the crime lab issues their report, but we're confident they'll confirm what we already know. Your fingerprints are a perfect match to those on the murder weapon. You see here…see those ridges?" Brennan pointed to two images side by side in the dossier. "Very distinct. No doubt in our minds." Brennan let his words sink in before asking, "Do you have any explanation for that?"

RG caught Daniels' eyes darting toward Brennan. Their coded stares didn't bode well. He regretted his decision to forego the lawyer thing, certain justice hung on his side, but in his preoccupied mind, he'd forgotten about all those innocent people sent to death row. He could feel his freedom ratcheting down to a nub.

"I already told you my fingerprints would be all over the place. Johnny and I both cut vegetables with several different knives."

"Several?" Brennan asked.

"Guess you're not a chef or you'd know you can't use a butter knife on everything. Check all the knives, especially the ones that didn't kill Johnny. You'll find pretty pictures of my prints all over those, too!"

"Funny thing is, the only other prints on the murder weapon matched Mr. Delvecchio's." Brennan let some time pass for effect. "Just yours and his. I can't imagine Mr. Delvecchio cut his own spinal cord, can you?"

RG squeezed his eyes shut, the image jolting him. Spinal cord? That's the first he'd heard of it. His gaze darted around the room, searching for a wastebasket in case his fried seafood came calling.

"I suppose Mr. Genius University Man Hero has a snide remark to that." Brennan glared at him with venomous eyes, like he'd caught him in an impossible riddle.

He had an explanation, but not one he could share. "So, the killer was smart enough to wear a glove before he used the knife Johnny and I used. Simple." Let them digest that for a minute.

Daniels produced an evidence bag, reached in and held up a serrated knife, blood still visible along the blade's jagged edge. "I tell you, if I tried to cut veggies with this, I'd cut my fingers off." He turned to Brennan with a smirk.

RG tugged at his shirt, sweat dripping down his back and sides. *Calm down, take a deep breath.* The interview had turned into an interrogation.

Chief Brennan ambled around the table. "Sounds real cozy, you boys cooking together." He took a long, slow sip from his coffee.

"What the hell's that supposed to mean?"

"Well, we call it overkill," Daniels chimed in, "what happened to Mr. Delvecchio. It's the type of thing usually seen with family members…or lovers."

Brennan leaned in. "Anything else you want to tell us about your relationship with him?"

"Like what?"

"I understand Mr. Delvecchio dated a lot of young ladies around here?"

"So what?"

"Didn't bother you at all?" Brennan raised an eyebrow.

"Why would it?"

"You're an educated man, Mr. Granville." Brennan grinned and eyed Daniels.

"I don't need to dignify your question with a response."

"So, you refuse to answer the question?"

"Who do you think you are asking me questions like that?" RG snarled.

"I'm the Chief of Police," Brennan snapped back, leaning over the table, "and I can place you in the home of a dead man the night he died. Who do you think you are?"

"Hang on a minute here, guys," Daniels broke in, facing RG. "What we're trying to say is people get angry with each other, husbands, wives, best friends. Things sometimes get out of hand." Daniels placed a hand on his chest. "We understand how this could've happened, especially if you were already angry when you arrived. We've all been there."

Daniels' ploy didn't faze him. "Well, I wasn't angry and it didn't happen that way."

"How did it happen?" Brennan pressed.

"Am I under arrest?" RG spoke in a clipped tone, his eyes fixed on the scratched wooden table top. If he demanded a lawyer this far in, they'd assume he was guilty. He had to sweat it out.

"Not yet." Brennan smirked.

"Not until we confirm the preliminary evidence." Then Daniels' tone softened. "But you don't need to wait for that. This guy's your best friend. Step up and take responsibility. Don't you owe him as much?" Daniels brought his chair around the desk beside RG and leaned forward facing him. "And you need closure on this, it must be eating you up inside. Talk to me."

RG let the ticking wall clock speak for him.

"How did it happen?" Daniels leaned back, folding his arms.

"How would I know?"

"Because you were there." Brennan pulled out his last piece of licorice, resting it on the table.

RG's jaw clenched and a vein in his temple began to throb. "When I left, Johnny was doing dishes."

Brennan changed his tack. "Was Johnny investing money for you?"

"Isn't that what friend's do? Help each other?"

"According to these financials," Daniels held up a stack of papers, "he wasn't helping you much."

Brennan stood and took a gulp of coffee as he circled the room. "Two things cause people to kill someone the way your 'Johnny' ended up. Love or money. You say Johnny wasn't your type." Brennan gave a quick wink to his partner. "So we're left with the money. Ten thousand dollars wasn't it?"

RG shrugged his shoulders. "Yeah, so what?

"Lotta money." Daniels shook his head. "Losing ten thousand would make a lot of people angry."

"Especially if they were already angry," Brennan added.

"Listen, I asked Johnny to invest the money into a risky venture. He advised against it, but I insisted." He scowled, his fists clenching underneath the table. "Can't fault a guy for following orders."

After a pause, Brennan spoke. "Do you know how many interviews I've done in my career, Mr. Granville?"

"You mean job interviews? I'm sure you've done a lot of those," RG snapped, glaring at Brennan. *Brilliant, RG, way to piss off the guy with the gun, handcuffs, and keys to the jail!*

Brennan smiled, eyeing Daniels. "Looks like our frat boy's a bit of a wiseass. Mr. Granville, I get to meet all sorts of people parked in that chair you're in." Brennan lowered his coffee, his stare boring into him like a laser. "Guilty, innocent...doesn't matter. Most think they're pretty smart, smarter than us dumb cops. Funny thing, though. I get a sense about people, and I'm never wrong."

RG locked onto Brennan's dead black eyes. In that instant, he read the man's intent as clearly as if he'd written it on the wall. Brennan had made up his mind, like a predator with his sights set on his prey, and RG was in a world of trouble.

"This interview's over." RG jumped to his feet, his chair skittering across the tiled floor. "I'm aware of my rights. Unless you're arresting me, I'm outta here. I'm requesting consultation with a lawyer before I say another word."

Brennan stood and hitched up his belt, addressing his partner. "Well, well, well. The smart guy lawyered up. Oh, you're free to go, but not too far. We're impounding your vehicle to check for biological material. May take a few days." As he left the interview room, he glanced over his shoulder. "Have a nice trip back to Boston."

RG collected his things and stormed out of the room, a cold sweat flashing across his body as it dawned on him he'd been promoted to 'official' suspect in his best friend's death.

Brennan called to him down the hall. "Oh, and you can bet we'll be in touch."

RG threw open the Falmouth Police Department's confining doors and let loose a profanity-laced diatribe, his muscles tense and vibrating like electric eels. The passersby on Main Street averted their gaze, quickening their pace to get a comfortable distance away from the menace. He paused halfway down the steps to the sidewalk, peering out along the street for a bus stop, train, rocket ship, anything to get him home. *Impounding my car...bullshit!* A costly cab or Uber ride could wait, right now he had to move his legs and clear the festering thoughts from his head.

Tromping down the steps, RG strode directly across Main, car horns and screeching tires registering only a vague rumble in his ears as his mind drifted to Walt and the thin line between the world of a free man and a prisoner. He now found himself caught up in something out of his control, with the outcome uncertain. Just when he'd built the confidence to step into the batter's box and face the supernatural threats before him, the earthly players had thrown him a curveball. And on top of everything, Johnny D was still dead and always would be.

He trudged along Falmouth Heights Road past the harbor, a walking pressure cooker, boiling blood flushing his skin a crimson hue, a steam cloud simmering in a halo around his body. He passed the Island Queen ferry boarding area and several sun-blistered motels and inns closed for the off-season. The harbor's beauty, along with its varied array of floating fortresses resting on the blue-green water, opened the pressure release valve inside him as an inner calm surfaced. Within minutes, the cold air pressing on his skin brought a shiver.

After a short trek through the labyrinthine side streets, journeying on auto pilot, he found himself on Crescent Avenue, overlooking an expansive park by Falmouth Heights Beach. On a cold, sunless December day, its vast emptiness brought with it a vague melancholy, like an amusement park ride closed for repairs or a local Mom and Pop going out of business. Winter ran off the playful activity of children holding hands, kites climbing the pastel blue sky, teens lounging in summer clover, or parents pushing their children in strollers. He closed his eyes, his mind taking him to a bright July afternoon, beholding everything before him that wasn't, all against the Atlantic Ocean's spectacular brilliant blue backdrop.

"It didn't go too well today?" Morrow's voice cooled the sting the interrogation had left. They stood beside each other, observing the park in its winter drabness, neither formally acknowledging the other.

"You're a master of understatement. I'm gonna need a good lawyer. I'll probably be losing my job…oh, and I don't have a ride back to Boston."

Morrow grinned. "Let's walk down to the water." Both men struggled against a steady headwind through the deserted park, Morrow holding his hand against his hat to avoid losing it to the buffeting breeze.

When they reached Grand Avenue on the park's opposite side, RG and Morrow crossed over to the boardwalk and seated themselves on a bench facing the Atlantic. The fierce cold wind mounted its assault, but the ocean quelled the mixture of anxiety, grief, and frustration brewing within him, reprising its role as elixir for whatever ailed him. His racing mind slowed to a stop as he stared out over the choppy surf.

"Johnny D's dead."

"I'm sorry." Morrow placed a comforting hand on RG's shoulder.

"It's Victor. He's making his way through my friends until he gets to Kacey and me."

Morrow nodded, lowering his head.

"Jesus, Morrow, can I at least get a reaction from you?"

Morrow flinched. "Pardon?"

RG glared at Morrow with a stunned expression. "I mean, my

friend Walt's attacked and you dismiss it. Now my best friend's dead, a killer is stalking us, and you have nothing to say! What the hell kind of caretaker are you? And what good is a caretaker who can't take care of anybody?"

"I'm not a genie in a bottle, and I'm not just anyone's caretaker, I'm yours. I don't have the power to protect others from their fate."

"Their fate? You've brought this upon them coming here. You're responsible for everything. If I died like I should have, all this would be over, but now people I love are getting hurt and dying, and God knows how many more will follow. Because of you! Now what are you gonna do about it!"

"There's nothing I can do—"

"And why is it Victor can be everywhere, know everything, but you can't?" RG interrupted, continuing his rant. "What, you finish last in your class in caretaker school?"

Morrow stood from the bench. "I'm tired of your petty insults. You treat me as if you want me to leave and never return."

RG hopped to his feet, pivoting to face Morrow. "What would it matter, I'm not getting any help anyway."

"Help? Right now, he can't get to you…because of me."

"I'm the one digging into Victor's past, trying to find his weaknesses. What have you found?"

"I can't get in. Victor doesn't give me access to his—"

"He's more powerful than you, isn't he?"

Morrow turned and stared out over the water.

"Isn't he? We're doing this little dance, training me to defend against him, but it's a charade, isn't it? It's David versus Goliath, it's Lake Placid, USA hockey vs Russia."

"Don't forget how those encounters turned out."

"Tell me the goddamn truth!"

"Okay, he's stronger than me! You want to hear me say it? He has the powers of the universe behind him and I don't, and he's undergoing a transformation that will make him even stronger." Morrow dropped back onto the bench, wiping the salt water spray from his glasses. "What do you want from me?"

RG placed his hands on his hips and stared at his shoes, then seated himself beside Morrow with a groan, the wind off the ocean picking up again. "I guess you've been keeping me alive for thirty-five years, you must be doing something right." He poked Morrow in the ribs with his elbow. "I'm sorry, I'm just frustrated, that's all."

Morrow placed a hand on RG's arm and gave it a squeeze. An overwhelming fatigue settled over the caretaker's eyes.

"I need your help, and Kacey does, too. She's ready to meet you."

"And I her."

"Can you teach her what you have been teaching me; help us create a dual force against Victor?" RG had no illusions how dangerous this mission would be, but he'd acquiesced to Kacey's wishes. He would give her a chance, but if he had to, he'd step in before it was too late.

"She possesses her own power, but I can teach her how to harness it." Morrow stuffed his hands into his pockets. "Tell her to dream about her favorite place tonight. I'll find her."

With his eyes closed against the biting breeze, RG sifted frigid, salty air through his frozen nose, unaware he'd missed Morrow's departure. Typical Morrow. He should have expected as much by now. On his feet, he strolled a distance down the lonely beach, just he and Jack Frost, miles from home.

Brennan lumbered from the interview room to his cramped, glassed-in office adjacent to the main entrance. He shut the door and dropped into his broken, un-reclining desk chair, staring absently around the room, a space he expected to be much larger and more comfortable at this stage in his career. The framed plaques and citations adorning his office walls defined a lifetime of achievements, but they meant little with respect to his thirty years on the job. His prized photos showed him mingling with the rich and famous, mere strangers in pointless photo-ops. He did value his framed picture of then-governor Mitt Romney, posed like long lost friends, both on the verge of cracking up at what might have been a lame joke. But the joke was on Brennan. A hundred other police officers also had the nerve to share the same prestigious Kodak moment on a hundred other office walls.

His examination continued down the wall: his famous poses with various wealthy Cape Cod businessmen, Brennan in his Chief's uniform—advertising his $67,500 annual salary—as he brushed elbows with multi-millionaire software developers and entertainment moguls in their Hawaiian shirts, sandals, and trophy wives.

Still, a gotcha moment surged through him as he tossed the manila folder from Granville's interview onto his desk. He had him, and Granville knew it. Brennan would wipe that wiseass look from the pompous professor's face. He rarely made himself promises, but this one had a special status.

The fingerprint evidence from BCI would confirm only two sets of prints on the murder weapon, the killer and the victim, and Granville's own words confirmed he'd handled the knife. The more Brennan studied the evidence, the more his game plan gelled into a solid case. Granville had placed his head into the noose, but Brennan would need one more item to pull the trap door's lever. He snatched the phone from its cradle and dialed Daniels.

"What's up Chief?"

"Chris, I need the Delvecchio evidence. Can you help me out? I'm taking it on a little trip up to BCI. Make sure to pack all biological samples in dry ice."

"Didn't think that was in your job description. I'm free to run it up there… or better yet, how about Smith or Gonzales? They need a new trick once in a while."

Brennan shifted in his chair. "What? And risk Gonzales leaving the evidence on a barstool in Wareham like he did last year. No fucking way. Besides, I could use a little change in scenery."

"Couldn't we all…"

Brennan softened. "I also need to talk to the CIOs over there about Detective Stahl's performance at the scene."

"Sir? Stahl has a pretty good reputation, he's a top notch—"

"He was a friend of both the suspect and victim," Brennan interrupted, "and to avoid compromising the investigation, I must follow proper procedure."

"Your call. I'm on it."

Twenty minutes later, Daniels whizzed into his office with the requested material, packaged as if a NASA team had been in charge. Brennan closed the door and sat down at his desk.

He had Granville dead to rights, but DNA evidence would solidify the case and convict the bastard. With *CSI* and *Law and Order* shows galore prompting jury members' sophistication and expectations, DNA earned its place as the main code word for conviction. For a professor, the amateur killer lacked basic common sense. Or did he? Granville had to have been covered in blood, but the ocean across the street from the crime scene might have been just the kind of problem solver he'd used.

If Delvecchio's DNA wasn't in Granville's car already, it would be by day's end.

Brennan took out his pocketknife and cut carefully across the seam tape holding the Styrofoam box closed. He opened the lid and reached through the dry ice's frosty air. Inside, several small storage units with multiple rows of plastic cuvettes containing Johnny D's serum, saliva, and whole blood. Brennan checked to make sure the ID number on the paperwork matched the ID on the blood sample. He took one of the cuvettes and placed it in his pocket where it thawed over the next several minutes. With Granville's car impounded, it would only take a few blood droplets sprinkled on the carpet or steering wheel.

Case closed.

Brennan smiled to himself. It's not like he hadn't done this type of thing before.

Later in the day when the station quieted down, Brennan entered the motor pool and searched for the white Subaru Legacy registered to Robert Granville.

～

RG plodded back from the Heights, Matty's office situated at least a half mile away on the other side of the harbor. He buried his hands deep into his pockets and kept moving, his eyes watering and cheeks beet red from the biting wind. When he finally arrived, Matty stood on the dock, loading up a small boat with supplies.

Matty glanced at his watch. "I'm guessing you weren't in and out in twenty minutes."

RG collapsed on a creaky wooden bench. "Brennan impounded my vehicle. They're looking for blood."

"That sonofabitch," Matty scowled, tossing a coil of rope onto the boat's deck and jamming his hands against his hips. "How could they think you had anything to do with it?"

"They don't know me like you do, Matty." The seagulls' distant cry overhead punctuated the silence between them.

"What happens now?"

"I wait for the evidence to come back and see if they're gonna arrest me," he said flatly.

The two men stared off in different directions as water lapped against the dock pilings. He could read in Matty's sagging eyes the dawning awareness that another friend was in a world of shit.

"Don't suppose you can give me a lift up to Kingston?" RG checked the time on his cell.

"Too many mooring inspections today. Here, catch." He threw RG his keys. "Just park it and leave them under the front wheel bumper. Livy and I will pick it up later."

RG gave him a hug. "Thanks, brother."

"Ain't nothing. Give Kacey my best." Matty stepped into the boat and pulled away from the dock. "It's gonna be all right," he said, his voice wavering. "You'll see."

He gave Matty a wave, crossed the parking lot, and hopped into his friend's GMC tank. His feet barely reached the pedals, but he managed to floor it all the way to the Kingston MBTA station, making the 5:02 to Boston with seconds to spare. At South Station, he took the Framingham/Worcester line to West Newton, where Kacey stood waiting for him on the darkened platform. She buried herself in his embrace, her eyes communicating the unspoken understanding that he might be moving into a jail cell, now the prime suspect in his best friend's death.

～

After dinner, Kacey snuggled underneath the designer sheets and feather-down comforter, retiring early, eager to meet Morrow in her dream, but the anticipation backfired. She tossed and turned, wide awake, oblivious to her final resistance. She slipped through the tenuous boundary of consciousness into a dream lying dormant since childhood, back to the Pancake Man, the restaurant alive with a welcomed familiarity and nostalgia. But a visual crispness accompanied this visit, a feeling of presence she'd never experienced before replacing the dreamlike quality of her childhood visions.

The dream sequence required Kacey to meet Mr. Morrow outside the restaurant. Reluctantly, she maneuvered toward the front door, her hand extended toward the door handle. A little girl stood beside her, shaking her head with wide eyes, mouthing the word 'no.' Kacey's heart fluttered in her throat as she grasped the handle, fearful she'd once again feel secret arms tug at her midsection and be forever lost in the brilliant whiteness. Fighting her instincts, she jerked the door open and slipped into a blinding white flash. Her hand released the door as the white shield engulfed her in a stark, swirling vortex until a calm and comfortable presence greeted her, guiding her through the nothingness.

"You must be Mr. Morrow," Kacey turned to the man twice witnessed in previous dreams.

"I am." Morrow doffed his hat. His suit conjured 1960's Savile Row, dark with thin lapels and a narrow tie dangling from a pearl-white shirt. Morrow placed his arm in the crook of her elbow as they walked through the brilliant white.

"You know, RG and I think you have an uncanny resemblance to the guy in *North by Northwest*."

"Cary Grant?"

"Uh, not exactly."

Morrow straightened his tie. "James Mason, then?"

Kacey tilted her head and studied his features. "Actually, the old CIA guy…can't remember his name."

"Ah, 'the Professor.' Hmm, well that's disappointing," Morrow chuckled and patted Kacey's hand. "Speaking of films, you must tell Robert I have identified who Yoda is."

Kacey couldn't stifle her amusement at whatever banter had prompted this discovery. "I will, I promise." Kacey gazed from left to right. "Where are we?"

"It's where I live. I'm sorry you can't see anything, but you will someday. You'll see how beautiful it is. You've chosen an interesting portal for entry into my world. It must be special to you."

Kacey melted into her childhood memories of the Pancake Man, the Sunday drives, the silver dollar pancakes. She'd preserved it exactly as she remembered, unchanging, the place representing the unspoiled past one longs to revisit. "I used to dream about the restaurant all the time as a girl. I was nervous leaving there tonight. You see, I tried to leave once years ago, but I got scared. I couldn't let go of the door handle."

"You weren't ready to come here. You see, as a child, you came to the portal solely in your mind. Back then, you couldn't leave the restaurant because you weren't strong enough to pass the mind through the portal while leaving the body behind. But now your growing powers allow transport of both body *and* mind."

"That's why it seems different."

"Now, if you choose to, you can fully pass into different planes, and not just this one."

"So, this isn't a dream or a vision like before?"

"Not anymore, it's the real thing."

Kacey glanced around her, the brilliant white world she traversed had taken on a three-dimensional appearance, like a shimmering mirage acting as a barrier, masking the shapes hidden behind it.

"Why was I chosen for this, to see things, the dreams and visions?"

"I can't say. I didn't have the caretaker abilities you have until I transitioned into this world. You're part of the next wave of caretakers, one developing earlier to face greater challenges. Jumpers are evolving and becoming more powerful, so caretakers must do the same."

"Jumpers like the burning man?"

Morrow nodded. As he answered Kacey's questions about life and death, caretakers and jumpers, and multiple worlds, a leak flowed from the corner of his mind, his deepest thoughts spilling into Kacey's consciousness.

"Is something wrong?" Morrow asked.

She'd caught a fleeting glimpse into his previous life, but she pulled away, uncomfortable violating his privacy. "I'm okay."

He'd had a family.

He directed her to a small bench. Kacey seated herself and glanced at Morrow, a peaceful radiance spreading across his features.

"You seem happy here. What do you see?" she asked.

Morrow grinned. "Very perceptive powers. This spot's my piece of heaven and exactly the way Robert feels when he's studying the ocean's swell." His eyes scanned a wide arc from left to right.

"Can I see?"

"Would you like to?"

Morrow waved his hand in front of Kacey's eyes and a world burgeoning with colors and textures opened before her, the mirage lifting and the hidden revealed. They'd been walking in a wooded area, through a small copse of trees high above a lush valley, the over-hanging branches and vines more vivid and dimensional than those on earth. The vibrant detail of every shadowed indentation in every tree trunk and branch, every vein in every leaf, exploded through her nascent visual field in indescribable color. Kacey's hand crept to her open mouth, unaware she'd risen from the bench. The green she expected in the leaves' canopy above appeared as something not quite green, a color unknown to her, but unmistakable in its faultlessness. The same held true for the fertile valley's hue before her, delivered to her eyes as nature meant it to be.

An unfathomable longing followed Kacey's sensory rebirth. She'd be *here* someday, after she'd fulfilled her present role. She'd somehow found a way to this existential plane, a world unknown to billions of her earthly neighbors living in the dark. Kacey immediately understood the experience of standing alone on Everest or the moon, being the first, the only one, the sole Powerball winner. This world would be her ultimate destiny, a place unparalleled in its beauty. And her role would be a caretaker, traveling among different realms to protect the living. The cosmic role bestowed upon her left her humbled, and her long-standing fear of the powers inside her immediately took wing, a weight hoisted from her shoulders. She'd embrace them, and now Morrow would help harness them. The emotional wave took away her breath, and she slowly dropped onto the bench next to Morrow, a tear spilling down her cheek.

He waved his hand in front of Kacey and the world resumed its vivid whiteness. "I'm sorry, Kacey. This may have been too much for you."

"Those weren't tears of sadness." Kacey's voice faltered as she spoke.

Another tear bloomed in Kacey's eye and Morrow gently wiped it with his handkerchief. "It's wondrous what the future holds for you."

"We live such black and white lives compared to yours."

"There are other worlds even more radiant. And someday you'll see them all."

"I want to, but not yet." Kacey stood and rested her hands on her hips, her voice strong and clear. "Look, I want to finish what I have to do in my world, to raise my child with my husband beside me. I'm here to find out how we stop the burning man."

"Are you ready?"

Kacey locked eyes with Morrow. "You're damn right I am."

"Then let's get started."

CHAPTER THIRTEEN

onday, December 11, 2017

RG threw on his jacket and killed the lights as he left the office, striding toward the fourth-floor exit. He pumped the elevator button, a ceremony, real or imagined, that somehow always seemed to hasten its arrival. His magic finger didn't end up saving him much time, the elevator shuddering to a squealing stop at every floor below. Once outside, he bolted across the street to the parking garage. As he trudged up the steps to the second level, the taillights of Wendell Abernathy's gaudy Dodge Viper flashed to his left, backing out of his reserved space. Another perk of being his father's son.

"Sonofabitch," he muttered.

Abernathy's car burst around the corner of the traffic barrier, tires squealing. RG blinked to clear his eyes, straining to identify the silhouette in the passenger seat. When the car sped around the bend, a light exposed none other than Brittany Thorne.

I'll be damned!

Revitalized, RG sprinted to his rented Ford Fusion. If he could land a paparazzi-style photograph of the two, his problems would be over.

Poking at the unfamiliar key fob, he struggled to unlock the door, losing valuable seconds. *Goddamn rental car shit!* Sliding into the driver's seat, RG jammed the keys home. Engine purring, he slid the gear into reverse only to freeze at the warning blare from the car coming up behind him.

The driver stopped behind RG's car, mouthing the word "Asshole!"

"Get the fuck out of my way!" Looking up, he'd completely lost site of the Viper. Swerving around Mr. Asshole, purposely creeping along like a snail lost in a swamp, RG crushed the accelerator and zipped into the exit lane moments before clipping a steel support column.

He hit the gas as his wheels straightened on Commonwealth Avenue, but came to an immediate crawl behind lanes of traffic funneling through the city's narrow corridors. He couldn't see Abernathy's Viper anywhere through the sea of flashing red brake lights. *It's fucking hopeless! Where the hell did he go?*

Shimmying his body up against the car seat, RG practically stood inside the cramped Fusion angling for a better view. As he scanned the gridlock, the Viper shifted lanes ahead. *I got you, you sonofabitch!* RG made an aggressive lane change to a chorus of honks and finger pointing, but the move paid off. He fell in a few car lengths behind.

RG had watched enough cop shows to learn you didn't camp right behind the car you tailed, but moved into different lanes to avoid detection. When a change in lane speeds positioned him directly beside the Viper on the right, a grin played on his lips, nothing separating him from Brittany but a glass window. One quick photo and he'd have his evidence, the two of them together miles from campus. RG's pulse ratcheted upward as he rooted into his back pocket for his cell, pulling it out and fumbling it onto the floor, his fingertips barely able to tickle the corner resting in the space between the pedals.

Pawing at the floor mat with his shoe tips, he kicked the device backward to an eager hand. In one smooth motion, he raised the cell and snapped a photo through the side window, capturing the crisp image of a basset hound in a beat-up Ford F-150. Abernathy's lane had picked up speed, the Viper hopelessly out of reach several car lengths ahead.

Shit!

After thirty minutes traveling north on I-93, RG exited the freeway in Andover and followed Abernathy through the winding suburbs until he came to Harrison Falls, a community consisting of the latest starter mansions for the upwardly mobile. A twitch flared across his cheek as he considered how much Wendell must be pulling down in his administrative position. Focused on the Viper, he only caught glimpses of the exquisite stone facades and Hogwarts-like archways and thatched roofs. After several turns down regally named side streets, Abernathy pulled up to his mini-mansion.

RG parked several houses down and shut off his headlights as the two strolled arm in arm along the short walkway and into the house. A light flickered in the first window next to the front door. He waited while an older couple strode briskly past the car, a pair of his-and-her shiatzus leading the way. He eased out and trekked across two spacious lawns separating him from Abernathy's home.

Skulking across Abernathy's property, RG eyed the lighted window, hoping neighbors had better things to do than notice him. He took a quick perimeter scan for unwanted eyes and found none, recharging his nerves. He tiptoed around well-tended shrubs and flowers only to slice himself on the spiky firethorn bush under the lighted window, the well-to-do's official 'guard shrub.'

Throwing a hand to his mouth, the bitter taste of blood hit his tongue. He peered through the glass into the lighted living room to observe Abernathy hovering over Brittany. Her body reclined like Cleopatra against the sofa, but a shadow from a floor lamp blocked her face. Abernathy extended a glass of wine which she accepted. He drooled at the thought of one good photo, just one. *Come on, turn around, show me your faces!*

As he pressed his nose to the glass for a better look, Abernathy raised his head and stared straight at him through the window, forcing him to duck out of sight back into the firethorn's wrath. *Fuck me!* Bleeding from a new assortment of lacerations, RG raised his head above the sill. Abernathy still fixed him with an unwavering stare. He ducked again but stopped, remembering his physics, how reflected light turns windows into one-way glass at night. *Sonofabitch isn't looking at me, he's marveling at his own reflection!*

Then Abernathy threw himself on Brittany, kissing her and running his eager hands over her body. *No, no, don't do this in front of me!* RG turned his head from the unwatchable. Not willing to let nausea get in the way of his Kodak moment, he turned back reluctantly. Poor Brittany. He had a twinge of sympathy for her, recalling Abernathy's stale breath from his encounters with him. How could she kiss a fire-breathing mauler? Nausea thrust back into his throat.

After several stomach-turning minutes, Brittany ran her fingers through her hair and straightened her shirt, but still didn't offer a clear line for a photo shoot. He needed both subjects in the best identifiable pose he could garner. *Come on, you two disgusting lovebirds. This way, just a little to the left Abernathy.* As if they'd heard him, Abernathy and Brittany turned and stood side-by-side, sipping their red wine.

RG pressed the phone to the window to snap his picture, subduing a cheer rising in his throat. *Yes, finally!* But he hadn't counted on the darkness triggering the automatic flash, light exploding through the glass, igniting the room like a lightning bolt.

Uh-oh. Not cool, RG.

Immediately, the lovebirds turned and stared in RG's direction. Brittany pointed to the window in an animated fashion. RG scrolled through his camera roll only to find a photo of whitewashed glass staring back at him. *Fuck!* He could sense their agitation through the window and figured he'd blown his cover. Abandoning subtlety, he marched to the front door and burst through it, breezing through the foyer and confronting the two surprised living room occupants.

"What the hell are you doing here?" Abernathy shouted, bolting to his feet and hastily smoothing his rumpled shirt. "Get out of my house."

Like a gunslinger, RG drew his iPhone and snapped a picture of Abernathy beside Brittany Thorne, his shirt untucked, frozen like a deer in headlights. Brittany had her hand on his arm, her disheveled blouse unbuttoned, the hair of a woman caught in a hurricane. As he examined the condemning photo, Abernathy stepped toward him and threw a haymaker, mashing his nose and pushing it to the other side of his face. RG collapsed to his knees, his eyes watering instantly, a burning sting traveling to the back of his brain. He raised his hands to his shattered beak, his cell phone skittering across the floor.

"Was that your best shot?" His head vibrated as blood jetted onto the hardwood floor. "You're finished. I have all the evidence I need." RG encountered a second wave of nausea, wondering whether the sight of blood pouring from his misshapen snout had brought it on, but he snickered at Abernathy, not about to appear weak.

"Brittany, don't just stand there. Grab his phone and delete that damn picture!" Abernathy shouted.

Brittany moved toward the phone and picked it up. RG stood and reached for Brittany's arm. As he gazed into her eyes, another blow rang the side of his head, Abernathy landing another loaded right. The crushing smack to his cheek twirled him around. *Holy shit, guy has a fucking cannon attached to his shoulder! Maybe he really was working out at the gym.*

For most there would have been no shame in staying down after absorbing two of his sledgehammers, but RG grew up in Revere and once considered himself a pretty tough sonofabitch. As Abernathy stepped in for another shot, he sidestepped the blow, pivoted to his left, and crunched him with a left-right combination dropping Abernathy to the hardwood with a thud.

"You've assaulted me, Granville, and I have a witness." Abernathy lay in a heap on the floor, massaging his bloody mouth. "I could have you arrested…harassment, trespassing, assault—"

"But you hit him first, Wendell," Brittany cried.

"What about that goddamn photo?" Abernathy twisted to his feet and sank his banged-up body against the couch.

RG turned to rescue his phone, but Brittany snatched it. Maneuvering away from him, she held her back towards him as she cupped the device in her hands, pressing and poking at it. "Needs a friggin' password."

"Brittany, give it up. It's over." He wrestled with her and pried the phone from her grip. "Do you really want to be one of those students who uses her body instead of her brains? Is that how little you respect yourself? Letting bastards like Abernathy take advantage of you?"

The waterworks in poor Brittany's eyes threatened to erupt. She stared at the monster in the room—Abernathy—then back at RG, wavering back and forth as if the floor were on fire. "You don't know a damn thing about me or about my life. What gives you the right? Maybe if you'd paid a little more attention to me, or if you'd picked up your own damn phone once in a while instead of your wife, things might be different."

"Is that what this is about? You want to pay me back for some delusional fantasy? You're better than that, Brittany. You have so much going for you, more than you give yourself credit for."

The tears shot forth with no end in sight. RG wanted to comfort her, but that's the last thing he needed. "My life is over if I don't get back into school." She whimpered and turned to Abernathy. "You promised me, you fuck! You said if I went along with the sexual harassment and…let you do what you wanted to me, you'd take care of everything. What a bunch of…"

RG glared with disgust at Abernathy. "It's over, Wendell. All of it." He had to squeeze his bloody palms into fists and hold them stiffly at his sides before he tore him to shreds and they had a real excuse to charge him with homicide. "Fucking withdraw the complaint now, or you'll wish you had a pot to piss in when I finish with you."

Brittany gazed at RG, crying softly now. "I'm sorry, Dr. Granville. I'm sorry about all this. It was his idea, not mine."

"I know, Brittany. The guy's a predator, it wasn't your fault. He found someone vulnerable to take advantage of. You aren't the first, but I'll make damn sure you're the last!"

She sniffled and reached into her purse for a tissue to wipe her mascara-smudged eyes and runny nose. She marched over to Abernathy still cowering against the couch, nursing his wound with a handkerchief.

Who fucking carries around a handkerchief anymore?

"The deal is off!" Brittany clenched her purse off the sofa and marched out the front door, slamming it hard enough to give Wendell one last punch in the gut. *That a girl!*

RG sidled over to the bruised man with deliberate steps. He leaned over to deliver one last message. "Sack of shit! You're finished. Your career just ran out of second chances."

He held up his phone and displayed the incriminating picture, then played the voice memo he'd activated to record the entire dramatic scene, a scene scripted better than a Hollywood screenplay. No Oscar award for this one, but maybe it deserved a token recognition.

"I think Brittany may be ready to file a different complaint by the end of the week. Knowing her, she's gonna talk—to your bosses, to the newspapers, to anybody who'll listen." RG gave Abernathy a wink and walked out the front door. "See you at your dismissal hearing."

Victor reclined on Abernathy's living room couch, impressed by Granville's ability to wangle his way out of a jam. He'd been following him, far enough away to avoid Morrow's detection, but close enough to watch the action, peek into his head from time to time. Granville left, confident he'd solved a problem tonight, but he'd soon learn how much worse he'd made it. When Victor finished with the vile man, Granville's troubles would descend on him like a hard rain. Victor beamed as the pieces of his plan tumbled into place as if by divine intervention.

Granville had sensed him tonight, the man's physical reactions a dead giveaway. Morrow had been working with him, teaching him to discern his presence, but the man wasn't tuned in yet, his development still raw. Granville attributed his nausea bouts to the amorous advances of a middle-aged man on a younger woman and then on the sight of his own blood, but he mistook the visceral for physical, instead of the intangible he'd been training for. Victor laughed to himself, like it mattered if Granville could sense him, anticipate his arrival. What could he possibly do about it?

After Granville departed, Victor entered the vile man as he stood by his living room window, gazing out into the night. He donned him like a wetsuit, straining the man's skin to accommodate his form. In an instant, Victor had familiarized himself with this latest living apparatus, like jumping into a borrowed car, hijacking every living system, sending flurries of scorching hot impulses careening along every nerve axon. Abernathy scurried away from the oppressive energy spreading throughout his body, but he found nowhere to hide.

Tapping into his mind, Victor stumbled upon a lifetime of pain and suffering, a little boy still very much alive in his adult costume. He joined twelve-year-old Wendell as he raced his bicycle through the winding Cambridge streets, the boy hugging the clay sculpture he'd made in school for his father's birthday. They arrived sweaty and out of breath at the ivy covered building and knocked on his father's magnificent office door.

"Come in," Alistair grumbled.

"Hi, Dad!" Wendell burst with excitement, shielding the birthday present behind him, a secret grin playing on his lips. He stared wide-eyed around the room at bookcases stuffed with thick hard-bound tomes and academic journals, and stacks of papers in piles on the Oriental rug blanketing the creaky hardwood floor.

A brand new oak desk had been delivered to Alistair's office, a piece exuding academic success and administrative power, its new owner eager to get situated behind it.

"What do you need?" Alistair snapped, placing his important papers in the pull-out drawers and arranging his desktop ornaments— lamp, blotter, pens, and calendar—in the proper position.

Wendell beamed at his father, the excitement on his face lighting the room. "Do you remember what day it is?"

"Son, I don't have time for this. Spit it out."

"Here you go, Dad. I made this for you." Wendell placed the sculpture on the desk, but as he moved the clay piece towards his father it scratched the polished oak desktop. Wendell's smile faded. He gazed up at his father. "Happy Birth—"

Alistair's open hand flashed across Wendell's face, and he cried out as he crumpled to the floor. Alistair inspected the gash, glaring at

Wendell, pulling his belt through the trouser loops. Victor could taste blood dripping from Wendell's nose to the corner of his mouth.

Alistair shook his head. "And this was a new belt," he mumbled, slapping it against his hand as he crept toward Wendell.

Victor fast-forwarded through Wendell's wretched childhood. After graduating top of his class at Harvard, Wendell earned his PhD and joined the Harvard faculty. Sometimes he would creep past his father's office and stare at the oak desk in the middle of the room. When Alistair lectured or attended a meeting, Wendell would take a razor blade and place a gash in the enormous desk, somewhere the old man wouldn't notice at first, but would discover eventually. Year after year, the scars accumulated, the beautiful oak desk becoming more and more unsightly, and the old man at a loss to explain it. Alistair introduced different items to the desk surface in an array of different patterns, but these attempts to hide the wounds only made the desk appear cluttered and disorganized.

Wendell snickered to himself every time he passed his father's office.

Victor drank with Wendell in the Harvard pubs and taverns, as he spent less time working and more time seducing the impressionable co-eds. With his academic career faltering, Wendell resorted to publishing questionable papers, exaggerating his conclusions, and finally falsifying research. Victor sat with Wendell in the inquiry hearings, Alistair himself spearheading the administrative process by which Harvard dismissed his son for research misconduct. They would never speak again.

But in the end, Wendell got the desk.

Victor wrestled with a fleeting pang of regret for what he must do, a brief moment of sympathy for a boy haunted by a monster under the bed, but the moment passed, his revulsion at the man fueling his wrath. He conjured what Wendell feared most, bringing it to life before him, intrigued the vile man would live his final moments in unbearable torment.

Wendell turned from the living room window and caught movement from the corner of his eye, a figure eyeing him from the sofa. His breath pulled from his body as he recognized his father as a young man, before the ravages of time had taken hold. He sported the brown wool slacks and tan sweater he donned in the evenings after work, the clothes he wore when he tortured Wendell. The silver watchband gleamed on his wrist, the metallic, twisty one that rattled with every violent belt swing. Wendell swooned at the sight of the man in his child beating outfit, a reminder of the daily terror his father would inflict.

The light dimmed in Wendell's eyes as the room transformed into the Cambridge brownstone's front parlor. Perched on an expanse of Persian carpet beside the grandfather clock, he gazed out the French window's wavy antique glass. He imagined the world outside his torture chamber, as he did every evening when his father came for him, beyond the panes to a place where fathers put their arms around their children's shoulders, tousled their hair, and built model airplanes with them.

A different world.

The Andover living room resumed in Wendell's vision as Alistair sprung from the couch and removed his belt, the silver watchband rattling. "It's time, son." Wendell's bladder let go, leaving an expanding puddle on the hardwood floor, a pungent odor wafting through the room.

"No, Daddy, please," Wendell begged as his father stepped toward him.

Alistair raised the belt in an arc above his head. Wendell's knees buckled and gave way, leaving him trembling on the floor in his own urine. The belt came down over and over in Wendell's mind, the watchband's metallic swish and the deadening memory of a thousand blows his father rained down on him accompanying it. Victor forced Wendell to raise his own hands to his throat and squeeze, constricting his windpipe. A much older Alistair Abernathy stood over him now, choking the life out of him, the watchband now hanging slack on the old man's spindly wrist.

"For all those gashes you carved into my beautiful oak desk," the old man roared at him, spittle flying from his mouth into Wendell's face.

It smelled like rotting earth.

As Wendell faded in and out of consciousness, he witnessed Alistair decompose in front of him, his face now a mask of black, rancid skin, his decaying body leaching an unmistakable formaldehyde odor mixed with aftershave. One of his eyes had been blanched white and the other missing from the ragged, empty eye socket. Wendell's hands throttled his own neck, compressing his own windpipe. Soon, the darkness crept in from his eyes' edges, his vision flickering on and off like a failing Christmas light, the movie reel in his brain slowing, the soundtrack winding down and finally stopping.

The show he'd been enjoying distracted him, and Victor nearly forgot to depart the vile host before it died, escaping at the last possible moment, a fatal mistake averted. Enraged at the near miscalculation, Victor initiated an explosion of internal heat, glowing flames bursting upwards to lick the ceiling, leaving blackened scorch marks on the walls and hardwood floors. Amidst his rage, he inspected the body on the hardwood floor. He'd done the man a service, giving his life greater meaning than he could've ever dreamed, his death representing a turning point in Victor's battle with Morrow, one changing the game in his favor.

RG returned home late and found Kacey in bed reading, the Kindle's soft glow bathing the shadowy room with light. He shuffled into the bedroom holding his shattered nose with one hand, ice cubes in the other, bloodstains spattering his blue button-down shirt and khaki pants.

Kacey snapped on the light. "Well," she said, taking in the scene before her, "how was your day?"

He shook his head as he detoured into the bathroom and ran the water.

"Correct me if I'm wrong, but this is the first broken nose you've gotten on the job, am I right?"

Trudging over to the bed, RG kicked off his shoes and teetered onto the cushy pillow-top mattress, arranging the scattered throw cushions to lean his weary head back. With labored effort, he pressed the washcloth bulging with frozen cubes against his tender nose, flinching as it touched bruised, swollen tissue. "One of the rougher faculty meetings we've had this year."

Kacey rose to her knees and leaned over, inspecting her husband's damaged face. "Here. Let me see. Does it hurt?"

"Like hell. With the crunches I heard, it has to be broken…it's like a balloon sitting on my face."

Kacey ran her hand over the prominent bump on the bridge of his nose. "It gives you that 'bad-ass professor' look. Students won't be arguing with you anymore about extra points."

"I'll have to get it reset in the morning. All I can do now is keep icing it." He repositioned the ice and described the evening's events, happening upon Abernathy and Brittany Thorne, the slow-speed chase, the compromising photo, and Abernathy's right hands to the face. He didn't fail to mention his combination punches dropping Abernathy to the floor.

Kacey glared into his blackening eyes. "Can you think of any better ways to improve your chances for promotion?"

RG considered the faculty serving on the promotion and tenure committee who regularly interacted with Wendell Abernathy. "Not really. This might've put me over the top." A grin crossed his lips as he leaned his head back, repositioning the washcloth.

"I think this picture says it all," Kacey stared at his phone.

"I've got audio, too." He cued up the voice memo recording.

Kacey's eyes widened as Brittany Thorne's voice filled the room. "You're home free! Nothing they can say will carry any weight now." Kacey leaned over and gave him a deep kiss. As she pulled back, she lost herself in his eyes for a moment. "You know, I can't help but feel for the poor girl. I'm proud of you being so encouraging to her after all the misery she'd caused you."

"I'm just too good to be true, aren't I?" Reaching his arms to Kacey in hope of more praise, he fumbled the bulging washcloth. "Damn!" He ran his wet hands across the bedding to coral the wayward ice cubes skating across the sheets.

Kacey maneuvered over to her side of the bed, propping herself against her pillows and headboard. "I've decided I'm going in."

"Going in where?"

"To peek into the burning man's thoughts, get a handle on what he's planning."

RG lowered the washcloth. "You've spent, what, a couple hours training with Morrow, now you're ready to face Victor?"

"I'm ready. Morrow convinced me to tap into the deeper powers."

"You mean, the stuff haunting you your whole life, the stuff you promised not to disturb?"

"It's different now. Morrow showed me a few things."

"He showed you a few…this is crazy!"

"So, what do you suggest? What's your brilliant plan?"

"I don't know, but you need more time to—"

"We're out of time!"

RG had struggled with his decision to place Kacey in danger, but he'd agreed with Morrow they needed her help. He couldn't compete with either of them when it came to their power, he had to give up the notion he had some control over this situation. They either sat on the sidelines waiting for Victor to call the plays, or they took it to him. The time had arrived to let go, let them do what he couldn't.

"Promise me one thing," he asked, leaning over and wrapping his arms around her.

"What's that?"

"You'll be careful."

"Of course." Kacey leaned over and gave him a kiss, then another. The ice cubes slipped into the bedding, but this time he didn't bother with them. "He'll never know I was there," she whispered between kisses.

Later, long after the lights had dimmed, a whisper tickled the back of his mind, repeating over and over. *But what if he does?*

CHAPTER FOURTEEN

Wednesday, December 13, 2017

For Kacey, she'd prefer hiking through nettles and bull thistles in her bare feet than dealing with the onslaught of demands the end of the school's second quarter dumped on her. Her duties ran the length of the school's soccer field, and then some, with parent-teacher conferences, student evaluations, committee meetings, curriculum review, and that didn't count teaching her regular classes. She hadn't completed her work until late Wednesday evening, cleaning up the classroom and removing the children's artwork from the walls.

RG, on the other hand, had skated through his end of semester. He'd finished teaching earlier in the week, his only remaining obligation to administer final exams on Friday, and he planned to recycle ones he'd written more than a year ago. *The sonofabitch and his cushy university job!* When she crawled into bed, she'd readied herself to shift gears and make an attempt at the burning man's thoughts, but once again, sleep did not come easily.

Her training with Morrow had been far more taxing mentally than physically, forced to confront her lifelong fear of the deep, hidden powers within. She'd suppressed her abilities for too long, fearing the use of a 'supernatural power,' denying the role she'd been intended to fulfill. Morrow, in his gentle manner, had been more therapist than trainer, teaching her to open her mind's door, welcome the unknown like an old friend, and not simply react to her power but to initiate and control it. Morrow helped her release her fear and embrace her innate skills to visualize the future, travel between worlds, and tap into the mind of others.

Morrow's training ushered in an acceptance her 'normal' life had ended. While she would take part in this world's earthly offerings while she lived, the 'something bigger' awaiting her here and in the next world pressed down like Boston's August humidity. But now as she embarked on her maiden voyage with her Morrow-honed skills, she recognized her ship would have to steam toward an iceberg named Victor. Not the best odds for success, or longevity.

Surrendering to unconsciousness, she entered sleep's swirling veil, like a surfer traveling a slow-rising wave, picking up speed as she dropped into the next world. In a growing light, Kacey found herself back at the Pancake Man getting ready to order breakfast. Much to her surprise, Mike Stahl strolled in and glanced around the restaurant. Spotting Kacey, he quickened his pace toward the table. The place buzzed with hungry diners and busy waitstaff, the faint smell of syrup permeating the room. In all their time together, Kacey and Mike had never eaten there, but this wouldn't be a social visit. Kacey understood she'd brought him here for a reason.

"Hey, Kacey." He slid one of the red-cushioned chairs away from the table and straddled it. "Wow! How long has it been since we had breakfast together?"

Kacey rewound the years like a wheel of ribbon gone wild, drawing it tightly and holding it together, those days too volatile and messy to ever let herself slip into that uncomfortable world again. His unkempt, bulky coffee-brown hair most men would die for hardly exhibited any evidence the man had aged a day since college, except for a random gray hair here and there. Where addictions tended to boost cellular degradation, she guessed his alcohol usage had worked more like the Fountain of Youth.

"Michael Francis Stahl, I'm glad you could join me."

"I didn't expect to run into you tonight. I must admit, it's a pleasant surprise."

Kacey turned to the menu. "You don't still soak your bacon and eggs with syrup, do you?"

Mike barked out a laugh. "Nah, I don't even eat bacon and eggs anymore," he said, clutching his chest in an exaggerated heart attack pantomime.

She chuckled at his performance, the man still able to make her laugh. "How about we order something? Since you're dreaming, I bet you can eat whatever you want—no calories or cholesterol to worry about."

"That does sound like a dream."

They ordered an artery-clogging breakfast and settled in to wait for it with a couple of steaming hot coffees. Kacey hadn't seen Mike as jovial and carefree since their days in college. Every time she'd run into him since then, a heaviness pressed between them, the weight of their history creating a palpable barrier to advancing beyond the past. *He thinks he's dreaming of me tonight. No wonder he's so happy.*

Stahl emptied two packets of sugar into his coffee. "Where are we? I feel like I've been here before."

"It's the Pancake Man in South Yarmouth. Everyone from the Cape has been here before."

He scanned the restaurant, his gaze falling on a young family in a booth near the kitchen. "Kinda looks like a young version of Bruce and Sandie, doesn't it?"

Kacey leaned over the table to pinpoint where Mike's gaze ended. An adorable girl about eight or nine fidgeted with her French braid and an overloaded plate of silver dollar pancakes. Kacey curled her fingers in a wave. "I'm not sure I see the resemblance."

As the food arrived, they sat in awkward silence, waitstaff unloading several large plates of pancakes, bacon, home fries, and eggs. Mike's table manners hadn't changed, wasting no time devouring a mountainous cheese omelet as Kacey stared in disbelief, as if his food might grow legs and run off the plate. A good thing they didn't have Facebook back then, or she'd have posted a few dandies.

"Same old Mike." Kacey blew the steam off her decaf before taking a sip. "You were usually finished eating by the time I'd placed my napkin on my lap."

"That's so I could sit and watch you and not get distracted by my food." He gulped another mini fried-potato mountain.

The weight of Mike's gaze settled on her from across the table.

"You don't mind if I stare, do you? I mean, it's a dream, right?"

Kacey leaned back from the table and folded her arms. "Isn't it time to move on, Mike? College is over, I've grown up and gotten married. Maybe it's time for you to grow up, too."

He finished chewing and leaned back in his chair. "Wow, why don't you tell me how you really feel?"

"It's time to get past this. Every time we're together the past sits with us like an eight-hundred-pound gorilla, pulling all the air from the room."

"It's not like I haven't tried, Kacey." He wiped his hands with a napkin as he searched for what to say. "Back when we were together, I had this feeling I belonged. I had a place here in this world…like being home." He pushed the remaining food around his plate with his fork. "I've spent the last fifteen years just trying to find my way home."

"You have to find a new address. You're driving past the wrong street."

Stahl dropped his eyes to the vinyl tablecloth, hard syrupy nodules embedded like braille on the material. "I know you've moved on, Kacey. It makes me wonder why some can fall in and out of love with different people and others have one shot at it."

"It doesn't work that way, Mike. We're wired to love, to connect with other people. You hold a piece of my life I'll never forget. I still think about you, what could've been, how my life might be different now. But we love people uniquely, and my love for RG isn't something I need to explain or justify. We blew it. Circumstances change."

"Well, my circumstances haven't. I'm still in Chatham, I'm still an alcoholic, and you're still every other thought that comes into my head." Stahl finished the bacon and eggs soaking in the syrup on his plate. "And I've got this gorilla following me around I can't seem to shake."

They sat in silence amidst the restaurant's bustle and commotion, each immersed in their own private universe. Kacey hadn't touched her food.

"Hey, this started off as a pretty good dream," he said. "What do you say we just enjoy the time we have together?"

"Good idea." She reached for her fork and dug in.

After breakfast, Kacey led Mike from the Pancake Man, the next world's brilliant white flooding the restaurant as they cracked the door, a swirling maelstrom drawing them from the waiting area, hoisting them off the ground. As Morrow had done for her, Kacey guided Stahl into the unfamiliar world, helping him find his feet. They continued through the desolate clarity until they reached the bench she and Morrow had shared.

Kacey reached for Mike and clutched his hand. "Listen, there's someone here I came to find. I think afterward you'll understand why I brought you here."

"Brought *me* here? What are you talking about?"

Kacey placed her finger to her lips. "Shhh! You can't make a sound or give us away. Just stay by my side. Is that clear?"

"This sounds more serious than a dream."

"If anything happens, wake yourself up, okay? It'll get you back home."

"You think I'm gonna leave you if something happens?" Stahl protested.

"You have to. Trust me."

Kacey could read in his eyes Mike didn't like his options, but he gritted his teeth and agreed. "Okay, it's just a dream."

"Close your eyes." Kacey ushered him into a deeper state of consciousness within her dream. Their bodies entered a swirling tunnel of light, their feet losing touch with the ground. Stahl's hand clutched hers in a vise grip. In moments, she found herself on solid footing inside a dark and humid, foul-smelling cave, not much more than a deep fissure hewn into a rocky cliff. Water trickled along the cave wall from the darkness above, running in rivulets beneath their feet, turning the cave floor's dirt and excrement into a fetid, muddy paste. The cave's damp, moldy smell reminded her of the descent into Kenmore Station, a palpable tension and fear alive within her.

She'd entered the burning man's lair.

Creeping across the cave floor, her fear and anticipation heightened, giving her mind clarity, but the weight of Victor's presence thrust itself upon her, countering any potential advantage. Victor had never fully ascended to the next world, living somewhere in between, paying an eternal price for his soul's confined vengeance and hatred. She peered at the man moving beside her, dismal and alone, his heart walled off from his world.

Maybe we all choose to live in varying degrees of hell.

Kacey froze. As Stahl turned to face her, she held a finger to her lips. Victor dozed on a tattered mat against the jagged cave wall. Closing her eyes, Kacey jumped into his mind, pushing against its doors until they swung open, allowing her access to rooms filled with his thoughts. Victor drifted in and out of a deep and restful sleep, exhausted from his work the previous day, enjoying the time of solace before the heat returned and the rage consumed him. Kacey pulled away from his mind and stared into his face, almost recognizing Victor Garrett's features through the burning man's opaque mask.

She closed her eyes again and went through the door, searching his mind as he dreamed. His thoughts replayed a crisp fall day as his nine-year-old boy prepared for his first fall soccer game. Sam joined the lines of rambunctious kids racing through their passing and shooting drills, Victor observing from a distance, amazed at how a child learns to navigate an uncertain world coming with few instructions. As the only extra player, Sam languished on the bench for most of the game, blowing into his hands and bracing himself against the churning wind.

Toward the game's end, the coach inserted Sam on the forward line. On the final rush of a tie game, the ball somehow squirted through a tangle of players onto Sam's foot. Without hesitation, he booted a shot past a diving goalkeeper and into the net to win the game. In an instant, his new teammates, and now his new friends, swarmed him, patting his back and rubbing his hair, a proud grin spreading across his face. In that sacred moment when Sam earned admission to a new world, he searched out his father and ran to him across the field. The memory soothed Victor's sleeping heart, but it also brought about a visceral ache.

Where are you Sam? Why can't I find you here?

A flash of fire coursed through the burning man's veins, the rage returning, the solace diminishing.

Time to burn again.

The burning man's thoughts shifted to his most recent activity in Kacey's world. He flashed a grin as he revisited his time with Walt Worthing, throwing him against the bars of his prison cell, basking in his suffering. The memories flew forward, like shuffling cards— Johnny D leaned over his kitchen sink, washing dishes, a force of energy driving him to the floor. Kacey stood beside him, a handful of half empty beer bottles still scattered on the kitchen table. She cringed and turned away as he picked up the serrated knife and slashed his neck.

On the floor, Johnny D lay in a blood pool spreading in all directions, running across Kacey's shoe tips. He lifted his wide and glassy eyes to meet hers. *"Kacey,"* he mouthed. No sound escaped his throat but the hiss of air from his tattered esophagus. His hand reached out to her. She wanted to comfort Johnny, hold him, but she couldn't engage the vision. She had to keep her emotions in check or she'd alert the burning man to her presence. She'd learned her lesson in Kenmore Square. She stood on the blood soaked floor in the burning man's mind as the light left Johnny's eyes, sensing his final thoughts.

Kacey disengaged from the burning man. She turned away in disgust, her whole body shaking. She fought to shield Victor from her emotions. Her rational mind told her to get out of there, to wake up, but she had more to learn.

She concentrated and focused again on his volatile thoughts. The fire raged inside him as he dreamed of his most recent cleansing, reveling in the vile man's killing. Sitting on the couch in Abernathy's living room, Kacey encountered an old man in brown slacks and a tan sweater watching his son. His head followed a slow arc as he turned to her.

One of his eyes was missing.

"Enjoying the show?" Alistair grinned as he rose from the couch and removed his belt. The watchband rattled as the ghastly old man, now long dead, beat his son with uncontrollable anger. The burning man grinned at the spectacle.

Snippets of the burning man's thoughts seeped from his mind, embedded themselves in Kacey's head. *They'll put Granville away soon for the murder of his valiant friend. The human scum, Brennan, will make sure the evidence points to him.* Victor marveled at the stroke of luck befalling him when RG confronted the vile man and the whore. *He placed the nail in his own coffin. With his blood on the floor next to the vile man, there's no doubt who they'll blame for my work.* Victor congratulated himself for his plan falling into place. *And when Granville's thrown into a cage with the other human vermin, then Morrow will understand what suffering means, every day.* Victor chortled, savoring the moment. *And just for fun, I'll have Granville kill his wife and son. It will be glorious.*

The fire exploded within Victor like a geyser.

Kacey recoiled, pulling herself from the hell of Victor's mind, her breath coming in waves. As black and white spots peppered her visual field, she reached out to Stahl, who steadied her.

Now she understood.

He wasn't going to kill RG, but set him up for murder, let the system take over, sending him to a place where nothing but violence and suffering awaited him. And he would use RG's pain to make Morrow suffer. Every day. For decades. With each assault, each beating at the hands of violent men, Victor would be there to smile at Morrow. To make Morrow remember his sin, his role in the boy's death.

Kacey recovered, but a fury brewed in her soul like none she could remember. *You sonofabitch! I'll find something in there to end you!*

She leapt back into Victor's mind, hijacking his thoughts, plundering his consciousness for anything she could use to her advantage. After kicking open every door to his thoughts, she crashed into a barrier, a locked, impenetrable door she couldn't access. She pounded and pulled but it wouldn't budge. Something powerful lay behind the door, something, she surmised, hidden even to himself.

As she stood there, tremors rippled through her body. Fear gripped the base of her neck and sent a chill deep inside. She shouldn't be here, a stunning secret lay behind the door, a truth Victor didn't want anyone to uncover. Kacey attempted to turn back, but in the swirling morass of Victor's mind, she lost her bearings, unable to find her way out. Horrific images flew at her—bodily invasions, sacrifices from different worlds, the deaths of children, families. So many. Losing her balance, she fell to his mind's floor, groping on her hands and knees for a way out. She glanced to her left at the gentle face of Morrow as a young man.

"Help me!" she whispered. In an instant, Morrow's battered body lay on the grass by the side of a busy roadway, his eyes open and head caved in, blood pouring from his ears and nose.

Kacey sensed a tickle growing in the back of Victor's mind, like a spider flitting across his thoughts. Awareness awakened inside him. She jerked herself from the grasp of his mind.

Victor sat bolt upright, his eyes darting about the dim cave.

Free from his head and once again back inside the foul cave, Kacey turned to Mike. "Go!" She shoved him from the dream as Victor's eyes locked onto her.

"Well, look who's back!" he snarled.

Now alone and vulnerable, Kacey's mind shut down, her fear impeding her logic, the confidence in her powers momentarily lost amidst her skittering thoughts rebounding inside her brain, failing to assemble themselves into a coherent plan. She reached out to Morrow with a desperate call moments before Victor entered her in a flash of heat and energy, throwing her against the cave wall.

Kacey's world faded to black.

CHAPTER FIFTEEN

Thursday, December 14, 2017

When RG awoke, the house exerted a throbbing stillness. He trotted downstairs to the kitchen, his starving dog padding about his empty food bowl. He seized the back door knob and shoved the door wide enough for Baron to bound into the yard and work off some steam while he replenished the mutt's food and water bowls. With an empty sink and coffeepot, he assumed Kacey had not completed her morning ritual. In the garage, her Outback rested on the garage floor in its space next to his. RG took the stairs two at a time on his way to the baby room, a special place she'd find any excuse to inhabit, but the room lay silent, undisturbed. Had she ventured out for an early morning walk?

I'm sure she'll be hungry when she gets back, I'll surprise her with a table full of food. Pulling out the griddle, he set about preparing a hearty breakfast buffet. It wasn't until he'd eaten most of the pancakes, eggs, and bacon, and finished reading the *Herald* that a sense of dread settled over him. It wasn't like her to go off and not tell him. He dialed her cell, its familiar ringtone squawking from the bedroom. She never left without her phone.

Grabbing his jacket and hat, RG attached a leash to Baron's collar, stepped through the front door, and jogged toward Centre Street. Kacey's daily stroll took her past BC's Newton Campus, so he back-tracked her usual route, hoping to catch her coming the other way. *Could I have missed her? No way.* After a half-hour trudging through the cold, he dialed her cell phone again, expecting she'd returned home and would pick up.

He still didn't receive her cheery greeting.

Jogging across Centre Street and back into the neighborhood, RG squinted to discern what looked like an unmarked police car in his driveway. He sprinted toward the house, his mind going a million miles an hour, trying not to imagine the worst. As he reached his driveway, two men in dark suits exited the car. Baron pulled hard against the leash, the men instinctively jumping back toward the safety of the vehicle.

"Easy boy," he coaxed Baron, giving his shoulders a rub.

"Are you Robert Granville?" one of the men asked.

Panic set it. "What's the matter?"

"I'm Detective Ray Harrington, my partner Paul Becker, Boston PD." With his stylish jet-black hair and five o'clock shadow, Harrington could have come straight from central casting. "Do you have a few minutes to talk?"

"Tell me Kacey's all right!"

Harrington tilted his head. "We're investigating the death of a Wendell Abernathy discovered in his home."

"Oh my God." RG's stomach dropped. "What happened?"

"Homicide. It appears the death occurred during a short window of time Monday evening."

"Can you tell us about your relationship with Mr. Abernathy?" Detective Becker asked. Becker, not the beneficiary of the genes his partner inherited, resembled a pug fighter in a B movie, short and stocky, with a face that may have gone a few rounds.

"He's a...he *was* a colleague."

"Would you mind if we talked inside?" Detective Harrington ran a hand across a square jaw.

RG ushered the men into the house and offered them seats in the living room, an array of interpretations flooding his mind about the conversation's layout.

Harrington rubbed his hands together. "Nice and warm in here."

Becker glanced out the living room window and gestured toward the driveway. "Car heater's busted."

"State budgets, huh?" RG shrugged.

Baron bristled at the strangers, a low, threatening growl rumbling from his throat.

"Come on, Baron. Let's leave these boys alone." He dragged Baron by the collar, countering his canine's braced paws against the tiled floor, and scooted him through the back door. Becker followed, keeping RG in eye's range, as if he would make a run for it or something. RG shut the door, more of a slam than a gentle push, wishing he could slam more than a door on this damn inquisition. He'd had his fill of questions from cops this week. *It has to be Victor's work.* He recalled the blood spatter on the front of his clothing. How much had he left on the hardwood floors? *Fuck me!*

"Sir, you asked if Kacey's okay. Who's Kacey?" Becker asked.

"Uh, she's my wife."

"She missing?" Harrington chimed in.

"I'm sure she's out for a walk. She should be back any minute." RG remained calm, hoping to avoid a new line of questioning. The detectives eyed each other, Harrington making notes in a thin spiral notebook.

"Figured you guys would be a bit more high-tech. What happened to those new digital e-notebooks our tax dollars went to?" *No car heater, paper notebooks, hopefully state budget cuts didn't affect the quality of detectives.*

"Mr. Granville, can you vouch for your whereabouts Monday evening?" Harrington asked.

"What part of the evening?"

Becker leaned forward. "All of it."

"Well, I worked late." *Here come the lies again. Why does it get easier?* "I headed into Boston to get some dinner, I don't remember what time—"

"Let's cut through the bullshit," Harrington interrupted, crossing one leg over the other, getting comfortable. "What time did you arrive at Abernathy's house?"

RG's face flushed. "What?" *Lying may come easier, but you still suck at it!*

The two detectives stared at him from across the coffee table.

Becker broke the silence. "What happened to your nose?" He gestured to his own.

"I got into a little fight."

"Who with?" Becker followed up.

RG sighed. "Wendell Abernathy."

Harrington and Becker exchanged glances.

"So, you had a fight? With the dead guy?"

"He wasn't dead at the time."

"You think it's a fucking joke?" Becker glared at him. "What were you doing at his house?"

You're getting into the bad habit of pissing off cops lately. RG exhaled. "Okay, I followed him home from work."

"You what?" Becker raised his eyebrows.

"So, you lied to us." Harrington shook his head.

"Look, he made accusations I'd had an improper relationship with a former student, when in fact, he'd been involved with her."

Where the hell are you, Kacey?

"So you followed him home?"

"To snap a photo of them together, that's all."

"Who's them?" Becker asked.

"He and Brittany Thorne, the student. I caught them driving out of the parking garage together and I followed them, on a whim. Thought I'd catch them in a restaurant or something, but they kept driving."

"You some kind of amateur detective, Mr. Granville?" Harrington continued to write.

"Or maybe a stalker?" Becker added.

"You just happened to decide you needed a picture of them on the evening he's killed?" Harrington asked.

"Well, I guess it worked out that way."

"And he hit you?" Becker inquired.

"Twice. Bloodied my shirt."

"Did you hit him back?"

"Only because he hit me first." He sounded like a child explaining a playground fight to the school principal.

"So, it's safe to say any blood found in the house could be yours?" Harrington asked.

RG shrugged. *They know.*

"What happened after you hit Mr. Abernathy?" Harrington asked.

"I left."

"Just like that?"

"Once I had my evidence, I left." *Where are you, Kacey?*

"Can we see the picture?" Becker reached out his hand.

RG scrolled through his photo library, producing the juicy image he intended to use in his defense. Becker accepted the phone and studied it with intense interest before tilting it for Harrington's benefit.

"Nice shot." Becker nodded his head.

"Did you have any interaction with…" Harrington checked his notes, "Ms. Thorne on Monday evening?" Becker continued to examine the phone.

"Only to ask her to tell the truth. She stormed out a few minutes after the fight, right before I did."

"Did you see her after you left the house?"

"Not after I left." *Victor has Kacey. She went into his head and never came back.*

"You said she left right before you. What, she just disappear?"

"Maybe she called Uber. They're pretty fast. How the fuck should I know?"

"You sure you didn't lose track of time in the house?" Becker added.

"I told you, I left right after she did." *They think I did it. I'm fucked.*

Detective Harrington continued to write in his notebook. After he jabbed a distinct mark at the bottom of his page, he said, "You know, Chief Brennan from Falmouth tossed us a bone. You seem to have a habit of hanging out with people who end up dead."

RG brushed his sweaty palms on the couch arm and dug his fingers into the decorative thumbtacks along the upholstered curve. "That a trick question?"

"Do you find these coincidences odd? You've been at the scene of two murders in the past week?" Becker asked.

"Obviously. I mean, what are the chances?" *Keep going, RG, talk your head right into the noose.*

"Million to one." Becker glared across the table, handing him his phone.

"You were clearly upset at Mr. Abernathy. How about Mr. Delvec-chio? Angry he lost your ten thousand dollars?" Harrington asked, the two detectives arriving fully briefed.

"Like I said to Chief Brennan, I wasn't there about the money."

"Would you say you have an anger problem?" Becker asked.

"That's it!" RG sprung from the couch. "No more questions without my lawyer."

Becker smirked and gave Harrington an 'I told you so' look.

"I need a minute to make a call." He stomped down the hallway into his office, the back of his shirt sticking to his body.

"We have all day." Becker leaned back and rested his feet on the coffee table.

RG slammed the door and collapsed in his office chair, sweat popping out along his hairline. *What the fuck's happening?*

He pulled his cell from his pocket and gripped it in his hand, hesitating. He let out a sigh and dialed his neighbor, Phil Goldwyn. The nightmare. The weekend do-it-yourselfer, always hauling some gas-powered mower, mulcher, trimmer, blower, or digger—anything with a noisy engine—revving it at the crack of dawn until the whole street smelled like a gas station. Despite the expletives he regularly hurled across the fence in the three years he'd lived next to Goldwyn, he'd never once considered the man's upside. He may have been a pain-in-the ass, but he taught criminal law at BC Law School across the street and RG needed a lawyer—and a bulldog. The man happened to be both.

Goldwyn answered his phone, an engine rumbling in the background.

"Phil, it's RG from next door."

"RG, didn't figure you had a phone. Usually when I hear your voice, it's shouting at me from your upstairs window."

"Yeah, Phil. Sorry 'bout all that. Listen, I've found myself in a tough legal spot. Could you come over for a sec and let me explain?"

RG resigned himself to a morning of mea culpas, compliments, begging, maybe a Hail Mary or two if it would get Goldwyn to the house. He also recognized Goldwyn loved being needed, the guy in the neighborhood everyone came to when they wanted to borrow a tool, or get advice on how to install a child's playset, Goalrilla, or fix an appliance. "I've been a bit of an asshole, I'll admit, but I'm damn glad I reached you. Can't tell you how much I *need* you right now."

A long moment passed, and RG couldn't tell if Goldwyn had hung up or not. "Phil?"

"Looks like an unmarked in your driveway."

RG grinned, Goldwyn was on the job. "Couple of hard-asses coming down on me pretty strong."

"Well, I'll have them pissing in their diapers and screaming for mommy by the time they jump back into their hunk of shit desecrating your property. Sit tight, RG, I'm on my way."

Within minutes Phil Goldwyn arrived at the front door. RG let him in and shook his hand, wincing at the solid grip the man offered. At six-foot-four, 220 pounds, with shoulder length hair and beard flowing over his leather jacket, he resembled more a Hell's Angel than a stereotypical lawyer, replete with a classic Harley—another engine he loved to rev.

"Thanks for coming over, Phil."

Goldwyn squinted as he examined his face. "What happened to your fucking nose?"

"You'll hear all about it."

RG introduced the lawyer to Harrington and Becker, but he ignored their outstretched hands. Known for dismantling police officers on the stand, Goldwyn's success as a criminal defense lawyer was in no small part due to his confrontational demeanor and intimidating presence.

He turned to RG. "Let's find a place to talk."

He led Goldwyn down the hall to his office. The lawyer leaned against RG's desk, half sitting on the desktop.

"Listen, Phil, these guys are asking me questions about a murder earlier this week. I swear, I didn't do—"

Goldwyn slapped his hands over his ears. "La, la, la, la, la! I don't care if you did it or not. I only care whether there's evidence to prove you did. Were you at the scene?"

"A couple hours before it happened."

Goldwyn stood, pacing back and forth across the Oriental rug. "Okay, okay. Not a problem. Anyone see you enter the home?"

"Just the woman in the house with him, but she left before I did."

"Any physical evidence you'd been there?"

"Maybe."

Goldwyn stopped. "Well, spit it out."

"I may have left some blood over there."

He stared at him. "What the fuck, RG?"

"I had a fight with the victim."

"When?" Goldwyn asked.

"The night of the murder."

Goldwyn resumed pacing. "At the scene of the murder?"

RG nodded his head.

"That's not good, RG." Goldwyn crossed his arms. "But hell, coincidences happen. You're an upstanding community member. It's not like you're showing up at murder scenes every week."

"Well…"

"Well, what?"

"Last week, I happened to be at the scene of a murder in Falmouth, too."

Goldwyn stopped. "Jesus, RG! What's going on with you? Did you get in a fight there, too?"

"Of course not."

"Okay, RG, keep your mouth shut until we figure out a strategy.

Have you said anything to the police today?"

"A little." RG replied, embarrassed he hadn't learned anything from the previous interrogation.

"How much?"

"Too much, probably."

"Have you talked to the police in Falmouth?"

"I did, Friday."

"What did you tell them?"

"More than I should have."

More pacing.

"Listen, the fact I'd been at both crime scenes is completely coincidental. You have to believe me!" RG pleaded. "I'm in deep shit here."

Please Kacey, come home. I need you.

"Let me talk to these assholes, find out what they got on you." RG and Goldwyn left the office and joined the detectives in the living room. "You, with the five o'clock shadow. You the lead on this?"

Harrington stood. "How'd you guess?"

"Cause this guy's too fucking ugly." Goldwyn pointed at a surprised Paul Becker.

"What the..." Becker's fingers curled into fists, veins standing out on his neck. "Fuck you!"

Goldwyn ignored Becker, his eyes never leaving Harrington. "What've you got on my client?"

"A dead guy named Wendell Abernathy, strangled on Monday night."

"Motive?"

"A former student, Brittany Thorne, filed a complaint your client initiated inappropriate sexual contact with her. Mr. Abernathy had been handling the complaint."

Goldwyn turned to RG. "She's the woman at the house with him?"

He nodded.

"She conveniently left before the murder. Your client had lots of alone time with the victim," Becker added.

Goldwyn glanced at RG, shifting his weight from one foot to another.

Harrington consulted his notebook. "Your client admitted his presence at the home on the night of the murder and described a physical altercation with Abernathy. We have a potential eyewitness in Ms. Thorne, and home security video shows his rental car in the neighborhood."

"Does the video clearly identify my client?"

"We're having it analyzed," Becker chimed in.

"So you have no idea if my client even drove the fucking car?"

"Location data on his iPhone puts Mr. Granville in the Harrison Falls neighborhood on the night of the murder."

"Who gave you the right to search his phone?"

Harrington glanced at Becker. "Your client volunteered it to Detective Becker to view a photo he took of Mr. Abernathy and Ms. Thorne in the home."

"Can't do that." Goldwyn waved Harrington away.

"He volunteered the phone to us," Becker countered.

"Not for you to search through it."

"That's fine." Harrington shrugged. "We'll remove it from our report."

But the damage had been done, no one doubted RG had been there.

"Any physical evidence in the house?"

"Blood spatter on the floor, and your client admitted it had been from an altercation with the victim," Harrington said.

Goldwyn glared at RG again. "Could have been from weeks ago."

"It wasn't," Becker added. "I'm sure Ms. Thorne will confirm the facts."

"Colleagues of Mr. Abernathy recently witnessed a verbal shouting match between Mr. Granville and the deceased in the days prior to his death." Harrington went on to tell Goldwyn the Falmouth PD had questioned RG in the death of John Delvecchio who'd recently invested and lost a large sum of money for him.

"Mr. Granville admitted to Falmouth detectives he'd handled the murder weapon," Becker offered.

"Any physical evidence from Falmouth?" Goldwyn paced across the living room's hardwood floor.

Harrington leafed through the pages in his notebook. "We have blood evidence in your client's car and fingerprint evidence on the murder weapon in Delvecchio's home. We're waiting for the lab results for both cases. Should hear something within the hour."

RG opened his mouth to speak, but Phil slapped a burly paw over his mouth.

"Don't say another word." Goldwyn glared at him. "Did you agree to provide blood and fingerprints in Falmouth?"

"I didn't see any reason not to."

Harrington continued. "We also found scorch marks in the Abernathy home."

"Scorch marks? What the fuck…?"

Becker crossed his arms. "Our theory is the perpetrator attempted to burn down the house to hide the crime."

Harrington checked his watch. "We're awaiting a court order to impound Mr. Granville's rental car and clothing to look for any accelerants or other evidence in support of this theory."

"A court order? You find any accelerant at the scene?"

"Nothing yet," Becker reported.

"So, what the hell you gonna search for here?"

Harrington searched through his notebook. "Um. Well…any type of—"

Goldwyn jumped in. "So, if my client has a can of Kingsford next to his Weber you're gonna arrest him? Judge will love that one. We arrested him for suspicion of grilling! Fuck off, both of you."

Harrington continued. "Listen, we're not going anywhere. We're staying to protect the integrity of any potential evidence until the court order—"

"It'll be a cold day in hell when I let you stand guard over my client in *his* home," Goldwyn interrupted, stepping toward Harrington. "Beat it, rookies."

Becker stepped forward. "You lawyer fucks are all alike. Think you're the gatekeepers to justice, but you don't give a shit about the victims. You just protect guilty assholes." Becker's gaze shifted toward RG with a laser-like glint. "Typical bullshit."

This showdown had flipped out of control. Goldwyn met him half-way, their noses practically touching.

Harrington stepped between them. "That's enough, Paul."

A twitch pulled at the corner of Goldwyn's mouth. "I need to talk to my client alone."

Phil Goldwyn stormed from the living room down the hall to the office, RG hustling to keep up. He slammed the door.

"What the fuck, RG?"

"It's not what it looks like."

"Listen, you never, ever talk to police without a lawyer present."

"I know, I know. I guess the horse is out of the barn."

"All the horses are out!" Goldwyn shouted. "You've completely laid out their case for them. You served them information on a physical altercation they had no idea about. You handed them a relationship between you, Abernathy, and the woman. All this gets weaved into motive. Don't say another word to anyone, anywhere without me present."

"I screwed up, Phil, I know." He held up his hands. "But I am completely inno—"

"La, la, la, la, la!" Goldwyn slapped his hands over his ears.

"Come on! Stop it, Phil. Someone killed my best friend. I'd never do that, and there couldn't have been blood in my car. It's impossible! The second guy killed happened to be a scumbag, I have to admit, but I only went to his house to catch him with Brittany Thorne." He explained the past history between him and Abernathy. "Someone's trying to set me up. I'm positive."

"Listen..." Goldwyn stared at the carpet. "I'm not sure there's much I can do for you. If any physical evidence links you to the crimes, you're gonna need more than some burned out professor who hasn't seen a courtroom in fifteen years. If the physical evidence comes back inconclusive, they have you on record admitting you weren't only present at both crime scenes prior to the murders, but you punched one of the victims and held the knife that killed the other!" Goldwyn threw his arms up and turned away. "Never talk to the police without a lawyer," he muttered.

"Will you stay with me while the detectives are here?"

"Of course, and better yet, we can have them wait in their goddamn car," Goldwyn snapped. "Fuck them. They're not paying for the heat in here."

Phil Goldwyn stormed back into the living room and ushered the two detectives from the house.

Becker turned to Goldwyn. "We'll be back. Either with a court order or DNA evidence. You better prepare your client for arrest and a bond hearing."

Goldwyn reached into his pocket. "Here's my card. I don't want to smell either of you assholes anywhere near this house until you have something. And get that piece of shit out of the driveway. We have standards in this neighborhood!"

Harrington and Becker reluctantly stepped out into the cold and headed toward their car. Harrington half turned as he headed down the steps, shouting back to Goldwyn. "You might want to ask him where his wife is."

"Fuck off," Goldwyn snapped. As they stepped back into the house, he turned to RG. "Where's Kacey?"

"I don't know right now."

Later, as RG lounged with Phil Goldwyn at the kitchen table waiting for the detectives' call, his cell chirped.

"RG, Mike Stahl. Kacey there?"

I'm in the middle of all this shit and Mike wants to flirt with my wife! The pressure inside RG finally spiraled to its boiling point, his cork about to blow. "She isn't, and why the hell do you want to know!"

"Take it easy, RG, it's not what you think."

It's always what I think. "Why the fuck are you calling my wife!"

"Just shut up for a minute and I'll explain!"

I can't wait, this should be good!

"I don't want to talk to her. I just wanted to make sure she's safe at home."

"And what are you, her guard dog? Why do you care?"

"I'm pretty sure something happened to her last night."

RG bit his tongue. *"How could he know that?*

"Is she there?"

"She isn't, and I don't have a clue where the hell she is."

"Listen, RG, I'm not sure where to begin, this will sound—"

"Trust me," he interrupted, "after the week I've had, nothing you say will sound crazy."

"Okay. Last night I had a dream, or at least I thought so. I may have been awake, I'm not sure anymore. Either way, Kacey's in trouble." Stahl expelled an audible sigh. "In the dream, we'd been out on the Cape having breakfast in this little restaurant and—"

"The Pancake Man?"

"How'd you guess?"

Victor's got her. She revealed herself and he caught her. "That's where she goes in her dreams."

"RG, I'm telling you about *my* dream, not hers."

"It's more complicated than that." RG left Goldwyn in the kitchen and scooted down the hall to his office. "This'll sound crazy, but I think it was her dream. And she brought you with her." A small pang of jealousy stabbed at him.

"That's not possible, RG."

"Believe me, Mike. That's why the dream felt so different."

"Okay, RG. I'm trying to get my head around this." He paused, collecting his thoughts. "In a fucked-up way it makes sense. She said something like, 'you'll understand why I brought you.' God, this whole thing's insane! If it was her dream, then she brought me there to show me something."

"What?"

"She needed me to peek inside the mind of someone called 'the burning man.'"

RG gave a sharp exhale. "I'm acquainted with him."

"How..." Mike's voice trailed off. "What the fuck's going on, RG?"

RG struggled to fill his lungs. "Tell me what happened."

"Well, we found him in this cave, and she'd been showing me his thoughts when somehow he caught wind of us. He woke up in a rage, but she pushed me from the dream before I could see what happened to her. I suspect he trapped her somehow."

Oh my God, I let her go through with her crazy plan!

"RG, I watched everything in his head, like a movie, memories from his past, things I wasn't meant to watch. It had to be a dream, RG, it couldn't be real…"

"Stay with me, Mike. Tell me what you saw!"

"I watched him kill Johnny Delvecchio…" Stahl remained silent for a moment. "This burning man killed some other guy, too. He called him the vile man. Any clue who he's talking about?"

How fucking appropriate. "Guy named Abernathy. Someone killed him the other night minutes after I left his house."

"I don't understand it all, but this guy's hell bent on setting you up for murder, making sure you suffer. I've never sensed such burning vengeance."

Now RG grasped the plan Victor had hatched.

"But there's more. He's gonna have you kill Kacey."

RG's vision faded. Dark spots converged from the corners of his eyes and danced across his visual field, his office now a snowy UHF channel. He dropped into his chair before he passed out. *He's gonna invade my body and make me do it. One more thing to put me away forever.*

RG hesitated as he considered what to say to Stahl. The time had come to tell him the truth, welcome him into the Twilight Zone. He'd already been in the burning man's cave. No reason to hold anything back now. Kacey had wanted Stahl to witness the burning man's thoughts, to get his help. If she'd chosen to take him there, RG would trust her decision. Stahl would assume he'd lost his mind when he heard what he had to say, but he'd already seen some unbelievable shit, and he'd been to a place seven-and-a-half billion people on the planet hadn't. It wouldn't take much to convince him of the rest.

"Mike, if you're not sitting down already, I suggest you do."

"Way ahead of you, man."

"Your world's gonna change after what I tell you." RG let out a deep breath before jumping in. "Mike, some people in this world are protected, they're watched over from the next world, sheltered from danger. They're protected by…caretakers, sort of like guardian angels."

"Guardian angels," Stahl repeated.

"Caretakers protect us from jumpers, vengeful souls from the next world who take over our bodies and initiate accidents, kill us for sport."

"Take over our bodies." A long pause followed. "RG, what drugs have you been experimenting with because they sound pretty fuckin' good?"

"Fuck you, just listen!"

"This is impossible!"

"Think about your dream, Mike. It's real and you know it. Don't hide from this!"

"RG, I can't—"

"Listen to me! The burning man is a jumper who's been after me my whole life. My caretaker, Morrow, has been protecting me, but he fucked up and can't protect me any longer. So, I'm dead, or will be."

"RG?"

"Wait, there's more. Kacey has caretaker powers. She can see things from the future. Morrow's been training her to help fight the burning man. He's coming for us, and he's gonna kill us."

RG could practically hear the gears turning in Stahl's mind, silently processing this new reality. "Mike?"

"And I thought my story would sound crazy. Jesus, RG! I'm not sure I want to know all this."

"Well you do now, and there's no turning back."

"One thing I'll have to admit if what I saw was real…you aren't a murderer."

The words came as a relief, but RG didn't care about guilt or innocence anymore. He only wanted Kacey back. "Like I said, all this shit is unreal, but real. Now you know what I've been going through, what Kacey and I have been dealing with."

"Must be why she took me with her...to show me what no one would believe otherwise...that there are forces out there we can't fathom or control."

"So now you know. Welcome to the club."

"The truth is RG, I'm not sure how to help you. How do I convince police officers or a judge someone I saw in a dream committed two murders? I can't convince someone this burning guy's even real. How do I do that?"

RG set his jaw. "All that matters is we know he's real."

"How do we get Kacey back?"

We? Sonofabitch! "I'll have to dispatch Morrow to see if he can get Victor away from her. If we can get Kacey back, there *is* something you can do."

"Anything. Just name it."

RG stood from his desk, gazing around his office at the accumulated worldly items defining his journey, novels lining the bookshelves, memories hanging in picture frames, the trappings of the world he inhabited. A few days ago, he'd faced a sure bout with death, full of angst, fearful of letting go, holding on with desperation to all he'd ever known and cherished. Today, death seemed like nothing more than a leaf caught in a maelstrom, insignificant. He would gladly face it to counter the enormity of what lay before him. He would make this nightmare end, his way.

RG braced himself for what he was about to say. "You need to kill me."

"What the fuck, RG? You *have* lost your mind."

"You have to." RG imagined the internal conflict going on in Stahl's mind. *Don't pretend, you sonofabitch. Don't tell me you haven't dreamed about wanting me dead. Now you have to find the balls to do it.*

"Mike, the only way to kill a jumper is by killing its host. The burning man plans to take over my body and have me kill Kacey and the baby. If you can kill me before he exits my body, he dies, and my family lives."

Silence filled the line for several long moments. "Mike?"

"Yeah."

"How good a shot are you?"

"RG...don't."

"It has to be instantaneous and a shot that counts. I have to be dead before I hit the ground, before the burning man figures it out."

"RG, I can't just—"

"It's not about you or me anymore! Do you want to save Kacey?"

"Of course, I do."

"Then can I count on you?"

"I need time to think about it. You can't suddenly throw something like this—"

"Okay, I'll take that as a yes."

"Fuck!"

A slow minute passed. "Mike?"

"Yeah."

"One more thing I need to ask."

"Well, I'm just full of favors right now."

RG chuckled. "I had a visit from the Boston police." He pulled back the curtain and gazed through the blinds at the two detectives struggling to keep warm in the car. "They're sitting in my driveway right now waiting to arrest me for two murders. Anything you can do to buy me more time?"

"They're waiting for the call from the crime lab, no doubt. I'm sure they have a warrant all ready. RG, can you get out of the house undetected? You can hole up here with me in Chatham while we figure this out."

"Well, they're sitting in my driveway. It's not like I can back out and drive past them. They'll follow me."

"Yeah, they will."

"Listen, Mike, I'll give you a call back. I have an idea."

RG dropped the phone and raced down the hall. Phil Goldwyn relaxed at the kitchen table, Baron's chin resting across his feet. He'd made a pot of coffee. "Need a cup?"

"No, but I need your car."

CHAPTER SIXTEEN

Thursday, December 14, 2017

Inside the burning man's cave, Kacey pressed against the jagged limestone, the unbearable heat worse than any inferno. Her head throbbed rhythmically, the slightest movement heightening her discomfort, a painful goose egg sprouting on the side of her head where she'd struck the cave wall. Sweat dribbled from her pores, her body striving to lower its core temperature, but proving no match for the intense incinerator in which she languished. She could sense her baby's distress, its furious kicking matched by her racing heart's rhythmic thump. She would have to come up with a plan soon or she would to lose her baby, and maybe more.

"Hot, isn't it!" the burning man chortled. "Isn't that what your people say when they have nothing to talk about? They fill the precious silence with talk about the weather." The burning man shook his head.

Kacey eyed him with caution as he paced back and forth.

"Don't feel like talking?" The burning man ambled toward her. "You know, my wife used to say that to me. She would prattle on and on about one goddamn thing after another. When I didn't respond she would ask, 'Don't feel like talking?'" He squatted down in front of her, heat pulsating off his glowing skin. "God, it's a wonder I didn't break her neck sooner."

He plucked a sickly rodent from one of the cages set up throughout the dwelling. "Hungry?" he snarled.

Kacey tasted sour bile rising in her throat, and without warning disgorged her breakfast.

"Never mind, looks like you've already eaten." The burning man chuckled and promptly devoured the creature.

His eyes narrowed and filled with flames as his laugh faded into a low growl. "Did you honestly think you could sneak into my mind and steal my thoughts? What did you see?"

"I saw a memory of Sam."

"Don't say his name!" His rage fanned the fire within him. Kacey cowered and fused herself against the wall, attempting to escape the shooting flames before they seared her flesh. "Did you learn how I'm planning to kill you and your child?"

Kacey instinctively wrapped her arms around her stomach. More than simply a part of her now, she would defend her child with every bit of the universe's power she had inside her. *You think you're taking my child? No way, motherfucker!*

She would need to buy them time.

"I figured jumping inside your hubby and helping him wring your neck would be a fitting way to ensure he's put away for the rest of his life. People in your world tend to frown upon killing pregnant wives. Won't be the worst way to go, I assure you. I'll make it as gentle as I can." The burning man moved toward her, his eyes glowing through a scorched mask, an inquisitive expression on his face. "What do you imagine would be the worst way to die?"

"Alone," Kacey said, "like you did."

The burning man's glimmering orange skin throbbed, flames erupting from his core. Kacey writhed in agony, screaming in pain as his heat engulfed her. Instinctively, she produced a cocoon of cool energy within her, enveloping her baby, protecting it against the hellish external bake.

"Wrong answer!" he shouted. "No, the correct response is to burn to death. The pain's unfathomable, unless you've grown to enjoy it as I have. There's nothing like burning." He closed his eyes and touched his simmering skin, his face a hideous mask of torment and pleasure.

He turned to her and gave her another blast of his internal heat just for fun.

The burning man snatched another rodent and stuffed it down his gullet, not bothering to chew. He strolled toward Kacey. "Hope you're ready to burn."

Kacey rose. "I am."

Victor raised a burning eyebrow. "What did you say?"

"I'm ready to burn with you." Kacey approached him with baby steps. "I've seen your power, I've seen it up close. I've been inside your mind, more than once. I want the power, too. I want to join you."

Flames diminished as quickly as they'd accelerated, a sneer replacing the vapors. "Join me as a willing victim?"

"What, you think you deserve all the power? All the glory?" Kacey took another tentative step toward him. "You have more than you need, enough to give to me."

"Share my Divine gift? With you as my burning bride? Why would you choose to join me all of a sudden? You don't fool me, I know more about you than you can imagine. I've seen your life force and its strength."

A fluttering invaded her stomach. *He sees right through you, everything you're thinking. He's gonna throw the fires of hell your way.* She struggled to keep her mind blank, to *not* think of the one thing rattling her mind and divulge her true intention. "I'm done with this world. I've been to the next one and I didn't find much there for me, either. I want fire inside me, I want what you have."

"What's in it for me?" The burning man stepped closer.

"We both possess powers, complementary powers. Together we'd be invincible."

He eyed her with suspicion. "I'm already invincible."

"But you're alone here. You don't have to be." She stepped close to him, her skin nearly touching his. "Let me join your mind, show you what it's like."

Kacey took his hesitation as tacit approval to move inside him, feeling him shudder as she entered him. A solid barrier wrapped around her mind, like a coat of armor, protecting her, masking her thoughts as she tolerated his humid stench, his mind's scalding touch. With a split-second scan, Kacey latched onto his racing thoughts, his cautious pleasure at the touch of another, his hesitant desire to possess her—the beautiful one—for eternity, his dormant longings for the earthly pleasures he missed.

Kacey exited Victor, tremors flitting through his body as she circled him like a hungry shark, his breath coming in gasps, his defenses penetrated. "Did you like it this time," she whispered, "with me inside?"

The burning man swallowed, his skin glowing red with his racing heart's beat. "You're ready to burn? To burn with me for eternity?"

"If it frees me from this hell, I'm ready for anything. Tell me when."

He turned to her with a crooked smirk. "When the time's right, but you need to understand something."

"What?"

"It's gonna hurt."

RG raced down the highway in Phil Goldwyn's Black Lexus SUV. He'd sensed his lawyer's doubt as to his innocence, but it hadn't stopped Goldwyn from lending him his car, granting him time to get his affairs in order before being absorbed into the justice system.

And he would be. Both men knew it.

After Mike's call, RG had burst out the back door, hurdled the fence into Phil's yard, and maneuvered the Lexus from the garage, creeping past the detectives' government issued Ford sedan idling in the driveway. Freedom, for the moment.

Speeding west on I-90, RG stood on the pedal, punishing the Lexus. His imagination ran wild, envisioning Kacey trapped, submitting to the burning man's brutality in another plane he couldn't access.

He pounded his fist against the console in rapid succession, leaving a dent, and a sting radiating up his arm.

"Fuck!" he bellowed, his sense of helplessness bringing burning tears to his eyes. "Morrow, dammit, where the hell are you?" Relying on osmosis to summon his caretaker didn't cut it when his once cushy, complacent world imploded around him.

He burst along I-93 S to the Cape, his tires screeching as he blew past the twin storage tanks on Dorchester's distant waterfront, a blur out his driver's side window. The blare of car horns receded one by one as he powered ahead, weaving through traffic. "Morrow, if there's one time to pay attention to me, it's now!"

RG sensed the air's displacement in the closed vehicle, a warm draft bathing his body in oscillating waves. Glancing to his right, he witnessed Morrow flip into his world, invading the passenger seat like sand streaming through an hourglass, filling his body's faint outline in an instant.

"Jesus Christ, Morrow, where the hell have you been? I've been trying to reach you. Kacey's gone." He held the steering wheel in a death grip.

Morrow nodded. "Victor's holding her."

RG glared at him, his eyes shifting between the road and Morrow, his teeth clenching. "How the fuck could you let her believe she could fool Victor? She wasn't anywhere near ready!"

"I disagree. She accessed his mind. She provided Detective Stahl detailed information—"

"Well, thanks to you, she's trapped!" he interrupted. RG pounded the wheel, fed up with Morrow's contentment sacrificing the people around him. "Victor's won!"

"Not yet." Morrow clasped his hands together. "Do not underestimate her power. She's very resourceful."

"What happened to her in there?"

Morrow exhaled, shaking his head. "It can be confusing in someone else's mind. I suspect the barrage of twisted, brutal images flustered her. I heard her faint call, could have been by accident, but that's when he caught her."

"How is it she's gone, did he abduct her? I thought these were just dreams?"

"Her powers have advanced to allow a complete shift across planes, body and mind. Victor didn't abduct her, but he is holding her, keeping her from reaching the portal. Now she can't get back."

"Can you help her?"

"I can't get to her. She whispered to me from deep inside him, like a distant radio signal fading into white noise. I'm getting stirrings of her, and she's no longer stuck in his mind, but she must reach out to me again if I'm to find her."

RG resisted the urge to tear into the sonofabitch, berate him for his limitations. "You trained her. You brought her to his world. This wasn't supposed to be a suicide mission."

"I told you before, nothing's guaranteed when it comes to Victor."

RG tapped his fingers on the steering wheel. "What do we do?"

"I can break his hold on her if I can find a way to weaken him somehow."

"How?" he asked.

Morrow paused a beat. "I'm working on it."

RG snatched his chirping cell phone from the cup holder. "Yeah."

"Phil Goldwyn. It's a good thing you bolted when you did, I just had a visit from Beauty and the Beast."

"Huh?"

"Harrington and Becker, for Chrissake! You expecting someone else at your door this afternoon? Crime lab results came back. You sitting down?"

"Well, I'm driving your Lexus, so…"

"Oh yeah. Well, they found your fingerprints on the murder weapon from Falmouth and in Abernathy's home. DNA from the blood samples found in Andover matches your blood type."

"What about blood in the Subaru?"

"Delvecchio."

"Impossible. Someone had to plant it in my car. I swear."

"Either way, they had a warrant. First-degree murder."

"What did you tell the detectives when they found me AWOL?"

Goldwyn chuckled. "I told them I took a nap on the couch and when I woke up, my car keys had disappeared."

"They buy your bullshit?"

"Nah, but I got a kick out of watching the veins in Becker's temple throb. I thought his head might explode."

"Are they looking for the car?"

"I didn't give them the license number or make. Fuck them, I don't need to do their job for them. But it's only going to take a few keystrokes before they find out what you're driving and get an ABP out on you. You gotta get it off the road, you hear?"

"Got it, Phil. And hey, man, thanks for—"

"Yeah, yeah, shut the fuck up. I don't want to hear it. Just say we're even for all those Saturday mornings."

RG grinned. "Fair enough."

"Listen, RG, I've made a few calls. I have a couple of criminal defense lawyers you should talk to." A long pause followed as RG barreled along the Route 3 breakdown lane as traffic inched its way toward the Cape. "I'll be honest, none of this will be easy on you. Your name's gonna be in the news by tonight. You'll have your tenure revoked, and you'll lose your job. When they catch up with you, you'll go to jail until trial. This whole thing will most likely break you financially, but these guys are the best, and—"

"Phil, I appreciate it, but I can't worry about it now."

"You have bigger things to worry about than two murder charges?"

RG glanced at Morrow and floored the Lexus. "Actually, I do."

The burning man dozed, finished with Kacey for the moment. He'd forced her to join him on his mat, his body smoldering, his murderous stench filling her nostrils, gagging her with every breath. Exhausted, every fiber of Kacey's body pleaded for rest, but with only a temporary reprieve from Victor's control, she had no time to lose. She summoned the courage to wrap her arms around her belly, pressing back and forth with exploratory pokes, hoping for a response. She slapped a hand over her mouth to stifle a laugh as she absorbed the spirited kicks, her cool energy barrier like a protective hammock around her slumbering baby.

She would have to reach out to Morrow if she wanted to make it home again, she couldn't get to the portal by herself. She cleared her mind and tried to descend into her dream state, but the cave floor provided no comfort, her pain unrelenting. As Kacey closed her eyes and dropped into the tenuous place between dark and dreams, a vision appeared before her. In it, RG dashed into the surf, side by side with a young boy seven or eight years old racing to keep up, seafoam exploding around them, the increasing depth of water slowing their momentum until they could run no further, both throwing their arms outward and diving beneath the waves. Kacey observed from the shoreline, RG teaching his son the only acceptable way to enter an ocean. The boy emerged from the water with a whoop, his arms holding his frigid body, the unforgiving, cold June sea wrapping him in an iridescent see-through cloak, dripping from him like a shimmering rain. RG stood beside his boy under a dazzling sun, arm draped around his shoulder, both sets of brown eyes locked onto Kacey's.

She'd witnessed too many other similar visions to misunderstand what this one had shown her, this one not a harbinger of death, but of life, a predictor of what could be, a possible future. Kacey's eyes swelled with tears, her energy revitalized, the fight inside her renewed.

As the vision dispersed, a yawning chasm opened before her, a fracture into the world she sought. Stepping through a heavy mist's pressing veil, Kacey tumbled into churning stillness, a place between worlds unique in its absence of sound or light. Through the unbounded calm, the familiar portal's outline took shape, the Pancake Man materializing in front of her. She clutched the door handle and twisted it open.

Kacey's footsteps echoed in the silent room. She stood alone in the foyer, her eyes tracking across the unfamiliar landscape, expecting the muffled din of family conversations, frenzied voices, clinking plates, and bells signaling the overworked waitresses to pick up their orders. Moving down the main aisle, her shoes left tracks in the dust along broken floor tiles. She stepped over shattered dishes and discarded silverware as she parted cobwebs cascading from the rotting overhead beams and rusty ceiling fans.

What had happened here?

The room wavered in her vision like a mirage. Kacey sensed the burning man's dominion kept her walled off from the childhood memories she'd known here, leaving only their abandoned remnants. She waited, confident Morrow would arrive soon. But he didn't. *Where the hell are you, Morrow?*

As she turned to leave the restaurant, a lone patron seated in a tattered booth by the wall caught her attention. Kacey tiptoed over scattered debris until her shadow drifted across the man, drawing his gaze upward.

His boyish physique and clean-shaven face defied an exact age, he could have been twenty or forty, but his haunted eyes confirmed the latter. She cleared her throat to get his attention.

"Lousy service…if you're in a hurry," he said. "Ten minutes and no one's even wiped the table yet."

"Mind if I have a seat?" Kacey studied the man's face, faded remnants of freckles scattered across his nose.

"Please." He flashed a grin, gesturing with his hand across the table.

Kacey slid into the cushioned booth.

He inspected his menu. "I'm pretty sure my dad and mom took me here a long time ago. Are we on the Cape?"

"Sort of."

"I remember this place." He glanced around the diner, nodding his head. "The silver dollar pancakes, too. Never could finish them myself, but never wasted, thanks to my dad."

Kacey found herself gawking, caught in the snare of his stunning blue eyes and golden blond hair. "My dad would finish mine, too."

"God, I miss him." He shook his head. "I had a feeling he'd meet me here. I've been waiting so long, but he hasn't come to find me."

Kacey reached across the table and grasped his hand. "Maybe he got lost."

He blinked away a hint of a tear. "I'm Sam, by the way."

There had been no doubt in her mind. "I'm Kacey, it's nice to meet you."

Sam craned his neck in search of a waitress, tossing the menu on the table. "Looks like I'm not gonna get anything to eat here today."

"I have a feeling you're here for another reason…to help me, and I think I'm here to help you, too. It's why I brought you here."

Sam scrunched his face. "Brought me…how could you—?"

"It's kinda hard to explain," she interrupted, "but if you want to see your dad, I can take you. He's told me a lot about you."

Sam's eyes widened, but then resumed a cautious wariness. "Yeah, right. Like you know my dad."

"I do…or someone who used to be your dad."

"What the hell does that mean?" Sam leaned back and folded his arms. "I dunno, this doesn't sound right."

Kacey scooted along the booth's soft cushion and stood in the aisle, motioning for Sam to follow. "You need to trust me."

Sam took a deep breath as he eyed Kacey, then slowly slid from the booth. They traversed the debris-laden floor side by side until they reached the front door. Kacey grabbed his hand as they exited the Pancake Man, in an instant, engulfed in the next world's vivid white milieu.

CHAPTER SEVENTEEN

Thursday, December 14, 2017

Brennan stormed out of his office, curious eyes glancing up from screens and tablets as he tromped down the hallway, bursting through the Falmouth Police Department's glass doors, plumes of steam fleeing his body as his blistering rage greeted the brisk December air. He stood facing his town with a sneer, searching for an outlet, a target for his wrath, maybe someone to shoot.

Brennan's superiors had informed him moments ago they'd assigned Detective Ray Harrington lead on both the Abernathy and Delvecchio cases, keeping the Falmouth boys at their desks to assist and support. Harrington's star had been on the rise for some time, a stylish package of youth and success the Boston PD had been eager to promote as the city's new face of law enforcement. Brennan had nothing against the detective personally, but a murderous love triangle among Boston's academic elite would now give Harrington the regional and *national* attention he craved for himself. *No way I'm sharing a seat with my ass on this one!*

As he turned to enter the station, he pulled the buzzing cell from his pocket.

"Yeah, Chuck, it's Ray Harrington. Hey, tough luck on this pecking order bullshit, I just heard myself."

Traffic noise through the receiver indicated Harrington and Becker were on the road. Brennan's body had chilled since stepping into the frigid air, but boiling blood still surged through his veins. *Fucking prick probably has the rearview mirror aimed at his face!* "If you're expecting congratulations, you might be waiting a while."

"Whatever," Harrington muttered. "Wanted to give you a heads up on the physical evidence."

What the fuck? "I didn't hear a goddamn thing from BCI about—"

"All communications come out of my office now," Harrington interrupted. "Fingerprints from the murder weapon came back positive, matching the prints found at Abernathy's place. DNA matched, too, inside the car and on Abernathy's floor."

Brennan roared back through the station, drawing more furtive glances. He jerked open his office door, slamming it hard enough to rattle the panes. "Goddammit, why am I the last one in line for information? It's my town, for Chrissake!"

"Look, I don't have to share anything with you. I called as a courtesy."

"Courtesy? What the fuck does that mean?"

"Listen, you gonna be a team player on this or not?"

Team player? "Funny, I never thought of it as a game." Brennan dropped into his chair, the metallic seams squealing under his weight.

"Anyway, we executed the arrest warrant. With Delvecchio's blood on the seat and steering wheel of Granville's car, we had enough probable cause."

Brennan's eyes widened. "Why didn't you tell me you nabbed the sonofabitch?"

"Because we didn't. The guy hijacked his lawyer's ride before we arrived, or we'd be posing him for his mug shot this very minute. But I could use your help. I need a BOLO on a vehicle to get the word out." He gave Goldwyn's address to Brennan. "It's going to be pleasure slapping the cuffs on that bastard."

Brennan sank noticeably in his chair, his role in the case relegated to secretarial help. "What, Becker forget how to work the onboard computer?" Brennan set his jaw, grinding his teeth.

"You wanna be on the team, Chuck?"

Only if I'm the starting QB, you bastard! Brennan bit his tongue. "You bet, Ray. I'll take care of it."

"Owe ya, Chuck. Thanks."

Before he could respond, the line went dead. He glanced up from his desk at Mitt Romney smiling at him from the wall.

Brennan refreshed the line and called Daniels.

"Yeah, chief, whatcha need?"

"I need you to get an APB out on a Black Lexus SUV, owner Phil Goldwyn of Newton." He gave Daniels the address and plate number.

"Jeez, Chuck, can't you get one of the—"

"Just do it!"

"Okay, chief. Goldwyn the driver?"

"Driver's Robert Granville."

"Sonofabitch! The guy's running?"

"And I'm gonna find him."

"Shouldn't we touch base with the Boston guys, they—"

"Don't worry about those bastards," Brennan cut him off. He slammed the receiver into the cradle and eased out from behind his desk, parking himself at the office window. He gazed across the street at the harbor's million-dollar boats, the sunlight reflecting off stainless-steel cleats and railings, so close yet so far out of reach. *Fuck this, time to make something happen!* Brennan picked up the phone, called a friend at the DOT, and learned Phil Goldwyn's Lexus used an EZPass transponder.

Brennan closed his office blinds, picked up his cell, and placed a second call.

He dialed a data management company in Fall River tracking vehicular radiofrequency ID tags inside EZPass transponders. Brennan understood little about the RFID technology, but as a private citizen, he abhorred the idea Big Brother could monitor law-abiding citizens' motor vehicle activity at tollbooths, highway overpasses, intersections, and signposts— anywhere they could place an electronic reader. But

Brennan wasn't averse to using his contacts to hack into databases and acquire the information when he needed to track a suspect. He didn't mind breaking the law when the law had already been broken. Sometimes you had to crawl in the mud to find the worms. When he'd brought the sonofabitch Granville into his jail and made the call to Harrington—after he'd called the media, of course—the end would justify the means. It always did.

The man picked up. "Len Kramer."

"It's Brennan. Glad to hear my voice?"

"Why're you calling this number? I told you—"

"Shut the fuck up, Len! Don't be so goddamn dramatic, just two friends talking."

"Friends?"

Touché, you fucking prick. "I need something from you."

"I figured."

"You're not getting all self-righteous on me now, are you, Len? Remember why you still have a job."

A deep sigh. "Listen, Chuck, I appreciate what you did for me. The company would've fired me if they found out, and I couldn't have done the time. But I'm clean now. I'm attending the meetings and back on track."

"Well, everyone deserves second chances," Brennan sneered.

"What do you need?"

Brennan told him about the Black Lexus SUV. "And I need it…yesterday."

"Got it, Chief, and I need…five hundred dollars. If I can triangulate activity and pinpoint location for you, it'll be a thousand. Deal?"

I save this maggot from a three-year stint and he has the nerve to charge me. "Listen, Len, this is a high profile collar, I need this one."

"Then you won't mind my asking price."

"You got a hell of a set on you."

"Supply and demand, Chuck. You can understand?"

"Sure thing, Len."

"All that publicity you like, Chief. It'll be worth it. Think of your future." Kramer chuckled as he hung up the phone.

A grin spread across Brennan's face. *We should all think of our future.*

~

When Kacey awoke, death and decay's fetid odor hung in the air, the burning man dozing on his mat beside her. Through the shadows dancing along the wall, a figure moved along the cave's opposite side, a man with his collar pulled up over his nose, his eyes darting back and forth at the bone remnants and animal carcasses strewn about. It dawned on her she'd never left the cave—at least her body hadn't—but in her mind she'd been with him at the Pancake Man.

Kacey raised her head and sat up, a finger pressed to her lips. She inched away from the burning man and crept over to Sam Garrett, pulling him toward her.

"What is this place? How'd you get here ahead of me?" Sam asked.

"Shhh! Keep quiet, I'll explain later. I need to tell you about—"

"Where's my dad?" Sam interrupted.

Kacey's eyes tracked to the burning man, a half-human ember glowing on the cave floor.

"What the hell?"

"Listen to me, Sam—"

"Enough!" Sam stepped away from Kacey, moving closer to the simmering body. "Dad?" Sam continued to press his collar against his face in the foul-smelling cave.

Sam pivoted, pointing his finger at Kacey with a scowl. "This some kind of joke?"

The burning man stirred, raising his head off the mat. He sat up, glaring at Kacey and the male intruder beside her. A flicker of recognition registered across the burning man's face.

As Sam caught sight of the creature's throbbing skin and devilish eyes, he backed away, averting his gaze. The burning man exploded in fury, fire and heat emanating from within, scorching the cave floor.

"Get out of here!" the burning man howled. He glared at Kacey with glowing eyes. Inside her head he spoke, *"Why did you bring him here! I can't let him see me like this!"*

"He's been waiting for you. He needs you."

"There's nothing here for him. His father's gone!" The burning man turned his back on them, his spiraling rage spawning a suffocating heat within the room.

Sam took Kacey's hand and stepped closer. "He looks familiar, the shape of his face and body."

The burning man stood up. "Why do you approach? Do you want me to incinerate the two of you?"

Sam continued to gawk at him in stunned shock.

"Don't look at me!" the burning man snarled, heat and fire billowing from him.

Sam took another step closer, squinting to make out the man's features beneath the flames. The burning man turned away, shielding his face.

"Go away!"

"Dad?" Sam stepped closer, leaning forward to peer around his father's shoulder.

As his eyes locked onto Sam's, violent tremors seized his legs, rippling upward to his torso and arms. The burning man quivered like a hooked minnow. Fire and heat erupted from inside, his skin glowing like a Chinese lantern, a war between fury and love waged from within, a thunderous, anguished cry bursting from his lips. The sound ricocheted off the walls, a yawning crescendo of torment, forcing Sam and Kacey's hands against their ears, eyes squeezed tight against the auditory assault.

Kacey opened one eye to witness the burning man's struggle in full force, his body undulating in rhythmic spasms as if it would explode. Liquid fire cascaded off him like lava flowing from a volcano, pools of flame burning out at his feet. She turned away to avoid the blinding white hot light. In an instant, the cave grew cool and dark, the cacophony silenced, the burning man's fire extinguished. The man who'd once been Victor Garrett sat shivering on the cave floor, naked. He reached over to his sleeping mat to cover himself.

In his weakened form with vulnerabilities exposed, every thought in Victor Garrett's head flew from his mind like ticker-tape caught in a breeze. Kacey grabbed onto them, witnessing his pain, the need for his son. She eased Sam toward him.

Sam stepped to his father and knelt beside him, snaked his arms around his neck, and leaned his head against his shoulder's cool skin. Victor recoiled from the initial contact, but then recognized his son's tender touch. Wrapping his arms around him, he pulled him close, tears caressing his face as he held Sam for the first time since his final day, when he'd given one last kiss to a dying boy in a hospital bed.

"I've missed you so much," Victor cried. The two held each other in a frantic embrace as he ran his hands through his son's hair. "My Sam."

"I've been waiting for you, Dad. Why didn't you come find me?"

"I couldn't." Victor held Sam's face with both hands.

"Why not?"

Victor lifted his head, scanning the room. "This place…it's as far as I got."

"I saw you on fire." Sam searched his father's eyes. "Why?"

Victor's eyes trained downward. "It's what I've become." From inside his head, Kacey sensed a spark ignite inside him. He would soon burn again.

"What happened to you, Dad?"

"Listen, Sam, we don't have much time. It won't be long until I return to what repulsed you earlier—the fire, the rage. I can't escape it."

"Fight it! Remember you used to tell me to fight?"

"It's too strong. I've done things, Sam, terrible things. I…I've gone too far now."

"Come with me," Sam pleaded. "We can leave here together."

A voice rumbled from the cave's mouth. "He can't leave here." Morrow stepped out from the shadows. "It's too late for him, Sam. He's not welcome in your world. You need to come with us."

Kacey broke her connection with Victor and turned to witness

Morrow enter the cave, his powerful voice booming in the enclosed space.

"But he's my dad," Sam shouted to the man. "I want to stay with him." His pleading eyes shifted to Kacey, as if she might convince the stranger to let him stay.

"You can't be here when the change occurs, when the burning man returns. He'll kill you."

Victor met his son's mournful gaze. "He's right. You can't stay."

Morrow motioned Kacey to join him by the cave's opening. He reached for her hands. "Are you okay? I heard you calling for me."

"I had a feeling you'd come."

Morrow's eyes dropped, inspecting the scorch marks on her clothes and body. "I'm sorry it took me so long to get here, but you did wonderfully. You directed me right to you, and you found his weakness. He's vulnerable now, but not for long."

"I'm stuck here, Mr. Morrow. I can only get out in my mind."

Morrow grasped Kacey by the shoulders. "He can't hold you in his current state, not until he burns again. I can get you back to the portal, but you must leave now."

"What about Sam?"

"We can't wait any longer!"

Kacey peered at Victor, clutching his son. He opened his eyes to meet her stare, his voice clear and strong in her head.

"You lied to me, didn't you? You never planned on staying with me." Spurts of fire welled up within him.

She shrugged. *"I had to survive...for my son."*

"What a fool I am." A pained expression migrated across his face.

"Let Sam come with us."

"And let you take all I have left?"

"He'll die if he stays. That can't be what you want."

Victor closed his eyes, acknowledging he had no choice. *"Give me a moment."*

Kacey remained linked with Victor as he witnessed his ten-year-old blonde, blue-eyed freckled boy merge into the young man before him.

"You're so big," he said proudly. "I wish I'd been around to watch you grow."

"Me too, Dad." Sam's eyes edged with tears.

"I'm sorry you had to witness what I've become." Victor turned his head away as fire rose in his eyes, the heat returning.

"I love you, no matter who you are."

Victor cried out as an intense burst of flames filled the room. "You need to go now."

Sam's head spun to Kacey and Morrow, then back to his father. "I never had a chance to thank you," he stalled, hoping to stretch the time, "for all the hours you spent with me in the hospital. Do you remember?"

Victor squeezed his eyes shut to block the gathering tears. They sizzled behind his burning eyelids. "Every minute."

"I may not have lived very long, but every day you made me feel loved."

"Then I did my job."

"Come with me, Dad." Sam pulled on his father's hand, like he used to as a child.

"I can't. A change is coming. I can't escape it." An unbearable heat soared within Victor. Fire pushed through his translucent skin, spreading throughout his body like electricity, seeping furiously into his arms and legs. "You need to let me go now."

"Please stay, Dad. Don't go yet." Sam leaned his head on his father's shoulder. "You can't leave me. Not now. Not after I've found you again. I need you," he whispered.

"It's time, Sam." Victor mapped his son's face with his eyes one last time, trying to take in every detail before it vanished in a white-hot evisceration.

"Will I ever see you again?"

Victor snagged Sam into a tight grip. Warm tears penetrated Sam's shirt as his sweltering thermal embrace flared.

Morrow called out. "Please, Sam. We're running out of time."

Sam stood, still holding his father's now burning hand. In an instant, an energy wave blasted through Victor, consuming him in fire, the dark cave illuminated in a hellish, blinding flash. The force blew Sam backward, slamming him against the cave wall. Morrow dashed to his aid, heaving and dragging him from the cave by his arms. Kacey stumbled out close behind. In bold retaliation, the burning man thrust exploding flames throughout the cave in a fiery ball, the rush of scorching gases sucking all oxygen in hungry gasps.

The time for reflection incinerated into an ash heap of torched memories; the love, pain, and sorrow burning into oblivion under Victor's flaming body. The change had arrived, freeing him, inciting an overwhelming desire to cleanse. Victor burned, now nothing but fire.

As the evening light bled from the sky, RG swung Phil Goldwyn's Black Lexus into Mike Stahl's driveway on Old Harbor Road in Chatham. Stahl rushed out the front door, waving him toward an open garage stall with the exaggeration of a NASCAR official. Once securely inside the garage, RG hopped out and accepted an ice-cold Coors Light from him.

"Thought you might need a cool one," Mike said, taking a sip from his own bottle.

"Hey, I thought you didn't—"

"I couldn't think of a better time to take it up again."

Stahl downed a long swallow and ushered RG inside, through the kitchen, gleaming countertops and appliances reflecting fluorescent lighting, pots and pans stacked neatly in the dish rack. He led RG into the living room, where a folded blanket and pillow rested on the sofa. "Hope you don't mind the couch. It's all I have."

"It's fine, Mike." RG removed his jacket, surveying the dimly lit house, a time capsule of 1980's Cape Cod decor—Linoleum floors, shag carpet, knotty pine, and gaudy flowered prints on the sturdy chairs and sofas. He half expected a velvet Elvis painting hanging over the fireplace, the ones they sold on every sidewalk back then.

"Nice spot, Mike." RG threw him a grin, but didn't divulge his musings about the environment's sterility, a house devoid of intangibles conveying a sense of home. He scanned the walls, a handful of canvas art prints filling the empty space. No framed pictures perched atop shelves or end tables; no Christmas cards lined the mantel. No Polaroids brightened the refrigerator door. A pristine calendar hung from the kitchen wall, thirty-one days empty of notations.

As he scoped out his surroundings, a thought occurred to him—Kacey had been here, right here, in a different time. The prospect brought with it a biting jealousy she'd been here with Stahl, maybe entwined with him on the couch where he'd sleep tonight. At the same time, the bittersweet joy of having shared a piece of where she'd once been gave him a tangible link to her.

Where the hell are you, Kacey?

Had Morrow rescued her yet? He rejected any depressing scenarios, the thought she could be...he couldn't say it. He wouldn't say it. Or was Morrow pacing outside somewhere, building up courage to deliver bad news? The butterflies flitted in his stomach and his anxiety level ratcheted up again.

"I grabbed us a couple of D'Angelo sandwiches. Turkey or Italian?" Stahl displayed two bulky, paper wrappers like a game show host tempting his contestants.

RG paced about the living room floor, his mind racing. "Kacey's out there somewhere stuck in an alternate world with a burning sadist planning to kill her." He pushed away the food. "Not feeling so peckish right now, Mike."

Stahl rested a hand on his shoulder. "Morrow's out there, too. You gotta have faith he's gonna bring her back."

RG buried his face in his hands. "This whole thing's fucking insane!"

"It's gonna be okay. You'll see." He handed him the wrapper marked with a large black 'T' drawn with a Sharpie. "You gotta keep up your energy. Eat."

Stahl finished his sandwich in record time, striding into the kitchen to throw away the paper wrapping, RG still working on his. "Listen." Mike's voice rose barely above a whisper. "About the plan we talked about on the phone—"

RG held up his finger as his cell chirped. "One second." He checked the screen, rising on unsteady legs. "It's Kacey!" Trembling, he raised the phone to his ear, counting on her voice coming back at him.

"Kacey?" *Please, please, please.*

"I'm back. Morrow got me out!"

"Thank God!" RG leaned his head back and took several deep breaths. "Thank God you're OK." He collapsed onto the couch and gave Stahl a thumbs-up. His body immediately deflated, the yoke of tension and anxiety hoisted from his shoulders. Stahl shuffled back toward the kitchen, allowing them privacy.

"Where are you?" Kacey asked.

"I'm at Mike's. He knows I didn't kill anyone...thanks to you. He's offered me a hideout until we can plan our next move. I'm a fugitive now, wanted for two murders and maybe grand theft auto for stealing Phil Goldwyn's Lexus."

"You stole a car? You mean I can't let you out of my sight a minute?"

"I'll explain later."

"Well, we have a bigger problem. The burning man's coming, and he's on a mission. It seems I've pissed him off."

"Hmm, I can't imagine that..."

Stahl's shadow graduated into the room. RG waved him closer, holding his hand over the cell's speaker. "If you're not keen on the plan, now's a good time to speak up. Otherwise, we're about to get a flaming visitor."

RG understood Stahl's ties to Kacey, how he still had feelings for her and maybe always would, but he also recognized he'd never let anyone harm her, so he gave him a voice.

"We gotta protect Kacey and the baby," Stahl agreed, swiping a hand through his hair. "I'm in."

"Not a word of this, understood?"

He nodded. "Tell her to get down here."

"Where are you, Kacey?"

"I'm back home."

"Get down here as soon as you can."

"Wait," Stahl interjected. "If she's home, they'll be watching the house. They'll follow her, and we don't want her leading them here."

"Kacey, do you see anyone on the street, sitting in a car, maybe?"

"Hang on, I'm gonna head into the baby's room where it's dark." After a moment. "Okay, I'm looking."

RG waited. "Well?"

"Down the street…there's a car. Could be watching the house, I don't know. I'm not sure I can get past without them seeing me."

RG deliberated a moment. "Call Phil Goldwyn. He'll know what to do."

"Will he talk to me, since you stole his car?"

"Just call him."

Two hours later, Kacey pulled up in front of Stahl's house in Ginny Goldwyn's Honda Accord.

Chuck Brennan perched on a barstool in Liam McGuire's Irish Pub on Main Street in Falmouth nursing a warm Jameson Irish whiskey. Swishing the golden spirits in his glass before taking another swallow, he'd lost count on how many he'd downed. He would need to be sharp since he'd be flying solo on this collar, but he raised the glass to his lips anyway. By the time his expected information on Granville's whereabouts came through, he'd be sober enough to man the wheel in a speedy run to arrest the asshole. He couldn't wait to read Granville his Miranda rights, slap the cuffs on the arrogant sonofabitch, and watch the smug look melt from his face.

He eyed the blonde behind the bar, one of the new ones, packed tightly into a form fitting tee shirt and faded blue jeans. He gabbed more than usual tonight, trying to impress her with details about the Delvecchio and Abernathy murders and the multi-jurisdictional task force he'd be heading up to solve the cases. His eyes wandered up and down her body, enjoying the sights as she leaned over to scoop up the generous tips he left at the bar's edge.

His phone finally buzzed, vibrating along the solid wood bar. He checked the clock above the cash register. Better to take this one outside, away from curious ears. "Hang on a minute, honey, be right back."

He slid off the barstool and filed carefully out the front door, his gait a bit more unsteady than he'd anticipated. The cold, crisp night countered the dull warmth spreading through his veins.

"Chuck Brennan," he barked, the slur to his speech noticeable.

"Chuck, Len."

"Where the hell are you? I've been waiting hours."

"Jesus, Chuck, I've been working all day on this!" His high-pitched voice exposed an overburdened man on the brink of a nervous break-down. "If you think you can master firewalls and multiple levels of security on the sly, by all means have at it." The man let out a deep breath. "Give a guy some respect."

"You got what I need?" Brennan shifted his weight from one foot to the other, not to fend off the cold, but to counter the nervous energy around his upcoming mission, the anticipation of finally getting his due.

"Yeah, I got it, but it's going to cost ya."

"What are you talking about?" Irritation shadowed his features.

"You want the goods, you're gonna cough up a little extra."

"You little fucking weasel—"

"Listen, asshole," Len interrupted, "it's my fucking job on the line. Dirty work costs extra. You're so smart, you try doing what I do without leaving an electronic fingerprint."

The town green and public library across Main Street sank like a cutout on the horizon, sucking Brennan down with it. "What are we talking about?"

"The amount's doubled."

Maybe quicksand offered a more appealing option. He gripped his phone with a superhero's strength, ready to crack the smart device in two, his buzz quickly wearing off. "Little steep, if you ask me."

"I'm not asking, I'm telling. Cash. Tonight. Take it or leave it."

Fucking prick, trying to pull a power play on me. Brennan

submitted to his demands, agreeing to meet in an hour. He couldn't miss his one and only shot at Granville. He wandered up and down the block to calm himself, then headed back into the bar, taking one last glance at the dream polishing glassware behind the mahogany barrier. The bills stacked in front of his barstool had diminished since he'd been outside. He didn't care; she'd earned it. He motioned her over and handed her his card.

"You ever need anything, honey, don't hesitate to call." He drank in one more comprehensive look before gathering his wallet and keys from the bar.

He hurried down Main Street to his car and made the short drive to the station, unlocking a drawer in his desk containing a shoebox full of cash. He counted out the bills, stuffed the cash in a white envelope, and threw it in his jacket pocket. He moved down the hall to a second room where he gathered more items he'd need for his trip. Sliding into the cruiser's front seat, Brennan rolled down the window, and hightailed it north to Fall River.

On Route 24, he drove less than a mile before guiding his vehicle into the Haggerty Sand & Gravel Company. He crawled through the dark, dirt lot past a line of three open-ended Quonset huts filled with sand, scanning the grounds. On the far side of the dented white trailer serving as the company's main office, the Hyundai Sonata sat idling, plumes of exhaust staining the chill night air. He flashed his headlights and pulled in beside it. Thick clouds partially blocked the full moon, creating a patchwork illumination along the frozen dirt.

Brennan slid from his vehicle and stepped around to the Hyundai. He glared at the mousy-looking, bespectacled man through the open window, thinning long brown hair combed over in an attempt to delay the inevitable. Brennan handed him an envelope. "You drive a hard bargain. Where is it?"

"You know, I don't appreciate being called a fucking weasel."

Brennan leaned on his elbows through the open window. "Well, you called me an asshole. Not very collegial."

"Yeah, well you try operating under all this damned stress," Len snapped, counting out crisp bills. "And couldn't you have picked a better place? It's really out of the way."

It is, isn't it? "Can't be too careful. Nothing personal, but if we're seen together, it's jail for me, the unemployment line for you."

Len finished counting the money and placed the envelope in his jacket pocket. "Get in and I'll take you to the Lexus. Least I can do."

Brennan scanned the premises for cars, people, any sign of life before struggling into the compact Hyundai, the car settling downward as he lowered himself into the passenger seat. The man had his laptop open and a map of New England on the screen, a series of red dots sprinkled across several major routes along the map.

Len turned the laptop toward the passenger seat. "Here's what you bought."

"What the hell am I looking at? I paid double for this shit?"

"You wanted to find the Lexus? These dots tell ya where he is. You do know how to play Connect the Dots, right?" Len said with a snicker, irritating Brennan all to hell. "Thousands of electronic readers around the state, each dot timestamped. Shows he started up in Newton, passed through the Brighton tollbooth into Boston, and got off I-90 onto I-93 South."

Chuck feigned interest, waiting for the man to identify the most recent timestamped location. His hand dipped into his jacket pocket. "Just get to the punchline." Brennan had grown irritable. "Where's the fucking car, Len?"

"You want your money's worth or not? Jeez." With a sag in his shoulders, Len pinpointed the Lexus' position. "He passed through Chatham about 5:30 p.m. Last electronic reader he passed, right along Old Harbor Road. You stake out both ends of Old Harbor and you'll nail him."

Sonofabitch! Mike Stahl lived somewhere near Old Harbor Road. Brennan immediately put two and two together. His instincts proved right, Stahl couldn't be trusted working on a case involving his friend.

"Now, was that so difficult, Len?" Brennan grinned as he reached into his pocket and pulled out the .25 caliber semi-automatic handgun he'd borrowed from the evidence room. He squeezed two quick shots into the man's forehead, the slugs exiting through the back of the skull and lodging in the headrest. He grabbed the laptop and reached into the man's pocket, scattering several bills into the growing blood pool on the car seat. Brennan fished around in his pocket for the second item stolen from the evidence room, a small white bag, placing it on the car's floor mat by the man's feet. He rolled down the passenger side window and stepped from the car, wiping his fingerprints from the gun and placing it onto the ground.

He'd done his homework on Len Kramer several years ago, arresting him for heroin possession, but making the incident disappear in exchange for his indentured servitude. Unfortunately, Len had over-estimated his worth. *Only a matter of time before I had to tie up this loose end.* Len's wife and young daughter would be shocked to learn their loving husband and father had slipped back into the life and had been using again, as he'd been doing well and attending his meetings. But hell, addiction was tricky. And here he was, dead in Fall River in a car full of cash and dope. Oh well, once a junkie, always a junkie.

Brennan's grin faded as he slithered back into his car. He'd needed a new contact anyway.

"That's what you get for calling me an asshole."

CHAPTER EIGHTEEN

Thursday, December 14, 2017

Kacey and RG hunkered on the couch in Mike Stahl's house reading the headline story on page one of the *Boston Herald*.

'FUGITIVE PROFESSOR' WANTED IN TWO MURDERS—Boston (AP)—A Boston University professor is now on the run in a sensational crime story about sex, money, and murder. Media outlets across the country have descended on BU in what has now been dubbed the 'Fugitive Professor' case.

Associate Professor Robert Granville, 35, evaded arrest late Thursday afternoon for allegedly murdering two people: a BU colleague and a lifelong friend. The story took a curious turn last week when Falmouth police questioned Granville, having found the body of his friend, John Delvecchio, 36, brutally slain in his home.

The murder is believed to be associated with a substantial financial loss in one of Delvecchio's investment schemes. At the time of questioning, the Falmouth police could not establish enough evidence to hold Granville, but forensic evidence later placed him at the murder scene. The lead detective, Ray Harrington would not comment publicly, but Falmouth Police Chief Charles Brennan told the Herald, "Mr. Granville is our primary suspect and although he's currently a fugitive from justice, we are confident an arrest is imminent."

Additionally, forensic evidence has also placed Granville at the site of the murder of Dr. Wendell Abernathy, 51, in his Andover home. Dr. Abernathy, Granville's superior at BU, had apparently been the victim of a hostile relationship with the professor throughout his tenure. Just a week ago, faculty at BU witnessed a verbal argument between the two men.

Authorities learned a former student, Brittany Thorne, 20, had admitted to having a sexual relationship with Granville, which Abernathy had been investigating. Another source at BU informed *The Herald* a finding of sexual misconduct with a student would likely result in a revocation of Dr. Granville's tenure and dismissal from the university.

Ironically, Granville had recently saved the life of a young boy who'd fallen onto the tracks in front of an oncoming train at Kenmore station.

RG slapped the paper onto the table. "Looks like I won't be giving my students their final exams tomorrow."

Kacey slurped her steaming decaf. "Not if you're the 'Fugitive Professor.'" She rescued the abused newspaper and perused the damning article. "I doubt your students will be filing any complaints."

He swiped both hands through his frazzled mane. "Whether I make it through this ordeal or not, the world will forever think I'm a goddamn murderer!"

Stahl entered from the kitchen. "Leave it to me, RG. I'll unravel how Brennan set you up and go from there. As for the other murder, the lead detectives might let me examine the evidence. We have to prove doubt."

RG dragged himself off the couch and into the kitchen, leaving the paper with Kacey. "Did anybody ever tell you your optimism's fucking annoying?"

"Once or twice. But listen, RG, we'll prove you couldn't have murdered Abernathy. We'll go through neighborhood home security video, eyewitnesses, whatever. As for the Falmouth evidence, it's dirty, and we'll have to prove that, too."

"Except they have DNA from both scenes, which pretty much seals my fate."

"Not if we can raise doubt how it got there."

RG rested against the doorjamb. "It'll take a miracle."

"Or a good detective." Stahl leaned against the counter and poured himself a coffee. "Ninety percent of wrongfully convicted suspects could've been exonerated if someone—anyone—examined all the evidence instead of making a rush to judgment. Let me work on that."

RG stepped into the kitchen, locking onto Mike's eyes. "There's nothing in it for you, but I'm counting on you to clear my name." RG's plea communicated the implicit understanding he'd never be arrested, he'd never go to trial, and no verdict would ever be reached. RG bought a one-way ticket for this ride, one Stahl agreed to punch for him. But he didn't want to be remembered as a murderer. He didn't want his child growing up with the shame.

"That's where you're wrong. There *is* something in it for me. I have a chance to put that sonofabitch Brennan away for good because there's no doubt in my mind he's framing you, and I'm gonna prove it. And don't forget, I witnessed the truth in the burning man's mind."

Stahl tossed back another coffee gulp. "You'll be disappointed to learn I ain't doing this because we're chums. If clearing your name helps Kacey, I'm gonna do it."

RG stared at the man who'd both kill him and clear him. *That would get you in good with her, wouldn't it?* He bristled at the idea of leaving Kacey alone in the world with Mr. Right-there-waiting. She'd love again someday, but did it have to be him? He'd have to give her more credit and trust he wasn't just a placeholder, sandwiched between relationships with Stahl.

"Well, I'm getting a little claustrophobic. I'm going to take a walk on the beach to clear my head. Anyone want to join me?"

"Too cold out." Kacey's posture remained stagnant, her nose still buried in the paper.

"Whoa, you can forget that." Mike occupied the doorway, preventing passage. "When your face is plastered all over the media for two murders, you don't go parading around town."

"You may be the bad-ass detective at the office, tossing around orders, but if I don't get some fresh air, I'm gonna need a straightjacket."

Mike sighed and sent an SOS to Kacey. "Can you talk some sense into him?"

"Who? Me?" She lifted her cup to her lips, still engrossed in the news.

"For Chrissake!" Mike flew to the closet and rummaged through shelves and containers. He tossed RG a hat, sunglasses, woolen scarf, unconcerned whether they landed in his hands or on the floor. The last item to fly across the entryway elicited a snicker.

RG pinched what could be mistaken as a mop head. "What in the hell is this? A Halloween wig?"

"Wear it, or stay in."

"Aren't you taking this disguise thing too far?"

"When you're sitting in a six-by-eight cell with a rusty toilet and sink, you can answer that question."

RG gathered the disguise pieces and tromped down the hall to the bathroom mirror. After coordinating the ensemble, he advanced with sheepish steps into the hallway. "Okay, how do I look?"

Kacey glanced up, dropping the newspaper into her lap.

Stahl held a hand across his mouth, eyebrows raised.

"Like the lead guitarist in an eighties hair-band," Kacey replied, breaking the pressing silence. "You just need the black leather pants."

"Maybe we should call him Slash?"

"That's it!" RG reached up, dismantling his ridiculous costume. "The hell with this!"

Mike intercepted him, haphazardly piling the hat, wig, and scarf back in place, flattening it down with his hands. He stood in front of RG, squinting and straightening until it passed inspection, like a parent fussing over his child before sending him out the door on Halloween.

Mike tugged on the wig's right side and nodded. "Okay, RG, I'm done. Now you're unrecognizable! Head out the back door and take Highland down to Seaview. It'll get you right across from Aunt Lydia's Cove. You can't miss the beach entrance."

RG growled as he walked out the front door into the dark.

Kacey's head swung around. "Be careful, Slash."

RG navigated the dark streets winding their way toward the beach, his hat and scarf keeping him warm and hidden from the world, his wig triggering a furious itch along his neck and scalp. Every few steps, he heaved the entire ensemble off his head and ran a set of eager nails through his hair to appease his discomfort. With each adjustment, the wig came down in a different position until he could no longer tell if it disguised or drew attention. *Unless a number of retired eighties rockers live in this town, I may be fucked.*

The wintery streets conveyed no signs of life as RG made his way to Aunt Lydia's Cove. He walked along Shore Road, the ocean's muted roar on his right. On his left, the dancing blue light of oversized LED screens illuminated the million dollar homes' darkened windows; TVs flickering, but no one marveling at the spectacular display of nature's starlight, ocean, and crashing surf.

He quickened his pace along the deserted beachfront. Glancing toward the sea, RG jumped as a shimmering outline appeared beside him. Filling with matter from shoes to hat, Morrow assumed his human shape as he flipped into the world from another realm.

"Holy mother, you scared the hell out of me." RG thumped his hand against his chest. "My heart rate just doubled."

"Rather me than the burning man, don't you think?"

"Right now, I could use him to heat this place up with a cozy bonfire."

"If you'd quit choosing the coldest days for a cardiovascular workout…"

RG shoved his hands deeper into his pockets, certain why Morrow had joined him. "What's on Victor's agenda now?"

"He's on the move, and you need to brush up on your training."

"I thought you said I'm ready?" They continued along Shore Road, passing the Chatham Pier Fish Market.

Morrow grabbed RG's coat sleeve and forced him into eye contact. "Since I've been hovering around you for hours now and you've failed to detect me, I'd suspect maybe you're not. Or, you're not paying attention."

"Checking up on me, eh?"

"It's a good thing, too."

"Then you're aware of my new nickname, the 'Fugitive Professor.' Has a nice ring to it, doesn't it?"

"I wouldn't be too hyped up about your adopted criminal nickname. You should be more concerned with your failure to sense Victor's presence at the murdered man's home the other night."

RG remembered the multiple bouts of nausea. "Well, at the time I'd been getting my ass kicked, I guess it didn't register."

"You can't imagine the ass kicking you're gonna get if you fail to tune in."

"From who? You or Victor?"

Waving his hand, Morrow dismissed RG's attempt at humor. "Now it's time to clear your mind and be alert. Time's dwindling. I won't be here to get you out of any more messes."

"Considering you've gotten me *into* all of them so far, I'm not sure if I should be too upset."

Morrow glared at him over the rim of his glasses.

The wind picked up, twisting RG's wig to the side, the long stringy hair whipping into his eyes, impeding his vision. He parted his hair like a curtain, curling the synthetic fiber behind his ears.

"You know, you look like the lead guitarist of an eighties rock—"

"Ah, kiss my ass!" He lowered his head against the sea breeze's frozen sting, gave an exaggerated flip to his jacket collar, and jammed his hands into his pockets.

Morrow kept pace as RG hurried down the road. "I understand you're relying on Mr. Stahl to help carry out a plan."

"Mike understands what's at stake here. He's ready to do what he has to do to save Kacey and the baby."

"But the question is, Robert, are you?"

"It doesn't matter if I'm ready. The burning man's coming."

Morrow placed his hand on RG's shoulder. "When he does, I'll be close by. I can't tell you how proud I am of you."

They strode in silence along Aunt Lydia's Cove, the wind-blown sand stinging their exposed skin. "I must leave you now, Robert."

RG lifted his hands. "You just got here. Walk with me a while."

"No, I mean I must leave you now—for good."

RG stopped in his tracks. "What?"

"I've been summoned back to my world. A new assignment has arisen. I told you we'd only have a brief period of time together before I had to return."

"Well, it's coming at a pretty bad time."

Morrow gave him a comforting smile. "According to you, I've done enough here already!"

"Can't you do anything? Ask for an extension or something?"

Morrow sighed. "If I could stay with you longer, I would. But there are some decisions even I can't challenge. Don't worry, you're ready."

RG glanced away, out over the ocean. "Will I ever see you again?"

"Not in this world."

RG steadied himself against Morrow's shoulder, his head spinning as if the wind blew straight through it, lifting his fragmented thoughts into the air and swirling them around. "I can't do this alone."

Morrow broke the mounting silence, "You're not alone. Ever."

A wave of numbing cold grew in RG's chest, nothing to do with the frozen December night. "Can I ask a favor?"

"Anything."

RG pulled his hands from his pocket and grasped the gold wedding band on his finger, struggling to shimmy it past his knuckle. "I guess my fingers were a little thinner five years ago." He squeezed it into Morrow's palm. "Listen, I have no idea what's gonna happen…you know, when I face the burning man. Will you hold this for safekeeping? That way it won't get all scorched or mangled."

Morrow rolled the ring between his fingers. "Of course, Robert."

"I'm thinking, if I don't make it through this, maybe you can meet up with Kacey some night in her dreams and give it back to her. Maybe tell her how much I miss her, too."

Morrow took the ring and placed it in the breast pocket of his coat. "I will."

"If I do make it through this somehow," RG smirked, "it can be an incentive to find a way to come back and drop it off to me. Maybe spend the day."

RG turned toward the ocean, shoving his hands deeper into his pockets to counter the biting wind sweeping in from the sea. He needed a moment, desperate to extend his final minutes with Morrow, but at a loss to fill the pressing silence. "I never asked you this, but is there a heaven?"

"The million-dollar question," he chuckled. "In my world, we worship our different gods and hope for salvation, like you do. I can't say if there's a heaven, but I can say there's always something on the other side of the door."

RG and Morrow scuffed along the cold asphalt road, their footsteps falling in a predictable cadence, but soon the sound diminished until he could only hear his own. When RG turned to Morrow, he'd evaporated into the chilled atmosphere without a word. He'd grown accustomed to the man's unannounced arrivals and departures, but now it would be forever. He stood in the cold, truly alone for the first time in his life.

Time to steer his frigid body home, but not until after taking a short detour.

RG exited the road toward a set of rickety, wooden steps leading onto the beach. They creaked with a sharp complaint in the thin, frozen air as he descended, trudging through the shifting sand toward the water. He surveyed the vast expanse of inky blackness, trying to differentiate the point at which the dark water turned to night sky.

RG contemplated the infinite number of times he'd stared out over the ocean, each viewing a unique experience, like seeing it for the first time, every time. In a world where few experiences stoke the senses with their originality, the ocean forever gave him such a gift. And tonight it appeared different still, providing a renewed sense of strength he wasn't sure he possessed until now. He savored the moment, a calm surrender falling on him, peace and strength coiled within him like DNA.

He stood ready for the burning man.

When RG left, Mike Stahl stepped back into the living room, refreshed Kacey's decaf and sat in the recliner across from her. She glanced at him as he checked a text message. How many times had she sat in this exact spot, inside this house? It hadn't changed one bit, from the familiar wear spots in the carpet to the splits in the wood paneling. It comforted her and repelled her at the same time. Kacey found herself trapped in a memory of a life long forgotten. She almost expected Mike's mom to shuffle in from the hallway and ask what they wanted for dinner. Maybe sitting in Mike's house again after all these years opened up a different type of portal for her, but she didn't want to travel through this one again.

"Quite a dream you had the other night." Stahl glanced from his device.

"It got a lot worse after you left, believe me."

He caught site of reddened marks on Kacey's arms and neck. "I'm pretty sure you saved my life."

"I brought you there, my responsibility to take care of you."

Stahl nodded his head in appreciation. "I wanted to say thanks… It's good to be alive." He ran a nervous hand across the stubble of his jaw. "Listen, Kacey, I'm sorry about the things I said in the restaurant. It wasn't fair to you. But I wouldn't have said them if I hadn't thought I was dreaming."

"It's okay. We finally talked, didn't we? Long time since we've been honest with each other." Kacey folded her legs underneath her and leaned against the couch's armrest.

"Hell of a breakfast, too, but when I woke up I'd gained five pounds." He pressed both hands to his belly. "I'm blaming you for that."

"Me? You ate enough for a small family!"

"You said it wouldn't count!"

Kacey grinned. "Looks like its back on the treadmill."

Kacey powered up her phone for the first time since she'd arrived at Mike's, text messages popping up on the screen, pinging and multiplying before her eyes, her friends and family now learning of the 'Fugitive Professor.'

What happened with RG?

Are you okay?

I never trusted that bastard!

Kacey buried the device in her pocket. She'd worry about the problems of this world, later, after taking care of the next world's. She endured the weight of Mike's eyes from across the room.

"Nice having you back in the house, it's like nothing's changed."

Kacey sighed. "Except everything *has* changed. You know that."

Stahl didn't seem to hear her, his mind snagged on a memory. "Do you remember all the times my mom would walk in on us when we sat over there?" He nodded toward the couch.

Kacey rolled her eyes and let out a forced exhale. "Mike...stop."

"I'll always remember the look on her face," he continued, "as if she'd seen the devil himself." He chuckled and leaned forward. "Do you remember how she'd mutter 'dear Lord' and bless herself?"

Kacey sprung from the couch, arms folded across her chest. "That's enough, Mike!"

He recoiled as if she'd slapped him across the face.

"I don't want to talk about our past, I don't want to reminisce about a life that's been over for fifteen years." Kacey held up her hand, showing him her ring. "I've been married five years. That man outside in the cold, the guy in the wig, he's my life, my world. And I may lose him." Tears swelled in the corners of her eyes as she held her arms around her stomach. "I may lose everything."

"I'm sorry, Kacey. I didn't mean to make you uncomfortable. I just had this flashback to when—"

"Your whole life's a goddamn flashback! I appreciate your helping us, Mike, but I can't be the reason you're doing this."

"You're not, Kacey. Well, maybe you are." Stahl threw his hands up. "I don't even know anymore." He turned and disappeared into the kitchen.

Kacey followed him, watching from the doorway.

Stahl grabbed the coffee pot, rinsed it, and tossed it in the dish rack. He leaned against the counter, his back to Kacey.

"Maybe RG and I should leave, find someplace else to hide."

"You can't, someone will spot you. You're safer here." Stahl grabbed a beer from the refrigerator, twisted off the top, and downed a gulp.

"Mike, don't!"

He pivoted to face Kacey, pointing his finger at her. "You can't tell me what to do!" He slammed the bottle onto the kitchen table, an explosion of golden foam erupting like a volcano, the bottle shattering. "The world's ending! The devil's heading to my house!" He kicked at the kitchen chair, knocking it onto its side. "And it's gonna kill the only thing I ever loved in this world. Why the hell shouldn't I start drinking again?"

Stahl wheeled around and stomped out into the cold, slamming the back door behind him.

CHAPTER NINETEEN

Friday, December 15, 2017

Chuck Brennan crouched low in the driver's seat of the Ford Taurus parked on Old Harbor Road. He conducted routine surveillance on Stahl's dwelling using binoculars and his side and rearview mirrors. He tossed two aspirin and swallowed them, his head still pounding from the Irish whiskey exacting its revenge and a restless, sleepless night.

Brennan had limped into Falmouth around midnight, and with his mind still fuzzy from alcohol, assembled a haphazard checklist to cover his tracks. After he'd jettisoned Kramer's laptop in the harbor, he pulled his car into the garage and scrubbed the driver's side seats and floor mats with ammonia and detergent.

He burned his clothes and shoes in the fireplace, took a shower, scoured the bathtub and counters, and then vacuumed the carpets to dispose of any trace evidence he may have dragged in. It had been a long time since he'd killed a man, and afterward Brennan lay in bed shaking like a wet kitten, thoughts of how today's DNA technology could turn an overlooked fingernail, hair, eyelash, or even blood mist into a one-way trip to life behind bars.

When his head finally hit the pillow just after 4:30 a.m., a fitful sleep awaited him, and in those fleeting dawn hours Brennan dreamed of Len Kramer and his family. The gunshots had been louder than he'd expected. Maybe the small car's enclosed space or the night's silence had amplified the blast, but the ringing in his ears hadn't stopped yet. Maybe it wouldn't. Maybe the image of Kramer's face would fade and let him breathe again, but it seemed to be getting stronger, choking him like a noose tightening around his neck.

Brennan closed his eyes, wishing the aspirin would hurry up and do its thing. He needed a clear head to outline his attack. He'd approach the rear of the house as soon as darkness fell. He'd first have to ascertain the two men's positions inside the house, then wait until the moment presented itself. He had his service revolver and a second gun in an ankle holster just in case. After what he'd learned from Detective Daniels that morning, he'd most likely be shooting at least one more person today.

Earlier in the day, Stahl had been busy working from home, the previous night's revelations leaving Kacey and him tiptoeing around each other. He'd embarrassed himself in front of her, a defeated man drinking out of desperation. Maybe he could turn it around somehow, find the evidence to clear RG's name, and salvage her respect. He'd made a promise and intended to keep it.

By mid-morning he'd escaped to his desk at the station, safe once again in the solitude of his cocoon, but he couldn't elude the anxiety gnawing at him. Leaning back in his chair, Stahl rubbed his face as if his calloused paws could scour away his vexing reality. His situation presented an unsolvable equation, a Zen Koan, a problem with no solution. His mind had played out every scenario, but no option had a favorable outcome.

RG had made it sound so simple—kill him, the burning man dies, and Kacey lives. But if he pulled the trigger, he'd kill the love of her life. He'd be the man who'd yanked her heart out, forever associated with her greatest loss. No way would she forgive him, allow him to make amends or reassemble the pieces of his life with her.

And how would he explain to his colleagues the .45 caliber slug they'd pull out of RG's head with the rifling from his HK45? He wouldn't be spending his time trying to clear RG's name, but fighting his own murder charge. He wouldn't have much of an argument against the ballistic evidence, but maybe he could tell everyone he did it to kill a supernatural being from the next world. Yeah, right! Slap on the straightjacket and take him away to Bellevue. Neither option too rosy in his view.

If he didn't pull the trigger, Kacey dies, plain and simple. He'd been inside the burning man's head, he'd heard the final solution for her. Could he live with himself knowing he'd done nothing to save the woman he still loved? Would a lifetime in prison be an appropriate trade-off for her life?

How much different would it be from the life I'm living now?

Stahl cleared his distracted mind and set about following through on his promise to sift through the evidence to help clear RG. He picked up the phone, finger poised over the punch keys. *God, what's the point? Why am I bothering?* If he could burn Brennan before all the shit goes down, then it would be worth it, and if the pieces fell into place for RG, so much the better. He stabbed at the buttons, placing the morning's first call to the Falmouth Police Department. Chris Daniels picked up on the first ring.

"Detective Daniels, Mike Stahl, Chatham PD."

"Detective Stahl, what a surprise. Really great stuff you presented at the BCI seminar on crime scene investigation last spring. I appreciate your taking time to talk to me afterward."

Stahl pictured the eager cop, recalling the same enthusiasm he had displayed in the same forum a decade earlier. "If I recall, you challenged me pretty hard on several topics."

"I'm hoping to go through the Bureau's CIO program someday."

"You'd be a good fit. Let me know if you ever need my support."

"Yes, sir. So, what can I do for you?"

Stahl leaned back in his chair. "I'm following up on the Delvecchio case. I processed the crime scene along with Russ Randle, and I need information about evidentiary chain of command."

"Any problem?"

He backed off. "Just a routine follow-up to find out when everything got catalogued and sent up to BCI. I don't want lawyers claiming procedural violations, especially when an investigator knew the suspect and victim. There's already been too much media coverage on this case."

"Then you need to talk to Chief Brennan. He's the one who took control of the evidence and delivered it to BCI."

Stahl stood from his desk. *Brennan, alone with the evidence.* "Isn't that unusual protocol?"

"From what I understand, he wanted to oversee it since, as you said, this is a high-profile case."

Yeah, I'm sure that's why. "Well, I can't think of anyone I'd rather have taking charge of the evidence," he lied. "As long as he handled everything personally, I'm confident there won't be any procedural tie-ups going forward."

"You want me to put you through to him? He could answer your questions better than I can?"

"Thanks detective, but no need to bother him." Mike hung up.

I got the answers I needed.

With the morning's second call, Stahl dialed Claire Simpson, an overworked laboratory director at BCI who processed forensic evidence from crime scenes all over Cape Cod and the Islands. A couple years on the far side of thirty, she could've passed for a college student with her youthful appearance and adventurous spirit.

He'd known Claire for the better part of five years, two of which they had spent in an on-again, off-again relationship. Mostly off. Claire had told him she'd no longer compete for him with a ghost, a haunting she sensed behind his faraway eyes and within the sturdy walls he'd built to keep the world at bay. Still, whenever Stahl had business at

BCI, he grabbed Claire for lunch, wondering whether the flicker behind her charcoal eyes could be the shadow of a flame she hoped might burn again.

"Well, well, Mike Stahl," Claire purred, "I hope you're calling to take me to lunch because I left mine on the kitchen counter today."

He could imagine her grin over the phone. "Is that all I am to you, a free lunch?"

"Consider it an upgrade. You used to be just a roll in the hay." She giggled.

"Lunch is an upgrade?"

"No offense, Mike, but you have no idea how much we ladies treasure our calories."

He cleared his throat. "Well, Claire, I wish I could satisfy whatever it is you hunger for today, but I'm calling for another reason. I need something from you and I need it fast."

"That was never your style." Another giggle.

He swallowed. "Now, Claire."

"Come on, Mike. Where's your sense of humor? What do you need?"

"How fast can you run a side-by-side blood comparison?" He doodled on a small notepad.

"Any particular case?"

"The 'Fugitive Professor.' I need you to find out whether the Delvecchio blood swab from Granville's car contained EDTA."

"The anticoagulant?" She lowered her voice. "What are you thinking?"

He let out a short breath. "Russ and I used EDTA blood storage vials at the scene, and they stored it back at the Falmouth Police Station. I have a suspicion it wound up in Granville's car."

"That's a serious accusation."

"And I need evidence to back it up."

"Well, I could compare the blood swabs from the car steering wheel to the whole blood collected at Russ's lab without the EDTA vials." Claire remained silent for a moment. "Mike, if the blood from Granville's car contains EDTA, then—"

"Brennan planted it," he interrupted. "That's what I need to find out. How fast can you do it?" Mike held his breath.

"Jesus, Mike, I can't sneak out samples to work on without authorization."

Stahl pressed. "You run the laboratory."

"Yeah, and it could cost me my job."

"Listen, there's no one I can turn to for authorization since Brennan's involved with the investigation. This has to be done off the books. Can you do it?"

"I don't know."

He pictured her chewing the end of her pencil. "I hate asking, but I need it."

Claire shed an exaggerated sigh. "I can get it done by mid-afternoon. But you owe me big, and not just lunch."

Her statement hung out there for a moment before her chuckle grew from the other end of the line. Stahl wasn't sure what it meant, but he agreed to it.

Earlier, Brennan had rested heavily in his desk chair, head in his hands, temples pounding through his fingertips as if they each had their own pulse. The wall clock ticked like repetitive hammer strikes on hard concrete. Brennan betrayed the evidence of his late night out, a touch more pink-eyed than usual on a Friday morning, but keeping with the legend surrounding his well-known carousing.

Daniels popped his head into Brennan's office. "Chief, you got a sec?"

"What do you need, Chris?" he mumbled.

"I talked to Mike this morning about CIO training up at BCI, and—"

"Mike who?" Brennan interrupted.

"Mike Stahl. He called this morning."

"What did he want?"

"Well, he wanted information about chain of command on the

Delvecchio case, the evidence transport. It sounded like he may have been trying to cover his ass since he knew both the victim and suspect."

"What did you tell him?"

Daniels cleared his throat. "Um, I told him you had it under control. Trust me, it made him much more comfortable when he heard that."

"Of course, it did." Brennan frowned. "Didn't want to talk to me?"

"Didn't want to waste your time, I guess."

I'm sure I'm the last guy he wanted to talk to.

"In any case, Mike offered to put in a good word for me up at BCI, and I wondered—"

"Let's talk about it later." Brennan rubbed his temples as he sank deeper into his chair. "I'll call him…reassure him we handled things properly."

"Sorry I didn't put him through to you earlier."

"No problem." Brennan snatched the receiver and punched in Stahl's number. He stopped halfway through and shot a sharp glance at Daniels, who nodded and backed out of the office.

When Daniels closed the door, Brennan hung up, no point in calling. *I'm sure Mike already suspects how we handled things over here.*

The change took full control of Victor, welcoming the fire burning freely in his body. It had been coming for a long time and he'd been patient, succumbing to its seduction entirely. And now he *was* the change, everything in his previous form dead to him now. He existed only as the burning man.

The time had arrived to balance the ledger with Morrow.

He would first kill the beautiful one. She had impressed him with her stealth, her ability to find him and sneak up on him, but he didn't fear her power. Her defenses would be no match for him now. She'd suffer his wrath in an explosion of burning pain the likes of which she could not comprehend. Nothing like the spa treatment he'd given her in the cave.

"That was just a warm-up." He chuckled at his pun, reveling in the sound of his contempt echoing off the cave walls.

But mostly, she'd pay for deceiving him, for fooling him into thinking there'd be more for him in his eternal limbo. He'd make her and the child die painfully. It no longer mattered whether he used Granville to kill her or not. He'd suffer the rest of his life either way. Morrow, too. Victor frowned as he anticipated how hard it would be *not* to kill Granville. It would require the restraint and efficiency he'd been cultivating in his recent cleansings.

But the change had come. He now bathed in nothing but pure fire.

An eternal fire, burning out of control.

CHAPTER TWENTY

F riday, December 15, 2017
Despite the serenity RG had savored the previous night on the sands of Aunt Lydia's Cove, a cloud of restlessness hovered over him. He stared out Stahl's back door as daylight leached from the sky, waiting for the incomprehensible, a confrontation he'd anticipated but could never fully prepare for. Kacey had spent the day on the couch reading, the antithesis of RG's nervous energy. But he'd lived with her long enough to diagnose the calm in her detached manner belied a terror she chose to keep hidden, the dread of what she'd already experienced in the burning man's cave and what soon awaited them.

RG had spent the day flipping through the *Herald* and checking the 'Fugitive Professor' coverage on the news, squinting to make out the picture on Stahl's antiquated twelve-inch cathode ray tube TV. *Another eighties relic in Mike's living museum!* Unable to stop snacking, RG had worn a groove in the shag carpeting, invading Stahl's pantry every few minutes to combat boredom and anxiety. He would re-stock if Stahl ever let him leave the house again, but after last night's humiliating game of dress-up, he crossed it off his list.

At 5:30 p.m., Stahl called to tell him he'd be coming home with pizza. RG collapsed on the couch beside Kacey. "Great, more food coming."

Kacey leaned against him. "We haven't talked strategy for the burning man yet."

"Strategy?" Guilt burned in his chest, his strategy already coordinated with Stahl. He stared into his wife's soothing eyes, which struck him like a view of earth from space, the solid blue broken up with hints of green and brown, maybe even a fleck of white, opening her inner universe. How he would miss getting lost there. He stole a precious moment to commit her intricacies to memory, recording details he treasured about her, even rare flaws, something to hold onto in case this was the last chance he'd have to spend with her. "Well, I'm going to divert his attention from you and the baby. That's the strategy."

"But I've faced him before, up close. What would you have me do, sit on the couch and watch?"

RG failed to keep eye contact. "I just want you and the baby to be safe."

Kacey rose and ambled into the kitchen, pouring herself a mug of decaf. "God, I wish I could pry open that door inside his mind. I'm sure we'd find a weakness, something we could use against him."

"I've tried to learn everything I could about him. I've done internet and library searches. I've met with detectives who worked his case. All I have are random facts that don't add up."

"Like what?"

RG rose from the couch. "Well, when Sam got to the hospital, the kid was so sick, there was little they could do, yet his type of cancer would have been treatable if caught early."

"Why'd they wait so long?"

"Maybe they were afraid of doctors. It seems Victor never went to one."

"Ever?"

"Not that they could find."

"Maybe they couldn't afford it." Kacey returned from the kitchen and dropped onto the couch.

"He worked in an insurance company. I'm sure he had benefits."

"What else?"

He paced the floor, taking his time. "His wife, Lucy, took out a protective order against Victor just weeks before the boy's death, before she took him to the hospital."

"Was he threatening her?"

"It was taken out to protect the boy."

"Sam?" Kacey frowned. "Didn't Victor practically live at the hospital with him?"

"He never left his side."

"So why the order? It's clear she didn't follow through with it."

"The day after Sam died, a neighbor witnessed Lucy and Victor arguing in their driveway, and she punched him. Somewhere, there's a story. I just don't know what." He shrugged as Kacey sipped her decaf.

Killing time, they assembled a theory from all the information, bandied it about it, and watched it fall apart. Kacey lay back onto the couch, deep in thought. RG continued pacing, but after several minutes, he stopped dead in his tracks. He squinted toward Kacey, mouth hanging open. In an instant, the seemingly random facts coalesced, making perfect sense. Victor had been hiding something behind the door, something big. *If I'm gonna die, at least the burning man is gonna hear the goddamn truth and face up to his past!* When Kacey glanced up at him, he explained his theory.

"Oh my God! He's been living a lie."

"And he's going to deal with the truth one way or another."

Brennan adjusted his view in the side mirror as the Crown Vic pulled into the driveway. He'd give Stahl a few minutes to settle in, take off his shoes, and hang up his sidearm. Brennan slid from the Taurus's front seat and crossed Old Harbor Road. Veiled in darkness, he made repeated passes in front of the house, attempting to triangulate Stahl and Granville's location, but he couldn't identify any shapes or movement through the drawn curtains and blinds.

He checked his watch. 6:22 p.m.

Brennan revisited the scattered string of thoughts from his protracted stakeout. Arresting Stahl for harboring Granville would not deter him from revealing the truth about the planted blood evidence. Stahl would dig, tests would be done, and fingers would point in Brennan's direction. He'd considered framing Daniels, but he couldn't do it to the kid, even though he'd handled the evidence and would be the perfect fall guy. The only solution? Make it all go away tonight. If he couldn't arrest Stahl, then he'd silence him. And if he silenced Stahl, he'd have to tie up other loose end. Brennan set his jaw and drew his gun as he crept slowly toward the back door.

As Stahl entered from the garage and slapped the pizza box onto the kitchen table, RG and Kacey descended like vultures. Somehow RG remained famished, despite clearing the house of nearly every morsel of food. He savored the taste and texture of every topping and cheese string pulled off its flatbread base, just in case this turned out to be his last supper.

Reaching for another slice, he pulled his hand away. His gut curdled with nausea and his head suddenly ignited. He clutched the back of the kitchen chair to keep his balance.

Kacey stood, gripping him by the arm. "What's the matter?"

"I need water." RG cradled his head as his world crept back into focus.

Stahl leaned toward him. "What is it, RG?"

"It's happening."

Kacey hurried to the fridge. "What's happening?"

"The burning man." RG then whispered to Stahl. "I need a few minutes to concentrate and draw him to me. You know what to do? Right?"

"Rehearsed and ready."

Kacey handed RG a water bottle, and he downed the cool liquid, quelling the just-eaten pizza rising in his throat. Pulling Kacey close, he squeezed his eyes shut as they settled into each other's arms.

"Remember, the burning man's gunning for you," he whispered, "and if he succeeds, he gets to the baby. I'll draw him to me."

"And I'll approach him from the next world, get into his mind again, see if I can—"

"No fuckin' way!" RG stepped back with raised hands. "I'm not letting you jump worlds and risk losing you again."

"I'm not going anywhere, RG, it'll just be in my mind." She reached for his hand. "I'll be right here with you. Maybe I can rattle his cage from the other side."

"Okay," he said, heart settling into its normal rhythm. "Whatever you do, be careful." He pressed his hands against her face and gave her a slow kiss. "I love you, Kacey Granville." He reached down for her hand, squeezing it twice.

Kacey nestled her head against him. "Any chance we could just hop a flight to the Bahamas tonight instead? Not that we can afford it…"

RG fought the emotional wave cresting inside, tightening his throat, stinging his eyes. "We'll have all the time in the world after tonight." He glanced over at Mike, who lowered his eyes.

"Okay, let's do this." RG paced the living room floor, a calm settling over him, the anticipation over, freeing him to focus on what Morrow had taught him. He concentrated on achieving a dreamlike state, eliminating all extraneous thoughts, his mind opening to a place beyond his vision. The burning man lingered nearby, his heat singeing the small hairs on his arms.

In the deep recesses of his mind, he made contact. *"Show yourself already. If you think I fear you, you're dead wrong."*

"Interesting choice of words," the burning man replied.

Chief Brennan stole around the house's perimeter, searching for a window to view the kill zone inside, but every shade had been drawn tight. With the necessary fix on their location, he could take them out quickly, no time to react or return fire. The first window on the far side offered a sliver of daylight between the drawn shade and window ledge. Brennan squinted through the illuminated crack, but could only observe the living room's lower third, couches, chairs, and a coffee table, someone pacing and another set of legs standing in the doorway to the kitchen. To his surprise, he discovered a third person, a woman sitting on the couch, very much pregnant.

Of all the goddamn luck! He flipped around and sagged against the house, a groan escaping his lips. He slid down along the weathered shingles until seated on a bed of leaves. Resting his elbows on his knees, Brennan grasped his head with his hands, rubbing his temples in slow circles, contemplating the mess he found himself in.

A pregnant woman, a goddamn pregnant woman...

Brennan steeled himself for the grim task ahead. It was either her or him—if he let her live he'd go to jail...not an option. He'd have to choreograph a shootout, take the men out first, and then use Stahl's gun to shoot the woman—collateral damage attributable to a wayward cop. Brennan rubbed his jaw. If he suffered an injury during the shootout, that would make things even more convincing. A through-and-through in the upper arm or right above the hip at the love handle would help justify the carnage. Either one would hurt like a bitch. A frown played at his lips, but turned to an ugly grin as he imagined the following day's headline story about a smart cop with a hunch taking out the 'Fugitive Professor' and the crooked detective harboring him. The story of a man putting his life on the line for his town, the story of a hero.

But first things first.

He moved with deliberate steps to the second window. Along the window's vertical edge, Brennan spied Mike Stahl standing between rooms, his sidearm holstered under his shoulder. *The sonofabitch must be expecting me! When I kick in the door, he's the first one I drop.* Then the other two. Afterward, he'd do a thorough search, room by room.

Just to be sure.

Brennan made his way to the back of the house, taking the steps to the raised, wooden deck leading to the back door. *Time to be a fucking hero.* He checked his sidearm and made sure the safety was off.

~

RG could sense the burning man in his head, surrounding him, but he couldn't see him. Kacey reclined on the couch, moving her mind toward the portal, where she could slip into the next world. He found himself in complete control of his mental focus, dialed in and aggressively relaxed.

"Should I call you Victor?" RG spoke deep into his mind. *"Or is there some other name you prefer?"*

"You don't get to call me by any name." The burning man's pulsating heat stabbed at RG.

"Why not? Are the names of twisted suicidal murderers like yourself off limits or something?"

"Taunting me?" he rumbled.

"Oh, I haven't even started." A fiery wave passed in front of RG, as if he'd placed his head inside a 500-degree oven.

"How stupidly brave you are! But it's not you I want. Today, you'll witness me roast your wife and child, so you understand what loss means. Then, torment will consume you the way burning flames would."

RG's knees bent like a folding jackknife.

"Is this all Morrow taught you? To distract me? Ha! You put your faith in a fool."

RG's heart sank, the burning man not biting. *"What do you know about faith?"* he spat. The burning man released a searing flame from behind, the scorching heat passing directly through him.

"I gave forty-two years of my life to faith!" the burning man growled in RG's head. *"You know what faith taught me?"*

RG could taste his stench just inches from him and sense his desire to enter him, char his insides.

"Faith taught me if there is a God, he can't be bothered. He sits idly by, unmoved by human suffering. A life of faith has no reward. There's only life and pain, over and over again. World after world."

The burning man circled him. RG closed his eyes, his muscle tendons and chords tense and tight. Silently begging the burning man to enter him and not Kacey, RG braced for the jolt when the demon threw himself inside his skin—and when the bullet pierced his brain.

The burning man spoke the words of a preacher from a different world. *"2 Peter, 3:10. 'But the day of the Lord will come like a thief in the night, in which the heavens will pass away with a roar, the elements will be destroyed with intense heat, and the earth and its works will be burned away.'"*

The heat was unbearable.

"Your people wait for God?" he chortled with a mountainous echo. *"I'm the cleansing by fire they're awaiting."* His face rested inches from RG's, a hot wind blowing through his hair.

"They await a savior, not a psychopath."

The burning man paused for effect. *"Well, what they're gonna get is me!"*

The air in the room fell upon RG with a heaviness, like the moment before a summer squall. In an instant, the oxygen sucked from his lungs with a whoosh as the burning man exploded into the center of Mike Stahl's living room, a soaring inferno of heat and fire towering over RG from floor to ceiling. The flames shot from him, scorching the carpeting, fixtures, and furniture, singeing RG's hair and skin. He jumped back instinctively from the heat's intensity.

The Beast unleashed himself into the natural world, an eventuality Morrow had neglected to include in his training. RG gawked expressionless at the unfolding spectacle, resigned to the fact there could be no defense, no protection from the hell let loose into their world. He shielded himself against the eye-searing glare with an outstretched hand, locking eyes with Kacey as the burning man turned his attention to her, grinning through the flames.

The burning man stretched his flaming arms and legs, the human body's boundaries no longer an impediment to him. He burned as he'd only imagined he could, the change freeing him, granting him his final form in the universal structure. He reveled in the infinite power he now possessed, how formidable he would be as he learned to navigate the tools of his new form. As he rollicked in his evolution's glory, a familiar tickling at the back of his brain distracted him—the beautiful one inside him once again, buzzing like a gnat he couldn't swat away.

He shook his blistering head. *Didn't she learn anything from the cave?*

His anger flared; her time to burn had finally arrived. He'd respected the fight inside her, but the time had come for a resolution. He'd work on her from the inside, his more familiar way of cleansing, where he could take his time, make it last.

She would endure his fury for her actions in the cave, her lies, her seduction, tempting him with a touch he'd learned to live without, and awakening feelings he'd buried. He'd make her pay for reigniting connections to long-forgotten secular pleasures, for reducing him from her captor to a punchline, a means to her end. No longer did the loss of an imagined future with the beautiful one haunt him, not after the change, but he'd make her suffer for the brief instance when he'd almost believed her. He'd told her in the cave he'd make her death as gentle as he could, that it wouldn't be so bad.

He'd changed his mind.

Kacey positioned herself on the couch and slipped across the misty boundary between waking and dreams to the portal. She fought her way through the bustling restaurant, sidestepped the busy waitstaff, and battled her way to the Pancake Man's front door, finally stepping into the next world's explosive pastiche of brilliant color.

From inside the burning man's mind, she beheld him standing before her like a towering conflagration, free in the world, reveling in his newfound form, like a child with a new toy. He'd been reborn into something beyond his wildest imagination.

He turned his rotting face toward Kacey. *"Well, look who's here. I've been expecting you. So, what do you think?"* The burning man shot flames toward the ceiling.

She spoke to him in his mind as he burned the world around her. *"I'm not impressed."*

"Doesn't matter. In fact, nothing will matter to you in a few minutes." He savored his magnificent flaming body. *"You got lucky in the cave, but your time's run out. You see, nothing can stop my power now."*

"If you're so powerful, why do you hide from yourself?"

"Don't be coy. Hide?" Flames danced as he laughed.

"Behind the door, that locked door in the back of your mind. I've seen it."

Kacey's words stoked the burning man's raging mountain of fire, flames shooting in all directions, scorching her with an unbearable heat, a white-hot light blinding her. *"Stay out of my mind, you insufferable pest!"*

"There's something there you refuse to face."

"Everyone hides things. You're no different. I've seen what's inside you."

"Then why are you acting like a coward? Open the door. Let's see what's inside."

"Only one door matters...the one I've opened unto your world, and all humanity will fall to their knees before me, starting with you!"

"I'll never kneel in front of you. I'm not afraid of you, but I think you're afraid of yourself."

"Oh, please! I'm tired of these mind games. It's time to finish what I've come for."

The twisting column of flames dancing in Mike Stahl's living room changed shape. Its energy channeled a narrow cone, aiming directly at Kacey. The fire swirled in front of her, spinning like a corkscrew, then pierced her body, hurling her onto the floor. The burning man positioned himself comfortably within her, stretching the shell of her body until it conformed to his new dimensions. She could smell his rotting and burned flesh inside her.

"Let her go!" RG's voice boomed inside her head. The mental connection between RG and the burning man still intact, she found

herself linked with both of them, RG in her mind, the burning man inside her body.

"Well, isn't this nice. The whole family's here."

As the burning man prepared to send a wave of fire through her, a surge of power welled up from deep inside her, part rage and part protective motherly instinct. She rose from the floor, envisioning ever muscle fiber in her body holding him like a fish caught on a million tiny hooks—precisely as Morrow had taught her. Her efforts left him paralyzed, sputtering, unable to breathe. She sent a pulse of her own energy into him, so icy and cold it scorched him. The burning man cried out in pain. She sent another wave of icy fire into him as he writhed in pain within her, a cry of anguish escaping his twisted maw. She felt him weaken.

"Send him to me!" RG shouted to her, his eyes darting toward Mike. *"Do it now!"*

Kacey sent a wave of energy through her body to expel the burning man, but at the last moment he slipped off her hooks, free once again inside her. He scurried away from her disabling internal clutches, bounding from her body like a blazing comet, reassembling himself in the middle of the living room. Weakened by Kacey's internal pummeling, the intensity of his flames momentarily diminished, but fueled again, swelling to double in size. RG hurled himself in front of Kacey, throwing his arms out to protect her as the swirling flames shifted directly at him.

Mike Stahl stood in the kitchen doorway, observing Kacey and RG, not altogether sure how to help, choosing to stay out of the way until RG gave him the signal. But when the burning man appeared before him, a raging firestorm of a man filled the living room. Stahl conceded their plan had no hope when he witnessed everything burning to ashes. They were back at square one.

In his panic, Stahl drew his HK45 and fired at the monster, the bullets melting in mid-air before reaching their target, his stopper proving to be as useful as shaking a stick at a charging Grizzly. The burning man gave him a dismissive wave, keeping his attention riveted on Kacey and RG pinned against the far living room wall. Stahl couldn't imagine a scenario where RG or Kacey had a chance against this supernatural force, and if they didn't have a chance, he wouldn't either.

As he contemplated the inevitable, an ear-splitting crack ripped the air as Chuck Brennan kicked in the back door. His face exhibited a look of frenzied contempt as he crouched and aimed his Glock at Stahl's heart.

The burning man hovered before Granville and the beautiful one, backs against the wall. RG swayed in front of her like a knight defending a maiden. *How brave he is, right to the end.* His flaming body thrummed as he debated how to proceed. He wouldn't be able to spend the alone time with Kacey he'd counted on—just the two of them—but in the end, it wouldn't matter; she'd burn just the same.

As he pondered their final disposition, he marveled at his free-burning form, running his blazing hands along his glowing skin. Once he eliminated the couple, he would make the world his new target, with a cleansing of epic, even biblical proportions. He was the End of Days for this miserable plane of existence.

The burning man recollected his time on earth, the people of questionable faith, the intellectually sparse, the pleasure seekers, the shallow, an entire population in existence for meaningless pursuits. The burning man would initiate a holy war of annihilation, scouring the life from the current world and the next, different realms, one after another until nothing remained. *And who could possibly stop me?* He would extinguish life as it currently existed, giving rise to the evolution of a species with greater depth, a species more like himself.

He would start with the two standing in front of him.

The burning man grinned as he accepted his destiny. "All right, who's gonna burn first?"

~

Brennan stood frozen in the kitchen, the splintered back door's remnants strewn on the floor, acting as tinder for the scorching air. His head swiveled back and forth across the smoldering room, eyes wide as saucers and mouth agape at the scene before him. Flames licked the floor and ceiling as a human torch ignited in the room's center, an explosive tower of uncontrolled rage. At first, Brennan pretended the room was simply on fire, but the overwhelming heat and rotted stench arising from the flaming form and its deliberate movements suggested it had life. Brennan wobbled from side to side as tremors descended through his body, his legs reduced to rubber.

"What is that? What the hell's going on here?" He rubbed his eyes with his free hand.

"Get the hell out of here, Chuck!" Stahl shouted, waving him toward the door.

Brennan's eyes glazed over, his mind shutting down, unable to connect to his surroundings or the reason he stood in Mike Stahl's living room. The primitive, reptilian portion of his brain took over, turning to the task of survival, seeking to identify the hierarchy of threats. The most immediate, the mountain of flames writhing on the living room carpet. Brennan waved his gun back and forth, shooting wildly through the room, a full magazine emptying into the ceiling and floor, bullets ricocheting off the wall, melting in the burning man's flames, missing RG and Kacey by inches. Two bullets slammed into Stahl's shoulder and thigh, dropping him to the floor like a broken glass.

"Sorry 'bout that, Mike," he mumbled, as calm as if he'd dialed a wrong number. He stepped over to Stahl and stared into his face as a fleeting thought reached his detached mind.

"I came here to kill you, didn't I? And the others, too?"

Stahl stared blankly into his would-be assassin's eyes.

Struggling to hold onto his last thread of sanity, Brennan took another clip from his belt and popped it into the Glock. Brennan focused on the foggy memory of his mission, blocking his surroundings to prevent him from thinking about the unimaginable, that *thing* in the room. He ignored the flaming man turning his glowing eyes toward him. *He's not there, he can't be.*

He steadied his sidearm, taking aim at RG and his wife. *One down, two to go.*

As he fingered the trigger, the raging column of fire spoke to him in a language he'd never heard before but understood nonetheless. "Sorry Chief, they're mine."

He aimed his hardware on the demonic wall of fire and unloaded the remainder of his cartridge. His bladder let go as a sheet of flame exploded in his direction.

RG glanced at Brennan, the whites of his eyes visible as he took in the unfathomable scene rising before him. He had his gun aimed at Kacey, while Stahl continued to squirm on the floor in pain. *So much for the plan, looks like I die another way today.* He calculated Brennan had at least two more shots left, starting with Kacey.

The burning man had other ideas. Winding up like baseball's Cy Young, he pitched a cone of fire toward Brennan, igniting him in a flaming collision as the man unloaded his automatic weapon. His high-pitched screams echoed off the walls. RG and Kacey blocked the horrific sound with hands clasped to their ears. Before Brennan could even think of escaping the flames or rolling on the ground, the burning man went into his windup again and delivered another fiery fastball, hitting its mark with astounding precision. Brennan's body writhed in a freakish dance from the flames until he fell, lifeless on the smoldering carpet.

The burning man pivoted his head back and forth between Granville and the woman. "All right, who's next?" He leaned over in an exaggerated pantomime of a pitcher on the mound looking in for the signs from an imaginary catcher.

RG stepped up. *Time for the truth you bastard!* "Victor! Look at me! Now!"

Taken aback, the burning man's swirling flames retracted to a mere smoldering circle. "I follow no one's orders!" He tossed a ball of fire up and down in his hand.

"Exactly the reason Sam's dead, isn't it?"

"Don't say his name!" Victor's figure ballooned instantly into a fireball, throwing scorching shards toward the wall behind RG and Kacey. The flames forced them to leap in different directions, Kacey tumbling in a heap beside Stahl near the kitchen, RG to the opposite side of the living room. The burning man's flaming wall stood between them.

The burning man pivoted to face RG. "You know *nothing* about my son."

"I know *you* killed him. Lucy knew it, too!"

The burning man dropped the ball of fire onto the carpet. "You're wrong. Your psyche mumbo-jumbo won't work."

"Why'd you wait so long to take Sam to the hospital?"

"What?"

"You remember, when he got sick. Lucy didn't see eye to eye with your decision to wait, did she? She even gave you a nice punch in the nose before you broke her neck, if I recall?

"She had it coming."

"What're you hiding behind the door, Victor?" Kacey shouted, pressing a kitchen cloth against Stahl's wounds.

RG stepped closer, enduring the unbearable heat. "Your son's coughing up blood for months, dying. You didn't think he needed to go to a hospital?"

"The hospital doctors killed him, the aggressive treatments—"

"No, Victor, it was your negligence," he cut him off.

"You haven't been honest with yourself, have you?" Kacey pressed.

"How could I have killed him?"

"Think about it, Victor. How come *you* never went to a doctor?"

The burning man stuttered. "I...I never got sick, I didn't have to go—"

"No checkups?" RG interrupted. "No prescriptions, no coughs or colds in, what, sixteen years?"

Victor held his burning arms out. "The power of God heals the chosen!"

RG paced in front of the burning man, one hand on his chin. "I get it now. I've read about people like you. Fire and brimstone types, won't bring their dying kids to the doctors, thinking faith will heal them."

Flames erupted from the burning man, the kitchen now catching fire.

"Lucy had to go to court to get you away from Sam, because you were killing him."

"Stop saying his name!"

"Open the door, Victor!" Kacey hollered.

RG continued. "I mean, God promises to heal the sick, doesn't he? Psalm 41:3, 'The Lord will sustain him upon his sickbed. In his illness, Thou dost restore him to health.'"

"God heals the righteous—"

"Your...experiment killed Sam!" RG barked.

"Stop saying his name! Stop!" The burning man held his glowing hands over his ears, his body quivering like a livewire.

"Everyone hides things," Kacey offered, "didn't you tell me that?"

RG shook his head, stepping closer to the burning man. "When you realized what you'd done, you stayed with Sam every minute, hoping for a miracle, hoping your God would reverse your mistake."

"I begged God to save him." Droplets of fire fell from his eyes.

"You haven't once accepted responsibility for Sam's death." He stood in front of Victor, jamming his finger at him. "Instead you blamed everyone else!"

"The doctors..." His voice trailed off.

"How many innocent souls had to pay the price for your denial, you sonofabitch?"

"God heals the righteous," the burning man whispered.

Kacey stood and approached him. "The door's open now, Victor. Take a good look inside."

The burning man collapsed to his knees as the heat grew from within, burning hotter. "I thought God would save him. Lucy begged me, but I didn't listen." Victor swelled like a flaming balloon, red liquid fire leaking from him, burning holes in the floorboards on contact. Buzzing like a guitar string, Victor's outer shell of fire oscillated in tight waves surrounding his body. "I think...I killed my son!"

RG latched onto Victor's thoughts, his hidden secret revealed—his denial, his responsibility for Sam's death—flooding his mind, like water bursting from a dam. A white-hot mass radiated from the burning man's belly, growing larger and hotter, throbbing inside him, like a nuclear reactor exposing its core. He recalled Kacey's description of his meltdown in the cave, but this transformation was different, in fact, the opposite. It would only be moments before he detonated with a catastrophic outcome, decades of rage directed outward now turning, shifting toward an internal target.

The hellish fire dissolved the floorboards into glowing ash, graduating to the basement cross beams. He shouted to Kacey through the flames. "You gotta run before the whole place goes up!" RG scanned the room. Solid walls encased him. He stood trapped. "There's no way out for me!"

"I'm not leaving without you!"

"Mike! Get Kacey out of here! Now!"

At the sound of her name, Stahl dragged himself to a sitting position. "I got this," he coughed. Through sheer force of will he rose to his feet.

A roar escaped the burning man's lips, flames searing into a white hue. Steam seeped from the fire, creating a scorching mist across the room. As the burning man's bizarre transformation intensified, RG's own hair and skin smoldered, moments away from igniting. Large oscillations now rocked the burning man and a pounding thump drummed the thick air as flames spiraled around him. With the escalating temperature and heat, something had to give. If RG was to survive, he'd have to put distance between himself and the burning man. His head swiveled back and forth surveying his flaming confines.

No exit.

"Go, go, go!" RG shouted, waving his hand toward the back door.

Shielding Kacey from the flames, Mike pulled her into the kitchen, his own clothing smoldering and catching fire. Kacey struggled against him, trying to peer around him, her arms flailing over his shoulders as if to reach out to RG one more time.

Just give me one more look into her eyes, please. Give me that, and I'll go in peace!

As Mike dragged Kacey out the back door to safety, she raised her head above his shoulder to find him, granting RG his fleeting wish. As their eyes met, the air changed, the fire's deafening roar funneled to a moment of deathly silence. RG closed his eyes seconds before the explosion flattened the house, consuming it in fire.

RG lay on the cold ground amidst the smoldering debris of Mike Stahl's house on Old Harbor Road, blown off its foundation from the ear-shattering blast. He stared down from above, silently observing as first responders worked on him, racing back and forth to emergency vehicles with medical trauma bags and life-saving equipment, administering oxygen, giving chest compressions, keeping him alive.

But they couldn't keep the life from draining out of him.

The overwhelming temptation to let go and find his peace beckoned him, but the magical comfort of Kacey's touch kept him tethered to this place for the moment. It had always been the thing he'd lived for, the means by which she passed her love into him and through him every day and in everything they did. She knelt beside his head, sobs obscuring the gentle words pouring from her mouth, her hands rubbing his hair, caressing his blackened forehead.

She had been scorched and burned, too, but showed surprisingly little damage, given the blast's ferocity. RG understood why when he glanced over at the paramedics attending to the burns along Stahl's back. He recalled Mike blocking his view of Kacey, pulling her toward the kitchen door, shielding her from the heat and flames. He'd also taken the brunt of the blast as they'd bolted from the house.

The scene below him grew dim and hazy. He was no longer on the ground sensing her touch and her cries grew louder and louder. Then, nothing. RG found himself somewhere between life and death. A force directed him toward something ahead, leading him through a doorway to satisfy his heart's deepest desires. He found it nearly impossible to *not* keep moving forward toward this infinite longing. On the way, images of his life filtered through his mind like snapshots tacked to a collage board, peppering him in a sensory finale. Confusing and yet crystal clear, a barrage of penetrating sound, taste, and color filling his mind and soul. The images' vividness magnified in their contrast, complexity, and dimension the moment Kacey debuted in the sequence. The depth of his heart changed the way he viewed and experienced the world around him, as if everything went from black and white to high definition in a flash. He instantaneously relived all the beautiful moments once again, leaving him thankful for the incredible gift his life had been. But one curious moment danced before him, a forgotten memory pushing forward in his dying mind.

His mother lay in a hospital bed, her life draining from her. RG perched beside her, holding her hand, reliving the memory as if it were happening for the first time. He'd been sitting with her for hours before she raised her head and strained to whisper a few last words.

"Did I ever tell you your father's favorite story?"

"I don't think so, Mom." The life-prolonging machines' beeps and hums provided a comforting background ensemble to his mother's soft voice. "Tell me."

"Romeo and Juliet."

He rubbed her forearm and smiled. "I didn't know that."

"Well, your father had a sweetness he didn't live long enough to show you, just a hopeless romantic." Helen's laugh won a temporary victory over the pain. "I never told you much about that side of him because it brought back too much sadness."

RG rested his hand on his mother's forehead. The heat and moisture dampened his palm.

"Back when we lived in Hartford, before you were born, your father would sometimes have to attend a medical conference or a childhood cancer seminar somewhere. Whenever we had to spend the night apart, he'd call me and recite from Romeo and Juliet." A sparkle of light reignited Helen's dimming eyes as she spoke. "Before he hung up the phone, he'd whisper to me, 'Good night, good night, parting is such sweet sorrow, that I shall say goodnight, till it be morrow.'"

Like an extinguishing flame, the memory abandoned him and let him travel on alone. Neurons in his dying brain flickered, the lights dimming in a mortal last call, nothing left but the compelling pull toward his final destination. As he transitioned, RG locked onto the words his father would whisper to his mother in his ritualistic display of affection. He let the words tumble from his lips, "Goodnight, good-night, parting is...

As another voice joined his chorus..."such sweet sorrow..." he opened his eyes, no longer alone..."that I shall say goodnight, till it be morrow." Daring to gaze into the celestial surroundings, his voice trailed off to see Morrow standing beside him, replete with his crisp dark suit, hat, and glasses.

"Dad?"

Morrow placed a hand on his shoulder. "I'm right here, Son."

CHAPTER TWENTY-ONE

F riday, December 15, 2017

His body convulsed as the defibrillator paddles delivered more than a thousand volts to a listless heart. The EMT lowered his ear to RG's chest, placing his fingers against the side of his neck.

"Nothing! Hit him again!" he shouted.

"Clear!" The paddles came down, jolting his upper chest and ribcage.

"Nothing! Continuing CPR!"

Kacey collapsed on the grass, numb, a wall of EMTs and paramedics separating her from her husband, doing all they could to revive him. Through the sea of moving legs, RG's prone body jerked into the air, a fraction of a second of artificial life imparted to him, then an unnatural stillness. They'd already hit him twice, and Kacey overheard the paramedics saying they'd try one more time. The EMT held the paddles over RG's chest.

"Clear!" he shouted.

Kacey closed her eyes before the jolt pierced the silence. "Don't leave me," she whispered.

~

"Why didn't you tell me?" RG stared intently at Morrow, finally disengaging from the embrace he'd waited a lifetime for.

"I couldn't. I would have been called back to my world immediately. I would have missed our time together."

RG regretted his impatience, the insults he'd hurled at him. "I'm sorry about the things I said back there." He threw a thumb over his shoulder. "I didn't always treat you so well."

Morrow smirked. "No different than most father-son relationships. I only had to take it for a couple weeks. I figure I got off easy."

"Where am I?" RG asked, glancing around his new environment.

"Don't you know?" They strode together through the space between life and death, not the next world, but not RG's world either. "You're on your way, as they say."

RG rubbed his neck, bending it to the left and right. "Funny, I don't have an ache or a pain…anywhere."

"You left it all back in your world. There will be new ones here, of course, if you choose to stay. If you choose to go back, you'll feel them all again, and then some. You've been blown through a wall and—"

"Go back?" RG interrupted, pulling on Morrow's arm to stop him. "What do you mean?"

"Well, you aren't too far along yet. You still have a choice."

RG sensed the numbing pull onward toward the infinite, fighting the overwhelming urge to surrender to its seduction. "Kacey's talking to me right now, up close in my ear." He raised both palms to his face and closed his eyes, the conflicting options thrown at him at every turn mystifying him. After waiting a lifetime for his father, he'd finally found him, but he'd have to leave Kacey if he wanted to be with him. Once again, no choice without collateral damage.

"I can't leave her, Dad."

Morrow gave his shoulder a squeeze. "I know."

"But I don't want to leave you either. It's not fair, goddammit! I didn't get my time with you. Can't you do something? Don't you have a little magic left?"

Morrow sighed. "Whatever I have left will be gone soon."

"What?" RG tilted his head. "You told me you had a new assignment, you'd been summoned back—"

"I wasn't completely truthful with you," Morrow interrupted. "Our Tribunal of Elders called me back for a hearing. They've decided to strip me of my powers, remove me as a caretaker, my punishment for revealing myself to you."

"Can't you file an appeal or something? Phil Goldwyn gave me the names of a couple of really good lawyers."

Morrow chuckled. "Oh, I'll be fine. I'll concentrate on living in my world for a change. It'll be like an early retirement." Morrow's cavalier façade failed to mask his pain.

"I'm sorry."

"Don't be. I'd do it all again in a second. To be beside you again in the world, and to get to meet Kacey, I have no regrets." The silence stretched between them. "But you're running out of time. If we blabber on too long, you'll miss your window. What do you want to do?"

RG dropped his eyes. "I've gotta meet my child, grow old with Kacey. I'm not ready to be here yet. I want to, but…" His voice trailed off.

"I'd be surprised if you'd made any other choice—it's the right one."

"Can't you come back with me? Fuck the Elders, jump back and stay with us, power or no power! I don't want to leave you." RG grasped his hand, daring Morrow to pry it loose.

"I've had my time in your world, I don't get a second go-round, but you do. Promise me you'll make the most of it."

RG nodded.

"Oh, one more thing." Morrow pulled the wedding ring from his jacket pocket and pressed it into RG's palm, closing his fingers over it. "I wouldn't have been able to give it to Kacey if you'd stayed."

RG turned it over in his hand, then slipped it on. "Thanks for holding onto it for me, it feels good on my finger."

"That finger will be the only thing on your body feeling good in a few minutes."

RG considered the state he'd be in upon his return. "Thanks for reminding me."

Morrow gave his son a pat on the back and turned to leave.

I'm leaving the sonofabitch forever and that's all I get? "Hey, wait a minute! A pat on the back?"

Morrow laughed. "Oh, don't be so dramatic."

RG shrugged. "But I'll never see you again."

"You will, Robert. You have the universe's power in your hands if you have the courage to use it."

"What the hell are you talking about?"

Morrow stood watching RG, a grin pasted onto his face. He glanced at the ring on his finger. "When you wake up beside Kacey, it will all make sense."

The look of confusion on RG's face turned to surprise as his body hurtled backward into space, weightless, as if a pair of hands had reached around his midsection and pulled him into a dark hole. Morrow's face pulled away, the light surrounding him forming a smaller and smaller circle until his face appeared as a dot within a pinprick of light. With a thud, RG landed on the frozen ground outside Mike Stahl's house on Old Harbor Road.

"I've got a pulse!" the EMT shouted.

Kacey flailed against the human barrier keeping her from RG. She burst through and dropped to his side as he opened his eyes. "You came back to me!" she cried.

RG's eyes rolled in his head, searing pain shooting the entire length of his body. "I had to say goodbye to someone."

~

Three months later

The sun shone brightly through the bay window, a measure of comfort against the late winter chill seeping through the living room walls. Kacey opened the *Herald* and dropped into her chair as RG reclined on the couch, Robert Jr. fast asleep on his chest.

'FUGITIVE PROFESSOR' CLEARED BY LOCAL 'HERO' COP—
Boston (AP)—Chatham Police Detective Mike Stahl is being hailed as
a hero for his efforts to clear the 'Fugitive Professor,' murder suspect
Dr. Robert Granville, of all charges related to the deaths of Boston
University colleague, Dr. Wendell Abernathy, and John Delvecchio, a
lifelong friend. The two murders are currently unsolved and the cases
have been re-opened.

Granville was initially jailed on murder charges after surviving
what appeared to be a tragic accident in Stahl's home in December, an
explosion claiming the life of Falmouth Police Chief Charles Brennan,
52. According to eyewitness testimony and ballistic evidence,
moments before the explosion, Brennan kicked in the door to Stahl's
home and shot the detective twice to prevent him from revealing the
police chief's plot to frame Granville for the Delvecchio murder.
Brennan also murdered Len Kramer, 47, who had provided him with
confidential information to locate the 'Fugitive Professor' at Stahl's
house. Security cameras at the site of the murder helped to identify
Brennan.

While recovering from the shooting, Stahl painstakingly assembled
the evidence and convinced police officials Granville could not have
committed Abernathy's murder, despite his presence at the home on
the evening in question.

Eyewitness testimony of Clarence Massey, 61, a neighbor of Abernathy, walking his dogs with wife, Joan, 57, proved critical. The
Masseys witnessed Granville leave the Abernathy house, cross their
front lawn, and drive out of the neighborhood with his lights off.
Suspicious, the Masseys approached the Abernathy home, where they
found a young woman, Brittany Thorne, 20, wandering along the road.
Believing a domestic dispute had occurred, Clarence Massey observed
Abernathy peering through the window of his home and contacted the
police, who later discovered his body.

Boston Police Department detectives Ray Harrington and Paul
Becker placed Granville under arrest in the hospital, largely based on
DNA evidence found at the Abernathy home. But despite the Masseys
repeatedly contacting the detectives to make a statement, neither

Harrington nor Becker returned their calls. Stahl located their names buried in the investigator notebook in Becker's possession. Massachusetts State Police spokesman Harry Quinn has called Harrington and Becker's investigation "a rush to judgement" characterized by "a significant lack of a thorough police work." Neither Harrington nor Becker, both on administrative leave since February, could be reached for comment.

Kacey stood and tossed RG the *Herald*. "Check out the headline article." He carefully unfolded the paper above Robert Jr., the rustling tabloid drawing no response from the slumbering child. Kacey grinned at the familiar positioning of the two men in her life and padded into the kitchen. She pulled out her cell, rolling it in her hand before punching in the number.

"This is Mike Stahl."

"Hey."

"Kacey?"

"Listen, I wanted to call and thank you...for what you did."

"You must be reading the *Herald*."

"And watching all the major news stations. You're all over the place."

"Well, I made RG a promise."

Kacey sighed. "You gave me my husband back."

"I just got him back where he belongs. Home. With you."

She stared out the kitchen window. "I should've called you...when everything happened. Asked you how you were doing."

"You had your hands full. RG's recovery, new baby, I understand. How's everyone doing?"

"Both doing great. Mike, I'm sorry you lost everything because of us...the house. I know it meant a lot to you."

"Well, sometimes we don't recognize the anchors in our lives, the things holding us back." Stahl hesitated a moment. "Losing the house forced me to move on from the past...from everything I'd been holding onto. It actually helped me *find* my way home."

"And your recovery?"

"Still got a couple bullets lodged in me and I'll always walk with a bit of a limp, but I'm grateful to be here."

"It's good to be alive."

He cleared his throat. "Listen, I'm staying with someone now. Her name's Claire, she's an old friend who works at our forensic lab. She's been kind enough to give me a place to stay and nurse me back to health. Although sometimes it feels like I'm living with Nurse Ratched."

A woman's giggle sounded through the line. Close.

"I'm glad for you, Mike."

A long pause. "I am, too."

~

RG lounged on the leather couch, milking all he could from his remaining injuries, reminding Kacey over and over how he'd saved the world and how most wives would be honored to bring him a Coors Light if asked. Holding her ground, Kacey reminded him the only thing he'd gain by her continual trips to the icebox would be more weight, which he'd been packing on like a Sumo wrestler during his convalescence.

While the cracked vertebrae, dislocated shoulder, broken ribs, and various burns on his body had healed, lingering discomfort and pain alerted him to the repercussions of his decision to return to this world. But as he glanced around the room, Kacey flopped in her chair next to the fireplace, Baron snoring next to her feet, and now Robert Jr., snoozing away soundless on his chest, he didn't regret his decision for a second.

He gazed at his son, his perfect little body moving up and down in a rhythmic cadence with every breath. This had been the payoff, everything he and Kacey had fought for and what others had died for—the joy of his laughter, watching his eyes lock onto his, and the touch of his tiny hands.

Easing himself off the couch, he placed Robert Jr. in the bassinet.

He stood and tossed the *Herald* onto the coffee table. "He did it, didn't he? He cleared my name."

"The evidence was all there. Mike just followed the breadcrumb trail."

"Speaking of breadcrumbs, are you hungry?" He placed his hands on his growing belly.

Kacey shook her head. "Remind me to never reference any type of food around you again!"

"How about a breakfast dinner?" He gave her a knowing wink.

Kacey grinned. "Should we get the whole family together?"

"Why not?"

"You want to drive, or should I?" Kacey asked.

"I'll get us there if you make the arrangements, help everyone get to the restaurant."

"Fair enough."

RG picked up the BabyBjörn and secured the harness around Robert Jr., nestling him comfortable and warm against his chest. He eased himself onto the couch beside Kacey. Then he reached down to his left hand, twirled his wedding ring around his finger, and clutched Kacey's hand. Together they dropped into the abyss, the air bending to accommodate the hazy coiling alleyway between this world and the next. At Kacey's portal, their paths diverged and Kacey continued on to the next world. As the darkness dissipated and his vision cleared, RG found himself inside the Pancake Man, frenetic with activity as waiters and waitresses ran back and forth between tables taking orders, busboys cleaned dishes off empty tables, and hurried voices erupted from the kitchen. A younger version of Kacey, her hair in French braids, sat with her parents on the other side of the restaurant getting ready to order.

RG ran his hand across his wedding ring. He'd learned of his newfound power the moment he regained consciousness in the hospital, Kacey seated bedside. When he woke and met her eyes, unrestrained thoughts from her brain flooded his head. At first, they came at him like confetti shot from a cannon, scattered and impossible to coral, difficult to discern. But within seconds, his brain adjusted to the assault, slowing every thought and image one at a time. When he uttered his first soundless word to Kacey deep within her mind, he immediately understood he'd come back from death with a gift, a ring connecting him with his wife and his father's otherworldly power.

During his recovery, RG and Kacey traveled to different worlds together, exploring their powers, familiarizing themselves with their complementary abilities and special skills. He advanced in stages, first reading the minds of the hospital staff and the police officers stationed at the door. With Kacey's help, he then learned to dream himself to the portal into the next world, never once skipping the blue-plate special. Finally, he graduated to transporting himself physically into distant worlds, long after the lights went out in his hospital room, when his absence wouldn't raise suspicions.

RG experienced different worlds and their various colors and hues, the universal language's diverse dialects, the universe's patterns of life, and human evolution in subsequent planes. They exercised caution to avoid detection from jumpers, but had help and guidance from Morrow's numerous caretaker acquaintances. Unhampered by his injuries' severity in the different worlds he traveled, RG's recovery turned out to be less taxing than he'd expected, having spent little time in his battered, but healing, worldly body.

RG didn't have to tell Kacey that Morrow had been more than his caretaker, she'd deduced as much. As he lay in the hospital drifting in and out of consciousness, Kacey had filled the time going through unopened boxes of his mother's photographs in the attic. She found cards and letters between RG's parents. When she read the ones concluding with a certain poem, she understood.

As RG perused the menu, the Pancake Man's front door opened. The next world's vivid colors flooded the restaurant, backlighting the man and woman jostling through the throng of people waiting by the door. The crowd parted as the well-dressed older man made his way from the waiting area and into the busy restaurant, Kacey's arm wound around the crook of his elbow.

RG waved a hand to his father, who doffed his hat as he made his way toward the table.

"Thanks for the invite, I'm starting to enjoy this place." Morrow leaned over and gave a kiss on the top of Robert Jr.'s head, peaking above the chest harness' front flap, before slipping into the booth beside his son. He ruffled RG's hair.

"Jeez, Dad." RG swiped a hand through his mane, smoothing it out again.

"You gotta be careful with the hair," Kacey admonished. "It takes him a long time to make it look like he didn't do anything with it."

RG reached into his pocket and scattered a handful of Hershey's kisses on the table in front of Morrow.

"Oh, you shouldn't have." His eyes widened as he corralled the candies into a small pile. "So, how are you coming along?" Morrow placed his hand on RG's forearm.

"It's overwhelming," RG admitted. "I see everything, people's pain, I spot their jumpers and caretakers. Sometimes I need to take off the ring just to *stop* seeing everything."

"You'll get used to it. You'll learn to dismiss most of the distractions as white noise, like a television in the background, as you get used to your power. You've gotten it all at once, not in stages like most caretakers, so I can imagine it's like being thrown into the pool's deep end."

"How did you do it?" Kacey asked.

"You mean the ring? Objects traveling between worlds are unique, they can confer its possessor's attributes to another. When Robert gave me his ring for safekeeping, he unknowingly allowed me to confer my powers to him upon its return."

"Could a human gift an object to a caretaker," Kacey asked, "send its attributes the other way?"

"A human can gift their compassion, their talents, artistic ability, anything they wish their caretaker to have within an object. This only occurs in more advanced worlds where caretakers and humans have evolved into more…interactive forms, where they can see each other. As you know, your world's inhabitants can't observe caretakers—"

"Unless the caretaker's a felon, like mine," RG interrupted.

"Ignore him." Kacey shook her head.

"Well, he's right, my situation offered a unique opportunity. No sane caretaker would ever gift all his or her power, unless—"

"Unless he's the aforementioned felon, about to be stripped of his power."

"Is he always like this?" Morrow inquired.

"Unfortunately."

A waitress arrived with plates of food, eggs, bacon, and hash browns for RG, a stack of silver dollar pancakes for Kacey, and a blueberry muffin for Morrow.

"Somehow, they know what we're gonna order, don't they?" Kacey pointed out. "I'm not sure why they bother putting out menus."

"Because that's how you remembered it," Morrow replied.

"And since they don't take money here, I'm kinda liking how it affects our food budget." RG wolfed down a forkful of hash browns.

"Cheapskate." Kacey grabbed her fork and dug in.

"Have you placed the ads?" Morrow asked, extracting a blueberry and popping it in his mouth.

"What ads?" RG raised an eyebrow.

"Didn't you tell him?" Morrow asked.

Kacey exchanged a sheepish glance at Morrow. "Not yet."

"What now?" RG eyed them with suspicion.

Morrow cleared his throat. "Kacey wants to advertise your services, place online classified ads around the world, cryptic messages, things only people seeking your assistance would understand." Morrow leaned forward, his elbows on the table. "We could work together, you from your world, me from mine."

"I thought you'd lost your powers."

"I have, but that won't prevent me from alerting you to dangers brewing over here, things posing a risk to your world. I can still detect the evil; I just can't act on it anymore. I can also put you in touch with caretakers who can help you."

RG opened his mouth to speak, but Kacey placed a finger over his lips. "I'm a caretaker, RG. I've seen the worlds I'll inhabit, experienced the powers calling me to act. I don't want to wait until I die before I can use my gifts and reach my destiny. And you have a gift, too."

"What if I tell you I'm not sure I'm wanting this gift? I already have a career I'd like to salvage."

"Grumble, grumble, how can you stand his complaining, Kacey?"

She rolled her eyes. "He grows on you."

"You may have a career, Robert, but you have caretaker blood, and you inadvertently married one of the most powerful caretakers I've ever met. Together you're linked through the ring, and you will do wonderful things. And since I cannot, I am relying on you now."

"If we're talking gifts, I'd have preferred a car on my sixteenth birthday."

"There are many out there in need of your power. You can help them, protect them. You'll hear their pleas in the back of their minds as they pass on the street. They will also come find you. People in your world can sense those with the power to help them, and they'll search you out."

RG pushed the food around his plate with his fork. "I'm not sure I want the responsibility."

"When you witness what your powers can do, you will."

"Do we have the experience to take this on? We only defeated the burning man out of sheer luck."

"That's why I'm here," Morrow offered. "Think of me as Obi-Wan Kenobi, sort of a Jedi master you can turn to when you need advice or guidance."

"Boy, after the Yoda thing you really brushed up on your Star Wars trivia, didn't you?"

Kacey reached over and grabbed RG's hand. "We can make a difference, RG. We can help foil threats to the world. Jumpers are evolving. The burning man would have destroyed our world if we hadn't outsmarted him, well, if *you* hadn't outsmarted him."

RG exhaled onto his fingertips and wiped them on his shirt.

"Together, we defeated a formidable menace. With Morrow's power on your finger, we have a responsibility to this world to protect it."

"It's only going to get worse here, I'm afraid," Morrow added.

RG rolled his eyes, tossing his fork onto his plate. "Fine. When do we begin?"

Morrow unwrapped one of the Hershey's kisses and threw it in his mouth, his eyes closing as he chewed. "How about after breakfast?"

THE END

ACKNOWLEDGMENTS

To my brother, Michael, for finding the mice, patching the holes and somehow knowing exactly what I am trying to say. To my editor, Linda, an inspiring mentor who I was fortunate to meet at just the right time. I am beholden to both of you. A special thanks to my readers: Jack Sayers,

Ruth Hanavan, Kim Roen, Kyle Gibson, Jeff Krug, Jeff Bridges, Chris and Kaylee, for offering their brutal honesty.

ABOUT THE AUTHOR

Stephen Paul Sayers grew up on the sands of Cape Cod and spent his first thirty-five years in New England before joining the University of Missouri as a research professor. When he's not in his laboratory, he spends his time writing and devouring his favorite forms of genre fiction—horror, suspense, and thrillers. His short fiction has appeared in Unfading Daydream.

A Taker of Morrows is his debut novel and the first in the planned Caretakers series. Throughout his journey, he has accumulated five guitars, four herniated discs, three academic degrees, two dogs, and one wife, son, and daughter. He divides his time between Columbia, Missouri and Cape Cod writing and teaching. For more about the author, visit https://www.stephenpaulsayers.com.